Sleeper Straddle

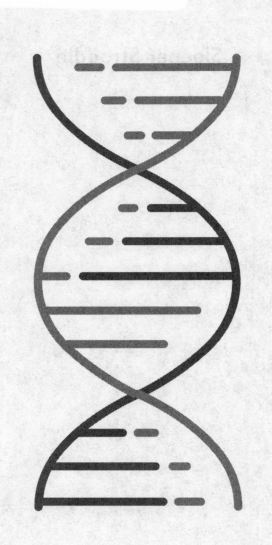

GEORGE R. R. MARTIN

Presents

Wild Cards: Sleeper Straddle

A Novel in Stories

EDITED BY GEORGE R. R. MARTIN

Assisted by Melinda M. Snodgrass

and written by

Christopher Rowe	Walter Jon Williams
Carrie Vaughn	Stephen Leigh
Cherie Priest	Mary Anne Mohanraj
William F. Wu	Max Gladstone

Bantam

New York

Published in the United States by Bantam Books, an imprint of Random House, a division of Penguin Random House LLC, New York.

BANTAM & B colophon is a registered trademark of Penguin Random House LLC.

Originally published in hardcover in the United States by Bantam Books, an imprint of Random House, a division of Penguin Random House LLC, in 2024.

LIBRARY OF CONGRESS CATALOGING-IN-PUBLICATION DATA

Names: Martin, George R. R., editor. | Snodgrass, Melinda M., contributor. | Rowe, Christopher, author. | Vaughn, Carrie, author. | Priest, Cherie, author. | Wu, William F., author. | Williams, Walter Jon, author. | Leigh, Stephen, author. | Mohanraj, Mary Anne, author. | Gladstone, Max, author.
Title: Sleeper straddle / edited by George R. R. Martin; assisted by Melinda M. Snodgrass; and written by Christopher Rowe, Carrie Vaughn, Cherie Priest, William F. Wu, Walter Jon Williams, Stephen Leigh, Mary Anne Mohanraj, Max Gladstone.
Description: First edition. | New York: Bantam Books, 2024. | Series: A Wild Cards mosaic novel
Identifiers: LCCN 2023029620 (print) | LCCN 2023029621 (ebook) | ISBN 9780593357859 (trade paperback) | ISBN 9780593357842 (ebook)
Subjects: LCSH: Science fiction, American. | LCGFT: Science fiction. | Linked stories.
Classification: LCC PS648.S3 S477 2024 (print) | LCC PS648.S3 (ebook) | DDC 813/.087620806—dc23/eng/20230914
LC record available at https://lccn.loc.gov/2023029620
LC ebook record available at https://lccn.loc.gov/2023029621

Printed in the United States of America on acid-free paper

randomhousebooks.com

1st Printing

Book design by Virginia Norey
Helix art: bsd studio/stock.adobe.com

This one is for Croyd's father
the late great Roger Zelazny
and Croyd's kin and cousins
Trent, Shannon, Devin, Corwin

Wild Cards

The virus was created on TAKIS, hundreds of light-years from Earth. The ruling mentats of the great Takisian Houses were looking for a way to enhance their formidable psionic abilities and augment them with physical powers. The retrovirus they devised showed enough promise that the psi lords decided to field-test it on Earth, whose inhabitants were genetically identical to Takisians.

Prince Tisianne of House Ilkazam opposed the experiment and raced to Earth in his own living starship to stop it. The alien ships fought high above the atmosphere. The ship carrying the virus was torn apart, the virus itself lost. Prince Tisianne landed his own damaged ship at White Sands, where his talk of tachyon drives prompted the military to dub him **DR. TACHYON.**

Across the continent, the virus fell into the hands of **DR. TOD,** a crime boss and war criminal, who resolved to use it to extort wealth and power from the cities of America. He lashed five blimps together and set out for New York City. President Harry S Truman reached out to Robert Tomlin, **JETBOY,** the teenage fighter ace of World War II, to stop him. Flying his experimental jet, the JB-1, Jetboy reached Tod's blimps and crashed into the gondola. The young hero and his old foe met for the last time as the bomb containing the virus fell to Earth. "*Die, Jetboy, die,*" Tod shouted as he shot Tomlin again and again. "I can't die yet, I haven't seen *The Jolson Story*," Jetboy replied as the bomb exploded.

Thousands of microscopic spores rained down upon Manhattan. Thousands more were dispersed into the atmosphere and swept up by the jet stream, to spread all over the Earth. But New York City got the worst of it.

It was **September 15, 1946.** The first Wild Card Day.

Ten thousand died that first day in Manhattan alone. Thousands more were transformed, their DNA rewritten in terrible and unpredictable ways. Every case was unique. No two victims were affected in the same way. For that reason, the press dubbed xenovirus *Takis-A* (its scientific name) the *wild card.*

Ninety percent of those infected died, unable to withstand the violent bodily changes the virus unleashed upon them. Those victims were said to have drawn the *black queen.*

Of those who survived, nine of every ten were twisted and mutated in ways great and small. They were called *jokers* (or *jacks,* *knaves,* or *joker-aces* if they also gained powers). Shunned, outcast, and feared, they began to gather in along the Bowery, in a neighborhood that soon became known as **Jokertown.**

Only one in a hundred of those infected emerged with superhuman powers: telepathy, telekinesis, enhanced strength, superspeed, invulnerability, flight, and a thousand other strange and wondrous abilities. These were the *aces,* the celebrities of the dawning new age. Unlike the heroes of the comic book, very few of them chose to don spandex costumes and fight crime, but they would soon begin to rewrite history all the same.

These are their stories.

The Sleeper

In poker, a sleeper straddle is a blind raise, made from a position other than the player "under the gun." Sleepers are often considered illegal out-of-turn plays and are commonly disallowed.

In Wild Cards, the Sleeper is Croyd Crenson. Croyd was a high school freshman on his way home from school when the virus was released over Manhattan on September 15, 1946. He witnessed all the horror of that first Wild Card Day firsthand, with death and transformation all around him. From that day on, Croyd has been continuously reinfected by the virus whenever he sleeps, his body reshaping itself into myriad new shapes and forms. Each time he wakes, he is changed. Sometimes he wakes as an ace, with astonishing new superpowers, different every time. Other times he wakes as a joker, malformed and hideous. He lives in terror of the day he draws the black queen, and does not wake at all.

Croyd can sleep for days, weeks, even months, but when awake he does all he can to keep sleep at bay. Unable to hold a normal job or have a normal relationship, he lives on the margins of society. He has been a bodyguard, a thief, a mercenary, a con man, a hero for hire . . . whatever it takes to survive. Everyone knows Croyd, and no one really knows Croyd. You never know what you are going to get when the Sleeper wakes. He is truly the ultimate wild card.

Sleeper Straddle

Swimmer, Flier, Felon, Spy

by Christopher Rowe

PART I

Tesla shut the folder. He took the string of the closure between his gray thumb and forefinger—no easy task given his long black nails, invulnerable to clippers as they were. Then he wrapped the string around the circular cardboard retainer, once, twice, three times.

The folders were an affectation, to be sure—as were the physical dossiers they contained, with their notes handwritten in pencil, and black-and-white photographs—but an affectation rooted in Tesla's deep-seated needs for security and secrecy. He was a great believer in computers and databases for research and surveillance, but a much greater believer in absolutely never storing any data electronically, even on those of his machines connected to nothing but the electrical outlets in the walls of his basement office. He had heard rumors that his erstwhile colleagues at the National Security Agency were making progress on technology that could access computers through the electrical grid.

Tesla was a great believer in rumors as well—at least when it came to the governmental intelligence apparatus that had once employed him, and for which he occasionally did freelance work, if anonymously, through a nested series of false identities and think tanks that existed only as post office boxes.

Satisfied that the thick folder was securely closed, Tesla stood up from his oak desk and took a few short steps to the door of the bank vault dug into one side of his basement. He turned the dial through the sixteen-digit combination, pleased with the complete silence of the tumblers even to his preternaturally sharp ears, then wheeled open the heavy door.

Nothing of his considerable wealth was stored in the vault. At least not of his wealth in various currencies, negotiable instruments, and specie. What it contained instead was a vast wealth of information.

Filing cabinet upon locked file cabinet lined the walls of the vault. Tesla approached one, selected a key from the ring hung around his neck, and, after unlocking the cabinet, pulled open the top drawer. He carefully placed the newly closed file, unlabeled like the cabinets, in the crowded drawer. He narrowed his eyes, making of the random placement of the file in a randomly chosen cabinet a conscious memory. The next time he needed it, he would cast his mind back and watch himself in his imagination: turning the tumblers of the vault's locking mechanism, taking a certain number of steps to a certain cabinet, tucking the file into a crowded drawer in a certain position, just so.

There were 4,622 folders stored in the vault, none labeled, all randomly filed. With a moment's thought, Tesla could locate any of them. An intruder would take days to locate a particular folder— and that after successfully cracking the combination of the vault; after successfully locating the hidden basement; after successfully identifying the anonymous house in the anonymous Northern Virginia suburb where Tesla, with a reasonable level of confidence, believed exactly one other person in the world knew he lived.

Of course, even after all that effort, the theoretical intruder would have to break the arcane cipher Tesla used in writing his research notes.

Vault closed, Tesla took his key ring from around his neck and stored it in a separate safe hidden in the basement's floor. He turned off the overhead light, red-bulbed and so casting light in the wavelength his infinitely adaptable eyes found best for close work, then pulled down the retractable staircase.

It was time to check the mail. Which meant it was time for lunch.

Tesla picked a cellphone from a rack of them on his kitchen counter. He powered it on for the first time, then used his nail tips to dial a number in the Netherlands. The ring that sounded reminded Tesla of an old-fashioned dial phone, which was easily explained by the fact that the number was for precisely that kind of device.

On the other side of the Atlantic Ocean, someone Tesla would never meet picked up the phone's handset and set it into a cradle. A tone sounded. Tesla dialed a thirty-digit number and patiently waited for the uplink that would send his call up to a satellite that had been launched from a Pacific atoll by no government and by no publicly known private enterprise. The signal bounced off the satellite down to an exchange, this afternoon's random one in rural Pennsylvania, and a third dial tone sounded. Tesla dialed again.

A woman's voice, aggressive, aged, and accented, came through the cellphone's speaker.

"China Star, may I help you?"

"I would like to order some food for delivery, please."

"Phone number?"

Tesla smiled. "This is Mr. Price."

"General Tso's chicken, steamed dumplings, right?"

"Yes, ma'am."

"Cash or charge?"

"Cash."

"Okay, thirty minutes."

Tesla pushed the DISCONNECT button. Then he dropped the phone into the industrial trash compactor that stood where a refrigerator would in someone else's kitchen and set it churning to destructive life.

The one other person in all the world who knew Tesla's address, the spectacularly well-educated daytime delivery driver for China Star, climbed the three brick steps to the front door. He did not knock. He did not press the button for the doorbell, which in any case was disconnected. Instead, he waved at the cleverly concealed camera above the lintel, set a brown paper bag on the wrought-iron table next to the door, and took a sealed business-sized envelope from inside the mailbox.

The envelope contained two $20 bills, one relatively new but not crisp, one relatively old but not creased.

The driver tapped the envelope once in his palm, moved it briefly near his left ear as if listening to it, then tucked it into a back pocket. With that, he left.

A moment later, the wrought-iron table sank into the porch. A moment after that, it rose up again, empty.

Tesla set his lunch out on the dining room table. As usual, the food was steaming hot. The broccoli in the chicken dish was bright green and he knew it would be perfectly cooked. His only complaint about the food from China Star was that, while they always had excellent vegetables, they never included enough of them.

He used a fork—his nails made him hopeless with chopsticks— to spear a dumpling and popped it in his mouth. His teeth, as

sharp and black as his fingernails and as the upturned horns growing from his temples, made quick work of the bite.

He ate quickly for a few minutes, but then slowed and contemplated the fortune cookie sealed in plastic that he had placed to
one side of his plate. He ruminated, with his mouth and with his
mind.

Then, with quick, precise movements, he picked up the fortune
cookie, removed it from its wrapper, and broke it in half. A small
rectangle of white paper, printed in red ink, fell onto the table.

Tesla could feel the electrical charge building up between his
horns and reflexively fought it down.

One side of the fortune had a series of numbers on it, meant for
lottery players. Below the numbers was a sentence, "Knowledge
blooms in new turned soil."

On the other side, there was a series of Chinese characters.
Below, in English: "Learn Chinese! What time does the train arrive?"

These things all taken together—numerals, fortune, phrase, and
Hanzi logograms—added up to a coded message. "Riverside observation deck. Old Town. Four A.M."

Tesla sighed. He hated going out. Especially so early in the
morning.

Going out, at least at the appointed time and traveling to the
appointed location, involved getting out the car. Tesla bought a
carefully anonymous upper-mid-range sedan every two years. On
average, each of the cars accumulated less than two hundred miles
while he owned them, which meant there was some obfuscation
involved in getting rid of them. Selling or trading in a car with that
little mileage recorded on the odometer was something the other
person involved in the transaction would remember. Tesla used
various methods of disposing of his old cars, including shipping

one overseas to a largely automated salvage yard, sinking one in Lake Ontario, and, once, sending one as an anonymous donation to a Jaycees chapter in Fayetteville, Arkansas, for use as a raffle prize.

He had carefully planned the fifty-five-mile route from his home to the meeting point with plans to arrive exactly ninety-five minutes early. He kept an eye on the screens of the three separate mapping devices he used for navigation as he backed out of his garage and drove out of the subdivision, observing the posted twenty-five-miles-per-hour speed limit carefully, but not *too* carefully.

One screen populated with moving dots showed him the locations of all local and state law enforcement vehicles currently moving around the road network between him and Alexandria. Another drew on various sources of data, mostly law enforcement but also media, to inform him of any traffic slowdowns or accidents. The third simply showed him the route he had planned out in advance, which ended in the long-term parking lot at National Airport. Convoluted, but not *too* convoluted.

The route from the airport to the park in Old Town, however, was not convoluted. Tesla was not entirely satisfied with that, but walking the multiuse trail two miles south to Oronoco Bay Park was a better solution than parking near the tourist area itself, even in the wolf hours of the morning.

He approached the appointed meeting site carefully, alert for signs of other watchers. The night was humid and warm, but Tesla was comfortable in black: jeans and a long-sleeved T-shirt he had sewn himself on a machine built up from parts sourced from auction sites all over the world.

Once he arrived at the park, he crouched at the base of the tree he had chosen from online tourists' photographs of the area. He would stay there, unmoving, for the next hour and a half, watching, watching, watching, before walking out to the short pier jutting into the Potomac River.

He did not ruminate on similar past encounters with clients. He did not let his thoughts wander down corridors of memory, with their endless doors and branchings and inevitable dead ends. He did not let himself think about *her*. He watched and watched and watched.

Nobody came into view during those ninety minutes he crouched. No night-haunting cats, no night-flying birds, no official patrols. No drunken carousers, out too late. No enthusiastic joggers, out too early.

Tesla knew when the moment arrived, but looked at his timepiece—a cheap watch carefully modified into an expensive one—to be sure. He stood and walked onto the pier.

Another slow, careful look around showed no sign of anyone approaching, no sign of any movement at all. Whoever this would-be client was, they had chosen their time and place carefully.

"You're good." The voice came from behind him, out in the river.

A boat. Tesla castigated himself over his elementary mistake.

But when he turned to face the Potomac, there was no watercraft. Instead, a man slowly rose from the water until he stood on its surface, gently bobbing in the current.

"Not good enough, apparently," said Tesla. He had seen stranger things than a man who could walk on water. It was that kind of a world.

The man shrugged as the water cascaded off him. He wore nothing but a pair of trunks of the type favored by competitive swimmers, so Tesla could see the scales along his torso, the fins at his feet, the gills at his neck. "You're a hard man to find," said the aquatic man.

Tesla decided that the man's words did not warrant a reply, so he just took a quick glance over his shoulder to satisfy himself the man had no allies creeping up on him unseen. He turned back to find that the man had come a yard closer to the pier's railings. Tesla began to let a charge grow between his horns.

"I didn't expect a joker," said the would-be client. "Or a jack, I guess we're supposed to say now, if you've got any powers. And I'm betting you do."

This time, Tesla shrugged.

"There's a lot about this situation I didn't expect, though," said the man. "When I started looking for somebody like you, somebody who knows how to track people down, I didn't expect to wind up in a pencil store. I didn't even know there was such a thing as a pencil store."

"There are stores for everything in New York City," said Tesla.

This particular store—the finest of its type in the world, though there were few establishments selling nothing but wood-cased pencils to give it any competition—was the point of contact for Tesla on the East Coast. It was how one reached him. A whisper of a rumor of a secret, hard-won, took people who needed to know things, eventually, to the store. The shopkeeper—an admirably closemouthed woman—listened to the inquiry, made a judgment as to its suitability as determined by the guidelines she had been given, and named a price. The inquiring party paid immediately and fully, or there the negotiation ended. The proprietor told the client where to go and when, never the same place twice, and that was it, except for her then ordering Chinese carryout at a restaurant owned by a cousin of the proprietor of Tesla's local China Star and placing a coded note in the envelope of cash she paid with. Things played out from there.

Things played out, in fact, to here and now.

"Pencils, though," said the man. "Who even uses pencils? Except bookies, I guess."

The man had a New York accent unadulterated by television or radio. In his diction, his pronunciation, and his emphases, he sounded to Tesla like a very old man indeed. But his voice was not that of an elderly man—though this meant little. There were very old aces and jokers in the world, and not all of them showed their age.

But Tesla knew most of the centenarians among his kind, and this man was not among their number. A mystery. To his dismay, he was growing interested in the situation.

"You don't talk much, do you?" The man bobbed another foot closer. He was almost close enough now to reach out and touch the railing. Tesla considered taking a step back, but the threat analysis he was running in one part of his mind told him that it was not yet time.

"As much as necessary," he replied.

"As much as I paid for this conversation," said the man, "I kind of thought we'd be chatting a lot more. It's not like we have a lot of time before people start showing up around here. I don't want to be seen, and I'm figuring you don't want to be, either."

Tesla nodded.

"Okay, then," said the man. A wayward ripple caused him to sink below the railing, then rise above it. "I doubt I'm going to learn much about you. In fact, I'd be disappointed if I did. But I need to tell you who I am if you're going to get anywhere with this job."

Tesla nodded again.

"My name's Croyd Crenson."

Memories, almost involuntary, came to Tesla. The door to the vault opened, the fourth cabinet in the second row to the left. The third drawer down. The first folder, and several more. Very, very thick folders.

"The Sleeper," said Tesla. "I suppose I should say it's an honor. It's certainly a notable event."

An annoyed look flashed across Crenson's face. "Used to be I could keep a low profile."

Tesla said, "You once caused a new outbreak of the wild card virus, eliciting a panic in the largest city in the country." He arched an eyebrow. "People *will* talk."

"Okay," said Crenson. "So you know my deal, right?"

Tesla mentally opened the file and read the précis on the first page. He came back to the pier. "You suffer from what Dr. Tachyon once referred to as a serial expression of the wild card virus. You are mutable. You sleep, you wake as a joker or an ace—or a jack, if you like—and you . . ." And here Tesla paused. "You influence those around you for a few weeks. You sleep. You wake. The cycle repeats, as it has for decades."

"Tachyon was a fuck," Croyd replied. "But yeah, that's pretty much it. 'Influence those around me,' heh. That's pretty good."

Out on the river, the low rumble of a passing boat sounded. Time was, in fact, growing short.

"What can I do for you, Mr. Crenson?" Tesla asked.

"There you go," Crenson replied. "Down to business. Two hundred grand's worth of business. That took me more time to get together than I wanted to spend."

Tesla waited. In perhaps ten minutes, he would leave the pier whether any job had been negotiated or not. He would disappear into the night, two hundred thousand dollars richer, and Croyd Crenson would swim out of his life, no doubt extremely frustrated. Tesla had frustrated many people in his life.

"Jesus, you're like a clam. Okay, I need you to find someone."

Tesla nodded. "Who?"

"I'll get to that," said Crenson. "First of all, can you do it? Someone in New York, I'm pretty sure. And I need you to do it pretty fucking fast."

Tesla did not hesitate. "Yes, of course. Without a doubt."

"You don't even know any details yet!"

"I know the person you seek is in New York, presumably alive. I know you are Croyd Crenson. I assume you will give me at least a hint as to this person's identity. That is more than enough to know that I can find this person." Tesla cocked a half smile. "And I know that I can do it pretty fucking fast."

"I like your confidence."

"The hint?"

"Hint?" A look of confusion passed over Croyd's face. "Oh! Who you're looking for! Easy enough. I need you to find me."

Tesla considered and rejected a number of obvious answers. Then he asked, "Will you be actively seeking to hide from me?"

"What? No! I'll give you my number and the address where I'm staying in the Bronx. It's the five other me's I need you to track down."

Tesla experienced an emotion, suppressed it, and noted it for later consideration. The emotion was delight. "And where were all of you last seen?"

This time, the look that crossed Crenson's face was surprise. "That's it? You don't want to know what I mean about there being five of me? Well, six of me. Counting me, I mean."

Tesla shook his head. "You slept. You woke. You were split into six bodies, presumably each possessed of consciousness and some notion of what and who they are. They dispersed for a reason you will now share. You wish me to find them for another reason you do not want to share. Problem being, I take very few jobs of this nature."

Crenson whistled low. "Fuck, you *are* good. But I don't want you to just find them. I want you to have them come meet me. All at the same time. There are no jobs like this."

Tesla hesitated. He'd been in his hideaway seeing almost no one for so long, but this was an intriguing opportunity. He might be the only one who could accomplish it. That alone seduced him. "I *will* find them and communicate their locations to you. In the Bronx."

"You don't want to know why?" In the distance, a dog barked.

"You've said. You wish to bring yourselves back together. Presumably so that only one of you will leave the reunion." Tesla turned and walked back into the park.

"Hey, wait a minute," called Crenson. "I didn't you give my number or address!"

Tesla didn't turn, trusting that the aquatic man could hear him even while he was facing away and moving with a swift stride into the dark. "I'll find you," he said.

Having used a powerful acid to remove the VIN and any other identifying details of the car—he would be driving across state lines soon, and he did not like to cross state lines in cars he owned— Tesla managed to make it home just before dawn. He had moved from shadow to shadow in his final walk, using hard-won tradecraft to ensure he was not seen.

Once home, he took an hour to make his breakfast—a porridge of steel-cut oats and millet—then sat eating it thoughtfully. He ran his eyes over the screen of a laptop, half reading articles on the webpages of a dozen newspapers around the world written in various languages. Nothing floated to the top of his awareness, though. He would recall the substance of the articles later if the need arose.

Mostly, he thought about the problem that Croyd Crenson had presented him with. The *problems*, rather. Croyds in the plural.

Tesla was made out of rituals. So, finishing his breakfast, rinsing the dishes and cutlery in the sink, placing them in the dishwashing machine just so, these things brought comfort. Tesla was also made out of pain, out of loss, out of losing *her*, and he took comfort wherever he could.

Now it was time to work.

In the basement, he turned the tumblers. He went to the appropriate cabinet and opened the appropriate drawer. He did not need to call the appropriate folder to mind because the four thick folders that took up all the drawer's space dealt with the same subject.

Croyd Crenson, a man who had disrupted the plans and troubled the minds of the mighty for nearly three-quarters of a century.

Tesla took the first folder out to his worktable, unwound the string, and opened it. He began to read.

These are the things Tesla read about Croyd Crenson.

He was a petty thief. He was a capable second-story man. He could barely walk. He was as fast as the wind. He weighed a thousand pounds. He could fly. He was a handsome man. He was a hideous monstrosity. He was a soldier, a fugitive, a fighter, a spy, a hit man, a ghost, a vector, and an addict. He evinced an unaccountable interest in algebra.

He was a villain.

He was a hero.

He was, in many ways, the living embodiment of the wild card virus. He was its greatest victim and its greatest success.

He was—and this is why, Tesla believed, he had agreed to the request of the Croyd Crenson he had spoken to a few hours earlier—a mystery.

How could such a man have even survived down the long years since the virus was released, much less had such a large role in recent history? How could he have been so many places, done such violence, and saved so many days? How had he been infamous among so many people and unknown to so many others?

Who *was* Croyd Crenson? How, at bottom, could Croyd Crenson *be*?

Tesla was near the end of the first folder now, having read what details were available on his subject from the dawn of the wild card age in 1948 until the early '60s. A few pages from the bottom of the stack, he came across a postcard.

He did not turn it over because he knew nothing was written on the other side besides the credit for the photograph depicted on the front. Tesla had ordered the postcard from the gift shop of the Museum of Modern Art when he had first assembled his Crenson folder. As far as he knew, the photograph it reproduced still hung in some gallery or another at MoMA.

The subject of the photograph was the subject of Tesla's inquiry. Crenson was always mutable, of course; it was his defining characteristic. But this picture—one of a series by a marginally famous photographer active in New York City in the 1960s and '70s—was rare in actually showing Crenson in media res. Lying on a couch, with a late-afternoon sunbeam falling across his face, was a man being both melted and molded. Here was the Sleeper, sleeping.

Now Tesla turned over the card and read the name of the marginally famous photographer. He took a moment to recall the pertinent details of every obituary of any substance published in *The New York Times* since the mid-'60s and decided that she was still alive.

He would determine her place of residence before obtaining another car, of course, but he was sure to a greater-than-reasonable degree that she would still be in New York. So few people ever left that city.

Except Croyd Crenson, of course, who had been active all over the world. But New York City was where he had been born. And it was where he always returned.

Over the course of the last fifteen years, since he had become what he had become—in more than one sense—few things had delighted Tesla. He was surprised, therefore, to find himself delighted to learn that there was a man in Brooklyn who made his living secretly sinking automobiles into the East River. He did so for cash only.

When he traveled, Tesla always carried a great deal of cash.

His wallet not noticeably lightened, Tesla went underground. Literally, in that he took the subway. Tesla was always figuratively underground.

He knew he would have to go to Jokertown eventually. He

would have to make personal contact with people who knew of or at least suspected his existence. This made him profoundly uneasy, but on the drive up from Virginia in a minivan liberated from a private impound lot, Tesla had had time to reflect on what, exactly, he was doing in pursuing half a dozen expressions of someone who could arguably be described as the most dangerous individual on the planet.

Tesla realized that he was taking risks.

He had not yet determined why.

He did not go to Jokertown, though; not yet. He went to another of the great neighborhoods that collectively made up the great city: the storied Village.

If his information was correct—and here Tesla allowed himself another small moment of delight, even a chuckle, at the notion that his information could possibly be incorrect—then the woman he wished to talk to lived on this street, on this block, in this building, in this apartment.

A chuckle. What was happening to him? He pressed aside the emotion.

He climbed to the third floor. It was late afternoon—about the time the photograph on the postcard in his breast pocket had been taken.

Tesla knocked, then stepped back from the door so he could be fully seen through the peephole, as was polite. He heard the sounds of movement within and saw the change in light in the little circle of glass that indicated he was being observed.

"May I help you?" The voice was that of an old woman, but with a quiet strength.

"Ms. Marshall," said Tesla, retrieving the postcard and holding it up. "I believe we have a mutual friend."

Days Go By

by Carrie Vaughn

April 1961

The apartment had somehow gotten crowded over the last hour, Iris Marshall observed from behind the kitchen table, sheltered by a barrier of bottles and empty glasses. It somehow always got crowded whenever Fletcher said he was only going to "invite a few people over." Word got around, the cheap bottles of wine came out, and the talk got louder and more passionate until they were all shouting to be heard. Someone had put on a record of experimental jazz, with a lot of high-pitched saxophone and notes in a jumble.

If Iris was completely honest with herself, she'd admit that she loved this: the noise, the ebb and flow of faces and styles as guests came and went and circled around the apartment, looking for people they knew, on the prowl for others they'd like to know. The up-and-comers, the next big thing. Parties like this were the thread that held the Village art and music scene together. They got crowded because no one wanted to miss anything.

She and Fletcher shared the loft on 8th Street, a block off Washington Square—bigger than most with an actual window overlooking the alley to let in some light and air. A kitchenette in one corner, a bathroom right next to it, a closet that was big enough to pretend to be their bedroom, and the rest of the space doubling as a living room and studio and whatever else they needed. They had a lumpy sofa and a couple of secondhand armchairs, but anyone who wanted to sit was just as likely to use the floor. Fletcher shoved his easel and canvases in the corner for parties like this. Sometimes, he even pulled them back out again to work.

"Miss Canvas, let me pour you a glass." A man with his collar unbuttoned stumbled against the table, rattling glasses, holding up a sloshing bottle of wine.

"No, thank you, I'm all right," she answered, her polite smile going lopsided with amusement. Gary, one of Fletcher's painter friends.

Very drunk, he seemed to get stuck a moment, leaning on the table and staring at her, his jaw going slack, his eyes going vague, as if hypnotized. If he weren't careful, he'd start drooling. "I could watch your face all day," he murmured.

She did not know what she looked like right at this moment, only that a never-ending pattern of shapes and colors passed over her skin all the time. Like a painting that was always changing, a spatter of lines shifting into blotches of color, impressionistic streaks transforming to pointillist shadows and back again. All of it abstract and entrancing. Or so she was told. She didn't much like looking at mirrors since she'd been diagnosed with the wild card virus two years ago. She glanced at her arms. On the left, a streaky hatch mark skittered across a backdrop of rust red, fading to gray. On the right, that same red formed splotches, an abstract splashing of paint à la Pollock. Made her want to put on a sweater, to cut down on the distraction. Maybe wear a hat with a veil.

"Have some crackers, Gary. Something to soak up all that wine." She offered him the nearby bowl, and this startled him out of his reverie.

"Right. Thanks." He grabbed a handful of crackers and wandered off again, looking for someone to pour his wine into.

The music stopped abruptly. Half the crowd booed and the other half cheered, and another record went on the turntable. More jazz, this one heavy on the drums. Iris got her camera out of its safe spot in the cupboard and considered what to frame with it. A laughing woman, her hair coming loose from its once perfect coif. Two men with cigarettes bent over the record player as if talking to it.

Fletcher stood in the middle of the room, like a sun watching all revolve around him, smiling magnanimously. He was a tall man with an athletic build. His shirt was crisp, his sleeves rolled up to give him a look that was somehow both polished and casual. A man at home in his realm. That was the image he liked to convey, at least. He made sure he spoke to everyone who came through the door.

"Dave, great to see you, glad you could make it!" he said, offering a hand to the scruffy bearded man who had just come in with a small entourage of young, equally scruffy friends, blinking around them with uncertainty.

"Fletch! Loud in here, isn't it?"

"And who're your friends?"

"This is Bobby Dylan, just moved to town a month or so ago and he's already playing gigs—"

Fletcher beamed at the kid. "Well, that's great! I'll be sure to come listen—"

He should have been a politician. A car salesman.

A couple of the newcomers scanned the room, and their gazes stopped dead on Iris. People's gazes always did. The Bobby kid was the only one who didn't immediately look away. One of the others backed up, tugging on the jacket sleeve of the man next to her. Boyfriend, maybe. "Eddie, I don't want to be here, not with one of *those* people." The woman was thin, artistically angular, dressed in a belted sweater over her tights.

"Aw, she's harmless. I heard about her, they call her Miss Canvas. Because she looks like a painting, you know?"

"But what if it's catching?" the woman hissed.

"I don't think you can catch it—"

"Eddie!" She was already dragging him back toward the door.

"Okay, hon, we'll go." They vanished out to the hall. Couldn't seem to get out fast enough. Iris pretended to fiddle with the film-advance lever. Head bent over, not noticing the scorn, not noticing anything at all.

Half the people in the room wouldn't talk to her. Would only look at her with a horrified curl to their lips, or an expression of wide-eyed pity. This was part of why she usually hid behind the table—to save them having to escape from her. Enough people did talk to her that she could pretend not to notice. It made the awkward leering of someone like Gary almost welcome. She took a picture of the doorway, and the last view of their retreating backs. It would come out blurry, they ducked out so fast. She could call the image *Flight*.

"Iris, do we have anything else to eat?" Fletcher was suddenly at her side, leaning on the table.

She quickly lowered the camera and smiled at him. "Just the crackers and peanuts. Everybody already ate all the sandwiches I put out—"

"Well, why don't you make more?"

"Because we're out of bread. I can't feed the whole neighborhood—"

His expression went hooded as the perfection he imagined for the evening stumbled. She knew that look. He was about to say something horrible, in a low voice so no one else would hear. He saved all his politeness for others.

"Anderson! Where the hell is Fletch Anderson!" The shouting voice carried from the hallway. Like a record scratch interrupting the impending argument, and Iris suppressed a grateful sigh. "Anderson! Where—"

A man swung into the loft, gripping the edge of the doorway. He was of average height, and he looked a mess, his shirt unbuttoned and his trousers stained, as if he'd been sitting on wet park benches. He needed a shave, and his eyes were bloodshot.

Fletcher grumbled, "Not now . . ." He put on his politician's smile. "Croyd Crenson. How are you?"

Unwell, clearly. Anyone could see that. The disheveled man focused on Fletcher and Iris, turning the intensity of a marksman on them. Their guests hurriedly parted as Croyd shot toward Fletcher, stumbling against the kitchen table.

"Hi," he said to Iris, studying her appraisingly and then looking away. He looked *away*, as if she were perfectly normal and had no deformity worth commenting on. With Fletcher, he made demands. "You got some? Whatever you got, I need it. Now."

"Croyd, you already bought up everything I had, I told you—"

"So when'll you get more?"

"A couple of days, I just need—"

"I don't have a couple of days, I need it *now*! Jesus, what kind of beatnik slum you running up here?" He blinked confusedly, as if he'd just noticed he'd walked in on a party. Arrhythmic drums continued beating out of the turntable.

"Croyd. Maybe you'd feel better if you got some sleep—"

"*No.* That's the whole point, I *don't need sleep.* Where you hiding it? You've got to be hiding something . . ." He pushed past Fletcher and started opening drawers under the kitchen counter, digging through cutlery, slamming each one shut before moving to the next.

"Fletcher, who is this?" Iris asked, hugging her camera protectively to her.

"Never mind, I'll take care of it." He reached, probably intending to take Croyd by the shoulders and steer him away. "Come on, Croyd, why don't you come on over and sit down—"

Snarling, Croyd turned to face Fletcher and heaved out a breath of thick, noxious smoke, yellowish and curling. Iris scrambled out of the way, holding her breath so she didn't get a whiff of it. But

Fletcher took it full in the face. He blinked a couple of times. Then his eyes rolled back in his head and he pitched over. Passed out, knocked against the counter, and collapsed to the floor. A woman screamed, which summoned the attention of everyone in the room. Even the record player hit a pause.

All those stares seemed to drive Croyd Crenson mad. He backed against the counter, his teeth bared. He lunged at the woman who had screamed and breathed a yellow fog into her face. Like Fletcher, she wavered a moment, then collapsed bonelessly.

"What *is* that?"

"I don't know—"

"Looks like mustard gas or something. From the war—the first war. My dad talked about it—"

"That guy's breathing *mustard gas!*"

This inspired a stampede for the door. Croyd must have seen it as an attack. He tried to fight through it, swinging wild punches, heaving more of the offensive breaths—a near-perfect weapon in a crowded space like this. Iris pressed herself flat to the kitchen wall and tried to figure out what to do. They didn't have a phone; she couldn't call the police. Not that the police would even come. She could try to get to the window—

Standing in the middle of the four other bodies he'd brought down, Croyd looked at her across the room. He panted, and each breath emitted a thick yellow puff. If he were drunk she could settle him down, but this was something else. He lurched, reaching, like he wanted to attack her next, and she started for the bathroom, which had a door with a reliable lock. But then he wavered. He stood planted, and his whole body seemed to sag, as if his weight had increased, or gravity had, and it was pulling him inexorably toward the floor.

"I just . . . I just need . . . just a couple more days . . ." His outstretched arm became beseeching rather than aggressive. As if Iris could give him those extra days.

Then he collapsed, just like the others.

— — —

It wasn't mustard gas, it turned out, because Fletcher was picking himself off the floor a few minutes later. So were the others Croyd had caught. They were shaking their heads and blinking confusedly, complaining of headaches. Some kind of knockout gas, then.

Croyd—he was fast asleep. Iris had dared to approach, tentatively reaching for his wrist to check for a pulse. She found one, so he wasn't dead, but no matter how much she shook him, he wouldn't wake up.

She put her camera away and tried to take care of everyone else, offering glasses of water and aspirin. Opening the window to let in what passed for fresh air in New York City. Wide-eyed and shocky, the other victims of Croyd's knockout breath fled as soon as they got to their feet. Fletcher remained on the floor, his back propped against the wall, for a good long time, glaring at Croyd's slumped form.

"Well. At least people will be talking about this," he muttered. "Yeah, that's Fletcher, the guy who throws parties where weird wild card freaks show up." He gave her a sidelong, chagrined look but didn't apologize.

"Should we call a doctor?"

"Oh, no, he's just asleep."

She didn't know how he could be so sure. "Do you think maybe we should put him on the sofa? Until he wakes up?"

Fletcher agreed. He took the man's shoulders while Iris took his feet, and they muscled him onto the sofa. He was just slightly too tall for it, and continued to look awkward and uncomfortable no matter how they arranged his knees and elbows. Iris unlaced and slipped off his shoes, tucking them neatly by the wall. Croyd snored softly.

Struck by the image, this man haphazardly slung on the sofa and oblivious to all, she fetched her camera and snapped a couple of pictures. The image would tell a story. What story, she wasn't quite sure. She could call the photo *Last One Not Standing*.

She pulled the blanket off the back of the sofa to put over him, but Fletcher began earnestly searching his pockets. It was definitely rude, and almost obscene the way he patted Croyd's shirt, reached around to feel his back trouser pockets, then started on the front.

"Fletcher, what are you doing?"

"He was trying to buy speed, he had to have cash on him. There." He pulled an impressive wad of bills out of Croyd's front trouser pocket. There must have been a couple hundred dollars there.

Iris winced. "Are you sure you should be—"

He pocketed the money. "Call it rent for the sublet on our sofa. He's going to be here awhile, if what I've heard about him is true."

"And what have you heard about him?"

"They call him the Sleeper."

Sure enough, Croyd was still asleep at the next big party, a week later.

"Are you sure we shouldn't call a doctor about him?" she asked, regarding the man still sprawled on their sofa. He was changing. His hair was falling out, brown strands scattered in a fall over the sofa cushion. His knees and elbows seemed to jut out even more; he fit on the sofa even less well than he had at the start, as if he was growing. His shirt and trousers seemed to be getting looser, as if he was getting thinner.

"I'm sure," Fletcher said, though his confidence sounded forced. "This is just what he does. Besides, what's a doctor going to do but let him sleep somewhere and see what happens?"

If Croyd changed like this every time he slept, no wonder he was desperate to stay awake. No wonder he'd been so crazy to get his hands on more pills. She hoped his temper was better when he woke up. "How long you been selling the guy speed?" She glanced at Fletcher sidelong.

"Never mind."

Iris hadn't been aware that Fletcher was selling speed out of their apartment. No, that wasn't entirely true. She had suspected. She had ignored the signs. The reason he was so friendly and inviting, why so many strangers showed up at their parties and left so quickly. She told herself it wasn't any of her business. Assured herself that it didn't mean anything and he must know what he was doing.

When she met Fletcher, he had introduced himself as a painter. He still did. Every now and then he pulled out a single painting to show off, the one he called *Three Tin Cans*, which was a textured smear of gray acrylic paint against a black backdrop. He'd been showing off the same painting for six months.

This week, Iris hoped she'd made enough sandwiches.

A newcomer to the party stopped in the doorway and stared. "It's true! He's really been asleep here for a week?"

"He sure has," Fletcher said, presiding over the man on the sofa like he was an art installation.

"I bet I can wake him up." The new guy produced a set of bongos. He must have been hiding them under his jacket somehow. A general chorus of groans and boos met this announcement. If they'd known he'd been carrying bongos he'd never have been let in. Undeterred, he sat cross-legged on the floor right by Croyd's head and started playing some boom-chicka basic rhythm. Mostly kept it, even.

This started a new game, a whole round of shouts and noise trying to wake Croyd. This only broke off when the Black woman who had a weekend gig at the Gate started singing. Everyone shut up to listen to her.

Croyd didn't wake up.

Iris watched it all from her shelter behind the table, simultaneously appalled and in awe. This was ebullient, this was life without fetters. It was rude, and it thrilled her. She took a few pictures, struck by the image of the singer, her head tipped back, hands clasped over her heart, singing to the sleeping Croyd like she was crooning a lullaby. Bohemian lullaby.

This was the best part of holding parties in the loft. Maybe Iris never got any sleep and was forever cleaning up empty bottles and spilled beer. But then she got a front-row seat to an impromptu concert, a round of performance art. The poetry and music that would be big in six months, and she got to hear it first.

She took a few photos of the table, trying to capture the way the light played off the dozens of empty bottles crowded on it, and the way the glass blurred the lines of the bottles around them and the wall behind.

An older man leaned on the counter in the kitchen and took a long draw on his cigarette. "Older" in this crowd meant over thirty. He'd probably been around for a while; might even have known Ginsberg and Kerouac. Wearing a wry half grin, he watched her taking pictures. Blushing—not that anyone could see her blushing—she set the camera aside and retrieved the platter of sandwiches off the kitchen counter.

"Would you like some—" She suddenly recognized him, the boyish clean-shaven face and receding hairline. The wry expression. "Oh, Mr. O'Hara. I heard you reading at Brata a couple of weeks ago. It was wonderful."

"That's sweet of you. Please call me Frank. Miss . . . ?"

Miss Canvas, she almost said. What everyone called her. Well, not usually to her face. Instead, she managed to offer her hand for shaking. "Iris. Iris Marshall."

"Nice to meet you." He looked her up and down, a skeptical furrow to his brow. "Don't take this the wrong way, but you don't really fit in with the girls I usually see around the Village." Her cheeks grew hot. She ducked her gaze and tucked a strand of hair behind her ear, trying to buy herself a moment to figure out what to say. "No, I don't mean that," he added quickly. "Forget about that. Head over to the Lower East Side, you'll see a dozen girls like you. I mean the finger sandwiches. Like you're hosting a cocktail party at some swank house on Long Island."

Oh, yes, that. There was nothing bohemian or Beat about Iris. She had on a pressed shirtwaist dress in a mild blue, with a full skirt and neat collar. Respectable pumps, hair that was neither too long nor too short. All she was missing was the pearl necklace. "I suppose so," she said, with a stifled chuckle. "I don't think I'm quite ready for the all-black artistic look."

He added, "So what's your story? Why aren't you at Smith, walking across campus with an armful of books?"

Her eyes filled with tears, which she quickly brushed away. She had thought she was over being sad about that.

Frank drew back. "Oh . . . you *were* at Smith?"

"I should have graduated last year. I was a junior when I . . . left." He waited, still with that skeptical arch. Like he could see right through her. "Was asked to leave. It was, and I quote, 'no longer possible for me to reach the ideal toward which the college encourages its young ladies to strive.' They were very kind about it, I'm sure."

"Aw honey, I'm sorry. That stinks."

"Thanks. It does stink, doesn't it?" She put on a smile, spreading her arms in a gesture of acceptance. "So I came to the Village to find myself. Just like everyone else."

"Let me know if it works. It hardly ever does. You a photographer?"

"Oh, I just dabble a bit."

"I'd love to see some of your pictures sometime."

"Is that a come-on, Frank?"

"You're not really my type. Your boyfriend, however . . ." He winked.

She'd heard rumors, of course. There were lots of men—and

some women—like him in the Village. It was part of why a lot of them came here. She wondered if she ought to warn him away from Fletcher, who wouldn't take that kind of come-on as a compliment. "Well, you can see some of my work in the advertising flyers for Manelli's Restaurant. I've become a master at capturing the way the cheese drips off a slice of lasagna in crisp black and white."

He laughed. "You know, I think I saw that one. Well done."

"It pays the bills. What I do . . . it's nothing special."

"Maybe that's what'll make it good. Everybody in this room wants to be special. Just like everyone else, right?" He grinned and drew another breath through his cigarette.

Now the singer was leading the rest of the partygoers in a round, and tapping the bongo player's shoulder to keep him on rhythm, which seemed a small miracle.

"I just . . . I would love to be able to capture this. One image, the thousand words and all that. I suppose that's what we're all trying to do."

"Preach. Thanks for the sandwich."

The sound of smashing glass, followed by a raucous cheer, meant a broken bottle, so Iris found a washcloth and went to track down the mess. A bottle of beer, quickly cleaned up, with help. No sign of Fletcher in the press of people. She lost track of Frank, too, but was still tickled that he'd been in the apartment and had actually spent a minute talking to her. It was nice of him to do that.

It must have been 3 A.M. by the time the party mostly petered out, and she was cleaning up what she could in the kitchen, making sure the last of the sandwiches went into the icebox—she'd made enough this time—and putting dishes in the sink to wash in the morning.

Fletcher waited until the last of their guests was gone, standing by to shut the door on their apartment, before stalking over to plant his hand on the counter next to her. He loomed, glaring. Furious. She could tell by the hitch in his breath, the tension in his arm. She couldn't figure out why. She stared back at him, blinking in a panic, a rabbit in the sight of a hawk.

"Do you know who that was?"

"Who?"

"That guy you were talking to."

She'd talked to a few guys. Fletcher wasn't usually one to get jealous. He knew she was a novelty, a freak, and that most of the men who flirted with her weren't serious. Were just making fun of her. He was the only one who'd ever asked to take her home. "Which one?"

"Do you even know who that was?"

"Fletcher, what—"

"The older guy, the guy in the kitchen who you slinked right up next to. The two of you laughing together—"

He's a homosexual, she almost told him. *He isn't interested in me.* "Yes, it was Frank O'Hara. The poet. He's really nice, Fletcher. I wouldn't have expected someone of his stature to be so approachable—"

Fletcher actually bared his teeth. His hand on the counter closed to a fist. "He's also a curator at the Museum of Modern Art. And you didn't think about introducing him to me?"

Vaguely, in the back of her mind, Iris must have heard something about Frank O'Hara the poet also being a curator at MoMA. An important person. Someone worth knowing. Someone who could open doors for an aspiring artist. A would-be artist.

Fletcher was the glad-hander between them. The outgoing host. The one who made sure to greet everyone who came through the door. How could he have missed someone with real status? She'd had such a nice conversation with the man, how could she possibly have been expected to think of Fletcher in that moment? She just assumed he'd already spoken with everyone who'd been here.

She met Fletcher's gaze, and hers hardened. "And if I had introduced you, what would you have done? Shown him your tin cans?"

He didn't hit her. He never hit her. But he growled—he actually growled—and hit the counter with his fist hard enough that she jumped. She put her hands to her ears—an inexplicably childish gesture that she wished she hadn't made. Then he marched to their bedroom and slammed shut the door. The whole building seemed to rattle. She knew better than to try to open it. It might not be locked, but the message was clear: She wasn't welcome, not tonight.

The living room smelled like beer, and the bongos had been abandoned in a corner, lying on their side. Absently, she went to set them right-side up. Wasn't much else here. The record player, the pile of canvases and crate full of art supplies in the corner. She suddenly wished Fletcher would find studio space somewhere. A lot of artists got together to rent studio space. Maybe he would actually work, if he didn't have to paint where he lived.

She'd have thrown off her shoes and slept on the sofa, but the sofa was occupied, which just seemed par for the course this evening.

Croyd had shifted some. An arm that had been tucked in was thrown back, his face pressed toward the cushion. This meant the blanket over him was freed from his grip. She wouldn't have to wrestle him for it. At least she could have the blanket. Before peeling it away from him, though, she found her camera. Tried to frame it like she had the last one. Snapped the shutter. *Last One Not Standing, Part 2.*

She wrapped herself in the blanket and propped her back against the sofa, which was a little softer than the wall. "I hope you don't mind. It's just . . . it's better if Fletcher has time to cool off alone. I'll be fine. I can sleep anywhere, you know. But I guess you know what that's like, hmm? Well. Good night, Croyd."

He snored.

– – –

The next day, Fletcher apologized for yelling and took her out to a nice dinner. Using Croyd's money, no doubt. She had long ago gotten used to the stares she got, going out with Fletcher. She didn't mind. Much. And Fletcher didn't seem to mind, either, for which she was grateful. Even if they did always seem to sit in the back of restaurants. She promised that the next time they ran into Frank O'Hara, she would introduce him to Fletcher. She hoped that would absolve her of any neglect she might have been guilty of. When she invited him to come along on a job she had at a gallery show a few nights later, Fletcher was all smiles. They walked down the street, her camera bag in hand and Fletcher with his arm protectively over her shoulder, and the night felt just about perfect. A nice New York spring, a hint of blooming trees in the air, and a deep-blue twilit sky overhead. If she were a painter, that was the sort of color she would try to capture. She hadn't worked much with color film—yet. Even with black and white, she could get the shapes. Looking straight up, the jagged edges of the buildings seemed like some kind of wall against that deepening sky. So she stopped and did just that, and thanked Fletcher for patiently holding her bag.

When they arrived at Limelight, the opening was underway, people already streaming in. Helen Gee, the gallery owner, wanted the photos for publicity and catalogs, and Iris was pretty sure she could place a couple in the social pages of one of the big dailies, especially if any genuine celebrities showed up.

"You don't mind if I go off for a little while, to take pictures? That would give you a chance to talk to people." She said this hopefully, worried that Fletcher intended to cling. Him looking over her shoulder while she shot always made her nervous. He'd make suggestions and be offended if she didn't take them. But he ought to be happy, being in the middle of a scene like this.

"Sure, hon. In fact . . . is that Warhol over there?" He took off across the room.

She spent the next hour engrossed in the frame of her view-finder and the comforting snap of the shutter. When she hid behind her camera, no one bothered her much, and she could watch the party without having to interact with it. Helen was on hand to give instructions—let's have a shot of this art critic in front of the work of that up-and-comer. It was a good exercise in composition, how to get a painting in the frame, along with the people looking at the painting, making the shot look candid rather than posed. She wanted to give the viewer the sense of being at a great party, and being jealous that they weren't there. The sense that, if they came to Limelight, they might get to be part of the next one. A lot to convey, in a single image.

"Miss Canvas, people call her Miss Canvas. It's like someone painted on her."

"I don't think it should be allowed, people like that being around normal people like us."

"She's harmless."

"How does someone get to be like that?"

"It's that alien virus . . ."

It was looking at the pictures of Jackson Pollock's work in that one issue of *Life* magazine, feeling like she was learning a different language. That the world cracked open and spilled out a bigger world, like something marvelous being born. She had majored in art history, trying to learn the language to explain what it all meant. And then she'd come to the Village because she hoped she could find a place that wouldn't reject her.

"Freak."

She found herself gasping. A hitch in her breath as she ferociously locked down on wanting to cry. As smoothly and casually as possible, her chin up and her steps even, because she didn't want anyone to think anything was wrong, she headed for the door, which thankfully was standing wide open, and then outside into the night air that just had a hint of coming summer stickiness.

And she kept going, suddenly deciding she needed to march across the street to the Riviera, to maybe get a cup of tea to calm her nerves. She wasn't in a good state of mind, and she wasn't paying attention. Only the squealing of tires on asphalt made her look up, and by then the car was nearly on top of her. Stupidly, she froze, blinded by headlights but still somehow glimpsing the equally shocked face in the driver's seat.

Then, with a *thump* and a crunch of steel, the car just *stopped*. Bounced on its tires and halted.

Frank O'Hara was standing between her and the car, his hand on the hood, which had a dent in the metal where he'd grabbed hold. He'd put out his hand and stopped the car, just like that. "How could you not see her!" he shouted at the driver. "Not like she blends into the scenery! Christ!"

He put his hand on her elbow and pulled her back to the curb, and the car squealed off, the driver shouting curses back.

"Iris. You okay?"

Only now did she start shaking, her breath coming out in a nervous laugh. Getting creamed on Seventh Avenue would have solved a lot of problems, wouldn't it? "Yes, I think . . . I just need to . . ." She turned her gaze on Frank. "You—you're an ace. Like Golden Boy."

He ducked his face to hide a smile. "Not very much like Golden Boy. I can stop a car; I can't lift it over my head. But yeah, I guess so."

"Nobody knows! You don't tell anyone. Why—"

"You were headed over to the Riviera? You need a coffee or something? Maybe a whiskey, after that?"

"Tea. I was . . . just going to get some tea. To settle my nerves." She laughed. The sound was brittle, on the edge of tears. She did *not* want to start crying, but holding her breath certainly wasn't the solution, and she gasped again. "No, wait. You have to come meet Fletcher. Fletcher will kill me if he finds out you were here and I didn't introduce you." She took hold of his jacket sleeve to pull him to the gallery.

He chuckled. "Fletcher. That very smug pretty boy of yours?"

She didn't know that Fletcher was really hers. She wanted to think so, but she wasn't sure. "He's a painter. At least . . . well, he's trying to be a painter. I think. Any advice you can give him . . . That would be great. He doesn't listen to me at all."

She plunged on ahead before she could second-guess herself and decide this was a bad idea. Fletcher was standing with a gaggle of other young artists and hangers-on, regarding a large painting full of muted colors, beige and pale orange, in vague shapes that seemed to travel down the canvas in a spiral. Like an autumn day, swirling leaves in a cold mist.

"This isn't so great. I could paint like that," Fletcher was saying. *But you don't,* she thought. She put on her best smile. "Fletcher! You wanted to meet Mr. O'Hara, didn't you?"

The crowd parted before them. Village royalty approached. Fletcher changed for his audience, from all-knowing superior art critic to fawning admirer, grabbing Frank's hand and pumping it like he was running for office. "Mr. O'Hara, it's great to meet you, I'm Fletcher Anderson—"

She'd done it. Fletcher was happy. All was well.

The pair of them talked for a time, and Fletcher seemed to be listening intently. Helen came by and asked Iris how she was doing, and she burbled a bit about the couple of rolls of film she'd already shot, how she was sure she got some great pictures, and what a great show this was. Iris didn't have to feign enthusiasm. This was just the sort of job she'd like to do more of, and said so. Helen seemed happy as she went off to see to her guests, and Iris turned back . . . to hear Fletcher's voice raised. Frank, who was shorter, had stepped back and regarded the younger man with a thin wry smile, like he'd heard this before and wasn't impressed. Fletcher had enough social acumen to pick up the mild contempt, and it made him angry. Iris was going to have to jump in, wasn't she? She felt ill.

"What is it you want, kid?" Frank said finally. "Take a minute to think about it. Exactly what do you want?"

Flustered, Fletcher didn't take a minute to think about it. "I want to be a famous painter, of course. Like Jackson Pollock."

"You want to be famous, or to be a painter?"

"Look, I just want to know how he did it, how I can do what he did—"

"You can't do what he did. It's already been done."

To his credit, Fletcher was restraining himself. He might have been gritting his teeth and turning red in the face, but he wasn't outright shouting. Then he glanced over and saw Iris looking on, with what must have seemed like pity in her eyes. It *was* pity, because Frank had asked, *Do you want to be famous, or a painter?* and Fletcher seemed not to even understand the question. He thought there was a secret, and that people like Frank were withholding it out of spite.

"If you'll excuse me," Fletcher said, and marched across the gallery and out the door.

Well, at least he'd kept his temper in check.

Frank smirked after him. "At least tell me he's good in bed."

She blushed hard, not that anyone would notice.

They went out for that drink after all. She got her tea, Frank got his whiskey.

"I think Fletcher would be a really good painter if he actually, you know . . . painted."

"I know the type," Frank said tiredly. "They sit at Reggio's in their black turtlenecks clutching blank notebooks and insist they want to be poets. Most of 'em get bored pretty quick. Your Fletcher—pretty as he is, he should own a gallery. Except I suspect he doesn't have any taste."

She smiled ruefully. "I don't really want to talk about Fletcher. He is what he is. He's kind to me." Usually. "But you—I hope it isn't rude of me to ask, but I'm so curious. I so rarely meet anyone else like . . . us. How long have you . . . you know. Had powers."

He shrugged. "Happened a couple of years after I moved to New York, back in '51. I'm not one of the originals; I picked it up later. Not sure when or how. You listen to the doctors, they say some people may get infected but not know it for years. That it's dormant, and then poof, one day, you're stopping cars with your bare hands." He made a dry snap of his fingers and seemed unconcerned.

"And you don't tell anyone."

"Habit, mostly. But lots of reasons, really. In some circles being an ace is worse than being a commie. The Conscription Act is still on the books, you know? A radical poet ace fairy from Greenwich Village? McCarthy would have loved to get his claws on me. God rot his soul."

She had been isolated from the politics of the decade past. What was there to know? It didn't concern her. She learned manners and worked just hard enough to get into Smith, where she had planned on working just hard enough to meet the right people and be invited into the right social circles, marry well, have children, and then . . . Well, none of that had turned out so well in the end. Polite society didn't care much for her plans, after what happened to her.

She hadn't considered that her being asked to leave Smith was political. It was just . . . the way things were. But she wondered now: What if she had put up a fight?

"The ones like me are lucky, I guess," Frank said. "We can hide it. Not like you."

"You know I tried? Put on a bunch of foundation and powder to try to cover it up, and I just looked like a demented clown." He laughed, but it was friendly, sympathetic laughter. Because the image she conjured *was* pretty funny. "Do you mind if I take your picture?" She still had her camera in her bag, and she wanted to capture this moment, the late night, Frank leaning back in his chair, with shadows under his eyes and wearing a wan smile.

"Sure," he said, and she snapped the shutter.

Fletcher wasn't home when she got back. The apartment was dark. She turned on the light and it was just Croyd on the sofa, the way he'd been for the last few weeks.

She had no idea where Fletcher was and maybe she should have been worried—maybe the car that had failed to hit her had run him over and left him lying in a gutter. He'd likely found a party somewhere. With one of those young women in tight pants gazing up at him adoringly . . .

She wouldn't think about it. Instead, she took Croyd's picture. She'd been taking his picture nearly every day, to document the transformation. His skin was darkening to a grayish brown and had taken on a glossy shine. Chitinous, almost, like some forest-dwelling insect. His hands and feet had curled in on themselves, stiffened by some kind of paralysis. His face was still human, though stretched, and still pulled into deep, slack unconsciousness.

Folding to the floor, she leaned back against the sofa. Croyd was always good company.

"Looks like it's just you and me tonight, then. Can I get you anything? A sandwich, a beer? No? Just as well. Can I ask you a question? How can things be going so well and so badly, both at the same time? The party tonight was wonderful, and I got to talk to Helen and Frank, and . . . then Fletcher. I just can't make him happy. I wish . . . he can be so clever and friendly. I wish I knew what would settle him down and get him to work. I'd help him, if I knew what to do. Then on bad days I'm pretty sure he has no intention of ever working, not really. He wants to be famous, is what he wants. Acclaimed. He doesn't care about the art at all, and

I think people see that. They'll come to his parties and buy his pills but never take him seriously. You should have seen him at the gallery . . ."

Kicking off her shoes, she folded her legs and told Croyd the story. He never once interrupted, and she could pretend he was listening intently.

"I don't know what to do. I can just keep doing what I've been doing. But a year from now? Five years from now? I don't even know what I want. No, I know what I want. I want my own darkroom. I want a gallery show. I want Helen Gee to hang my pictures in Limelight. I want people to look at my pictures and remember them. I want . . . I wish they wouldn't call me a freak."

She wiped her eyes before she could start crying, said good night to Croyd, and went to get herself to bed.

Fletcher stumbled back to the apartment after daybreak, making enough noise that the downstairs neighbor yelled. Still drunk. Iris put on a robe, settled him into a chair, and poured him a couple of glasses of water. He smelled like someone else's perfume, which was such a cliché it made her tired.

"Iris, you love me, don't you?" he said tiredly, looking up at her with bloodshot eyes. "Of course you do, I can always count on you . . ." Suddenly he squinted. "Your face . . . your face just went weird . . . It's, like, purple . . ." His head nodded, and he slumped back and started snoring wetly.

There she stood, in a cheap apartment with two unconscious men and a half-drunk glass of water. This was her life, she supposed. For what it was worth.

She spent the afternoon in the darkroom and returned to Limelight to deliver prints. Helen had a message waiting for her. "I spoke with a gentleman this morning, he's maître d' of a nightclub over on the Bowery and is looking for someone to take pictures for their ads. He likes your work, and I think you'd like him."

"The Bowery. Isn't that where . . ." She couldn't quite figure out how to say it politely.

"Where people like you live. Yes, dear. Here's his number." Helen smiled kindly and patted Iris's hand.

Well, she could always use another job.

She took a cab to the Funhouse to make sure she got the address right. And because she wasn't too sure about the neighborhood. She shouldn't have worried. A quick glance told her she might be safer here than she was in the Village. First person she saw was a man who looked for all the world like a bipedal walrus, with blubbery grayish skin, tufts of red hair, and tusks protruding over his lips. Dressed in a garish green-and-gold Hawaiian shirt, he was hawking newspapers from a corner stand, and the scene was so incongruous and charming that it made Iris smile. She wanted to take pictures.

There were others. Deformed. Afflicted. Covered in fur or feathers or scales, with the wrong number of limbs, or a body too big or too short or too long. *Say it*, she murmured to herself. *Say the word* . . . They were jokers. Half the people on the street wore masks, so you couldn't see them at all. Were they hiding themselves, or trying to blend in?

Nobody would look at Iris twice in this neighborhood.

The Funhouse was a bright spot amid the run-down tenements along this section of the Lower East Side. The sign, FUNHOUSE in a big sans-serif font, was outlined with neon and carnival lights. All turned off now, in daylight, but at night the glare would be visible for blocks. Large mirrors flanked the double doors on either side, giving the front a feel of depth, like the place went on forever and you could just fall in.

The man she assumed was Xavier Desmond, the club maître d',

was waiting outside the red-painted front doors. He startled her. In most respects he was nondescript, a man in his thirties, well turned out in a suit and tie, slicked-back dark hair, clean-shaven. His eyes were kind. His nose . . . was a trunk. An elephant's trunk in miniature, drooping past his chin, with what looked for all the world like a hand at the end of it, with prehensile digits, grasping. She hesitated a step; she couldn't not. His eyes held the same expression, regarding her. A moment of wide-eyed surprise. Even if a wild-card-spawned deformity was described to you beforehand, confronting the reality always shocked. A moment when the back of your mind, a prehistoric instinct, tried to decide if what you were looking at was even human. That moment, that hesitation, was always awful, always embarrassing. And for both of them it was gone in a moment, and they schooled themselves to politeness.

She smiled and strode forward. "Hi, I'm Iris Marshall. You must be Mr. Desmond."

"A pleasure to meet you, Miss Marshall. Why don't you come inside and I'll show you around."

The interior was just as gaudy as the exterior. What first caught the eye: an immense chandelier glittering with a hundred crystals. Desmond turned a couple of switches and the lights came on. Mirrors, the place was filled with mirrors and glass and silver, reflecting the light back and forth and back again, drawing you into a sparkling, glittering world of reflection. Some mirrors gave back normal reflections—she caught a glimpse of herself, blue and yellow swathes of color distorting her face. Others were funhouse mirrors, the images tall or fat or blurred, too many curves or too many angles.

Look in those mirrors, everyone became a joker.

In the farthest booth, right outside the kitchen, a man appeared to be asleep, wrapped in a blanket, hugging himself. He had the most amazing hair, down past his shoulders and bright red. He was so odd, with fine skin and a delicate face, but he seemed gaunt somehow. Fragile, like he might blow away in a wind. Iris raised her camera to take a picture of the intriguing figure, but Mr. Desmond gently put a hand on her arm and lowered it back down.

"Not him. We let him alone."

"That is Dr. Tachyon, isn't it?"

"It is. He's . . . had a rough time of it lately."

"I'm sorry to hear that."

"Maybe another time, he'll be up for introductions. Assuming you want the job?"

"Of course I want the job." She didn't have to think about it. "There are so many possibilities. All this light and texture . . . I just hope you like what I come up with."

He smiled; the expression translated into his trunk as a kind of sinuous twitch. "Some photographers won't work here. They say the lighting and angles are too difficult. They can't get a clear image."

"No, not at all. I wonder if you even want a clear image." She walked along the front of the stage, looking back toward the seating, then looking sidelong at herself in a dozen scattered angles on the glass. The colors and patterns racing across her skin made the images even more dizzying. "I can keep myself out of the frame, if I stand at an angle. But this . . . you can get a doubling, the performer onstage and the image in the mirror, and you won't be able to tell which one is real. You'll look at the picture and wonder, does she really have eight arms or is that some crazy reflection?"

"Yes, exactly. That's what Angela—she's the owner—thought when she put the mirrors in."

"It's like Picasso, where you can't tell where the figure ends and the background begins. All lines running into each other. Or . . . have you seen any of Grace Hartigan's work? All the lines and colors just crashing into you . . ." She turned to him, determined. "We can make this art. If that's the sort of direction you want."

"I think that sounds marvelous." Under his trunk, he smiled. "Miss Marshall, if I might ask you a rather rude question . . ."

"I suppose." She wouldn't have to answer.

"Your skin . . . the patterns. Do you have any control over what appears? Or is it random?"

She shook her head. "No control at all. It seems to happen randomly. Just as well, I think. If I turned all red when I got angry or blue when I had a crush on someone . . . that wouldn't go so well. This is fine."

His trunk lifted in a shrug. "Because if you could control it, that'd be quite the act."

What a horrifying thought. "You could call me Miss Canvas," she said, chuckling. At his querying brow, she explained. "That's what some of the artists in the Village call me. Miss Canvas. Because I look like someone painted on me." She winced a little; she didn't have to explain it. It was obvious.

"Do you like the name?" He asked neutrally, without judgment.

She almost rattled off the quick, casual answer: *Oh, it's fine, I don't mind* . . . But she bit her lip and shook her head. "Not really, no. It could be worse, I suppose. But . . . somehow the word *freak* seems to get tossed out in the same conversations where people call me Miss Canvas. They don't see me, they only see . . . this. I suppose you understand." For the first time, she was talking to someone who clearly, undoubtedly, understood.

"The silly nicknames . . . it's fashionable," he said. "And if you choose and embrace the name yourself, that's one thing. But if someone else chooses the name, without any care for what you want . . . well. Being called the name you wish to be called seems a fundamental right, I should think."

"You don't have a nickname," she said. She could imagine the names others would give him: Elephant Man, the Great Schnozz. Nothing good.

"I am Xavier Desmond," he said. "Now and always."

"Do you mind if I take your picture? Just a portrait. I'll put it with the rest of the publicity shots, and you can do whatever you like with it."

He hesitated, eyes widening in what might have been fear. He almost physically drew back from her, as if she had threatened him. She wondered if he'd ever had his picture taken since the wild card virus had transformed him. She certainly hadn't let anyone take hers, so she understood the reluctance.

"You're the maître d', right?" She smiled gently, donning what Frank had called her Long Island hostess attitude. She tried to set him at his ease, to reassure him. Usually, her subjects couldn't wait for her to take their pictures. But they were actors, musicians, performers. "Do you have a spot you're usually at? From which to survey your domain? If I'm really going to document this place, you should be part of that."

His narrowed gaze was skeptical. "My podium is over here by the bar . . ."

She coaxed him onto a barstool and told him to look toward the stage, as if watching the next act. She clicked the shutter a couple of times without warning him—he only flinched at the noise the first time. He finally relaxed—she could tell, because the folds and furrows in his trunk smoothed out, and the hand came to rest holding the edge of his jacket. For all the world like a stately gentleman.

"Now then, let's see how some of those turn out."

"If I don't like them you'll destroy the negatives?"

"We'll discuss it. I should come back during a rehearsal, to get some pictures of your performers . . ."

Buoyed by a new and unfamiliar confidence—the new setting, the new job, the *interesting* job, the kind Mr. Desmond—she decided to walk a little through the neighborhood and then take the subway back home. It was seedy. There were vagabonds clutching bottles wrapped in paper bags. Trash had accumulated in the gutters. Not a quaint flower box or bookshop in sight. But no one stared at her. No one gave her a second look, even. She walked with her chin up, face turned to the world. Smiling a little, even. She was just another joker walking down the street. It made her giddy.

Along with the nightclubs, flophouses, and liquor stores, there were mask shops on the Bowery. Another quirk that had sprung up in the neighborhood when it became the place where jokers congregated. A thing that tourists looked for and gawked at. But she wasn't a tourist.

She stopped at one that had its door open and seemed inviting, with a welcome mat on the pavement and classical music playing on a radio. The carpeting was worn, but the walls were vibrant: shelf after shelf, all full of masks, cloaks, hats with veils, and then more masks besides, from dainty dominoes to full-face masks with elaborate headdresses. Feathers, fur, leather, and silk, in every color as well as black and white. Simple paper masks, the kind children would wear for Halloween, on a rack by the door. Amazing, ornate works of art on a high shelf where no one could reach. Venetian Carnivale, crammed into one little storefront. She desperately wanted to take pictures, but she'd used up all her film at the Funhouse.

One shelf held blank masks. Full face, they only had holes for the eyes, like expressionless ghosts. Made of plain buckram, they came in several colors: white, black, red, gray. She picked up a white one, absently tracing its glued edge.

"I kind of like those blank ones. Sometimes people get them and paint things on them—" An older woman spoke, and Iris turned around. The clerk's counter was almost hidden behind all the masks and cloaks, and Iris only saw her when she moved. She had a long snout, with whiskers and rich, shining dark fur. Like mink. When the clerk saw her face, her beady dark eyes blinked, startled. "—but I guess that wouldn't be a thing for you."

"No. But I'm rather enjoying the idea of the empty canvas."

"For you? Half off."

Iris beamed at her. "I'll take it."

— — —

Back home, she checked on Croyd, who was indeed still alive, and still asleep, his chest inhaling and exhaling, steady and strong. Somehow. He hadn't had anything to eat or drink in weeks, but the strange hibernation continued. She didn't like to think of anyone dying in her apartment, so checking on him had become habit, along with taking his daily picture. His legs, grown sticklike, were draped over the arm of the sofa now. He had begun to smell faintly of dried leaves.

She settled to her favorite spot, leaning against the sofa near Croyd's head, pulling up her knees.

"I have had the most amazing afternoon. Do you know Xavier Desmond, maître d' at the Funhouse? I imagine you do, you seem like the kind of guy who knows lots of people . . ." Surely he knew all about this, but she told him anyway. She showed him the mask she'd bought, the clean surface. Blank, expressionless. Anonymous.

"I don't know why I never went to Jokertown before this. I suppose I heard so many stories. And, well. There are some parts of town girls like me are just told not to go to. There are so many things girls like me are not supposed to do. Or rather, girls like I *was*. I hardly know what I am now. Well, anyway, I can't wait to get to the darkroom and see how the pictures turned out. I've got some ideas to change the lighting for next time. Oh—Mr. Desmond gave me tickets for a couple of shows. I'm not sure if Fletcher would like to go. It's trendy enough for him, certainly. It's the kind of thing he'd brag about doing. I'll ask him. Worst he'll do is say no." No, the worst he'd do was tell Iris he didn't want her going back, didn't want her hanging around in that neighborhood.

She would have to practice telling him that she was going, one way or another, with or without him.

— — —

One afternoon, she came home from picking up a few groceries and found a dozen people arranged around the front room, which wasn't at all normal this time of day. Far too early for parties. The angle of light from the window filled the space, making it the best time to use the room as a studio. In fact, there were easels set up, and others had big sketchbooks in their laps and charcoal in hand, and they worked in silence. Their subject: the increasingly sticklike, insectoid man stretched out on the sofa.

Even Fletcher had a canvas set up on an easel and was mixing paint on a board. Some reds and yellows, looked like. Didn't much match the more brown-and-beige palette Croyd had grown into, but that didn't matter.

Iris set down the bag and wandered over to see what people were drawing, painting, or whatever.

"Word got out," Fletcher said. "A model who will absolutely stay still and not complain."

"Croyd didn't sign up to be a model. Are you sure this is—"

"Eh. He'll never know. Besides, *look* at him. He's so *interesting*."

Croyd had stretched, limbs growing attenuated. His hands had unclenched, displaying fingers with joints in the wrong places. His mouth still hung open slightly in a distinctly human gesture, and his snoring continued faintly. Wouldn't it be something if the guy woke up right now? And gave them a taste of that temper he'd shown off when he arrived?

"Fletcher, I don't like this. What if Croyd doesn't want people painting him?"

"Well then, he shouldn't have passed out here, should he? I'll give him a cut of the fee, that'll make him happy."

"You're charging a fee to paint here?"

Fletcher just grinned.

"What's this, Miss Canvas doesn't like painters?" one of the men said.

"I like painters just fine, usually. And I'd really appreciate it if you not call me that. My name is Iris."

"Aw, it's all in fun."

Another of them sat back in his chair and blew out a frustrated breath. "The wild card virus has ruined abstract expressionism. I paint a portrait of a guy like this, go for realism, and people will think it's a de Kooning."

"No, they won't," Iris said flatly, glancing at his canvas. The guy glared back at her.

She took a peek at Fletcher's canvas. He'd painted a corner of it, a series of yellow shades, each one a tone darker. Like sunlight moving across a room. She felt a hopeful flutter. He was really painting, and it might even turn into something good—

"Don't stare," he muttered at it. "I hate it when you watch me work."

"Then I won't watch." She hurriedly marched away, to hide in their room until the studio session was over.

"Too late," he said, dropping his brush. "I've lost the mood now."

Iris closed her eyes and sighed.

The painters stayed all afternoon, and she calculated whether she had enough spaghetti and marinara on hand, because if they were still here by nightfall Fletcher would want her to cook dinner for everyone. Fortunately, one of them said something about catching a show, and that was the signal for them all to pack up, leaving crumpled rags and spatters of paint behind. Gratefully, she emerged. She hoped that maybe Fletcher had gone out with the rest of the painters on some adventure or other. But no, he was still here, setting the quarter-painted canvas and the rest of his supplies in the corner where they usually stayed.

She just wouldn't talk about the afternoon at all. It was over, done. If she said nothing about painting, he'd have no reason to lose his temper. Bustling in the kitchen, she filled a pot with water. "I've got some marinara. How does that sound for dinner?"

A pause. She held her breath. "That sounds fine."

She let the breath out.

They had an almost pleasant dinner, with a bottle of wine left over from some party or other. Cheap stuff, but it went well with the pasta, and Fletcher relaxed enough that he almost smiled. She was cleaning up over the sink when he came over, moving close in. For a moment she thought he might actually help wash dishes.

But no, he touched her wrist and moved his hips against hers. "C'mere."

"Oh, Fletcher. My hands are wet—"

He kissed her, and she melted. She was tired, still annoyed with him, filling their place with crowds without ever asking if she minded, and she paid just as much rent as he did, if not more. All his schemes and deals and where did the money go? She was always buying the food, talking to the landlord . . . But he kissed her, and she melted, like always.

He reached down and hitched her skirt to her hips. Began stroking her thighs, easing them apart, tugging at her stockings, revealing skin. Black lines and blue splashes traveled hypnotically across them. She froze. "Fletcher . . ."

"I really want you." He was hurriedly unfastening his trousers.

"Then let's go to the bedroom."

"I want you *here*."

"But Croyd is here."

He glanced over at the sofa and chuckled roughly. "It's not like he's watching."

She had gotten so used to talking to Croyd; it didn't matter that he didn't talk back. He was *here*, he was present. She wasn't an exhibitionist. But there was no arguing with Fletcher. He pulled her legs up around his hips as he braced her against the counter, and she held on to him. She was just so grateful that anyone at all wanted her.

— — —

They were good, she was sure. Everything was going to be fine. She was even hopeful, with so much to do, so many pictures to take . . .

She spread prints across the counter from her second shoot at the Funhouse, during a matinee performance, lining them up based on what effects she was able to get from changing the angles and lightings of the various mirrors. Some of them didn't work, turning out too bright and confusing. But some looked great, a tripling of a laughing face that seemed to imply that the laughter sounded bigger, louder. Cosmos and Chaos, the juggling jokers, threw three times as many balls and pins between them, and Chaos's six arms reached for them all. In another, a green-skinned singer—known as the Girl's Choir—held an operatic note, her face haloed by sparkling chandelier lights. She held her hands raised, and the mouths on her palms sang counterpoint. In the blazing lights she looked like an angel. Mobia, the acrobat with the triple-jointed spine—the image gave no clue which way she was going to bend next, which was very mysterious. Singers, comedians, dancers, all of them strange and wondrous, made fantastical under the mirrored lights. And an image of the audience, full of both jokers and naturals, but against the backdrop of their images in the mirrors it was hard to tell which was which, and who was onstage and who was watching. It was abstract art in photographic form. The camera didn't just record reality; it could be used to shape it.

Fletcher had slept late, but finally wandered out around lunchtime, tucking his shirt into his trousers and blinking blearily. "Any coffee?"

"Yes, in the pot." She didn't look up from her prints, pulling out the ones she most wanted to show Mr. Desmond.

Coffee cup in hand, Fletcher came to look over her shoulder. "What the hell is this?" He picked up one of the portraits she had taken of Mr. Desmond. It was the one where his trunk's hand loosely held the edge of his jacket. It made him look whimsically distinguished. She hoped he liked it.

"Oh, that's Xavier Desmond. He runs the Funhouse nightclub; he hired me to take some pictures. That reminds me—he gave me tickets. If you're up for an outing, we can go any night we like."

"That joker place over on the Bowery? What are you doing going to that dive?"

"It's not a dive. It's really nicely done, and the mirrors and lighting are so impressive—"

"And you were there."

"I told you, I was taking publicity shots. Mr. Desmond wants me to come back—"

"I don't want you going back there. Ever."

"Why not?"

"It's not safe."

Exactly what she was afraid of. She had played out this exact conversation in her mind. She swallowed back bile, licked her lips, and said, "How do you know?"

"They're jokers, honey. I just don't want you hanging around them."

Carefully, she said, "Darling. *I'm* a joker." She had never said this out loud before.

"But you're different."

She tilted her head. "Oh?"

"You're . . ." He trailed off, gesturing absently.

She could supply a whole dictionary of terms. She was interesting, polite, accommodating. She didn't turn stomachs. Having her as a girlfriend made Fletcher interesting, memorable, noteworthy. She was harmless.

"I see," she said softly.

"Promise me you won't go back there."

"I can't do that."

"I'm only thinking of you, of your best interests—"

"Are you?" She met his gaze. She wondered what he saw, what patterns were dancing across her skin, right at this moment. "I think you're worried that if I spend too much time there, I might make friends other than you. That I won't need you any-more."

This time, he would hit her, she was sure. His teeth bared, he looked as if he wanted to spit words, if he only knew which ones. He crumpled the print of Mr. Desmond, then tore it in half. Her heart jumped for a moment. But it was fine, she had the negatives, she could make another.

With a great snarl he swept all the prints off the counter in a flurry and marched out of the flat. Iris covered her face and let out a sob. Just one sob, then collected herself with a deep breath. He'd left the door wide open, so she calmly went over to close it. Then sank next to the sofa, near Croyd.

And Croyd moved. She nearly screamed when the blanket shifted, when the fabric rustled. For the first time in two months he moved, propping himself on his elongated, sticklike elbow and blinking open his eyes.

He met her gaze. "Honey. You have got to get away from that asshole."

First thing Croyd did was stumble to the bathroom. The faucet ran for a time, then came silence. She used the moment to clean up, gathering the photos Fletcher had scattered and putting them in her bag. Croyd still hadn't emerged, and she was about to knock to see how he was doing when the door flew open and he lurched out. He had to bend to get under the frame.

"Sorry. Just had to look in the mirror. This one . . . this isn't so bad. It's not great, but it's not bad. You got anything to eat around here? I'm *really* hungry. And do you maybe have some suspend-ers . . . or a coat . . . something . . ." He fidgeted awkwardly. The shirt hung off him like it was on a wire hanger, but the trousers—he had to hold them up, the fabric bunched up in both strangely bent hands. How did someone like this even *dress*? Off-the-rack cloth-ing certainly wouldn't fit him. She found suspenders in Fletcher's things, and helped Croyd rig them so they at least held his trousers up, however much they looked a circus tent on him. An overcoat ensured that he would remain decent out on the street.

She suggested they go to the diner around the corner.

Walking with this new version of Croyd was interesting. He moved constantly, flexing his legs, testing out the new limbs. He blinked at his strange hands for a moment—his eyes were dark and incongruously human. He was clearly deep in thought. Pausing, he put them up against a brick wall. Leaned in, clenched the fingers. And then he climbed. Straight up the wall, turning left around the first-floor window and looping around to turn right over the second floor.

He laughed. "Would you look at that?"

Gasping, she clapped her hands over her mouth, tamping down on a spike of panic—what if he slipped and fell? But he seemed in no danger. Head down, he crawled along the wall back toward the sidewalk, pushing himself off when he reached about head height and landing solidly on his feet. He spread his hands in a little *ta-da*, and she clapped, laughing.

"Gotta think about what I can do with this," he murmured, surveying the wall again.

"Cat burglary?" she offered. He pressed his stiff lips into a line.

People stared; of course they would. She felt a bit odd because they were staring at Croyd and not her—for once, she wasn't the freak. They wouldn't stare in Jokertown, she reflected.

The waitress at the diner gaped at them when they stepped inside but couldn't stop them. Iris had a moment of wondering if she would try, but smiled sweetly at the girl and walked confidently in, leading Croyd to a booth in the back. He was still experimenting, using his sticklike legs to lift himself to the back of the booth, reaching up to touch the ceiling, moving to the wall to perch for a moment, looking dispassionately at the other patrons staring back at him with round shocked eyes.

"Maybe we should sit down," Iris suggested, sliding into the booth. Croyd lowered himself to the seat across from her. The waitress crept over cautiously, and Croyd proceeded to order . . . all the food. Mountains of food. One of each, it seemed like. And why not? He hadn't eaten in two months. Iris ordered coffee and an English muffin.

Croyd had gotten through a dozen eggs, two stacks of pancakes, a chicken-fried steak, and a plate of hash browns as big as his head when he finally came up for air and met her gaze across the table. "Why do you stay with him? The way he talks to you? You shouldn't have to put up with that."

She blanched. "You heard that?" Maybe he just heard that last argument, right when he was waking up.

"I heard everything, over . . . how long was I asleep, anyway?"

"Two months."

"Christ. Yeah. *Everything.*" He arced an eyebrow in a knowing leer. "I . . . don't know how. My brain just . . . feels little bit like a record player right now, it's playing back all this stuff, all this noise. I usually don't remember anything from when I'm asleep, not even dreams. But then I'm usually by myself." He took a long drink of coffee. "You guys have a lot of parties. Were there bongos? God, so much jazz."

"So you know about the painting sessions?"

"I'm never falling asleep in the Village again," he muttered.

"I was worried that you wouldn't want people painting you. Not when you didn't know what they were doing. Or . . . taking pictures?"

He paused with a strip of bacon halfway to his mouth. "Pictures?"

"I take pictures. I'm a photographer, but I suppose you know that. And . . . you were right there, and it was just so strange, what happens to you. No offense."

"None taken. It's definitely strange. You . . . have any of them with you?"

She dug in her bag for the envelope of prints she'd made. Each new one went into the stack. Three dozen in all. She'd never really looked at them all in sequence until now. Croyd stacked plates and pushed them to the side, and Iris wiped up a puddle of syrup before setting the pictures down and fanning them out. Croyd as he was, asleep. Then, the changes. He hadn't been immobile. An arm stretched; his legs curled up, then flopped off the sofa. From one print to the next, the metamorphosis wasn't visible. But taken together . . . they were like the frames in a film. It was like she'd made a flip-book that revealed his transformation.

Croyd was enthralled. He went back and forth, studying one or another, then drawing back to regard the whole collection. Iris kneaded her hands nervously, waiting for him to say something.

"I've never seen it," he said. "What I look like, I mean. I was infected in '46, the first Wild Card Day. I've slept . . . I don't know how many times. But nobody ever sees themselves sleeping, right? Unless they have a camera. This. Huh."

Speechless, apparently. "I know it must be strange . . ."

"Can I keep these?"

"Of course."

Sated at last, Croyd offered to pay, then patted his pockets down. "Wait. Where's my cash?"

She should have warned him about that. Remembering how he acted at the party, she braced for yelling. For him to jump up and storm around and break things. "Guess."

Instead, he laughed. "Typical. Hmm, Fletch and I are going to have a little talk later."

She had just enough to pay their bill. He promised to pay her back, and maybe he would, but she didn't expect it. All settled, they left and took the long way back to the apartment. Iris's feet dragged. What was she going to do, without Croyd to talk to?

You have to get away . . .

She made enough to pay rent on a place, she thought. If she

asked around, maybe someone needed a roommate, just until she got herself sorted out. Maybe they wouldn't mind a joker roommate. Maybe, maybe . . .

Croyd alternated between walking on the wall beside her and walking on the sidewalk. And scaling a lamppost, just because. He seemed to revel in his extraordinary agility. It made her a little dizzy to watch, but he was so much like a kid playing, she had to smile.

"So what'll you do now?" she asked him.

He shrugged—a particularly broad gesture with his spindly arms. "Do some catching up. See if I can make some cash. Speaking of which . . . you think Fletcher's back yet?"

"Only one way to find out."

She wasn't looking forward to confronting Fletcher. Croyd's words kept rattling in the back of her mind. She didn't have that much. Her clothes, some records and books, her portfolio. The furniture came with the apartment. If she had help, she could probably get it all in one trip. And how sad was that, a whole life packed in a couple of suitcases? She thought of her parents' house outside of Boston, with all its fine furniture and tasteful decorating, two cars and trimmed lawn—the accoutrements of the life she'd been preparing for when she got kicked out of Smith . . . She couldn't remember now if she had been exiled from that, or if she had fled. Was still fleeing.

Life with Fletcher had been playacting that suburban domesticity she had thought she wanted, at one time.

Fletcher was not at the apartment. She had no idea where he was, and she found she did not care. Croyd went to the bedroom and started searching, digging in the pockets of discarded trousers and rummaging through the drawer of the nightstand.

"No cash, but . . . How about this?" He held up a crinkled envelope that seemed to be filled with pills.

"What're those?"

"No idea. But they might come in useful later."

Standing in the doorway, Croyd surveyed the living room, evidently looking for someplace else Fletcher might have stashed a wad of cash. He went to the turntable to flip through the albums, to peer under the stand. Glanced out the window, clinging to the wall to shorten the distance. Then he found the stack of a dozen or so canvases tucked in a corner. A few finished, a few half painted, the rest blank.

"I thought he was supposed to be a painter."

"So did I," she murmured. "I think he could be pretty good if he just spent a little time—"

"Why are you even with him? That's what I don't get. You could do so much better."

"Could I?" She shook her head. "If you saw the way people look at me when I walk into a room—"

He crossed the room to stand in front of her. "I think I turn up a joker maybe a little more than half the time. I don't know, I've never really counted. So yes, I know exactly how people look at us. But Iris . . . you're beautiful."

She laughed. Just laughed. Beautiful. That was just what people said to young women to be polite. It didn't mean anything. "It's nice of you to say so, but—hey!"

He reached around her arm and into her bag; she flinched, but he only drew out her camera. Studied it a moment, then stepped back and clicked. It happened before she could hide her face or tell him to stop.

"I don't like having my picture taken," she said weakly.

"Develop that and see how it turns out. Just see."

He handed the camera back and she took it, uncertain. The case was hard, the lens gleaming like an eye. Usually, she trusted that eye. All right, then.

On impulse, she went up to Croyd, stood on tiptoes, and kissed his cheek. His skin was cool and surprisingly soft. No stubble to speak of on this new face.

He stared. "What was that for?"

"Thank you. For listening to me all those weeks. For . . ." She shrugged. "Just because."

"Okay, I'll take it. I guess."

He might have looked odd and moved so strangely, but that face was wry, and his features human. Ears and nose, dark eyes, lips, and everything else. He smelled male, skin with a bit of sweat on it.

He seemed so bemused that she couldn't resist, and kissed him again, on the mouth this time, brushing her lips against his. He put his clawed hand gently on her shoulder and kissed her back. He wasn't demanding like Fletcher was when he kissed her. His touch encouraged, invited. His hold on her—his other hand had moved to her hip—was light. When he stepped into her embrace, he seemed to be waiting for her to flee. His body was thin, wiry, strange. But she seemed to fit against him just fine and held on tight.

"Do you want to?" he whispered.

"Yeah," she said, and disengaged just long enough to lead him to the bedroom.

When she was naked, she was enthralling, she had to admit. Lying back, she folded her hands behind her head and let Croyd watch artwork travel over her skin. A shaded curve passed across one breast and along her ribs. Watercolor splashes of red moved around her thigh, up her hip. He traced a sketched line as it disappeared into her pubic hair, and her breath caught. Smiling, he kissed her belly.

Naked, he was thin, all angles. Incredibly limber, she remembered, blushing. His sticklike legs flowed into an incongruously muscular backside. Those long, lithe legs needed that power to anchor them. His penis was as human and expressive as his face. Their legs were still entwined, so she couldn't quite reach it, to stroke it. For now she could continue to enjoy this sensuous, quiet, moment . . .

A door slammed open. "What's going on here?"

They'd left the bedroom door open, and Fletcher stood in the middle of the loft, gaping. Iris had a moment of panic. Just a moment. Then she relaxed into a moment of delightful fatalism. Nothing to do now but see what happened.

"Oh, hello, Fletcher." She met Croyd's gaze over her naked chest, and they both grinned.

He slid off her and started pulling on clothes. Reluctantly, she did the same, digging through the sheets for her bra and slip.

"Iris!" Fletcher's voice was rough.

Dressed now, she ignored him. Straightened the sheets a bit. Then she found a suitcase and started folding her clothes into it.

Croyd blocked the doorway—giving her time, she realized. She didn't have to rush. She was able to make sure she got everything that was hers.

"Fletcher Anderson," Croyd said. "Where's my money?"

A beat. A gaping, guilty expression that only a guy like Fletcher could manage. Then, "What money?"

Croyd laughed. "Yeah, that's what I thought."

"What the *hell* are you doing with my girlfriend?"

"I'm not your girlfriend anymore," Iris called over Croyd's shoulder.

"Iris! How could you . . . with that . . ." Fletcher jabbed a trembling finger at Croyd.

"With that freak? Hmm."

"She's a lot of fun; I don't know if you noticed that," Croyd said amiably.

"You bastard! You've got a lot of nerve—"

"You want to fight a duel over her? Because I'm game if you are."

"Get . . . out! Both of you, just get out!"

"Oh, certainly," Iris said. "I was just getting ready to leave."

Camera. She definitely had her camera, tucked in her bag, and the folders full of prints and negatives. She rather wanted to take a picture of Fletcher right now, to try to capture the twisted expressions passing over his face.

Two suitcases and three bags, set in the middle of the room. Her whole life fit in her arms.

"Ready?" Croyd asked, a suitcase in each hand and one of the bags slung over his shoulder.

"Ready," she said, the last two bags in hand.

Fletcher had to yell, one more time, "Just get out. And don't come back! I never want to see you again, Iris!"

She and Croyd left the apartment. Not even a backward glance.

They sat on a bench in Washington Square Park for a while, where some poor college kid was playing folk covers on bongos and harmonica and it just wasn't working. He had a small crowd of friends with him, forming their own little party on the lawn. It was nice.

She'd made some calls to a handful of women she knew, and one of them offered her sofa for the next week or so, until Iris could find her own place. It seemed terribly ironic, but Iris was grateful. They'd already dropped off her bags.

Croyd had invited her to stay with him, and she politely suggested that maybe she ought to be on her own for a while.

"Will you stay in the Village? When you get your own place, I mean. Or go somewhere else?" He meant go live in Jokertown, where she fit in better.

But maybe she didn't want to fit in. She thought about the parties, coffee at the Figaro and the Bitter End, the jazz clubs, showings at Limelight, and everything in between. Random meetings with poets and artists and singers.

"No, I think I'm going to stick around here, if I can. My career's just getting off the ground. I can't lose that momentum."

"You might run into Fletcher."

She probably would; this wasn't a big circle she moved in. "Well, if he doesn't want to see me, he'll have to be the one to leave the party."

"Atta girl," Croyd said and patted her knee. "I suppose . . . I need to get going." He looked up to the sky, which was clouding over. Looked like rain.

"When will I see you again?" she asked. Before he slept again, she hoped. Because the next time he woke up, she wouldn't recognize him.

Croyd winced. The expression seemed odd on his beige, stiff face. "Here's the thing, Iris. I like you."

"Oh? I'm glad—"

"And that's a problem. I'm not a good person. I . . . get into a lot of trouble. And I don't want you to get hurt."

"It's fine, Croyd. You are a good person. You got me away from Fletcher—"

"That night we met, when I was coming down off the pills and at the end of my rope—that'll happen again. I don't . . . I don't want to hurt you."

"But . . ." She tried to argue, then realized she didn't really know what she was talking about. She listened to awful harmonica music for a moment and worried that Croyd might not say anything else at all. Just get up and leave. It seemed like something he would do.

Before he could, she said, "I've got a couple of tickets to the Funhouse. Of course you know about that; you heard that argument. But maybe . . . would you like to go with me?"

For a moment she thought he was going to say no. But he smiled his thin, stiff smile and said, "Yes, I would."

Swimmer, Flier, Felon, Spy

PART II

Tesla stood on the street outside Iris Mar-shall's apartment building and considered his next move. Much of what she had told him was interesting and much of it was useful, but not immediately. He had certainly learned more about the Sleeper's cycle of reincarnation than he had known before, and he had learned something of how the man interacted with other people.

But how to use this information to find Croyd—or *a* Croyd, or *some* Croyds—eluded him for the moment.

Tesla walked down the street, careful to move quickly and to avoid eye contact with other pedestrians, so as to blend in with the native New Yorkers as much as possible. There was little he could do about his appearance, but New Yorkers were used to both seeing extraordinary things and not seeing extraordinary things, depending on which was likely to be safer. Tesla envied their superb inherent threat-assessment abilities.

He decided there were two courses of action available to him, both involving visiting information sources. He had never visited either, not even the very public and well-known one, and was still working to overcome his active resistance to this mysterious urge to do his own fieldwork.

Both choices held dangers. Both held opportunities.

He decided to visit the more dangerous place first. The visit would involve potentially exposing one of his most closely held secrets. It would involve the deliberate abrogation of rules he had set for himself and certain others that he had declared absolutely inviolable.

It involved visiting the pencil shop.

Tesla had long ago taught himself to avoid habits. This was elementary. But he had also taught himself to avoid *enthusiasms*, and this was more difficult, especially since such enthusiasms he had ever had—those not involving other people at least, or, most important, a particular other person, *her*—were quite esoteric, and thus easily trackable.

Tesla enjoyed French films of the 1930s and had not seen one in decades. He fancied himself a competent sushi chef for a Westerner, and had not so much as sharpened a knife for just as long. He was passionate about pencils, and here, well, here he fell down.

Tesla had never met the woman who technically owned the pencil shop in Midtown. She was his most trusted associate, and as the point of contact for his clients she had served both her own interests and his ably and discreetly for as long as Tesla had made his living as a specialized freelance intelligence operative. Tesla's world had contracted for the last fifteen years, down to contact with almost no one but her, and that through esoteric means.

But he wasn't always that way. When the CIA recruited him, based on his background as an academic expert in many things, but especially the history of economic warfare, he lectured at the Citadel while he moonlighted for them on special projects. Then he met *her*, a woman with secrets he didn't know, secrets as deep as his own. It was learning her secrets that caused his card to turn, and his association with the CIA to become more . . . distant. It was difficult to care about any of that when the love of his life had vanished. Tesla, who could find anyone, had no idea where she had gone.

And so the man who was once known as Eliot Rice became Tesla, the man he was now. A jack with gray skin, sharply pointed features, and a pair of metallic horns growing from his temples, sweeping up and around in the manner of a bull's. Whenever he was conscious, a constant charge of electricity crackled between the tips of his horns in the manner of the high-voltage traveling arcs usually known as Jacob's ladders. As with everything in his life, Tesla developed fine control of the powers of these bolts—powers he rarely used.

But enough rumination on the past. He and the woman in the pencil shop, his primary contact with the outside world, had enjoyed a long and fruitful correspondence, all evidence of which had long since been obliterated. He couldn't help but think of her as something like a friend, though they'd never met. The negotiations that had led to her being in his employment had been indirect, complicated, but fruitful in that now she owned the finest pencil shop in the world. Not that there was much competition for that honor.

But it *was* an honor, they both thought.

The finest pencil shop in the world.

How delightful.

The pencil shop had an enviable corner storefront, with plate-glass windows on each side and a wooden doorway flanked by elegantly carved, seven-foot-high pencils. The pencils had been produced at the workshop of a master woodworker in Beijing. This man was a cousin of . . .

No. Tesla was working, not remembering who left him without a trace.

A bell jingled when he pushed through the door. He paused and breathed deep, taking in the scent of thousands and thousands of pencils, pencils of every imaginable variety from manufacturers large and small all over the world.

Tesla had known about the recent renovations, but had not known that they included, in addition to lovely bespoke display cases for the shop's wares along the walls, a small section of stationery. He wasn't sure how he felt about that. The shop had formerly sold pencils only.

The store's owner and manager stood behind a low wooden counter. She was looking at him with a smile on her face, gray hair frazzled, glasses slightly askew, a pencil tucked behind each ear. She was not unkempt, precisely. She looked, instead, very comfortable in her clothing and in herself.

"Good evening," she said. "You're a new customer! Or perhaps. Are you here to peruse, to perhaps purchase, or simply to gawk? Gawking is fine, you know. I'm aware mine is an unusual shop."

It certainly was, though not for the reasons she was implying. Not solely for those reasons, anyway.

Tesla refrained from returning her wide, toothy smile, knowing that his own was, to say the least, disconcerting. He walked along one wall, holding out a hand to let his fingernails play across the displays, click, click, click.

When he reached the counter, he said, "I have quite a collection already."

Her expression became curious. "I'm sure I should know you then."

"Perhaps," he said. "But my collection is incomplete. I am looking for a pencil from between the wars."

Now her expression was cautious. "There are so many wars," she said.

Tesla nodded, acknowledging the point. He was directing the conversation toward something she clearly suspected, and that she was clearly not pleased about. "These later wars all run together, don't they?"

The woman sighed. "You are looking for a particular pencil? From between the wars?"

So sad that the pleasantries, the preliminaries, had been exhausted already.

"It's Soviet," he said. "From a factory in the Caucasus."

There was not now, nor had there ever been, a pencil factory in the Caucasus.

"Just a moment," she said. She walked to the door and hung up a sign written in elegant, penciled script. It read, CLOSED, FOR NOW. She turned three locks.

The light switches were between two of the display cases. Tesla imagined this was inconvenient but was no doubt a relic of the wiring put in decades after the building that housed the shop was constructed. The woman walked briskly past him, jerking her chin at a curtained passage behind the sales counter. He followed.

In the back room, which smelled even more strongly of pencils than the shop floor, she took a seat at a small desk. She turned on a lamp. There were no other chairs.

Leaning over, she opened the bottom drawer of a short filing cabinet and reached behind the folders of invoices and receipts. She brought out a small metal box with a grille on one side and a single switch on the other. This, she set on the desk. She flicked the switch, and a low hum filled the air. She took the pencil from behind her left ear and looked at Tesla. She tapped the distal end of the instrument, void of ferrule or eraser, against her teeth.

Then, finally, she spoke. "I thought the arrangement was that you would never come here."

"The arrangement," said Tesla, "was that I would only come here in the direst of circumstances. Thus, the passcode."

She nodded, looking sad. "Does this mean I can't keep the shop?"

"Not at all," said Tesla. "I must admit that I am violating the terms of our agreement in coming to speak to you tonight."

"Ah," she said. "The circumstances are not so dire as they could be. Or should be." She was, of course, a very clever woman.

Tesla shrugged. Now that he thought about it, he actually wasn't sure.

"You haven't ordered takeout in the last few days," she said, carefully. "Not particularly unusual, but . . . well. Your fortune awaits."

Perhaps he had been correct in coming here after all.

"There's a new collector?" he asked.

"A man with very similar interests to the one I recently wrote you about."

"A sleepy man?"

"It was my impression he was barely keeping his eyes open. Though of course, when one has gemstones for eyes, perhaps it's impossible to close them."

Tesla nodded. He suspected that she could continue their conversation in this vein all night. He suspected she might even enjoy it.

Another surprising revelation. He would enjoy it himself. But time being of the utmost importance . . .

"Tell me where he is."

She frowned. Then she took a sheet of the heavy stationery Tesla wasn't convinced she should be selling from a lacquered box on the desk. She chose a pencil from a coffee mug on the desk that had the words WHAT'S YOUR POINT? printed on the side. She turned so that he could not see what she was writing.

When she turned back, he saw that she had folded the paper into neat quarters.

"I'm afraid we're closed, sir," she said, standing.

On the street, Tesla spared a glance back into the shop, seeing the woman disappear behind the counter. He had thoroughly enjoyed their encounter. He hoped never to see her again.

The sky threatened rain, so he stopped beneath the awning of a bodega doing no business at all. In the neon light of a beer sign, he unfolded the paper. There was a word written in the precise center of each of the four quarters.

Uptown.

Underground.

Troglodytes.

Trouble.

Tesla had never been a smoker, even in his grad school days when many members of his cohort, ridiculously he'd thought then, had all taken up pipes. But he always carried matches.

First looking up and down the street, then into the bodega, where a teenager sat on a stool staring down at her phone, he struck a match. He passed the flame under the paper. To his surprise, the scent of sandalwood rose up from the burning page.

The fire grew, consuming the whole sheet, the flames licking at his fingers.

He did not flinch. Physical feelings were by far the easiest to suppress.

Even though he was hundreds of miles from home, that did not mean Tesla was completely without resources. It did not even mean he didn't have access to his files.

He sat in a lounge chair in a room of a small hotel that was not known for its discretion because it was barely known at all. Tesla was not the only visitor to New York who wished to remain anonymous.

He sat, and he thought. His memory was prodigious, but what he was doing was a charlatan's trick, something even a boardwalk mentalist could accomplish. Though he vastly preferred physically handling the coded papers and photographs, charts and maps, in his files, he could remember the substance of most of them by *going there*.

He closed his eyes. He went to the appropriate cabinet, opened the appropriate drawer, withdrew the appropriate folder. Opening it, he read "Gangs of New York." His lips quirked. He didn't remember penciling the joke on the title page. Then he realized it wasn't a joke. At the time, he just hadn't thought of it.

He turned the pages. Joker gangs, nat gangs, gangs whose membership was made up exclusively of various ethnicities and countries of origins. Prostitution, protection, drugs, drugs, drugs.

At last he came to a page headed with the phrase "of unusual composition and methodology."

He ran his eyes down the page until he found the word "Troglodytes."

Troglodytae. "Cave-goers." Much mentioned by the ancient Greeks and Romans, from Herodotus to Tacitus. An almost certainly legendary people said to inhabit caverns in Africa and Europe. Pomponius Mela had written that they were nurtured by serpents.

Troglodytes. "Trouble." A mixed gang of jokers and nats who lived in utility passages and abandoned subway tunnels deep beneath Uptown Manhattan. What nurtured them, Tesla couldn't say.

He opened his eyes.

He couldn't say. But he could find out.

Tesla called down to the desk. A smooth and professional man's voice said, "How may I be of service?"

"I need a powerful flashlight, gear for light urban spelunking, and a loaded handgun."

"Very well, sir. Is an hour too long? We don't have the spelunking gear on hand."

"Yes," said Tesla. "That will be fine."

He sat down at the room's writing desk with his hands folded in his lap. Anyone looking at him might guess he was asleep, or perhaps in a meditative state. In fact, he was slowly and carefully putting himself on edge. This involved electricity arcing between his horns with increasing intensity, but then finally disappearing.

He was fully charged now, capable of emitting a blast that could turn a cinder-block wall into rubble. Unfortunately, it would take him hours to build another charge up of sufficient power to be useful. Thus, the gun.

There was a discreet knock at the door. Tesla waited a moment, knowing that whoever was outside would not wait for him to answer. Opening the door, he found a rucksack, a holstered nine-millimeter, and a tactical flashlight as long and thick as his forearm neatly arrayed on the plush hallway carpet.

He arranged these items about his person and took the stairs down to the lobby. There was no one at the desk, but then, there never was.

Shouldering the rucksack, Tesla walked out into the night.

There were a number of means of egress to the network of subterranean passages that made up New York's undercity.

Some were obvious. Tesla could, if he chose, jump off the platforms of a select number of subway stations—this took careful timing—and walk the track until he came to an electrician's service door with a broken lock. There were a number of Uptown buildings with extensive sub-basements that had been altered without the knowledge of owner or superintendent. And, of course, there was always the option of prying up a manhole cover and clambering down a ladder.

Tesla did not find any of the obvious options particularly attractive.

So he took the elevator.

He had known of the elevator's existence for a few years, but had never actually investigated its provenance, its ownership, or its operation. He only had so much time, after all, and there were so many mysteries in the world.

A mystery he had to immediately solve was how to find and call the conveyance. He knew that it moved at different times to different locations. A conversation with the concierge at the hotel gave him some basic information. This particular morning the elevator call button would be found on the wall of the Early American Collection room of the New York Public Library's main branch.

The precise books to withdraw and reshelve, and the appropriate sequence, had been more difficult to track down. It had taken Tesla almost forty minutes and required him to make two phone calls, which annoyed him mightily. But now here he was.

A biography of Phillis Wheatley, a volume of John Adams's letters, and a folio of portraits of the first three presidents. The folio was to be reshelved in its rightful place but with the spine facing inward. The biography and the letters were to be transposed. Both of these actions were offensive to Tesla, but he followed the directions he had been given to the letter.

The lights in the room went out, and the librarian and the one researcher who had been present when he arrived muttered to each other in annoyance. It was not completely dark, but dark enough that only someone gifted with eyes such as Tesla's would bother staying there.

Once the patron and librarian stumbled their way to the door, Tesla caught sight of a glowing button on an exterior wall, which was not nearly thick enough to house anything more than wiring and insulation. It was set in a rectangular metal plate next to a downward-pointing arrow.

After he pushed the button, a discordant hum sounded, following by a thumping noise and screech that sounded unsettlingly like the scream of a horse in distress. Then, against all reason, a set of elevator doors appeared. A rusty accordion gate was pulled open, and Tesla entered the cramped compartment.

The elevator attendant was so tall that she had to bend over double to fit inside the old-fashioned cage. Her skin and hair were pure white, as were her eyes, which were absent iris and pupil. Her lips, though, were ruby red, and Tesla did not believe it was because she applied lipstick.

The operator closed the gate as soon as he boarded, and the doors closed.

"Going down," Tesla said.

"It's not like I go up," said the operator.

She held out her hand and Tesla placed a thick stack of $100 bills, bound in a paper banker's band, on her palm. The price of using the elevator was, from what he had been able to determine, unfixed but always high. He hoped he was paying enough for his trip. A distressing number of long fingers closed around the money, which swiftly disappeared into the woman's robes.

"Down *where*?" she asked.

Tesla paused. "I'm looking for the Troglodytes," he said.

The woman made an exasperated sound. "So, *sideways* first, *then* down. Why didn't you say so?"

Machine noises sounded, the compartment jerked, and Tesla sensed the elevator moving swiftly. He could not exactly track the direction they were traveling, given the way the elevator shook and shifted. The only thing he could tell for certain was that it seemed largely to be moving left, which was not particularly helpful.

"How long?" he asked the attendant.

She glared up at him with her all-white eyes. "You didn't pay the expedited rate," she answered, which of course was no answer at all.

The elevator did not seem to be moving more quickly—even sideways—than any other old elevator. Tesla idly considered the operator, who seemed in turn to be considering *him*, but with much more intensity. A joker, obviously, but was it some wild-card-granted gift of hers that explained the elevator's existence? It seemed impossible that there were actual machine works powering its operation, as that would require a vast network of hidden passageways, a no-doubt-stolen energy source, and a general conspiracy of silence among many important players in New York City.

Then he considered his destination. Hidden passageways, stolen energy, a conspiracy of silence.

An actual physical conveyance or some by-product of the alien virus?

Tesla decided first that anything was possible, and second that it didn't really matter.

At last, the elevator began to clearly move down. And down. Down for an uncomfortable amount of time.

"Are you sure they're this deep?" Tesla asked.

The operator did not answer.

Finally, the elevator stopped with enough force that Tesla felt it in his spine.

The doors opened onto a narrow, dimly lit passage crowded with horizontally running pipes. A slight scent of sewage floated in the dank air.

Tesla let the charge between his horns become visible. He leaned out and looked left and right. He saw no one.

Abruptly, he stumbled into the passageway, having been kicked in the backside. How had the bent-over woman managed that?

He turned. She was closing the gate. "Will you be here when I come back?"

As the doors closed in front of the grating, she said, "You didn't pay the return rate."

Then the wall was just cinder blocks, weeping water.

The source of the light was a flickering, wall-mounted bulb about fifty feet to the right of Tesla's position. "Right," of course, being purely subjective. The only sounds were the faint hum of wiring within the conduit pipes, and a sloshing, as of open water though a channel, beyond the light.

And breathing. Tesla could hear his own breathing, fast and shallow.

He took a moment to calm himself. He considered whether or not to hold the pistol in his hand when he began exploring the tunnels but decided against it. The charge he held between his horns would do as a first resort if things turned violent.

Slowly, carefully, he made his way toward the flickering light.

He averted his eyes from the bulb itself in an attempt to keep his vision clear. When he reached it, he saw that graffiti had been painted on the opposite wall in tall, tightly spaced, looping letters. It took him a moment to realize what he was seeing.

The letters were, in fact, Greek characters. Tesla made the mental translation into Latin letters.

Ageōmétrētos mēdeìs eisítō.

Or, in English, "Let no one untrained in geometry enter." According to Elias's *Commentaries,* the sign over Plato's Academy.

Another mystery.

But Tesla was an accomplished geometer. He continued down the passageway.

"Stop, in the name of the law!"

The voice was a boy's and came from above Tesla.

Tesla stopped. He looked up and saw a large, open pipe jutting out from near the ceiling, which was quite high here. Two bare and very dirty feet dangled out of it.

"I've never actually heard that said aloud," Tesla said calmly.

Then, from behind, he heard a great intake of breath, like a giant sniffing.

"Joker," said a low, rough voice. "Joker with *power.* Smells like ozone."

"Is he electric?" asked the child. The person who sounded like a child.

"Smells like ozone," said the voice from behind.

There was a small grunt and a kick of the filthy legs. Tesla heard the Trog with the child's voice hit the concrete floor before him. But he did not *see* the gang member. At least not all of him. The bare feet and legs stopped just above the knee. Above that, Tesla could clearly see the tunnel beyond.

"I think you're electric," said the invisible boy. The *mostly* invisible boy. "I'm gonna call you Sparks. Hey, Nose! This is Sparks!"

"I'm gonna call him Ozone."

It was impossible for Tesla to guess the extent of the boy's power. Were things he carried rendered invisible as well, meaning he might be carrying a weapon? Why was he barefoot in this filthy and fetid place?

"And what shall I call you?" asked Tesla.

"That's Nose behind you," the boy replied. "Turn around and say hi."

Tesla slowly turned, not knowing what to expect. What he saw surprised him more than any monstrosity might have. Nose was, by all appearances, a middle-aged Black man, perhaps a little shorter than average, wearing a Dodgers T-shirt and khaki work pants stuffed into rubber boots.

Which made him an ace. Which meant that Tesla's information about the diversity of the Trogs' membership was correct.

"How'd you get down here, Ozone?" asked Nose. "Take the elevator? We told that woman to cut that out."

"We told her to cut it out unless she was cutting us in," said the boy. "You got any money left, Sparks? That's a high-dollar trip, getting down here. It's even higher dollar getting back out."

Tesla said, "The operator told me she wouldn't be returning." He needed time to figure out the situation. Were these two guards? Guides? Did he dare hope for the latter?

Nose laughed. "Which meant she kicked your ass out of her elevator."

"You were watching?"

"Nah," said Nose. "She always does that."

"Customer service," said Tesla, "has taken a turn for the worse since the last time I was in the city."

Nose looked surprised, and then he laughed again, this time heartily. He even slapped his knee. "Customer service!" he said. "Did you hear that, Knees?"

The boy—Knees, Tesla surmised—was laughing, too, a high-pitched giggle. "I heard it! That's a good one! Customer service!"

Tesla looked from one Trog to another, from Nose to Knees—or what he could see of Knees. He was surprised the droll joke had elicited such an enthusiastic response. Maybe humor was in short supply in the undercity.

"Okay, okay," said Knees. "We don't have you figured out, but we do have you held prisoner. You understand that? You understand that you're our prisoner?"

Tesla felt the held charge bouncing around his brain. "I understand that," he said.

"Okay, Sparks." The feet turned away from Tesla and began walking down the passage. "Let's go see some women about whether or not you're going to live to see daylight again."

There was a prodding at Tesla's back. Even through his jacket and vest, he could tell that the caliber of the pistol Nose now held was much larger than that of the pistol he himself carried.

Nose shouted after the retreating, mostly invisible boy as he guided Tesla after. "Let's call him Ozone!"

As they made the long trip through the passages and tunnels of the undercity, Tesla became aware that they were entering a more populated area. Once, in a large, cavernous space where there was actual bedrock underfoot, he caught sight of a fire high above him. There were catwalks up there, and a number of people were surrounding an oil barrel with flames flickering out of its open top.

Then, in a low place where he and Nose had to crouch—Tesla could not tell whether the same was true of Knees—a chorus of loud hissing noises came from a side tunnel. "That's Mr. Orange-blossom," said Knees. "Sounds like he likes you."

Tesla glanced back over his shoulder but could see nothing in the pitch-dark side tunnel. He did see that Nose, while he still held his enormous handgun, was pressing a handkerchief over the lower part of his face, a distressed look in his eyes. Tesla sniffed but smelled nothing beyond the general miasma that had by this point become familiar enough that he could almost ignore it.

Finally, after a number of splitting passageways and turns, all of which Tesla memorized, there was light ahead that was much brighter than the series of dim bulbs that had lit their way so far. The tunnel they were traveling opened up into an enormous chamber. Strips of LEDs were stuck to the ceiling and at various places on the concrete walls. A single gigantic pipe made a U shape, extending from the right-hand wall, turning, then reentering the same wall.

Dozens of people, some obviously jokers, some to all appearances nats, stood or sat everywhere in the chamber. Most of them were working at benches, sorting what looked to Tesla like trash, assembling or disassembling small machines, preparing meals. Others were sprawled on thick carpets that spotted the floor or sat in reclining chairs that had seen better days.

It was to a pair of these chairs, set side by side, that Knees and Nose guided Tesla. The left-hand chair was empty, but in the right sat a plump, fiftyish white woman whose gray hair was wound around her head like a thick rope.

"So here he is," said the woman, evidently to Knees. "We got your telegram."

Tesla saw that the woman held a square of buff paper in her hand printed in block capitals, by all appearances an actual telegram. When could the boy have sent such a message? Sent *any* message?

"Why'd you leave him his gun?" asked the woman.

"Least dangerous thing about him," said Nose. But he reached inside Tesla's jacket, pulled out the pistol that had been provided by the hotel, and deftly unloaded it one-handed. Then he returned it to Tesla's shoulder holster.

"What *is* dangerous about him? I mean, he *looks* dangerous, but who makes it this far down here that doesn't?" The woman was looking Tesla up and down, pursing her lips. Her eyes were a surprisingly bright green.

"He's electric!" said Knees. "That's why we're calling him Sparks!"

"Come on, man," said Nose.

"What's your name?" asked the woman.

Tesla hesitated. Then he said, "My name is Tesla."

The woman rolled her eyes. "Why does every joker in the world come up with some goofy nickname for themselves?"

Tesla cocked his head to one side. Did she actually expect him to answer? Did she actually not know?

The woman waved her hand. "My name is Monica Carrot. That's my actual birth certificate name, even the Carrot part. Ellis Island."

"It's an honor to meet you, Ms. Carrot," said Tesla. "You are the leader here?"

"Troglodytes have a rotating committee chair beholden to the whole membership of our anarchist collective."

"Ah. Then it's an honor to meet you, Madame Chairwoman."

"I'm not the chair," said Monica Carrot.

Tesla simply nodded in response.

"I'm the vice chair. Chair this month is my sister, Elizabeth."

Tesla waited a moment, but everyone he could see—and Knees—appeared to be waiting on *him*. So he said, "I look forward to meeting her."

"Good," said Monica Carrot. "Because here she comes."

Suddenly everyone nearby, except the vice chair, jumped, ran, or otherwise scrambled outward in a panicked circle from the two reclining chairs. Tesla decided it best to do the same.

A wise decision, because something—some*one*—plummeted from overhead to land in a crouched position, one knee and both tight fists against the floor. The figure was cloaked in a voluminous red robe and was by all appearances a woman whose hair was on fire.

The Chairwoman, for this was surely she, shot a look at Tesla. She shared those startling green eyes with her sister, as well as a general shape of face and manner of bearing. She dropped the robe to the floor, revealing that she was wearing a brown pantsuit.

When she sat down in the empty chair beside her sister, her flaming hair instantly caused smoke to rise from the headrest.

A man darted up out of the crowd, took station behind Elizabeth Carrot, and held out both of his hands, fingers spread wide. Thin streams of water flowed from his fingers, and the smoke subsided.

"Thanks, Tommy," said Elizabeth Carrot. She even sounded like her sister. She gave a dismissive look at the upholstery under her arms and added, "Fire-resistant my ass."

"Thanks for joining, sis," said Monica Carrot.

The Chairwoman smiled and patted her sister's hand. Then she looked at Tesla with evident curiosity. "What's his story?"

"Knees says he's electric, whatever that's supposed to mean," said her sister. "Claims his name is Tesla."

"That's a cute one," said Elizabeth Carrot. Then she looked at Tesla. "You're working that theme pretty hard, aren't you? If you have electrical powers, anyway."

Tesla shrugged.

Elizabeth Carrot cocked an eyebrow. These were not on fire. They weren't gray, either, but brown. This was the only clue Tesla had that she might be the younger sister.

Smoke started to rise from the chair again, and Tommy hurried to do what was evidently his assigned task. Elizabeth Carrot didn't say anything to the man this time.

"So," she said. "Are you leaving here dead or alive?"

Tesla did not hesitate. "Alive," he said.

She laughed. "You think you can fight your way out of here if I give the thumbs-down? You must have a hell of a lot of the old alternating current at your command."

"What I have at my command," said Tesla, "is a hell of a lot of knowledge."

Elizabeth Carrot looked over at Monica Carrot. Both of Monica Carrot's penciled eyebrows were raised. Seeing her sister's glance, she gave the barest of nods.

"Well," said the Chairwoman, "that's a better power than electricity *or* flaming hair."

Negotiations, Tesla had always believed, were at their heart very simple. Everyone wants something. Everyone can *provide* something. The art of it—frequently delicate and always fascinating to him—was learning what needs and provisions existed on each side of the table (or all sides of the table in particularly fascinating circumstances), then opening ways for all involved parties to depart having gained something.

What the Troglodytes needed was money, which on the face of it was simple enough. Though the demands of the community—a much larger community than anyone above suspected—were considerable, Tesla's resources were considerable as well. The sticking point was this.

"We don't want your money," said Monica Carrot.

Tesla did not respond. He was seated on a low divan that had been pulled up in front of the sisters' paired reclining chairs.

"To clarify," said Elizabeth Carrot, her flaming hair now dimmed somewhat compared with the spectacular pyrotechnic display that had accompanied her entry, "we don't want you to, what, cut us a check or something."

Tesla did not own a checkbook, but he took the Chairwoman's point. "You want me to provide information that will lead you to opportunities to earn"—he did not emphasize the word aloud—"your own way. You wish to build a self-sustaining economy in the undercity."

Monica Carrot looked at him with some surprise.

"I've done this before," said Tesla. And he had, more than once. Among South American Natives, supposedly "uncontacted," and in the nowhere between the Gobi and the Himalayas. Tesla had found that his interests often coincided with those of peoples who lived on edges, though this was the first time the edge presented was between the upper world and the lower.

"We do okay for ourselves," said Monica Carrot, somewhat defensively.

Tesla said, "You rob poor people. You sell drugs to helpless people. You profit from hopelessness."

Monica Carrot looked affronted, but it was her sister that answered her. "You missed saying that we're poor ourselves. And many of us are hopeless."

"Leaving . . ." Tesla trailed off.

"No," said the Chairwoman. "We are not helpless. But as you seem to realize, we're no longer able to continue doing things the way we have been."

"An attack of conscience?" asked Tesla.

Surprisingly, it was neither of the sisters who answered, but Tommy, the man whose watering fingers kept Elizabeth Carrot from setting her ersatz throne afire. "We have always had a conscience," he said. "We have never had the option of following it. You seem to offer us that opportunity."

Tesla looked at the sisters.

"Tommy's the immediate past chair," said Monica Carrot.

Tesla nodded. "You want to cease being criminals," he said.

Elizabeth Carrot laughed. "Now, now, we didn't say that. We just want to be different *kinds* of criminals."

Then it was just a matter of showing them how to set up anonymous brokerage accounts.

"And what can we do for you?" Elizabeth Carrot asked Tesla.

He told her he needed a simple introduction to a man he believed to be associated with their community and safe passage to that man's location. He then provided the description of the gem-eyed Croyd who had visited the pencil shop.

"You want to meet the Miner," said Elizabeth Carrot. "Sure, safe passage and an introduction are easy enough. Realize, though, that he's not one of us. We can't guarantee he won't kill you."

"And he's been getting crazier and crazier since he showed up a while back," Monica Carrot had added.

Then they had said their goodbyes, these marked more by wariness still than goodwill, and detailed off a pair of foot soldiers to lead Tesla to the distant passage where the Miner was believed to reside.

The foot soldiers were Knees and Nose.

"You must be pretty fancy," said the boy. "I mean, you're wearing a fancy suit, but even Nose there has a fancy suit stashed somewhere, don't you, Nose?"

"Real fancy," said Nose.

They were walking through an unlit passageway that angled down through bedrock, Nose and Tesla each carrying flashlights. Knees ranged a short distance ahead of them, but apparently couldn't see in the dark—or at least the dirty feet never went beyond the doubled circles of battery-powered light.

"How'd you get the Chairwoman to let you go?" the boy asked. "And with us as an honor guard?"

Tesla considered his answer. "She let me go for money. I don't know what I did to rate you two."

Nose said, "Not the types to accept bribes, those Carrot sisters."

"I didn't say it was a bribe," said Tesla, and when neither of the others answered he considered the matter closed.

Which was a good thing, because they had apparently reached their destination: a ragged hole on the side wall, with tailings spread out all around and making the footing treacherous. It was uncomfortably warm. Perhaps the source of the heat matched that of the dim red light emanating from the horizontal shaft.

"This is as far as we go," said Nose.

Tesla wondered if he'd been out-negotiated after all. "I keep forgetting to arrange for my return passage," he muttered.

"Nah," said Knees. "We're gonna take you up top after. I mean, if you come back out in a reasonable amount of time."

"How long is a reasonable amount of time?" asked Tesla.

"I guess we'll find out," said Nose, shutting off his flashlight.

"You're going to wait in the dark?"

"Oh," Knees piped in. "We're used to it. All of us down here are."

"Except for the Chairwoman and her flaming hair, I suppose," said Tesla.

He saw Nose look past him, and realized that if the boy had been visible, the two Trogs would have been exchanging a freighted glance.

"Nah," said Nose. "She's used to it, too."

Which was cryptic enough, thought Tesla, and, aware that he might have already taken an unreasonable amount of time deciding to do so, he gingerly entered what could only be described as a mine shaft.

It took a few moments for Tesla to puzzle out what the round, amber scales he was seeing were, with their accompanying circles of white and what looked like strips of paper suspended inside. They were melted prescription medication bottles. There were a distressingly large number of them, pebbling the path between the tailings like landscape stones.

The red light grew brighter and the heat grew more oppressive. Soon Tesla could see that the source of the light was twin cyan stones, apparently floating about six feet above the ground. The stones turned toward him.

Ah. Eyes. Of course.

"Mr. Crenson, can you hear me?"

Tesla played the beam of his flashlight over the Miner's body. In this iteration, Croyd Crenson looked like a large statue carved from bituminous coal, human but only vaguely masculine in outline. Crenson's body was vibrating—a most disconcerting sight. Also disconcerting were the sounds of small stones falling up and down the shaft, the occasional small cloud of dust, the rumbling underfoot.

"Have we met?"

The Miner's voice was like wet concrete being poured onto a gravel substrate.

"In a manner of speaking," said Tesla. "Do you remember the circumstances under which you woke this time?" He figured there was no point in doing anything besides directly engaging with Crenson. Time, after all, seemed to be very much of the essence, for so many different reasons.

"You mean you met one of those other bastards," said the Miner. "The imposters."

Interesting.

"I was hired by a man claiming to be Croyd Crenson, yes. He tasked me with finding you."

"Just me?"

"I concede the point. My assignment is to find all of you, and to arrange that you meet with . . . with the man I first met claiming to be you."

"Why should I want to meet him? Which one is it, anyway? The swimming one? The one with all the arms?"

One part of Tesla's mind was busily filing all of these facts away, pleased that so much progress was being made in the investigation in just this brief exchange. Most of his mind, though, was playing out various scenarios that ended with him surviving this encounter.

"He was a . . . swimmer, I suppose you could say."

"Oh, that bastard. Yeah, he got blown out the window but I saw him land in the river and take off."

"There was an explosion?" asked Tesla.

"Wind. He got blown out the window by wind. Do you have any speed?"

"Alas, no," said Tesla, and made a mental note to lay in a supply for the next time he encountered Crenson. *A* Crenson.

"Who are you, anyway? How did you know to come down here looking for me?"

"Well, Mr. Crenson, it's my understanding that you came looking for *me*."

"I don't think so," said the Miner.

"You simply recently developed an interest in high-end pencils, then?"

Tesla did not realize he had assumed the Miner was already standing until the figure actually *did* stand up, the coal-black body shifting and molding. Where a large mutated man had stood before him, now there was a giant, head cocked at an angle so that his skull didn't brush the ceiling.

"That's who you are? The guy who knows things?"

Tesla paused. He settled on saying, "I'm genuinely flattered."

"So one of the others got to you first. The swimming guy, you said."

"I'm curious as to why *you* were looking for me," Tesla replied. "How can I be of service to you?"

"I want you to find out where all those other bastards are so I can go kill them."

"You don't think that's perhaps a bit extreme?"

"Why do you think the swimming guy hired you?"

Tesla usually chose not to directly question the motivations of his clients, for they couldn't be trusted to truly know or disclose them. He might have made a mistake in not doing so in this particular instance.

But he could put this to use. His job was to get all the Croyds to the same place. "I am simply a messenger, though one whose message seems to dovetail with your interests."

"Stop talking like that," said the Miner.

"My apolo— I'm sorry," said Tesla.

"What do you know about my interests?"

"Just what you've told me. I was hired to find you and to arrange it—to fix it so you would meet up with the guy who hired me. It sounds like you want to meet him, too."

"Oh, hell yes. Where is he?" asked the Miner.

"I don't know where he is right now. But I know where he'll be at midnight two nights from now."

The Miner grumbled, the sound matching the groaning of the rock around them. "Tell me where."

Tesla recited an address in Midtown Manhattan. "Do you remember that place?"

The Miner nodded. "Yeah. Yeah, I remember it. Of course I do."

"So I can go?"

The Miner began sinking into the ground. Tesla felt a new and worrisome vibration through the soles of his feet.

"Wait!" Tesla said. "Croyd!"

The Miner stopped. "That's me. You're fucking right that's me!"

The giant, Tesla realized, was barely holding things together, both physically and mentally.

"Tell me, if you will. Why were you looking for me? And how did you know where to find me?"

The Miner shrugged. "Guess I had the same idea as the swimming guy. Find somebody that knows shit. As for how I tracked you down, well, you ain't the only guy who knows shit. I asked the Walrus. Coo coo ca-choo."

Then he was gone.

Tesla found Knees and Nose where he had left them. The rumblings of the surrounding earth had subsided when Crenson disappeared into the bedrock. Even the heat was dissipating.

"I believe my adventures underground have come to their end," he told the Trogs.

"Glad you're still alive, Sparks!" said Knees.

"Why, thank you, Knees, I genuinely appreciate that."

"We're supposed to take you up to wherever you want to go now," said Nose.

"Ah," said Tesla. "Well, I suppose I can't put it off any longer, then."

"Sorry to be leaving us?" asked Nose.

Tesla actually was. But he didn't tell that to the two gang members—to the two *collective* members—who had accompanied him for what he now realized must be better than a day.

"He's not going to say if he is!" chortled Knees. "Where do you want to go next?"

Tesla didn't really know the answer to that question. He knew a place he did *not* want to go next. Unfortunately, it was also the place he *must* go next.

"Jokertown," he said.

Though Tesla had only ever seen the operator of the newsstand from across a busy street, had never spoken to him, and had just a thin file on him as one of the older jokers in the world, he considered Jube the Walrus a colleague, after a fashion. Wearing a Hawaiian print shirt and a porkpie hat, tufts of orange hair sprouting about his head, Jube was famous in Jokertown for knowing things.

Part of that, of course, was his trade. It had been many years since Tesla had seen so many different newspapers for sale in one place. They were all of them, no matter the language or sophistication of design, much thinner than they used to be, of course. Since the internet had eventually convinced the world that data and information were the same thing, the sad, slow demise of newspapers had become something of a preoccupation of Tesla's. He was unable to subscribe to any, of course—that would mean that someone else had his address—but he read their websites widely and, when such was available, deeply.

He would not have guessed the state of the newspaper industry from looking at the wares of the Walrus, however. There were two dozen from New York alone, serving populations ranging from the whole of the world to communities of people living in the city who barely had enough members to merit the name *enclave*. Tesla wondered how many people who wandered by Jube's newsstand read Hmong, for instance.

But then, a newsstand that looked like it came straight from the 1950s could hardly have profit as its sole motive. Whatever else might be said or not said about Jube the Walrus, he was clearly engaged in a passion project.

"What are you looking for today?" the Walrus asked, eyes up-turned so they met Tesla's. "All the news that'll fit is right here! Democracy dies in the dark, all that jazz!"

Tesla said, "I'm in the market for more specialized information, actually."

"Well, why didn't you say so? Feast your eyes. You read Polish, Thai, German, Armenian, Mandarin, Cantonese, Québécois?"

"Yes," said Tesla. "But what I'm looking for isn't in a news-paper."

There was a change of expression on the Walrus's face, subtle, but Tesla had been watching for it. "There's an awful lot you can learn reading newspapers," was all he said.

Surprisingly, Tesla was growing tired of seeing every conversa-tion he'd had since having been hired for this adventure turn into verbal fencing. "There's even more you can learn by listening to the right people."

"You know," said Jube, "all the time I've been knocking around this planet, I gotta say I've met more people who were right than were wrong. Or at least they think they're right."

There was something odd in the way he'd said "knocking around this planet," but Tesla let it pass. He was not investigating

Jube the Walrus. "Let me say, then, I'm looking for someone who knows the whereabouts of a mutual acquaintance of ours. I won't burden you with his name."

"Best not. I am terrible with names." Jube plucked a tourist's map from a stack on the newsstand, his thick fingers surprisingly deft. The cover of the plasticized map said, "Because You Don't Want to Be Lost in Jokertown!" Then he produced a grease pencil and circled an intersection five blocks away.

"It's a diner," he said. "Look for a man seated near the middle, with his back to the door."

"An uncommon habit in Jokertown, I imagine," said Tesla. "Will that be the man I want?"

"Him . . . or someone who might know where to find him. If he cares to." Jube held out his hand. "Six fifty for the map. They were a dime when I started this stand."

Tesla peeled seven $1 bills off the roll in his pocket and handed them over. "Keep the change," he said.

"I was going to anyway," said Jube.

Tesla oriented himself to the map and started up the street.

"Hey!" came the cry from behind. "Mister!"

Tesla turned.

"Do you know what the ram said to the electrician?"

Tesla shook his head.

"I've got baaaaaad news!"

The diner would have made a good subject for a Hopper painting if it had been better lit. And if the windows were cleaner. And if the patrons had been nats. But then again, when *Nighthawks* was painted, nobody had been called a nat because there were no jokers yet to deal with.

The man seated at the center table with his back toward the door would never pass for a nat—his great curling ram's horns ensured that—but his suit was pressed, if not quite so sharply as those of the men in Hopper's famous picture. And, of course, he couldn't wear a hat. He was in a booth staring at a partly filled-in *New York Times* crossword puzzle.

Tesla knew who he was. Not Croyd; a retired detective from the NYPD's Fifth Precinct, Fort Freak.

He took the seat opposite him without asking and without introducing himself. He sensed that he was running out of time, that he didn't have any more time for games.

"I know you?" Leo Storgman asked, not looking up from the paper.

"Wouldn't you remember me if you did?" Tesla replied.

The old man looked up. "Probably," he said. "I've got a pretty good memory."

"I'm looking for someone."

"I'm out of the missing persons business, friend. Retired. And I haven't seen Croyd Crenson in years."

Tesla sat back, trying not to let the surprise he felt show in his features. "News travels fast in Jokertown," Tesla said.

"Bad news does, anyway," said Storgman.

I've got baaaad news, thought Tesla.

The Hit Parade

by Cherie Priest

1.

Monday, December 5, 1983

NYPD detective Leo Storgman made a slow, meticulous sweep of the narrow radio booth—where shelves were loaded with show notes, commercial scripts, station schwag, and assorted electronic equipment. Beneath a microphone the size of a hoagie, a shiny pink mug read GLAMSHELL GLITTER GALA, 1982, so it came from last year's drag ball. He leaned over to give it a sniff without touching it. The dregs at the bottom looked and smelled more like whiskey than coffee. He stood up straight again and used a dull pencil to poke at a box full of cables and cords. He surveyed the jumbles of headphones and batteries, a cup full of ballpoint pens, and boxes of badly labeled files.

Satisfied that he'd now seen everything important, he shook his head at the fresh corpse that rested facedown on the DJ desk. He asked his partner, "Shouldn't the coroner's office have been here by now?"

Detective Ralph Pleasant twisted his lips into a crooked bow. "Maybe," he said. "But this close to Christmas, the morgue is always hopping. They'll be here any minute."

"Hey, man, don't talk like that. I've still got three weeks to finish shopping."

"Slacker."

"As always." Back to the subject at hand. "Will he go to county, or . . . ?"

"The clinic, I bet. They know how to handle bodies like this." Ralph meant the Jokertown clinic, but not because it was the closest facility—even though it was.

"His body's not that weird," Leo observed.

Ralph snorted. "Relative to what?"

"Relative to *me*." That shut him up. This time. "He has two arms, two legs. One head."

A little carefully: "So do you."

Fair point, Leo thought. He threw him a bone. "You've got me there. No horns, at least."

The dead fellow may not have had Leo's thickly curled head-ornaments, but that didn't mean he was ordinary. Ralph told him, "The producer says he had a face like a trench, if you dug one through a minefield. And skin that looks like it was hit with a blowtorch. Look." He slipped a gloved finger down the back of the body's collar, revealing a strip of red, bubbled skin.

"I've seen worse." Leo crouched down beside the DJ. The man's hands had fallen to his sides, and his knees were tucked under the desk. The back of his skull was a misshapen pulp of gore. Clotted blood spilled down his cheeks and pooled around his nose and chin. "Somebody caught him by surprise."

"Probably. No signs of struggle, but . . . they hit him from behind," Ralph agreed. "Murder weapon's probably something like, like . . . a hatchet, or . . ."

Leo used his pencil to gently shift a lock of matted hair. "I don't know about a hatchet, but it was sharp and heavy. Hang on, there's something else here. Some kind of dust."

"Leave it for forensics. Anyway, who even knows what this guy's head was shaped like in the first place?"

Leo resisted the urge to reply. Some things weren't worth bickering about, not when you had to ride in a car with a guy every damn day.

Terry Wilson, the station manager, tapped a greeting from the far side of the booth window. She was a small and dark-haired nat, with round glasses and a frumpy polyester sensibility that was probably charming to someone, somewhere. "Detectives?" Her voice was piped in through a speaker.

Ralph perked up first. "Ma'am?"

"Someone's here from the coroner's office." She sounded tinny and faraway. She was taking great pains to avoid looking at the dead man. "Are you finished? Can I send him in?"

Leo nodded without looking up. Over his shoulder, he said, "Go ahead." Under his breath, he added, "It's about time."

His partner, the senior member of the pair, added, "Yeah, it's all right. Don't worry, ma'am. They'll have him out of here in an hour. After that, the forensics team will swing by, and then you can have your radio station back. Hey, lemme ask you a question."

Leo heard the muffled click of a speaker being engaged on Terry's end. "Yes?"

"What does it sound like, right now? Your station, I mean. Are you playing music or something? Commercials?"

For a moment, she looked confused. "Oh? Oh. What you hear is what we're playing, Detective. Nothing at all."

"Dead air," Leo muttered.

Ralph laughed.

Leo frowned. He hadn't meant it as a joke. "I'm sorry about the programming disruption."

Another soft click. "Not half as sorry as I am, I assure you."

He glanced over at the window and promptly wished he hadn't. She looked stricken and lost. "I'm sorry about your . . . DJ, too. Your friend," he guessed.

She didn't say anything in return, just nodded and looked away.

She disappeared through a side door. It closed slowly and silently behind her.

Ralph gave the corpse another quick look-over. "What are you thinking, kid?"

Leo tucked his pencil into his shirt pocket. "Gonna go out on a limb and say he was murdered."

"That's why we pay you the big bucks. Your keen investigative eye. You want to chat at the boss-lady, or go through call logs and threat reports?"

"Don't really care. Wait. You don't want to talk to Miss Wilson?" Leo asked. "She seems nice enough."

"Eh. I'm tired of dragging details out of shell-shocked survivors. It's your turn."

"Yeah, all right. I'll talk to her. You enjoy your paperwork. Did they file these threats with someone at the precinct, or . . . ?"

"She said they don't bother, because no one ever follows up. I will take it upon myself to prove her wrong," he declared with seriousness that sounded suspiciously like mockery.

"You do that. Leave the bereaved to me." It usually worked best that way. Leo was younger than Ralph by fifteen years, but his bedside manner was considerably better.

Ralph said something about collecting those threat logs and left the small booth that smelled of body odor and blood . . . and something else, some odd stuffiness with a metallic edge—the weird, warm sizzle of electricity and hum of audio equipment. It almost felt like humidity.

Leo was idly glad to see him go. Ralph only wanted the easier of two gigs, and he wasn't creative enough to realize that a left-leaning radio station in Jokertown probably received a metric ass-load of hate mail. The thought put a faint smile on his face.

Only a faint one. A final look at the dead guy wiped it off again.

He shut the door on the way out, and passed Mickey and George with a gurney as he headed for the station manager's office. "That way," he gestured, pointing around the corner. "He's in the booth."

"Thanks, Storgman," Mickey said, kicking at a rusty wheel. "Is it a bad one?"

"You ever see a good one?"

George said, "Fair point," and pushed the wheeled bed past him. A folded black body bag fluttered on the thin, hard mattress as they disappeared down the hall.

Terry Wilson was sitting in her office, swearing into a phone. The office made the DJ booth look squeaky clean. Tall file cabinets lined one wall, and each cabinet was stacked with boxes, files, and folders. Radio equipment was parked on carts. A coatrack was overloaded with raincoats, winter coats, hats, and scarves. An oversized set of headphones rested at the edge of her desk, its cable dangling over the side and into a round trash bin that over-flowed with marked-up scripts, a busted cassette with its curly plastic contents unspooled, and half a dozen losing scratchers. The wadded balls of paper surrounding the bin suggested that Terry's three-point shot could use some work.

The station manager saw Leo standing in the doorway, mo-tioned him in, and wrapped up her call by saying, "I'll give you the details later, all right? He's dead, the cops are here, and I have to go." She smacked the handset back down onto the receiver. "Sorry about that."

"No problem. Was that your boss?"

"The station owner," she confirmed. "I had to call them and tell them about Jake. I know it's awfully late, or . . . or awfully early? I don't know what time it is anymore. But still. Better he hears it from me than the front page of the *Jokertown Cry*."

"I hear you. I know Ralph wanted your threatening call logs. Did you give him tapes or what?"

"Yeah, I gave him a box and told him to have fun. He looked disappointed."

Leo grinned. "Only one box?"

Terry shrugged. "It was only overflowing a little bit."

"I think he was hoping for something a little less time-intensive. But he'll be fine."

"Should I go down to the station to help him?" she asked a little anxiously. "I'm supposed to give a statement, right?"

He nodded and pulled out his notebook. "Yeah, but we've got a minute or two. Could I trouble you for the highlights? Just give me something to start with."

"I don't know where to begin."

He settled into the seat across from her desk, kicking away some paper balls and an old racetrack form. "Well, ma'am, you found the body, right? Start there."

She took a deep breath and placed her hands flat on the desk, steadying herself. "Okay. Right. Of course." Her eyes began to water, and she cleared her throat. "Jacob Riskin. He's been my overnight star for almost six years, and we have this routine, you know? Sometimes the shift is long, and the calls are shitty, and the morning seems like a thousand years away, so he'd fly the donut flag. The donut flag, it's just—" She laughed, but it was a small, wet sound. "It's just a pencil with a sticky note on it, and there's a drawing of a donut. He'd wave the flag and I'd go to the twenty-four-hour place down the block, you know?"

"Is that a cops-love-donuts joke?"

"I didn't mean it that way, I'm sorry."

He shook his head. "I was just kidding, I know the place. Jack and Jilly's, right? Next to the big construction site, where they tore down that old hotel. My partner's a big fan of their Boston crèmes."

She relaxed a little, seeming both rueful and relieved. "It's not so crazy, right? Late-night people like us, well. Sometimes we need a sugar fix."

Leo tried to steer her back onto the subject at hand. "So Jake needed a sugar fix, and he raised the donut flag. You left to go get him some donuts?"

"Yes, that's right. I was in the production booth, and he waved the donut flag, and I gave him a thumbs-up. I went and got a dozen, because I wanted some for myself."

"How long were you gone?"

She took on the faraway look of someone doing math in their head. "Maybe ten minutes? Couldn't have been much longer than that."

"What was Riskin doing while you were gone?"

"Just . . . hosting his show, like usual. Played a song or two . . . and some commercials, I assume. I haven't had time to listen to the tape yet. When I got back with the donuts . . ." She petered out, as if she wasn't sure what to say next. She looked small and lost in her oversized office chair.

"That's when you found him."

"That's when I found him," she confirmed, misery dripping from every word. "The station was quiet. When the queued-up commercials quit playing, Jake usually would make a five- or ten-second bump and put on a record. The only cardinal sin of radio is silence."

"Then he died at some point while the commercials were playing. How long would those run?"

"About three minutes. Commercial airtime is cheap in the wee hours of the morning, so it's usually oddball stuff in thirty- or sixty-second packages. Party lines, video dating services, pawn-shop specials, that kind of thing."

"Is there any chance at all that he recorded what happened in the booth? Because if we have actual audio of this guy's murder, that would be fantastic."

She shook her head. "No such luck. He muted everything because he knew I was bringing him food. We have a strict no-food policy while live on-air."

"Makes sense." Behind him, on the other side of the open office door, he heard the squeaky wheels of the coroner's gurney heading out a little slower than it came in. "Who else had access to the DJ booth?"

"Dozens of people, if I'm honest. Our security protocols aren't very secure. We've gotten comfortable here—we've been in this building for twenty years, and we share it with a number of other offices and businesses, as well as some storage."

Terry closed her eyes, struggling to tune out the squeaky wheels as they retreated down the corridor. When she opened them again, she turned them on Leo. "What am I supposed to do? We're short-staffed at the best of times, and I only have three daytime people to swap back and forth. Maybe we'll just . . . play the national anthem and go off the air at midnight like TV stations do. At least until I can find someone else who's willing to stay up all night for an insulting paycheck, taking abuse from random callers and local politicians alike."

Then she started to cry.

2.

Tuesday, December 6, 1983

Ralph Pleasant staggered into the office an hour late, looking rumpled and ducking swiftly past the captain's office. Captain McPherson might or might not have cared, but it was always best not to risk it. Safely unspotted, he found his desk and shrugged out of his overcoat, then let it flop damp and sagging on the back of his chair. He sat down heavily and scooted the seat under his desk with a groan. Leo looked up from his notes. "Any luck with those threat reports from WAJT?"

"I thought I picked the easy gig."

"Oh, come on. It couldn't have been *that* bad."

"It was bad enough," he groused. "Mostly the radio station gets assholes complaining that Jake wouldn't play their requests, but I did find a few callers I wouldn't mind talking to. One's some kind of gentrification crusader who's running for office . . . because *of course* he is. The guy's mad about some fundraiser Jake was running, I couldn't tell you why, but I think we ought to find out. Another call came from a tweaker who sounded half out of his gourd, threatening to kill the DJ if he wouldn't help him out."

"Help him out with what?"

"No idea," Ralph concluded. "But the station manager said she thought the tweaker might be Croyd Crenson."

Leo leaned back in his seat and folded his hands across his chest. "The Sleeper? Shit. I didn't see *that* coming."

"You ever met him?"

He shook his head. "Heard about him, is all."

"Yeah, he's a legend. I met him once. Weird son of a bitch. Then again, I would be, too, if I woke up with a new wild card every time I tried to catch a little shut-eye."

"Poor bastard," Leo agreed. His life had become weird enough when just the *one* wild card turned on him; it was hard to imagine waking up each morning with a new one. Until his own transformation, he'd never appreciated the joy of being an ordinary-looking man. The horns were the worst of it—they seemed extra visible, now that he was losing his hair—but he didn't appreciate the pallid complexion with the greenish tint much, either. Thank God his wife hadn't cared. She liked to say she hadn't married him for his looks, anyway.

"Poor bastard or no, I put in a call to a buddy of mine a couple of hours ago. Right now, God knows what he even looks like, much less where we can find him—but let's see if we can get a lead on him. Meanwhile, you want to have a chat with Angus Hood?"

"Is that the crusader? Politician? Whatever?"

Ralph Pleasant nodded. "He's doing a ground-breaking cere-mony at the edge of Jokertown."

That rang a bell. "The fancy grocery store? The one everybody says jokers can't afford?"

"Yep, it gets underway today. Let's check it out while I wait to hear back from my guy about the Sleeper."

"Sounds like a plan." Leo stood up and reached for his coat.

"The third caller, we don't know. Threw a lot of Bible verses around, sounded like a preacher, maybe. Didn't identify himself." Ralph's phone rang. "That might be my source. You want to hang out and wait, see if you can figure out caller number three? Or do you wanna go the ground-breaking by yourself?"

Leo was happy to let Ralph take the lead on finding the Sleeper. "I'll hit up the ground-breaking. See if you can find Crenson, and I'll have a word with this Hood fellow. Caller number three can wait."

When Leo pulled up in his sedan, the ceremony was just about to begin.

He parked at the curb and got out to join a smallish, well-dressed crowd of people with dollar signs in their eyes. All of those eager faces were pointed at an empty lot, cleared by bulldoz-ers and staged for construction, with a couple of big machines parked on either side of some cinder blocks, a cement mixer, and a pallet of bricks. Beside the bricks stood a small man who was held upright by a pair of crutches anchored on his upper arms. His torso was twisted three times around like a corkscrew, but by for-tune or surgical intervention, his face and feet were still pointed in the right direction.

Rumor had it that sometimes, a card's turn could say something about the person whose body it changes. Like a guy who couldn't mind his own business would get big, crazy ears; or someone who grew up religious might take on characteristics of a demon, or a saint.

Ordinarily, Leo didn't like that line of thinking. It sounded too much like blaming some poor joker for their affliction—and anyway, what did his horns say about *him*?

But all he knew about Angus Hood was that he'd been a real estate developer until his semi-retirement—and now he was taking steps to gentrify his old stomping grounds. A line flickered through the cop's head, something his grandfather used to say about people he didn't like: *That guy's so crooked, he has to screw on his socks every morning.*

Maybe there was something to it, and maybe there wasn't.

Either way, he tried to smother any unqualified dislike of the man, because you just couldn't do that with suspects. Even when you really wanted to.

Instead, he made his way toward the front of the crowd with a series of gently pointed elbows and firm but polite apologies; and there he stood shoulder to shoulder with what he assumed must be investors, employees, and other interested parties whose motives he could not imagine. Speeches were offered by the woman who owned the grocery franchise, a representative of the construction company that was building the place, and then finally Hood stepped forward to say his piece.

"Welcome everyone, and thank you so much for being here!" His voice was on the high side, and he spoke quickly, like he was in a rush. Leo got the feeling he always talked that way. "I'm so proud to get this party started at last. It's taken a lot of work, a lot of time, and a lot of money . . ." he added with a wink at the front row. "But we've finally got all our ducks in a row and today's a beautiful day for a new beginning. This is a great day for New York City, and a great day for the citizens of Jokertown!"

With some assistance from a stiffly smiling assistant in a pair of inadvisably high heels, considering the terrain, Angus Hood took a narrow shovel and tossed a little bit of dirt over his shoulder.

A cheer rose up. Leo clapped politely.

When much of the milling crowd had thinned out, Leo closed in on the man of the hour. He was still chatting with somebody from the *Jokertown Cry*. Looked like it might've been one of the editors, but it was hard to say; he was wearing a stylized mask that gave him the face of a rabbit.

Leo shuffled his feet and scanned the rest of the scene.

A couple of suits talked with the kind of excited exaggeration that suggested they shared cocaine as likely as a tailor. Some woman with a messenger bag and a frazzled air was handing out pamphlets, but he couldn't see what kind. A shaky guy in jeans and a hoodie tripped over a stray cinder block, swore, and hustled past while hiding his face, but that didn't mean anything. A lot of people in Jokertown hid their faces. Plenty of folks didn't want to be looked at.

Then again, plenty of folks enjoyed an audience, thought Leo, as he watched a sharp-dressed bigwig talk too loudly into one of those new mobile phones, just to make sure he had everyone's attention—even if that attention was made entirely of irritation.

"Might as well hold a whole damn pay phone to your skull," Leo said to himself. He glanced again at Hood, who was finally left alone. With a couple of swift strides, he reached the real estate developer, who was gathering a briefcase and clearly preparing to leave. "Excuse me, Mr. Hood?"

"Yes? Can I help you?" His voice, though high and swift-paced, had a solid salesman mode.

"Detective Leo Storgman, NYPD."

Hood's polite smile froze but didn't slip. "And what can I help you with today, Detective? Are any laws being broken, in addition to a little bit of ground?" The frozen smile thawed and jiggled, as if he was pleased with his own cleverness.

"Not that I'm aware of, but that's not why I'm here. I wanted to talk to you about Jacob Riskin."

Hood's confusion appeared genuine. "Who?"

"Wide Awake Jake," Leo clarified. "Overnight DJ at WAJT."

"Oh. That guy. What about him?"

"He's dead."

"Natural causes . . . ?" Hood asked with a squeak.

"No such luck. What was your beef with him?"

"Beef?" Angus Hood snorted. "Oh, dear. Well, it's awful to hear that he's dead, that's never a good thing—but you overstate the case, Detective. Mr. . . . Riskin? That was really his name? Goodness. Mr. Riskin and I disagreed on a number of things, not least of all . . ." He gestured broadly at the area where the made-for-TV ceremony had just occurred.

"Spell it out for me."

"It's only that this project is not . . . universally approved of, in Jokertown. I understand the opposing view, I really do, but it's terribly shortsighted. Jokertown can't remain a lawless ghetto forever, and furthermore, it *shouldn't*. Businesses like this store will soften the boundaries between neighborhoods, leading to more foot traffic, more tourism, more citywide flow as people—regular people, you understand—feel safer about coming and going."

Leo pulled his notebook out of his pocket and said "lawless ghetto" as he scrawled something there.

"Oh, I didn't mean . . ."

"I know what you meant. You want more money pouring into the neighborhood." Before Hood could protest, the detective continued. "Tell me what Jake thought about your grocery store."

Angus Hood hemmed and hawed, and shifted on his crutches. "As I said, it's a narrow view. He didn't like the idea of the store purely because it's fancy, and he didn't like the idea of the crowd it would attract."

Leo didn't buy it. "That's why you called in to his show? To tell him off?"

Now he blushed. "I didn't . . . I didn't 'tell him off,' sir. I was trying to finish a conversation he'd walked away from, when I tried to have a calm, measured, logical talk with him. He'd set up a tent in an empty lot a couple of blocks from here, and I only wanted to reason with him, but he got upset. It was clear there was no talking to him."

"What was Jake doing in a tent?" Leo asked.

"Oh, it was some kind of on-site broadcast giving out T-shirts and stickers, begging for donations. Some charity group is looking to build a men's shelter here in the neighborhood, and their grant money fell short."

"Sounds like a worthy cause to me."

But Hood objected. "Worthy for *some*place, to be certain. But here? In a neighborhood already widely regarded as a blight upon the city?" He shook his head sadly. "Detective, I'm a joker myself—as you can see, obviously—and I understand the needs of these people better than anyone."

Leo offered a dubious "Eh."

"*I* am trying to move this community forward, and yes—to bring in money, and strengthen the economy. I want to change the public perception that Jokertown is a dangerous place to live, or visit, or shop. Jake, on the other hand, wanted to concentrate the poverty and misery into this precise locale, thereby attracting even more of it."

"You want to jack up property values, and Jake wanted to bring them down. Got it."

"That's . . . that's a significant generalization."

Leo shrugged. "Still more true than not, though. If it wasn't, you would've argued with me."

Now Hood was getting flustered. "That's not fair, and I think you know it. If you must generalize, then say that I want to make things better, and that Jake wanted to make things worse."

"Worse for who? It would've been better for homeless jokers. And there's more than a few of those, hanging around."

"Now you sound like *him*," Hood sulked. "Homelessness is a problem in almost every neighborhood, in every city. But not every neighborhood has—or ought to have—such a shelter."

Leo cocked his head at the jerk on the mobile phone. "I bet it's not a problem in *his* neighborhood." He made a mental note of Hood's carefully tailored custom wardrobe and thought it must have cost a mint. "Or yours, either. I take it you don't live around here anymore."

"*My* neighborhood is not on trial."

"Neither is this one. Social services are thin on the ground, and Jake Riskin wanted to help pick up the slack. You want to build a grocery store with fancy imported vegetables that cost a week's salary. Does that more or less sum it up?"

He repeated the accusation. "You aren't being fair."

Leo tried to keep a glint out of his eye when he asked, "Just like Jake?"

"I didn't hurt that stupid DJ," Hood declared bluntly, and perhaps more loudly than he meant to. He dropped his voice for the rest. "Look at me, Detective. I can barely manage a short flight of stairs unassisted. You think I just . . . what? How did he die? Do you think I held a gun and aimed it with any degree of success? Because I assure you—"

"No, he wasn't shot. Someone snuck up behind him and bashed his brains in."

"Oh, God, that sounds . . . messy. And like something that would require upper-body strength."

Leo nodded, but also said, "Not much, if he was caught by surprise."

Just then, the young assistant in the high heels interjected herself with careful apologies. "Excuse me, I hate to interrupt—but Mr. Hood? The reporter from ABC is here, and he's hoping for a quote."

Relief flooded Hood's face. "Ah! Yes, of course. Detective, if you'll excuse me."

"Sure." He could always drag him down to the station later, if push came to shove. Facedown over his notebook, Leo jotted a few lines as he walked back toward his car. He was almost there, keys in his hand, when he heard a hard whisper.

"*Hey.*"

He paused and looked around.

"Hey, buddy. Over here."

Against the nearest wall, at the edge of the nearest alley, stood a man in a long gray overcoat. A scarf was wrapped high around his neck, and a knitted cap covered his head. The addition of some aviator sunglasses meant that only his nose was immediately visible. Or his nose and what looked like a couple of greenish tentacles waving slowly from under the coat. Their tips darted back and forth, like a cat's tail when it watches a bird.

Leo didn't love it. "Get out of here, Bozo. I'm not a guy you want to flash."

"No, man. It ain't like that. I want to talk. I think you're looking for me."

Skeptically intrigued, Leo put his keys back into his pant pocket. "What for?"

"Got a tip about some Fort Freak uniform sniffing around, but I've got more sources in Jokertown than the NYPD does. I always stay one step ahead."

Ralph wasn't one of the uniforms, but that didn't mean he hadn't sent some meter maid to run his errands. He sure as hell wasn't above it, so Leo asked, "Ralph Pleasant? Is that who's asking about you?"

"I don't know. But he's looking for me, and he's asking about Jake."

Leo sucked in a small, short breath. *Holy shit.* "Does that make you Croyd?"

His eyes glanced left and right, again, and a third time. He nodded, and his mouth bobbed in and out of the scarf. "That's me. Come over here, man. What happened to Jake? Nobody's saying, except that he's dead. Nobody knows anything."

"Why don't you just come on down to the station, and we can have a talk."

"Yeah, that's not gonna happen. Come on, please? I don't have all the time in the world."

Leo kept one corner of his brain on his gun. The Sleeper was an old guard legend, in Jokertown and elsewhere. Much like his appearance, his reputation was all over the place and you couldn't be too careful. "All right. But no funny shit, okay? I'm not in the mood."

"Nobody is," Croyd assured him. He backed up and stepped aside, into the alley's shadow. The illusion of privacy made him a little less tense and twitchy, but he still stood so stiffly that he vibrated—like he was clenching a muscle.

Leo joined him and faced him. "Jake was murdered. You know you're a suspect," he said flatly.

"Shit. Why would anybody . . . ? Never mind. I guess I'm not *surprised* to hear I'm a suspect. That's . . . actually less surprising than what happened to Jake. But why do I look good for it?"

"You know how you call in to a radio station, and they record it?" Now that he was in the Sleeper's immediate proximity, Leo could see that what ought to be the whites of his eyes were the color of pistachios, and the appendages under his coat weren't tentacles. They were vines.

"Sure. Wait. They record *all* the calls? Not just the ones they use on air? I didn't know that. Or did I know that? I *should* have known that." He smacked the side of his own head, self-recriminating as he fidgeted.

"Croyd, why did you threaten Jake?"

He stared briefly into space. Then he snapped back into focus. "Threaten him? Did I do that? I didn't mean to. When did I threaten him?"

"Not long before he died."

"When did he die?"

"The other night," Leo said vaguely. "Shortly after you called him, raising hell. You want to tell me what that was about?"

The Sleeper nodded hard enough to rattle his brain. "I do! I'll tell you right now: I was upset with Jake, that's true. It's totally true. He's doing that fundraiser for the homeless shelter, right? The station is partnering with the clinic. Get it?"

Leo nodded. "Not even a little. Keep going."

"So he's got friends at the clinic, that's all I mean. He could've used them to help me, but he wouldn't do it. He said it was because he couldn't this time, but I don't know, man. I don't know. Should I have believed him?"

"Maybe? What help did you need?"

"Same help as always," he said bitterly. "I don't know how much longer I've got, you understand? The clock is ticking. It's always ticking."

"Are we talking about how much longer you can stay awake? I've heard you have trouble with that."

He laughed, and it sounded like gravel running through a clothes dryer. "Trouble! Sure. Call it that. I can't do it alone. I need help. *Medicinal* help. And my usual guy got busted last week. Son of a bitch is in Rikers."

"Gotcha." Leo hadn't read too deeply into Croyd's criminal dossier, but you heard things, here and there. People talked. "You thought Jake could get you pills, speed, whatever. Something to keep you awake."

"He was my *friend*, man. And I had a real bad day, real bad. Even worse when I found out Tommy was in Rikers, and I was shit out of luck. I was desperate, okay?"

"Desperate enough to kill him?" he asked, but his gut already doubted it. Croyd was shaky, stretched out thin. The guy was in no mental state to plan a murder, even one of opportunity. Besides, as far as Leo knew, the Sleeper's criminal record ran long, but mostly minor.

"No! God, no. Desperate enough to make a phone call, that's it. Then, then, then," he chattered, "Tommy's guy put me in touch with a distributer for the Demon Princes, and *that's* how I got what I needed. Shit, maybe I shouldn't have said that to a cop."

"It's fine. That's not what I'm chasing right now. Point is, you got your drugs and you're still awake. How long have you been up this time?"

"Not sure," he admitted, scratching at the side of his neck. Doing so shifted the scarf, revealing a weird texture to his skin. "Maybe a week or two. Less than that. More than that? I'm running up against a wall, see? I can't hold out forever. I never can. I never do. I have to sleep sometime, but I gotta put it off. Gotta put it off. And usually? Jake didn't mind. Sometimes, he'd invite me down to the station and I'd hang out in the booth with him overnight, or we'd kick around upstairs in his crash pad. It's not like I'm catching any Z's anyway. We were pals. I wouldn't have hurt him. I was just . . . just . . ."

"Lashing out?" Leo offered.

"Sure, sure. Lashing out. I want to help you, man. I want to know who killed Jake, too. But you've got to keep me out of the station, out of the spotlight. I don't deal with cops on cop-turf unless I have to. Don't make me deal with more than one at a time. Don't make me come into the station. Don't try it. Don't."

Something about the phrasing gave Leo pause. "Croyd? You think you could stop me, if you wanted to?"

"Pretty sure I could, yeah," he said with just a hair too much enthusiasm.

Now suspicious, Leo asked, "Why are you wearing all those . . . layers? What card did you wake up with this time, Sleeper?"

"A weird one, like usual. Kind of cool, though." He gave the alley a furtive check, then opened his coat like the flasher Leo had first thought he might be. Underneath, he wore a plain white shirt and a baggy pair of shorts. Without the coat to cover him, it was clear that Croyd was growing vines. Mostly small, curly ones that weren't any bigger around than a piece of yarn. But also some big ones, as thick as a man's wrist. The big ones sprouted from his back and fell past his knees.

Croyd waved a few around, even fashioning one into a shape that was close enough to a thumbs-up. "I think this time I drew a monkey crossed with ivy or something."

"Looks like kudzu to me." Leo had seen it exactly once, on a road trip south to see his in-laws. It'd stuck with him, the way it blanketed everything and killed everything. Not with poison, but with strength and shade. The leaves that feathered down Croyd's exposed bits reminded Leo of that trip, those vines.

"Ivy, kudzu, whatever. I'm growing green shit. It's almost as good as extra hands. They're so useful, I'm not sure if this is a joker thing or an ace thing."

"We can all use an extra hand sometimes, right?" Leo came to a decision. He pulled a card out of his pocket. "Here, take this. You got better sources in Jokertown than I do, right? Maybe you'll hear something sooner than I do."

Croyd used one of his tentacle-like vines to take the card and tuck it into a pocket on his shorts. "Does this mean I'm not a suspect anymore?"

Leo wanted to say no. He knew he ought to say, *No, and you're coming with me.* But he didn't. He couldn't. He wasn't hard enough yet. "It means I think you're probably innocent, but neither one of us can prove it right now. Call me a soft touch. But *call me.* If you hear something."

"I'll do that. No, really. I will. I promise."

3.

Wednesday, December 7, 1983

Back at the Fifth Precinct, Ralph was hanging up the phone and grumbling to himself when Leo rolled in the next day. "Goddamn son of a bitch. He can't hide forever."

"Who?"

"The Sleeper. I requested his file in case that might give us a hint, but Mole's down there in records with his thumb up his ass. I put the word out on the street, too, but nobody who's seen him is talking. It's worse than a needle in a haystack, tracking down a joker in Jokertown. Especially when you're not sure what he looks like."

"Do we know for sure that he's a joker?" Leo asked innocently. "For all we know, he might have gotten up on the ace side of the bed this time. We'll keep looking. Any progress on that final caller?"

"Nah, he could be any idiot with an ax to grind. Doesn't like queers, doesn't like jokers, doesn't like much of anything. I listened to it half a dozen times." Ralph nestled back into his chair, a thoughtful look on his face.

"Any accent?" Leo tried. "Any background noise that might point us to a location where the call was placed?"

Still thoughtful, he tapped a pen on the edge of his desk. "Nothing *that* useful. But you know who it reminded me of? My pop. He was like that, his whole life. Worked up about what other people were doing, or who they were being. My mom said it was nobody's business, but Pop didn't see it like that. He was of the mind that if God said something was wrong, then that made it Pop's business to tell the world."

That didn't sound much different from Ralph, except Ralph didn't use God as an excuse. But Leo chose not to say so. "I didn't know you had a religious upbringing."

"As long as I wasn't a fag or a hippie, Pop mostly left me alone. He had tunnel vision, let's put it that way."

Leo mulled it over. "Then it could've been worse. You got the tape?"

Ralph reached for a handheld voice recorder that was sitting beside his nameplate. "The tech boys put it on a little cassette for me, real nice. Here you go. Hit PLAY and be dazzled by some asshole's war against immorality."

Leo took the recorder and adjusted the volume down a few ticks from "full blast."

The first voice he heard was smooth and radio-savvy, clearly belonging to Wide Awake Jake. The second belonged to someone with big opinions and the time to share them.

> Wide Awake Jake, who's on the line?
>
> Your station is a tool of the Antichrist, and everyone who works there will go all the way to hell, and then you're going to burn there! Forever!
>
> Good to know, thanks, man. I'll pack light.
>
> You're a dead man. All of you are—you unnatural freaks, doubling down on your sinfulness when absolute submission to Christ is your only option for salvation!
>
> I don't want to burst your bubble, but there are a lot of other options out there. Why would you pick on us, anyway? Who pissed in your Wheaties this morning?
>
> Jokers, idolators, masturbators, homosexuals, deviants—
>
> —now you're just listing some of my favorite people; I love it. Must've made a whole bucket full of piss-Wheaties.
>
> You're all dead, and you're all burning in hell!
>
> I'm still very much alive, and when I'm not, you won't know a damn thing about where I've gone.
>
> Not for long, you're not alive. Not for long! God's army has many soldiers—and I count myself among them!
>
> Okay, well, that's enough of that.

And the DJ hung up.

"Couldn't agree with you more." Leo reached over and stopped the cassette. "Ralph, I hope to God your father didn't sound like that guy."

"You could see it from there, when he got real worked up."

The elevator chimed. Leo looked past his partner's shoulder and changed the subject. "I think your Sleeper file has arrived."

Indeed, Sergeant Mole shuffled forward—bearing an over-stuffed folder in his rodent-like hands. "Here you go, Ralph."

Ralph snatched it up before the records specialist could set it on his desk. "Took your own sweet time, didn't you?"

The gray joker in the portal-thick glasses shrugged it off. "It's a big file. Happy reading," he concluded, and then he wandered back down to the basement.

"Happy reading," Ralph grumbled, a sarcastic echo. He flipped the folder open and ran his fingers through a few pages. "Christ, the Sleeper's been a busy guy."

"He's an old guy. Been around forever."

"Watch who you're calling *old*," Ralph warned as he skimmed. "Me and him aren't that far apart."

"All right, I take it back," Leo told him. Then, in an effort to return to the previous subject, he asked, "Hey, Ralph, did your pop ever hurt anyone or threaten to kill anybody?"

Ralph cackled and set the folder aside. "All the damn time. Usually, he was threatening to kill *me*."

Leo nodded. "I believe it. Hell, that's why I asked. Listen man, I've got an idea. Why don't we go down to the joker church, talk to the priest down there."

"Squid?" His partner shuddered. "You ever see that guy?"

"I've met him in passing a couple of times. He seems all right."

"That *face*, though." Ralph held his hand up under his chin and wiggled his fingers. "Gives me the willies."

"Put on your big-boy pants, because he might know something useful. His church gets picketed and threatened at least once a week. He might recognize the voice. Might have even talked to this guy." Even though he'd just peeled off his overcoat, he tucked himself back inside it and pocketed the recorder. "I know it's a stretch but let's give it a try. I'll protect you from the big bad octopus preacher."

"Sometimes I hate this job. I hate talking to jokers." Swiftly, he added, "The real crazy-looking ones, anyhow."

Leo bit, but not very hard. "Then put in for a transfer. I think we're the only precinct in the city with any on staff."

Ralph feigned surprise as he stuffed his arms into his own coat. "And lose such an easygoing partner? One who'd never drag me along for an afternoon of legwork he could do his own damn self, without me?"

"You'd get over me eventually, and meet somebody new. Maybe someone who leaves you all the Boston crème donuts and everything."

"Don't tempt me."

It wasn't that far to the church, and the church was mostly empty when they arrived—quiet and dimly lit, with tidy rows of pews and an enormous statue of Christ on a crucifix hung up behind the pulpit. But it wasn't any Christ that Leo or Ralph had ever seen anywhere else: This one was mutated as if by the virus, a strange monster only vaguely human, nailed to a double helix instead of a cross.

Ralph couldn't take his horrified eyes off it, so he didn't see Father Squid slip into the sanctuary from a side door.

Leo saw him. He elbowed his partner and gave him a quiet, "Heads up." Then to the priest, he said, "Hello, Father Squid. Don't know if you remember me; I'm Detective Storgman."

"Storgman, that's right." The priest had been a large man once, and now he was a large joker. Physically imposing, even if he hadn't been wearing a long black cassock that made him look as big as a mountain, and even without a curtain of tentacles hanging from his face—hiding everything except his eyes. He held out a hand for a shake, and Leo took it as Ralph cringed. "I remember. You brought me the lost child, last year."

"That's me. And this is my partner, Ralph Pleasant."

Father Squid almost offered his hand to Ralph, but something about the man's tight posture stopped him. He settled for a head-nod instead. "Good to meet you, Detective. Your partner was stopped on the street by a little girl. She'd gotten separated from her mother."

The poor kid had a face like roadkill, with stubby legs and long arms. But she was maybe five or six, just a little older than Leo's own daughter at the time. His gut had said she'd have better luck at the neighborhood hub where someone might recognize her, or (at the very least) look out for her without treating her like some kind of monster.

"Since you never followed up, I assume you found her parents."

"Oh, yes. All was well. I gave her some ice cream, made a couple of phone calls, and she was home in time for the dinner I'd accidentally spoiled. Now what can I help you with today, Detectives?"

"No lost kids this time," Leo told him. "Got a dead DJ, though. Wondered if maybe you could help us identify a threatening caller."

"Ah, yes. I heard about Jacob. It's a shame, really. He could be an abrasive fellow, but it was mostly for entertainment purposes. He was trying so hard to do good work, in whatever ways he could. The last couple of years, he even ran a holiday fundraiser for the food pantry, I believe."

Ralph said, "This year, he was shilling for a homeless shelter. Not everyone was thrilled about it."

Father Squid shrugged, sighed, and said, "No two people can ever agree about what can—or should—become of Jokertown and the people who call it home."

Leo reached into his pocket and pulled out the voice recorder. "I don't know if this guy was pissed about the shelter or not, but he was pissed about something—and he's a real God-botherer. I know this is a little . . . out of left field, but something tells me he might've given you grief at some point. Could you listen to this, and tell me if it reminds you of anyone?"

"Of course, I'm happy to help." Father Squid took the recorder and pressed PLAY, then held it up to the side of his head for better listening. The angry, tinny voice rang out in the sanctuary, punctuated with Wide Awake Jake's interruptions. When Jake ended the call, Father Squid stopped the tape.

"Recognize him?" Leo asked hopefully.

"Hm. The voice is familiar, to be sure—but we get so many threats, accusations, and unfocused angry rants that it's difficult to separate one from another. I'm sorry, but I just don't know who this is."

Ralph sighed, and Leo said, "Well, it was worth a shot."

"Thanks for your time, Father," Ralph said as he turned on his heel. "But I'm getting out of here. I mean, I'm heading back to the station."

"I understand," the joker said. Then, to Leo, he offered a parting handshake. But it wasn't empty. He used the gesture to pass along a folded note. "I hope you find your killer, and I hope you find this unfortunate, angry speaker. If I hear any useful gossip, I'll pass it along."

Leo pocketed the note without reading it.

Ralph was waiting at the door. "You coming?"

"I'm coming." Leo gave Father Squid a knowing head-bob and rejoined his partner.

He did not open the note until he was back at his desk—where he pretended it was just another piece of paper, pulled out of his overflowing inbox. He scanned it quickly and was about to open his mouth when Ralph said, "Coroner's report came back."

"Yeah? Anything useful in there?"

He flipped the folder open. "Blunt-force trauma. Big surprise."

"Let me see it."

Ralph shut the folder and tossed it across his desk. "It's all yours."

Leo gave it a fast perusal. "Okay, so. Somebody beat him to death with a brick."

"A brick? Where does it say that?"

"The residue on his head. There was some dust around him, on the desk, too. It was a dried and fired clay mixture. Which is a long way of saying 'a brick.'"

Ralph nodded thoughtfully. "Beaned with a brick. What a way to go."

"If the first blow coldcocked him, there are worse ways to check out, I guess." Discreetly, he slipped the note back into his pocket. "It beats getting a piano wire to the throat, or a set of concrete shoes."

"If you have to pick, I guess."

Leo stood up and collected his coat.

"Where you going? Any chance you've got a lead on either of our mystery callers? The Sleeper or the God-botherer?"

Leo didn't answer those last two questions. "I'm not going far, and I won't be gone long. Got a thing to take care of. It's for my kid," he lied.

"Oh, shit, are you two still jumping through hoops, trying to get her into that preschool?"

He was happy to let Ralph fill in the phony blanks. "We're almost done, but there's always one more goddamn thing. I'll be back in a few."

On that note, he headed out the door and into the street.

The city was cold and nasty, more wet than frozen. The wind cut sharp around the precinct's gray walls. It was the middle of the day, but the sky was the same shade of white that it'd been since dawn and it would stay that way until dusk. Sure, Christmas was coming. Sure, there were wreaths and lights and garlands hanging around, dotting the gray with warm specks of gold and red and green. But goddamn, it was not a beautiful day.

Everyone on the street was bundled to the nines, boots to hats, fattened up with layers of winter warmth—so Croyd Crenson didn't stand out as much as he might have otherwise.

He lurked on the corner, leaning against the Fifth Precinct building all casual-like, except for the intermittent twitch that might be mistaken for ordinary shivering. He wore the same clothes as the day before. His face was nothing but a pair of oddly colored eyes and the very tip of a nose that was starting to turn pink from the chill. He said, "You got my message."

"Yeah, the priest is good for that." Leo leaned beside him and jammed his hands into his overcoat pockets. He should've brought gloves, but he never remembered to grab them in time. "How'd you know I'd pay him a visit?"

"A hunch, is all. Squid's ground zero for Jokertown information."

"I thought that was Chrysalis," the cop gently argued.

Croyd chuckled. "I meant the *free* kind of information. If it makes you feel better, I left notes with a couple of other guys, too. I haven't been following you, and I don't have any psychic abilities. Not this time." He looked and sounded tired, rather than twitchy. Leo had a real hard feeling that the Sleeper was going to crash sooner, rather than later.

"What have you got for me?" he asked.

"Couple of things. For starters, something's funny with the money."

"What money?"

Croyd shifted his weight against the wall and shivered. His prehensile vines were tucked up tight under his coat. "The fundraiser money. Grapevine says, Jake told the charity group that he'd raised almost fifty thousand dollars. They only got twenty-eight."

"Now, that *is* interesting," Leo said. "It opens some possibilities."

"That's what I was thinking. Money makes everything stickier, right? And that's a big chunk of change. The shelter won't happen without it. You got any special accountants, or something like that? Somebody who can check the books?"

"Maybe. I'll ask around, but even if we can track where it went, that doesn't mean we can get it back. When people steal money, they usually spend it or hide it pretty quick."

Croyd hugged himself tight. "But there's always a chance, right?"

"Anything's possible. Why the interest, though? Are you thinking about checking into a shelter, one of these days?"

A small plume of frozen breath blew through the Sleeper's scarf. "Put yourself in my shoes. I don't sleep unless I have to, but sometimes . . . *I have to*. And I don't always look as pretty as I do right now."

Leo shot him a look. Croyd waggled an eyebrow.

"You don't have a fixed residence?"

"Sometimes I do; usually I don't. I've been stuck in a loop for forty years, man. It's hard to hold down a day job like this, all right?"

"That's a long time to run from a good night's sleep."

"And more cards drawn than anybody else in the world, I bet."

Leo let out a low whistle. "I'd ask why you fight it so hard, but I don't have to. Do you ever know what you'll wake up with, ahead of time?"

Croyd shook his head. "Once in a while, I can steer it a little bit—if I'm really, really focused. But that doesn't happen very often anymore. One day, I'll draw the black queen and that'll be it. Game over, curtain's down. That's all she wrote." He took a deep breath, and let it out loudly. "But for now, I've got a spot down at the station."

"What? Terry's letting you crash there?"

"Nah. Jake kept a little flat upstairs. Every now and again, we'd hang out and have a drink. It ain't much—shit, I think he was only squatting—but it's private and quiet. Until Terry remembers it exists."

They were both quiet for a moment. Then Leo asked, "You said you wanted to talk about a *couple* of things? Is there something else?"

"Oh, yeah, right: I talked to Squid again, after you left the church. He said you had a recording, or something? Can I hear it?"

The voice recorder was still in Leo's pocket. "Sure, but . . . why? You think you know the nut on the line?"

"I spent a lot of time listening to Jake at night. I probably listened to more of his shows than anybody except the producer. Maybe I'll know the guy."

He fished out the recorder and handed it to Croyd. "I thought they didn't put those callers on the air."

"Oh, Jake would air them. Not every time—but the first time or two they called, he'd give 'em room to hang themselves. He used to say that if you're *that* confident in your shitty opinions, you ought to put your name on them."

"It's a shame I never met this guy. I think I would've liked him."

The Sleeper hunkered a little tighter against the building. "He was a good one. And for what it's worth," he said quickly, "if he thought anybody was stealing from the charity fund, he would've raised hell about it. You can quote me on that." Then he took the recorder and held it against the wall between them, out of the wind. He hit PLAY, listened for about ten seconds, and said, "Oh, it's *that* asshole."

"Care to elaborate?"

He stopped the player and handed it back to Leo. "You ever hear of the Holy Bough Church of the Redeemer?"

"No, but that's quite a mouthful."

"Everybody calls them Holy Bough for short. It's run by a real shithead named Lewis Perry." He turned to face Leo, still keeping one shoulder against the wall like he needed it to stay upright. "Yanno, he got into it with Terry the other day. At some club event."

"What do you mean, they got into it?"

"You know that charity poker game they got running every year at the Elks Club? Another fundraiser, but 'tis the season."

"There's a couple of games in town. One of these days, maybe I'll be important enough to join one," Leo said wryly.

"You play?" Croyd asked, then changed his mind. "Doesn't matter. There's a game, and the producer was there representing the station. All I heard through the grapevine is, they got into an argument and it was so bad they kicked Perry out. That's it. That's all I know. But that's him," he said, pointing to Leo's hand.

The recorder was frigid in his grip. He put it away, and it was cold on his thigh through the fabric of his pants. "Thanks, Croyd. This was actually helpful."

"Good, I'm glad. I'm not a suspect anymore, am I?"

"You will be, if anyone figures out you're the guy in that other phone call."

The Sleeper said, "Shit. Don't . . . don't bring me in, right? You can't bring me in. I don't have another day or two left in me. Don't make me crash and come around in a cell. Come on. Don't do it, man."

Leo couldn't make him any promises. "I'll look into your leads, all right? If we can figure out who really killed Jake, then you're off the suspect list for good."

4.

Thursday, December 8, 1983

Lewis Perry's office was located in an old building a block away from the Wet Pussycat porn palace on 42nd, a fact that gave Ralph a case of the giggles. "Been in there once or twice," he admitted. "It's not for the faint of heart."

"Yeah?"

"Nothing I haven't seen before, but still. All in one place like that. Nice folks working there, I'll say that much for it—but it's basically a big fat wonderland of filth. Speaking of." He peered up and down the block. "I think Ackroyd set up shop around here someplace."

"The PI?"

"That's the one. I wonder how he's doing."

Almost surprised, Leo asked, "Do you really care?"

"No. But I'm a little curious."

"Well, you can satisfy that curiosity when you're off the clock, because I think this is the place."

The building in question might've been mistaken for a Victorian tenement, except for the electric lighting and the NO SOLICITORS sign beside the main entrance. The façade was dirty and its bricks were loose, hanging wild like a little kid's teeth, waiting to fall out. The windows were close together, and the first-floor corridor split off into offices with old-fashioned frosted-glass windows in the doors. The wreckage of midcentury letters lingered in peeling flakes and alphabet-shaped shadows.

"This doesn't look like any church office I've ever been to," Ralph Pleasant said warily. His eyes roamed the ceiling cracks and the badly worn floor tiles.

"The church itself is outside the city. This is just the office. Maybe it's more of a tax dodge."

Ralph wasn't having it. "Tax dodgers usually have the dough to pay for better digs."

"So look on the bright side, would you? He doesn't have enough members to have a lot of money."

"That's true. Silver lining."

They were looking for office number 103 and soon they stood in front of the correct spot, staring at an elaborately painted sign announcing THE HOLY BOUGH CHURCH OF THE REDEEMER, DR. LEWIS A. PERRY, MINISTER. A crucifix was mounted on either side of the door, and just below it, a handwritten note tacked just south of Jesus's bleeding feet: "God hates the Blasphemer, the Heretic, and the Bearer of False Witness."

Ralph held up the back of his hand and rapped on the glass. "This must be the place. Good thing we're not vampires."

The door swung slightly open in response to Ralph's light knock, revealing a large, heavy-looking desk flanked by bookshelves that overflowed with Bibles and what appeared, at a distance, to be religious reference volumes of some sort. The two detectives stepped inside and Ralph announced their presence.

"Hello? Anybody here? New York PD . . . is anybody home?"

"What are you doing here?"

Both cops spun around. Lewis Perry had come in behind them, silent as a ghost.

"Ralph Pleasant, and this is my partner, Leo Storgman. Are you Lewis Perry?"

"You didn't answer my question." He was a man of ordinary height, slender and tense, with a sour expression. "What are you doing here?"

Ralph was feeling confrontational. "We're the ones who ask the questions. Why don't you have a seat over here at this big desk, we'll sit down, too, and we'll all have a real pleasant chat, okay?"

"I don't have real pleasant chats with jokers," he said, giving Leo the hairiest of all possible eyeballs. "You're not welcome here."

"I don't really give a damn," Leo told him. "I'm here to do a job, and you're going to help me."

"If I refuse?"

Leo shrugged. "Then we throw you in cuffs and take you downtown. But decide fast, if that's how you want to play it. I've got other shit to do today."

Lewis Perry's eyes narrowed, and he sidled past the cops— giving Leo a wide berth. "On the one hand, it might be a good opportunity to raise awareness for my cause. The world would see," he said, pointing a finger at Leo's forehead. "It would know you for what you are, if you dragged me out of here in chains. A brute, punished by God—now existing purely to oppress the righteous." He took a seat behind his desk and straightened his back, squared his shoulders. "But I have an appointment this afternoon, and I don't wish to miss it. I think handcuffs would prove inconvenient. Very well, let's talk. If we must."

Leo pulled up a chair. "We must."

Ralph did likewise, though he scooted his seat back another foot—like he wanted to stay as far away from that desk and those books and that preacher as possible. "First, I want you to understand that you don't get to talk to my partner like that. He's a cop, and you're going to treat him like one, you hear me?"

"You can make me speak, but you cannot make me change my views."

"They're shitty views, but they're all yours. You can keep 'em," Leo said, privately pleased by Ralph's defense. He would've been more pleased if it'd been a defense of jokers, rather than cops—but he'd take what he could get.

"And second," Ralph continued. "To answer your question, we have some questions about Jacob Riskin."

"Who?"

"Wide Awake Jake," Leo clarified. "A very dead DJ with whom you had a problem."

"Ah. Another ghastly joker, murdered by his own kind, I'm sure. I heard somebody beat him to death with a bat. What does that have to do with me?"

Ralph didn't correct him. "That depends. Where were you three nights ago, around two in the morning?"

"In bed, sleeping, next to my wife—who will *cheerfully* confirm this fact."

Leo doubted the "cheerfully" part. He pulled out the voice recorder, set it on the desk between them, and hit PLAY. Perry's own voice rang out in the little office. It was loud enough to shake the glass in the old door. Neither detective turned down the volume. They let it run until Jake cut the line.

Lewis Perry played stupid. "So what? I called into a radio show to express my disapproval of its operation."

Maybe he *was* stupid. In Leo's opinion, he was crazy at the bare minimum—and sometimes the two went hand in hand.

"Does your disapproval always come with a side of death threats? Or are those reserved for jokers?" Ralph asked.

"I did not *threaten* him. Listen very closely. Technically, what I said was—"

Leo stopped him right there. "Knock it off, buddy. By the time you're splitting hairs with 'technically,' we all know what you're up to. Why were you being so hard on the guy? What did he ever do to you?"

The minister's nostrils flared. The right one went a little higher than the left, lifting his lip enough to show one yellowed tooth. "It's bad enough that he was a joker. But the way he supported those disgusting people, those disgusting causes . . ."

Ralph gave him a hard stare. "I warned you once, and I won't do it again. You're talking to two cops. Keep that in mind."

Leo thought Ralph was just itching for an excuse to deck the guy, and on the one hand, it would've really brightened his morning. On the other, Ralph was right. He was there to be a cop. So rather than let the situation escalate, he tried to redirect it. "This year he was shilling for a homeless shelter. Surely you don't have a problem with *that*?"

"It was going to serve jokers, and no one else. They're a filthy accident, and they should not be coddled."

This line of questioning was going nowhere fast, so Leo tried another angle. He turned to his partner. "I don't remember Jesus saying anything about jokers in my Sunday school lessons, do you, Ralph?"

Staring stiffly at the preacher, Ralph replied, "I do not."

"I *do* remember a whole lot of stuff about feeding the poor, caring for the sick. That kind of thing." When Perry didn't take the bait, Leo pushed his luck. "Is that what your spat with Terry Wilson was about? At the Elks Club? She wasn't the one responsible for the homeless shelter, you know."

"Oh yes. *Her*." He sneered. "Whore of the unclean."

Ralph rolled his eyes. "We aren't here to speculate about her after-hours activities, Mr. Perry. We want to know why you had a problem with her."

"It was perfectly civilized small talk," he said with a sulk. "Or at least it *was*, until I asked about her advertising rates."

"You wanted to run some commercials? For your church?" Ralph asked. "With the . . . what did you call her? Whore of the unclean?"

"I may as well send out the word to the people who most need to hear it. But she got very high and mighty on me, and insisted they don't *do* commercials for people like me."

Leo said, "People like you? Is that how she really put it?"

"In so many words. 'No religious stuff.' She was adamant that her station should remain God-free, and that was her choice, obviously. It was a poor choice. A choice frowned upon by decency, but what could I do about it? Nothing."

It occurred to Ralph to ask, "Wait. That was a poker tournament, right? What were you doing there? Doesn't God have opinions on gambling?"

Perry's face twisted into a mask of revulsion. "I most surely was *not* there to gamble. I was there to cancel my club membership. They started allowing jokers, did you know that? And they're not supposed to allow women at all, but this event was open to the public, and it was an absolute embarrassment. I was on my way out the door when I overheard someone mention her role at the station, and I changed my mind. I asked for a moment of her time."

"Had you ever talked to her before?" Leo wanted to know.

"Not personally. I went down to the station a few weeks ago, but she was too busy to see me, and the DJ told me to beat it or he'd call . . . well . . . *you*. I only saw her in passing. She was supposedly on the phone in her office. We didn't speak at that time."

"So you stalked her to the Elks Club," he said flatly.

"Two passing encounters in the span of a month is scarcely *stalking*, Detective."

Ralph held up a finger. "Two confrontations, and at least one screaming phone call."

"I did not scream, and my call was not directed at her. I spoke my truth, and I did so with the confidence of Christ at my side. But in the end, it's her station and she can run it however she likes. Likewise, this is my voice, and I can use it to shout the gospel if I so choose."

Ralph had just about enough. "Yeah, I know how this works. I grew up with guys like you. I was *raised* by a guy like you, and I'm not going to sit here and listen to you act all self-righteous when any idiot can see you're just a shitty little hustler." He stood up and slapped his card down on the desk. "Call me if you're ready to start talking sense."

Leo followed suit, rising more slowly, watching the minister as he did so. He was a little surprised to see Ralph so pissy, but only a little. Maybe if you grew up religious, you used up all your patience with it while you were still young. "We'll be in touch."

Back out in the hallway, with office number 103 shut and locked behind them, Ralph had more to say—and he shook faintly while he said it. "Guys like that, they always say that everybody hates them for no reason. But if you never learn another goddamn thing while you're working with me, learn this: There's *always* a reason. At least one. Probably more than that."

"Jesus, Ralph."

"I'm not wrong."

He sighed. "No, you're probably not."

"He's a total asshole, exactly the kind who'd do violence if he could get away with it in God's name. He'd feel like a hero for it, too. Probably thinks it'd buy him a first-class seat on the fast train to the pearly gates."

But Leo wasn't sold. "I don't like him, but I don't know. He's a special kind of rotten for sure, but it's a reach to say he'd take a run at Jake because he was mad at Terry."

"Terry *and* Jake," Ralph said. "He said Jake sent him packing, the one time."

"True, but if that's all it takes to spur this guy to murder . . . you'd think he'd have a sky-high body count by now. Or a rap sheet for assault as long as your arm—not just a reputation for shouting."

Ralph realized he wasn't moving Leo's needle, but he was still wound tight as a clock spring. "You're lucky you don't know it firsthand, Leo. But I'm telling you, guys like him? They don't just shout. They *never* just shout."

5.

Friday, December 9, 1983

Leo Storgman hung up the phone and said, "Huh."

"What was that about?" Ralph asked. He was filling out a report, and he didn't bother to look up from his two-finger hunt-and-peck typing.

"It was a guy from the group that's building the homeless shelter. You're not going to believe this, but you know how I told you they didn't get all the money Jake promised them? Well, most of the missing cash just turned up."

"Turned up? Like it dropped out of the sky, or they figured out it was a . . . I don't know. A clerical error?" Hunt, hunt. Peck, peck.

"Turned up, like it arrived in a big envelope with an apology note."

Hunt. Peck. Pause. Ralph looked up. "Who signed the note?"

"Nobody."

"Not Terry Wilson?"

Leo frowned at his partner, confused. "Why would she have signed it?"

He grumbled irritably. "You told me the money was short, so I talked to the charity head. He said he got the reduced donation from her, the day after Jake died. I tried to follow up with her yesterday, but she wasn't in the office and I couldn't find her. Figured I'd try again today."

"Huh." Leo drummed his fingers on the phone receiver.

"You think the money had something to do with the murder?"

Leo stood up and stretched. "There's probably some formula, somewhere. Something that says when there's two crimes in close proximity, they're probably part of the same crime."

Ralph stayed where he was, hands hovering over the typewriter keys. "Wow, that's deep. Did you come up with that all by yourself?"

"Just something I noticed, that's all. Come on. Let's saddle up and check in on Terry."

"Nah, go without me. I need to finish this, and I've got two more of these to go. Let me know how it shakes out. Then I can type that up, too."

With a real weird feeling knocking around in the back of his head, Leo drove back to WAJT headquarters. All the way there, he played the case over in his head, poking at the edges. He tried to file, sort, and process all the fine details and his broad impressions.

By the time he got there, parked, and found the front door, he was barely surprised at all to find a small crowd gathered on the sidewalk.

Everyone was looking up. A few people were pointing. Someone shouted to call the fire department. Or the cops. Or . . . or . . . *somebody*.

It was starting to snow, just fits and starts. Flakes flew and billowed along the building fronts, dashing down alleys and catching in drifts on windowsills. Leo looked up like everybody else, and flurries caught on his lashes.

He blinked them away and shielded his eyes with his hand.

"Terry!" he called. She wasn't that far up, so far as New York buildings went. The radio station was headquartered on the ground floor, but the station building was only half a dozen floors. Still, it would be enough. "Terry, get down from there! I just want to talk!"

She shook her head, so she must've heard him over the wind and distance.

Someone behind him breathlessly announced that he'd called 911, and the fire department was on the way.

Leo didn't think it'd get there fast enough. He stalled her. "Terry, why don't you tell me what happened?"

She said something back. He thought it was "no" but couldn't be sure.

"Louder! I can't hear you!"

She stopped pacing back and forth. She leaned over the side of the roof, and even at a distance of six floors, he could see that she'd been crying. Her hair was wild, and she wasn't wearing a coat. "I fucked up!" she shouted. It was a desperate, almost pitiful thing to hear. "It's all my fault! Everything's my fault!"

"It's hard to talk like this! Take the stairs back down, and we'll . . ." Behind him, people were whispering back and forth. In the distance, he heard a siren. But in this city, there was always a siren someplace. It didn't mean someone was coming to save you. "We'll sit down, just the two of us!" he swore. "I'll um . . . I'll get some donuts!"

Leo had never talked anyone off a ledge before, and he had a real bad feeling that he was real bad at it. Frantically, he scanned the horizon—hoping and praying for a fire truck or a helpful ace. He'd seen Turtle flying around the district lately; maybe that guy could swoop in and save the day.

But the sirens were still terribly distant, and the sky was empty of heroes.

She stepped away from the ledge, but he could still see the top of her head.

Where the hell was the fire department? Traffic was a shit show, but the nearest station wasn't a mile away. Get the woman a net, for chrissake, or a parachute, or whatever you used to catch somebody when they threw themselves off a roof.

Terry leaned back over the side, and sobbed at top volume, "I killed Jake! And I took the money, but, but . . ."

"But you gave it back! They got the cash! If there was an accident, or if there was a fight . . . we can talk about it!"

"It's too late for that! Too late for Jake." He barely heard the last part, but she spoke up again when she added, "And too late for me!"

Then two things happened, nearly at once. First, at the periphery of his vision, a window ratcheted open on the second floor. And next, Terry closed her eyes. Finished talking, she opened her arms and stepped off the ledge.

She fell like a stone.

She passed four floors in less time than it took the crowd to gasp.

But the window.

Something snapped out of the window and seized her—almost an instant too late. Too late to catch her, certainly. But in time to break her fall. Barely.

Her body lurched and the crowd shrieked as she smacked into the façade. She bounced against it once, twice, and then fell the remaining fifteen feet onto a cluster of four big guys who wanted to be heroes and mostly got clobbered for their efforts. She hit them hard. They all five tumbled to the ground, bruised and moaning.

The crowd swarmed, everyone eager to participate in this wreckage. Was she dead? Were her saviors hurt? How badly?

Leo fought his instinct to dive in with the rest of them, and instead he looked up. On the second floor, the broken window was shattered. One side of its frame dangled out over the street. Bits of glass tinkled down with the snow. Something long, green, and snake-like curled up the side of the building and disappeared over the sill.

Terry was semiconscious and gasping. The men who'd tried to

save her looked only a little worse for wear. A fire truck rounded the corner, so there'd be medics on the scene any second.

There wasn't much Leo could do for her, short of arresting her in her sleep.

He looked up again.

The green tentacle was gone. The broken frame swayed back and forth. Snow blew into the hole where the glass used to be.

He made a decision. He pulled out his badge. "NYPD!" he announced, prompting people to clear a path. "NYPD! Everybody move! Out of the way!"

He pushed past a few slow rubberneckers and grabbed the front door, threw it open, and ran inside. There were stairs, and there was an elevator that looked like it hadn't worked since the Second World War. He chose the stairs and he climbed them two at a time. It was only a single flight. It didn't take him ten seconds to reach the landing—where he skidded to a stop.

Which way? Where was the room with the open window?

His first guess was wrong; his second guess was unlocked. "Bingo," he muttered. He whipped it open and flung himself inside.

Now he stood in a disused space with a dirty futon and a rattling mini fridge, along with boxes, crates, and shelves full of vinyl records. Beside the busted window, Croyd Crenson flopped like a rag doll. Two of those weird tentacle-tails looked like elastic that'd been terribly overstretched; they splayed beside him, unmoving.

He looked up at Leo and grinned weakly. "Thought I could catch her," he wheezed. "So I gave it a shot." He put his hand over his heart and clutched it, which worried Leo enough that it showed on his face. The Sleeper stopped him from asking about it. "Too much speed, and not enough sleep. Don't worry about me, I'll be all right. I'll wake up soon, and this'll all be . . . all be gone." He waved his hand to show that he meant the tattered vines.

Leo crouched beside him. "Croyd, you need help. Let me take you to the clinic. They'll know what to do."

"*I* know what I need. It's all . . . here. Yeah." He nodded and closed his eyes. "I'm done. Sorry."

"What can I do?" the detective asked. "How can I help, if you won't go to the clinic?"

"Cover the window," he suggested. "Space heater," he spit out, and with tremendous effort, he pointed one of his undamaged vines at a small unit beside the fridge. "Pretend . . ." He started coughing. When he caught his breath again, he said, "Pretend you never . . . saw me. Shut the door behind you."

This was exactly what Leo wanted to do, for all that he knew he shouldn't. Croyd hadn't killed anybody. But Leo had kept him out of the investigation. He'd used him as an informant when he should've brought him in as a suspect.

Once in a while, the right thing was the easy thing. It had to be, didn't it? By the sheer law of averages. One time in a million. "Okay," he concluded. "Okay," he reassured himself. He gave the Sleeper a little shake to bring him around as much as possible. "Croyd? Hey, Croyd?"

Bleary-eyed, he answered. "Huh?"

"I'll do it, all right? I'll do something about the window. I'll shut the door and, I'll cover it with police tape or something. But you've gotta do one thing for me, you hear? You've got to understand that *this never happened*. We never talked. You never called in and talked shit at Jake. I never let you off the hook. This never happened. None of it. Croyd?" His eyes were slowly closing again, so Leo shook him some more. "You get it? Croyd, do you get it?"

The Sleeper nodded with all the speed and gravitas of a glacier. His eyes slipped shut, but his smile said he was still listening. "Who are you, again?"

"Attaboy," Leo smiled back, even though the Sleeper couldn't see it.

As a final gesture of goodwill, Leo hefted him onto the futon. Then he did what he could with the window, closing the one unbroken pane and stacking some record boxes in front of the other. He tucked a moth-eaten curtain into the gaps. It wouldn't be warm in there, but the boxes were heavy. The wind wouldn't knock them over. He plugged in the space heater and made sure there was nothing close enough to melt or catch fire. By the time he shut the door, Croyd was quietly snoring.

"Good luck, Sleeper. It was nice not meeting you."

6.

Saturday, December 10, 1983

Terry Wilson had three broken ribs, a concussion, and a fractured hip. She also had one hand cuffed to her bed at the Jokertown clinic. She wouldn't be there long. Dr. Tachyon told her she'd be released to police custody within a day or two, and she seemed resigned to this. "It's the very least I've got coming," she said, sinking deeply into the pillows.

Detective Leo Storgman sat alone beside her. Ralph was home with the flu, or just as likely, a hangover. "On the bright side," he told her, "you returned the money, you showed considerable remorse . . . the DA may cut you a break. Manslaughter, if not murder."

Maybe if he'd known the DJ, Leo would have handled her differently. Maybe not. Maybe he was just a sucker for a woman who fucked up, tried to fix it, and could only do so much.

"I don't deserve a break," she told him.

"So? You might get one anyway. I've still got a few holes in the report, though, if you don't mind." He put his now-trusty voice recorder on the bedside table and pressed the green button to start recording. "Let's start with the murder weapon. Where did you get it? What did you do with it?"

"I . . . I got the brick at the construction site. The one next to Jack and Jilly's."

"Then you *did* actually go for donuts."

She nodded. "I told him that's what I was doing, and I even walked all the way down there and grabbed a dozen. But I was so distracted, so scared."

"Tell me why you killed him."

Her whole body shuddered, and the cuffs jingled against the bed rail. "I've had this problem for so long, I don't even know how to talk about it anymore. I'd gotten in deep with a couple of loan sharks—"

"For what? What did you need all that money for?"

A flush crept up her neck, past her chin and toward her cheeks. "Gambling," she whispered. "I've been gambling, and it's been so long since I've had a hot streak—I thought I was due at the track." She started sniffling. "Like my dad used to say, 'The sun shines on a dog's ass every now and again.' I always hated that expression. But I thought, the next race, I'd make it up. The next hand, I'd pay it all back."

"A common mistake."

"Except," she said, a little more brightly, "it worked! Eventually."

"Is that how you made up for what you took?"

"One lucky horse, and my last thousand dollars." Her voice choked. "Why didn't it happen a week ago? If it'd only happened a week ago, nobody would've ever noticed. But I *had* to take it from the fund drive. They were going to break my legs, or worse!"

He couldn't argue with her there. "Yeah, I've seen it before. You were scared. You were sitting on a pile of cash, even if it wasn't yours."

Now fully in tears, she said, "I thought I had time to pay off the sharks and win back enough to make up the difference. But Jake already had a rough idea of how much we'd raised," she sobbed. "He noticed some was missing. We got into a fight about it, during a commercial break. He knew something was up. He knew I was lying, that I was hiding something—and he told me so. I told him that he should stick to his job, and I'd stick to mine."

"Then you offered to go get donuts."

"I needed to clear my head. I told him I'd be back soon . . . and we could . . . we could talk about it then—I was buying myself time to think." Her speech was breaking up. Leo handed her a tissue from the box beside the bed. She blew her nose loudly and wetly. "Thanks."

"Sure. Now keep going. You went to the donut place, and you saw the construction site next door, and you got an idea."

"I barely remember it. I remember seeing a stack of old bricks. A few had spilled out onto the sidewalk. I remember it was cold and hard and heavy. I remember I hid it under the box. When I got back to the station, he was talking to some caller, queuing up the next songs. I put the donuts down. I picked the brick up. I went in behind him, and . . . and . . ."

"You have to say it."

"I hit him, over and over again." She began to lift her cuffed right hand, as if to show Leo how she'd done it, but the cuffs stopped her. She let it rest on the blanket again. "Then I saw the recorder running, so I pulled the tape and ripped it all out, just in case. I let the next song run and then I pulled the plug. Then I called the police. Then you came. That's everything, I swear. It's everything."

Leo reached for the recorder and almost turned it off, but changed his mind. "What did you do with the brick?" he asked.

"Threw it into the dumpster behind the station. It won't be there now; they picked up the trash yesterday, but you don't need it. I confess. I killed him. I killed him," she said again. One more time for good measure. "I killed him."

7.

Christmas Eve, 1983

Ralph was back at his desk and Leo gave him the report to skim, in case he was curious. Ralph didn't read too much faster than he typed. He was mostly happy that someone else had taken care of the paperwork. "Looks good to me. All wrapped up with a bow, just in time for Christmas."

"Barely."

"Still counts. One thing though. One loose end."

Leo raised an eyebrow. "Is there? I thought I got everything . . . ?"

"The Sleeper. We never did find him."

"So? He didn't do it. Who cares if we never found him?"

Ralph returned the report, then leaned back into his chair and put his feet up on the corner of the desk. "All I'm saying is, it's not quite perfect."

"Nothing is, Ralph. Nothing is."

Ralph held up his wrist and looked at his watch. "Oh, hey, look at the time. I think I'll run and grab some lunch. You want a sandwich or something?" He dropped his feet to the floor again with an enthusiastic stomp. "I'm starving."

"I'll take a raincheck. Got another stack of these to type . . . since you tossed a couple of yours at my inbox."

"You noticed that, huh?"

"I always notice."

Ralph cackled as he slipped into his overcoat, one arm at a time. "All right, suit yourself."

When he was gone, Leo flipped through the report sheets, saw that there weren't as many as he feared, and remembered that he actually knew how to type. He didn't have the fastest fingers at the Fifth, but he could outpace Ralph any day of the week—and he planned to.

Later.

He grabbed his own coat along with a hat his mother-in-law had knitted for him last year, and headed out into the street.

The snow was heavy enough to finally start sticking, even though it was still a degree or two above freezing. He wound his scarf around his neck and let the ends knock against his chest as he walked. It wasn't a great day for a walk. The weather was hard. The snow was halfway to sleet. No matter which direction he turned, the wind somehow hit him head-on.

But now it was Christmas Eve. The green and red lights were bright even at noon. People smiled and hollered "Merry Christmas" back and forth. Carriages were tricked out with jingling gold bells, and their horses blew hot steam when they snorted and stomped.

Back home, Leo's wife and daughter were making holiday cookies that would look like a crime scene by the time his kid was done with them. Their living room held a little tree with silver tinsel and bright-red ornaments. The gifts underneath were mostly for Melanie, which was just how Leo and Vicki liked it.

But he didn't go home.

He went to the WAJT, even though it'd been shuttered for a couple of weeks, ever since Terry had taken her unsuccessful swan dive off the roof. The building wasn't locked. Leo let himself inside and climbed the stairs to the second floor. He tried the door to Jacob Riskin's hiding place. It swung open to reveal a room full of crates and boxes, a few shelves, a mini fridge, and an empty futon with yesterday's paper lying unfolded on the dirty cushion.

The Sleeper was in the wind.

Leo wondered where he'd gone. He wondered what he looked like this time. He wondered if it mattered, or if they'd ever cross paths again.

"Merry Christmas, Croyd," he said, and he shut the door behind himself.

Swimmer, Flier, Felon, Spy

PART III

"So you know who I'm looking for, but you don't have any information that will help me find him. I assure you, my finding him will benefit everyone in this city."

"I have no doubt you believe that," said Storgman.

"What can I say that would convince you?" asked Tesla.

Instead of answering, the ram-headed man picked up the cheap ink pen lying beside his newspaper.

"How about a little quid pro quo," he said. "Help me out with something."

Endless side games. Tesla felt the beginnings of despair that he would ever get anywhere in this cursed place. Why had he left home? Taken this job?

"What," asked Storgman, "is a six-letter word for a writing instrument?"

Tesla blinked. "Pencil," he said.

"That fits," said Storgman, but he did not write anything on the paper. Then he went on. "Seven-letter word. Ends with the *E* in pencil. A popular world cuisine."

Tesla felt the detective's words like a hammer blow. He realized he'd barely thought of *her* during his trip below the city, a rarity. But he went ahead and said it. "Chinese."

Again, Storgman wrote nothing on the paper. He said, "A lot of people underestimate New York's Finest. You know they say a couple hundred brutal assholes spoil the bunch. But I'm not an asshole. And I'm good at . . . puzzling things out."

Tesla let that slide. "What about brutality?"

"Excuse me?" Storgman replied.

"You said it's the brutal assholes that spoil the department's reputation. Or that's essentially what you said. Then you said you're not an asshole, but didn't say anything about brutality."

Storgman looked Tesla directly in the eye for an uncomfortable moment. Then he smiled. "No," he said, "I didn't."

"How do you know who I am?" Tesla asked.

Storgman shook his head. Tesla wondered if the muscles in the old detective's neck and shoulders had been strengthened by the virus to account for the great weight of his horns.

"I don't know who you are," Storgman said. "I know *what* you are, more or less."

"And what is that?"

"Some people think you're a fixer. But I think you're more of an information broker. Which is why it's surprising to see you here, in the field as you types say."

Tesla asked, "What's this business with the pencil and the Chinese food?" He needed to know how badly his network had been compromised. "And what does the Walrus have to do with anything?"

"Jube is an information broker himself, of a sort," said Storgman. "There's nothing that goes on in Jokertown that he isn't privy to, and precious little he's not aware of in the whole city. Above or below. In a way, you owe him. It's mostly him who sends people to the pencil store when they need your services."

Tesla knew, of course, that in order to receive the inquiries that made up his work, his services must be made known to the wider world. Or at least to a narrow section of the world. Part of the reason he lived as he did was the hope that if he stayed put, if the right people could get to him, maybe *she* would one day return. He rarely admitted this to himself, and certainly would not admit it to this man.

"Here's how it works, as near as I've figured out. Well, me and a few others. Somebody needs to know something real bad. They check around all the usual places, but nobody can help, for blood or money. Eventually, somebody in the know—the Walrus or one or two others—directs this somebody to the pencil store. So the woman who runs it is your agent. They ask their question and fork over a lot of money. At the end of the day, she closes up shop and goes to a particular Chinese restaurant, one not too far from here, actually, and orders takeout. She's in there maybe five, ten minutes tops. She heads to her apartment in Chelsea—usually in a cab, sometimes on the subway. If it's a nice night she's even been known to walk. But no matter which way she goes, she ditches her order in a trash can before she's gone a block. Some people think that's part of it, but me, I think she just doesn't like egg foo yong. Because it's not always the same trash can."

As a matter of fact, she was allergic to eggs, but Tesla figured that Storgman knew enough about his operation already and didn't volunteer that information.

"Of course there will be some changes in my agent's operation," he said.

Storgman shrugged. "That's none of my business. Any information I need, I track it down myself. But there's still the question of why you're here instead of whatever hole you live in, and why you're going around asking questions instead of just providing answers. Oh, that reminds me. Nobody knows how or when your clients get their money's worth. So you've got that going for you."

That was something of a relief. If the detective was telling the truth. Changes would have to be made in that area as well, of course.

"The question of why I'm 'in the field,' as you put it, will have to remain unanswered, I'm afraid," said Tesla. He wasn't sure he could explain it if he wanted to—not even to himself. "I need to know the whereabouts of the Sleeper. I've been told you would be able to help me. I'm prepared to pay for the information, or to offer some sort of quid pro quo."

"How about your name?"

"Alas, that is information I cannot divulge. Shall it be cash then?"

Storgman held up his hand, as if fending off a mosquito. "I'm plenty comfortable. And you've already waved that wad of bills around where anybody could see it enough."

"Then we are at an impasse," said Tesla.

"Nah," said Storgman. "He's working in the kitchen at Mister Yum's Noodles, which is two doors down from the pencil lady's favorite restaurant. Short and pudgy this time, smells funny. Or so I'm told. I haven't seen him or spoken to him in a long time."

The border between Jokertown and Chinatown was indiscernible. Tesla felt as though walking down the street was sort of an act of osmosis, as if he weren't so much crossing from one neighborhood to another as pushing through a motile membrane. Mask shops gave way to Chinese apothecaries, but then there would be a bar clearly catering to joker clientele, then a grocery with signs in Mandarin plastered on the windows.

Soon enough, though, all the signs were in Mandarin, and soon enough, Tesla was swept away by familiarity, by longing, by pain.

Mandarin was far from the first foreign language he had learned to read and speak, but it was the closest to his heart. It was his expertise with the language that had first brought him to the attention of the Central Intelligence Agency. It was the language that had led, eventually, to his downfall. For Tesla, it was the language of love.

Years ago—years before he'd gone freelance, years before his card turned—he had been one of many experts posted to the China desk at Langley. His specialization had been the tremendous economic strain the world's largest military placed on a planned economy. A so-called planned economy. Even before Western-style capitalism had begun its slow encroachment, money moved around the Chinese military in a fashion more akin to feudalism than it did with the Maoist version of Marxism, with generals and top-level bureaucrats behaving more like independent warlords than good communists.

In his research, Tesla discovered that there was another expert active in his field working at a think tank in the District. He read two white papers she had written on the subject before he decided he must meet her. Emails were sent, eventually phone calls were made, and a business lunch was planned.

She could not be said to have been stunning, but then neither was Tesla—then Eliot. She was Taiwanese, educated in the States, living and working on an extended visa. She was, unexpectedly, brash. She was witty. She was generous. Her laugh was loud, joyous. Her name was Li Min. She moved into his house. Into his life. He thought they were happy.

Tesla had never expected love, but he found it with her. He loved her then. He loved her still.

It turned out she was a spy.

Tesla had a long-standing policy of ignoring everything his father had ever said to him. This was part of a larger project of forgetting everything that had ever happened to him prior to his meeting Li Min.

But whenever he entered a Chinese restaurant, his father's voice floated up. *All Chinese restaurants are the same.*

This was untrue and even ridiculous. But it was more than that.

All Chinese restaurants are not the same. In fact, all Chinese restaurants are different from one another. They are all unique.

The unique thing about Mister Yum's Noodles was that it smelled strongly of cinnamon—something Tesla had never encountered in a noodle shop. He thought of what Storgman had said about this version of Crenson smelling "funny" and wondered if there was some connection.

Then he stopped wondering. If there was one thing Tesla had learned in his years of gathering and studying information, it was that coincidences were rarer than most people—especially statisticians—believed.

A man behind the checkout counter nodded at Tesla, then jerked his chin into the dining area, telling him to sit wherever he liked.

The restaurant was mostly empty, and everyone in sight was ethnically Chinese. A couple bent over bowls of soup, not talking as they ate. In a booth, an older man with nothing on his table but a teapot and a cup twisted his napkin, making different animal shapes in quick succession. They were startlingly realistic.

As Tesla took his seat, the door to the kitchen swung open. He expected the smell of cinnamon to grow stronger, but instead it subsided, overwhelmed by a new fragrance, lavender.

The many cuisines of China were extraordinarily varied even within the same region, so it was not impossible that somewhere in that extraordinarily varied country there was a dish that used cinnamon and lavender. But it would certainly be unlike anything Tesla had ever encountered.

Smells funny.

No one was paying him any attention. Boldness occasionally being the better part of valor, he walked into the kitchen. It was small and hot, and three large woks were set over active burners. A fireplug of a man, Caucasian with light eyes and light hair, was stirring some vegetables into one, hissing steam rising up.

As Tesla entered, an aroma of rosemary reached him, clearly emanating from the man. "Croyd Crenson?" Tesla asked.

With no hesitation, the man took the wok by its handle and flung the contents in Tesla's direction. Tesla stepped backward, avoiding the worst of it, and when he looked up, Crenson was running through a screen door into the alley that backed the restaurant.

"A chase scene," said Tesla. "Lovely."

As it turned out, Crenson did not run far. Instead, he hid. Or tried to.

The alley was dark, dank, and noxious, like every other New York alley Tesla had had the misfortune to enter. Crenson must have counted on the odiferous nature of the place, which backed on not one, not two, but three different restaurants, to keep him concealed behind an overflowing garbage dumpster.

The overwhelming scent of cardamom, however, led Tesla right to him.

"Get away from me," Crenson growled. "I'm not who you're looking for."

"I believe you are," said Tesla, keeping his voice even and calm. "And I'm not here to hurt you, or to steal from you, or to bother you in any way whatsoever. I just want to talk to you for a moment."

Crenson surprised Tesla by stepping out into full view. "I ain't in the mood to talk," he said.

The enormous weight that struck Tesla from behind instantly knocked the breath from him, even before he landed full on his face on the rotting asphalt that paved the alley. He tried to breathe, then to move, and couldn't accomplish either task.

Then the weight that was pinning him was gone, but only for an instant. A large, clawed paw hooked him by the rib cage and spun him onto his back. Then the weight returned and Tesla could see that what was imprisoning him was an enormous tiger. It leaned in, its breath hot, its claws terrifyingly sharp.

Tesla rarely missed when he released a lightning bolt from between his horns. This time, there was no chance of it all.

White and bright, an enormous electrical charge arced from between Tesla's horns into the tiger's face, blowing the huge beast up into the air, flipping it a complete 360 degrees so that, despite the blast, it still managed to land on its feet.

It did not stay on its feet though, but collapsed, whining.

Tesla started to turn but found that there was a large kitchen knife at his throat.

"Thought you weren't here to fight," said Crenson.

"I'm not," Tesla replied, using the same tone of voice he'd used earlier. "But you'll of course excuse my reluctance to be made a meal of."

A citrus smell Tesla couldn't specifically identify filled the alley. "You'll of course excuse my reluctance not to be suspicious when some unknown character shows up and calls me by name. People don't recognize me, friend."

"I hope we *can* be friends, Croyd, of a sort. I believe I can help you."

"You have any speed?" was the reply.

"No," said Tesla.

"Cash?"

"Rather a lot."

"That's a good answer. The others hit all the easiest caches before I could get to them. Hand it over."

Tesla did so, keeping a careful eye on the knife. He had minimal training in hand-to-hand combat but wasn't under illusions about how he'd come out unarmed against an unhinged Croyd Crenson equipped with ten inches of razor-sharp steel. He'd need time to recharge his horns.

Croyd pocketed the sizable roll without looking at it. "Feels like a lot," he said. "I like it when there's enough cash in my pocket that I can feel the weight of it."

"If you'll excuse the cliché," said Tesla, "there's more where that came from. And I can get it to you if you're willing to meet me again in two days' time."

Croyd's eyes narrowed, and now the alley smelled of something rich and complicated that Tesla did not recognize. What an odd power. If could be said to be such.

Then a sound joined the scent, a faint flourish like paper folding. Tesla risked a glance back. The tiger was gone.

"Yeah," said Croyd.

"Yes, you'll meet me?"

"Yeah, he does that."

"The tiger?"

"Tiger, sure. This time."

Curious.

"Look," said Croyd, "what you've given me already should do for those two days, so just tell me where to meet you and be prepared to suffer if it's some kind of setup."

Tesla told him.

Tesla made his way back through the kitchen, pausing long enough to turn the burners down under the industrial woks, which were already smoking. The only smells in the kitchen now were of garlic and chili peppers. He deposited the knife Croyd had given him on a butcher's block. *I only took this job for a little scratch,* Croyd had said before trotting out of the alley, *but I don't want to steal from them.*

A curious set of morals.

In the dining room, almost all of the customers had disappeared and the man behind the desk next to the door was clutching a rolled-up menu, sweating profusely.

Tesla started for the exit, and then noticed that the man with the paper animals was still in his booth, lying back now like he was exhausted. Tesla remembered the sound of folding paper, remembered what Croyd had suggested about the tiger not always being a tiger.

He approached the booth. "You look as if you've been in a fight," he said in Mandarin.

The man looked up at him. "I don't speak Mandarin," he said in English.

Ah. "My apologies, I shouldn't have assumed," Tesla said in Cantonese.

"I don't speak Cantonese, either," said the man, again in English.

Things hadn't been going well for Tesla in general, and this trip into Chinatown wasn't improving them any.

"You look as if you've been in a fight," he said.

"You're looking a little wrung out yourself," replied the man. "You got any more electrical blasts to hand out?"

"I remember something about a shapeshifter who favored a tiger form working for the gangs in New York, oh, thirty or forty years ago now," said Tesla. "But not a word about him for decades now."

The man gave Tesla a long, level stare.

"I'm not in town much anymore. Moved to Kansas City. Turns out I like barbecue better than I like this kind of stuff." He gestured in the general direction of the kitchen. A burning smell was floating in the air, but Tesla was positive it did not herald the return of Croyd Crenson.

"Perhaps you'd like to prevent your woks from scalding too badly," Tesla said to the man by the door, who nodded and quickly crossed the dining room, disappearing through the swinging doors. Tesla doubted he'd see him again.

"Kansas City barbecue," he said to the man who could become a tiger. "That's vinegar-based?"

An annoyed look flashed across the man's face, but then he grinned. "You're joking."

Less of a joke than a salvo, but Tesla said, "I am. How did you know?"

"You're an American who speaks Mandarin and Cantonese both. You talk like a British schoolmaster. You're wearing a three-thousand-dollar suit covered with restaurant alley gunk and it doesn't seem to bother you. You've got a lot going on. People who've got a lot going on usually know about all kinds of things."

Tesla shrugged, acknowledging the point. "Perhaps it's my wild card power."

The man laughed. "Knowing different types of barbecue? You know, I can actually imagine situations where that might come in useful. But no, your wild card power is that electric blast you let loose back there."

Tesla shrugged again, and the man narrowed his eyes.

"So that's *one* of your wild card powers?"

"One of my powers, at any rate. Let's say it's an ability." Uninvited, Tesla took a seat opposite the man. He studied the origami sculptures for a moment, letting his gaze linger over one of what appeared to be a woolly mammoth, the shaggy hair suggested by minute, masterful creases in the paper. "I'm glad you chose the tiger," he said.

"That one is wishful thinking," the man said. "I've never managed anything that large. It would have been hard to negotiate my way through the kitchen like that, anyway."

Tesla considered the height of the ceiling and the width of the swinging doorway. "Yes, I imagine it would have been."

"What do you want with Crenson?"

"Ah," replied Tesla. "There we come to a matter of client confidentiality."

"This has to do with the other guy claiming to be him? Floating around the park?"

Tesla kept his features carefully neutral, rapidly considering his options. "Yes," he said. "It has to do with someone else who says he's Croyd Crenson. You say he's wandering around a park? Do you mind telling me which one?"

The man looked down his nose at Tesla. "When New Yorkers say 'the park' to tourists, they mean the big one in the middle of Manhattan, pal. And I don't mean wandering, I mean *floating*." Here, he made a motion with his hand mimicking a falling leaf.

Tourist? Well, perhaps that was true.

"How do you know that the Croyd in the park isn't the real one?"

"Maybe I've got some client privilege, too."

"Touché."

"British schoolmaster. If you must know, the one here told me some things about me that only the real Croyd Crenson would know."

"Old acquaintances, then?"

"Let's just say he's a friend of the family."

Yin-Yang Split

by William F. Wu

September 30, 1990

Vivian Choy rarely felt scared. Now she stood before the front door of 8800 Glenhollow Road and was more worried than usual. The house was two stories, imposing. She had come up a long front walk through a smooth, green lawn. A high hedge surrounded a large area she supposed was a patio area. The warm, late-September day belied the danger she faced.

"Maybe I'm crazy." Vivian spoke to her twin brother, Ben, through the mental link they had always shared. "He has no idea who the hell I am. There must be better ways to get some money."

Not this kind of money, said Ben. *The cash you can get selling one of Quinn the Eskimo's designer drugs? You want to work fast food instead?*

"As long as you can steer me to customers later." Vivian steeled herself for walking into an unknown situation. Desperate for cash just to pay basic bills, she hoped to join the circle of drug dealers around the man known as Quinn the Eskimo.

Ben had controlled the body they shared for long periods of time while she "rode," as he was riding now. Whoever was riding could sometimes take over in times of stress. When that happened, their body changed gender. She had ridden while Ben, with his taste for trouble, lived outside the law. He had worked for the Shadow Fists until recently, when she had taken an opportunity to take over their body.

Vivian had dreamed of becoming a cop someday, but having a twin brother who was a known criminal inside her mind, ready to take over their body when he could, turned that dream into a bad joke. At least he had never been arrested. He had a small stash of cash in the tiny apartment where they lived, but it would not last long. Right now she needed money to survive, no matter what she had to do.

They had managed to keep secret the nature of their shared body. As the ace Lazy Dragon, Ben could make a small image of an animal out of folded paper or soap or wood and move his mind into it to bring it to life. Vivian had a similar power with mechanical objects. Except for their late parents, no one knew she was the ace called Tienyu, meaning "Heavenly Jade." When either of them used the ace power, however, their body would lie limp where it was, vulnerable to anything or anyone.

You got to look confident. Nobody wants a scared drug dealer.

Vivian leaned against the button and then pounded with an oversized brass knocker to make her point. Whoever was riding at a given time always helped out in the end, because danger threatened both of them. "When I think of all the times you took me into risky situations, well, maybe you should have been scared when you weren't." She fidgeted with the pendant they always wore, an old Chinese coin hanging from a chain through an opening in its middle. Their grandfather had given it to Ben long ago.

Forget all that. You're my sister. You're looking for me and you're short of cash.

"This place seems weird to me. He doesn't have any fences or walls around this estate. You think he'll trust me because I'm your sister?"

The front door opened. "Yeah?" The guy inside had East Asian ancestry, with a stocky and muscular build. He wore a jacket in a distinctive shade of blue. His bloodshot eyes focused on hers and he gave her a wide, phony smile.

"I'd like to speak with Quinn the Eskimo," she said. She was sure this guy belonged to the Chinatown gang called the Immaculate Egrets. A white bird emblem on the back of the jacket would confirm it. Word on the street was that some of them were working as Quinn's soldiers. Ben had worked with them at times, though he had declined to join.

The guy's smile remained. "And why should I let you interrupt him?"

He's Darren Yang, Ben said. *I know him. Use it.*

She thought he looked vaguely familiar. "I'm Ben Choy's sister. He might be here."

"No way. What's your name?" He did not move, waiting for her response.

"I'm Vivian. My brother worked with Quinn at Chickadee's." That was an upscale whorehouse where Quinn had introduced a new drug called rapture to potential users.

"There we go." Yang stepped back and opened the door all the way. "Step up."

Vivian entered and was startled when he frisked her. *I should have known,* she told herself. Her tight black jeans and snug, long-sleeved gray pullover could hardly hide even a very small weapon. She did not count the pieces of paper slipped into the front of her jeans, where she could slide them out easily. One piece of folded paper represented a chain saw on wheels, the other a small helicopter with inch-long missiles. She had also folded a little cash around her apartment key instead of carrying a purse.

Asshole, Ben said as Yang let his hands linger on her breasts and the inside of her thighs. *He's on something. Watch your back.*

Vivian knew this was not the time to make a scene. *My back's not the problem,* she said to Ben.

Yang pointed from the foyer to a hallway. "You first."

Vivian understood he would not turn his back to her. At his direction, she walked down the entrance hall past portraits of Edgar Allan Poe, Sherlock Holmes, Elvis Presley, and Tom Marion Douglas, among others. She turned at his direction and walked through the living room where some Immaculate Egrets were talking with a quiet intensity. Eventually she stepped outside into a lush, meticulously tended garden. This was the area surrounded by the high hedge.

The garden dazzled her with its range of colors and precise pruning. Her gaze took in roses and chrysanthemums, then snapdragons and sunflowers and more. The plants were laid out with a precise blending of colors, shapes, and textures that gave the whole a feeling of serenity. Some ornaments were interspersed between the rows of plants, including a four-foot-high concrete mushroom and the hookah-smoking caterpillar curled up on it.

"Hey, Speedo," Yang called out. "Girl here to see the boss."

Several more of Quinn's soldiers, also Immaculate Egrets by the jackets they wore, turned to look. Several were cleaning firearms. Two studied her with intense expressions. Some other soldiers were not Immaculate Egrets and wore no insignia of any kind. Several, however, were Werewolves, a joker gang that always wore identical masks on any given day. They wore Dan Duryea masks today.

Vivian realized she was the only female present.

The cease-fire is still good here, Ben said. *So far.*

She knew the Egrets and Wolves had agreed to a cease-fire when they joined the Shadow Fists as an umbrella organization. With the Shadow Fist leadership killed, no one seemed to know if that umbrella still existed.

Watch them all, said Ben. *Quinn must be keeping them high so they'll stay loyal. But don't count on a damn thing.*

Do you know anyone besides this Yang? Vivian asked him.

I've met them all. Don't really know them. Only know Yang a little.

A big joker stood in the middle of the garden. Above the waist, he was fairly good looking and appeared to be a fit, middle-aged Caucasian male. Below the waist, he had the body of a goat. He looked like a faun out of Roman mythology except for a thick, long tail with big spikes. The only concession to the present was a leather wallet at his hip, hanging on a chain crosswise over one shoulder. As he looked her over, he shifted his weight back and forth quickly on his split hooves.

Behind the joker, a man in a blazer and slacks crouched with his back to her in front of some mushrooms growing in a shaded area.

Yeah, that's Quinn back there, said Ben.

The joker called Speedo came closer on his furry goat legs. His eyes were bloodshot and he was covered in sweat above the waist. He had an air of contained energy about him. "I wouldn't interrupt him when he's tending the mushrooms. He likes to say they call for precise judgments."

"This is Vivian," said Yang. "Says she's Ben's sister."

"I don't know any Ben around here," said Speedo. "Granted, I'm kinda new. What do you want?" His speech was quick, as though he was in a hurry.

Vivian glanced past him and saw Quinn was standing up and brushing dirt off his hands. "I'm looking for Ben, you see? But if he's not here, well, I'm hoping for some help."

"Help, you say," Speedo said with a grin. "This is the right place. I happen to like speed and I get super-duper, whooper-duper, personally tailored speed here. There's no need to bother Quinn yet. What's your obsession?"

"No, no, I don't mean using, you see? I'd like to sell some product. I need to make some money and, without Ben, I don't know where to turn."

"You're a street dealer where?"

"Actually, I haven't done this before," said Vivian. "But I know people who would never buy on the street. Upscale, you see?" That was a lie. She knew the same lowlifes her brother did. She would worry about customers after she got something to sell.

"What have we here?" Quinn, a tanned, thin, wasted-looking man in a Peter Max T-shirt under his blazer, avoided Speedo's large spikes to come forward.

"Vivian," said Speedo. He spoke her name as though she was an exciting discovery. His tail swung faster. "What we have here is Vivian. As your bodyguard, I declare I'm sure you're safe with her."

"Remember Ben?" said Yang. "Her brother."

"I remember Ben." Quinn took in her appearance. "He handled security at Chickadee's when I introduced rapture. Ah, that blue stuff proved to be popular. And pretty soon I might just have something else to introduce." He took her under her chin and tilted her face upward. "Well, now."

Speedo, still intense, turned his attention elsewhere.

"Do you suppose I could get something to sell?" Vivian forced a little smile and stepped back. "I need some money to get by, at least until I find Ben."

He held her gently by her upper arms and leaned down close. "You need a little taking-care-of, I get that. And I might be just the guy."

"I don't intend to be a burden," said Vivian. "Tell me how much money I need to score something I can sell myself. Just a little to start because I'm almost broke. I've heard of rapture. How about that? Or anything you have a lot of?"

"Come and see." He put one arm around her shoulders and walked her to a big flower bed. "Smell those wonderful roses?"

"Yes, very nice," said Vivian. She tried to turn slightly, hoping to loosen his grip, but he held on.

"And here, my gardenias. Quite aromatic also."

"They smell great."

"And do you recognize these beautiful blue blossoms running along the front?"

"I don't," said Vivian.

"So your brother told you about me. Do you know what I do?"

Vivian knew some street talk about Quinn from Ben's experiences. His real name was Thomas Quincey and he was a scientist, a chemist. As an ace, he created drugs inside his body and supposedly could inject them into people with needle-like bones from his fingertips. As Quinn the Eskimo, he had been the head of science in the Shadow Fists, manufacturing his designer drugs in bulk to help fuel their income. The Shadow Fists' leadership had been killed during events related to the destruction of the Rox and now no one seemed sure of whether the organization was continuing.

"Tell me about yourself," Vivian said in a cheerful tone. She again tried to escape his arm without being rude and failed.

Vivian could pull out one of her folded-paper items and take control of the entire situation. The problem was that when her mind went into the mechanical object, her body would lie in place, defenseless. Not to mention, she would still be broke.

"The blue blossoms, and those white ones, are opium poppies. And the mushrooms, I wouldn't fry these in butter and serve them with a steak. I think you take my meaning."

"You make the product yourself?" She tried to sound naïve. "I would really appreciate having something I can sell for living expenses, you see?"

"See? Do I see? I want to see you in a cheongsam," said Quinn.

Shit, said Ben. *I didn't know.*

"You like Asian women?" Vivian kept her tone matter-of-fact.

"Some people call it yellow fever," said Quinn. "I call it good taste. You know what, little flower? I think we can work something out."

She started to reply but found his tongue in her mouth and his arms embracing her. Caught by surprise, she tried to loosen his grip but he held her too tightly. One of his hands went to her butt.

You want to bail, now's the time, said Ben. *Otherwise, you want the street life, then no goody-goody bullshit.*

Vivian had always believed her best future lay in staying out of trouble—the opposite of Ben's attraction to the risk and excitement on the streets. In this moment, she understood Ben's point. Idealism was not going to pay the rent.

Get him alone, said Ben.

Quinn disengaged and ran the fingers of one hand through her rather short hair. "You ever wear it long? It would be so beautiful long."

She forced a smile. "And what do I get for working something out?"

"I take good care of my pets," said Quinn.

Ben, she said, *what's one of those terms for white guys, again?* Neither of them spoke any form of Chinese, but they had picked up a few phrases from time to time.

Bok gwai lo. He won't know the difference.

She remembered, then. It meant "old white ghost," and was originally an insult. Common use had made it less so. "So where do you take your pets, bok gwai lo?"

Quinn grinned and put her arm through his. "Come with me, little flower."

Goddammit. She was about to trade her body and hated the idea—but not as much as she hated starving. If she had to hate herself, she could do that later.

If you really want out, let me take over, said Ben. *We'll get of here.*

Vivian ignored him. She was walking, with her arm locked through Quinn's, up a flight of polished hardwood stairs. At the top, she found herself in a large room with an old-fashioned, canopied four-poster bed.

Quinn turned and held her at arm's length. "Give me a show, little flower."

What the hell does that mean? Vivian asked Ben.

Striptease, said Ben. *Now I'm going to hibernate. Be back when it's over.*

That last comment was nothing new to Vivian. Her love life had been limited by the way they traded control of their body back and forth, but he always managed to shut down somehow when she was having sex.

A striptease, she thought to herself. She had never done anything remotely like that, even playfully. *If he's a tit man, he's going to be disappointed.* Then she spoke aloud. "You know what, bok gwai lo? How about some music?"

A clock radio was on a nightstand. Quinn found a rock station and turned it up. "What does that mean, anyway?"

Vivian began by swaying her hips from side to side. "It means 'white devil.'" She gave him a smile.

"Love it." Quinn shucked his blazer and pulled off his T-shirt. "Say it again, little flower. Before you love me long time."

"Bok gwai lo." Vivian stifled a wave of disgust. Did he think she was a whore of some sort? *But I am about to be just that.* Keeping her forced smile in place, she took the long tail of her pullover and lifted it to show her midriff. Then she lowered it again and used two fingers to pull her folded-paper chain saw and helicopter, and the cash folded around the key. She palmed them and continued. Though she felt completely out of her depth, Quinn's eyes were on her every move, slight as they were, as he unfastened his slacks.

A guy thing, she said to herself. Working with the music, she gradually got her pullover off. She never wore a bra, so she was now in her jeans, socks, and sneakers. As she unbuttoned the waistband of her jeans, she saw that Quinn had let his pants and underwear drop to his ankles. He was pleasuring himself as he watched her.

When she eventually got her jeans down to her ankles, she had to stop swaying so she could kick off her sneakers. That struck her as very unsexy but she shucked her jeans and socks, put her folded paper with her cash and key under the jeans, and stood up again. Now she wore only plain white underpants, from a discount grab bag.

Quinn's face was shiny with sweat. "Come here, little flower."

Reluctantly, she walked up to him. She struggled to keep anger out of her voice. "You want little flower fucky-fuck, love you long time, bok gwai lo?"

"Your pussy's going to like this," said Quinn.

When he reached for her, she reminded herself this was about survival.

After Quinn had enjoyed her, with no interest in her part of the experience, she got out of bed and found an attached bathroom. After a long shower, she returned to the bedroom and put her clothes back on. She stashed her paper figures, cash, and key like before.

Quinn took a quick shower and got dressed. "You like, little flower?"

"Sure." She sighed. "Yes, bok gwai lo. And you're going to take care of me now, right?"

He shrugged into his blazer. "You know why my soldiers like me? Because I like soldiers on speed. And they like it, too."

"Are you offering speed I can sell?"

"Let's go back to the garden." He took her hand.

You back yet, Ben? Vivian asked.

Yeah, I'm back.

Outside again, she saw that the Egrets who had been in the living room had joined the others in the garden. They were checking out mushrooms and talking about them. The Werewolves were joking among themselves.

"Hey, homies!" Speedo shouted at the Egrets. "You going to let me in on the talk?" He was rocking his weight back and forth on his goat legs and swaying his big tail fast.

Alarmed, Vivian looked up at Quinn.

"Speedo loves speed," said Quinn. "Sometimes my concoctions make him even more touchy than usual."

Satisfied, Vivian decided to be more demanding with Quinn.

She turned and blocked Quinn's way. "You said you take care of your pets. I'd like to see a product."

"Of course you would. And I have a brand-new one. I call it quiver. A hallucinogen that's partly under the user's control. Who wouldn't like to choose a part of their dreams?"

"How much do you want for just a little?"

"I can do better than that." Quinn pressed his fingers against her neck. "What's your fantasy? To fly? To kill your enemies? To get screwed again by Quinn the Eskimo? It'll only hurt for a moment, little flower."

Even as she tried to jerk away from his touch, she heard shouts from the far corner of the garden. Immaculate Egrets and Werewolves drew guns on each other and began firing at nearly point-blank range.

Guns! Get out! Ben yelled. *Run for the front door!*

Before Vivian could respond, Quinn's drug was in her, and a stinging sensation in her neck was followed by heat that seemed to spread through her neck, up to her scalp, and down to her chest. She gasped for breath. When her knees buckled, she fell to the soft grass, aware of pops and rattling sounds that seemed a long way off.

My fantasy? To be alone, Vivian thought to herself as she felt a sensation like sinking into a huge bed of feathers. Having her own body, and Ben having his, was their mutual lifelong dream.

To be alone, Ben echoed.

Vivian felt someone fall next to her. Though on her back, she no longer saw the garden or the sky above her. In a dreamlike state, she heard more rattling sounds and shouts that seemed distant.

She was running into an empty place, all white except for a dark figure in silhouette. She found herself chasing a hazy duplicate of herself, identical down to her pullover, jeans, and sneakers. While they ran, the figure in front grew younger and smaller. She pushed herself to run faster. A black-and-white yin/yang symbol rose ahead of them, like the sun at dawn, to loom over her until it became gigantic.

Vivian stared upward at the yin/yang symbol, with the black and white curved teardrop shapes within a circle and a small spot of the opposite color in each one. In front of it, she saw herself as a child, wearing a boy's white shirt and black pants. She was running and crying as her mother and father watched. Then her little form changed to become Ben. He was wearing a yellow dress as he ran in circles. Their mother and father stood by, helpless.

Against a sky of deep red, the color of celebration, the yin/yang symbol began to spin and the human figures vanished. As the symbol spun faster, the halves became images of Ben and herself, bent forward to fit the shapes. Little by little, the two versions of them separated slightly and then joined again as though the power of the spin could move them apart.

Vivian was beyond forming words, but she understood the choice. She could depart from the symbol or crash it. For a long moment, she watched the symbol spin faster. Her heart pounded as the chance for the wish of her life opened in front of her.

She launched herself into the crack between the halves, flying into the expanding space between the two. Everything around her spun. She became the white teardrop shape and spun even faster, trying to catch Ben in the black shape.

The force of the spin threw her aside. Her body thrashed and she hit her arms and legs on the ground.

Ben let out a wordless roar, as though in pain. His voice seemed different somehow. When she opened her eyes, she found herself on her back looking up at the deep-blue sky and a scattering of white clouds.

Vivian pushed herself to a sitting position and gasped. Her clothes lay in tatters around her. Her pullover had been ripped apart at both side seams. Her jeans were torn apart, her underpants, too. Even her socks and sneakers had come off. She was dizzy and confused. The rattling had stopped. People were shouting.

Next to her, Speedo was helping Quinn to his feet. She found the remains of her pullover to help cover herself. When she looked down, she saw that she was ungodly thin—her arms and legs were scrawny and her ribs showed. She put a hand to her face and found that her cheekbones were prominent over narrow cheeks.

"Sis?" Ben's voice came in a hoarse whisper nearby, not in her mind.

Vivian tried to speak but she could barely put any thoughts together. This couldn't be real. Was she still hallucinating?

When she turned, she saw the young guy she had often seen in the mirror when she was riding and Ben was in control. He was nude—her height, his face an oval, his nose slightly broad, his hair longish and indifferently combed, as emaciated as she was. Her brother Ben was just getting to his feet, staring at her with no concern for modesty.

Still not trusting her perception, Vivian looked around the garden. It seemed Ben had been right about the guns. All the Werewolves lay motionless on the grass, bloody. Two Immaculate Egrets were down, one with open but unseeing eyes.

"Hope I didn't body-slam you too hard," Speedo said to Quinn.

Vivian saw that the biggest spikes on his tail were red with blood.

"You're a great bodyguard," said Quinn. "Like another hit?" Needle bones extruded from the fingers of one hand and touched Speedo's wrist.

"Nobody leaves," said Speedo. He was serious, on the edge of anger, as he strode around the garden. "Not yet. Got that, homies?"

Quinn looked down at Vivian. "What the hell? My quiver did this? Did your wild card just turn?" He turned to Ben. "And who the hell—Wait a minute. I know you, don't I? Aren't you Ben?"

"Yeah."

"What the hell happened to you? You haven't eaten in a week or two?"

"Long story," said Ben.

"Both of you stay right here," said Quinn. "You're not going anywhere. I need to sort out some shit."

Vivian tied part of her pullover around her waist by the arms with the open area at one side. She held another piece of fabric in front of her chest. Then she located her folded-paper figures and the cash that was still folded around her key. "Ben. That's really you?"

"And it's really you." He picked up some fabric from her jeans and covered his privates. Then he found the coin pendant on its broken chain and picked it up. He called out. "Hey, Yang!"

Darren Yang walked over, looking back and forth between them. "Where the fuck did you come from? And what the hell happened to you?"

"Quinn said stay here," said Vivian. "Like we're prisoners."

"I can handle that," said Ben. "I need some goddamn food, but what the hell. This is a big estate."

"What are you talking about?" Vivian said in a loud whisper.

"Chill," said Yang. "A truck is on the way to pick up the Wolves. They'll be dumped outside the city somewhere. We'll take our guys out and report them shot to death somewhere else so their families can have them. Meantime, Quinn's having Speedo keep watch."

"Quinn knows me from before," said Ben. "He can still trust me."

Yang turned to Vivian. "He has to decide about you." His toned eased up a little. "There's cold pizza and beer in the kitchen. I'll tell Quinn you both need clothes."

By the time Vivian got to her feet and followed Ben to the kitchen, Egrets were stationed in several places around the house. All the doors to the outside were guarded.

Vivian woke up after a sound sleep, still among the remains of her clothing. At first she had no idea where she was. Then she recognized the canopied four-poster. The shock of seeing Ben, and realizing they had split into two individuals, returned to her. She had satisfied her hunger with pizza and beer, which made her very sleepy. Now she had no memory of coming to this room, whether she had walked or was carried. She was still clutching her paper figurines, cash, and key in one hand.

When she sat up, she discovered a cheongsam laid out on the bed next to her. It was a deep red with white embroidery. A three-pack of underpants was next to it.

Darkness had fallen. She got up to lock the door and found it locked from the outside. Throughout her life, a moment like this got a comment from Ben, maybe snide and sometimes helpful. She was very aware of the silence.

After another quick shower, she pulled on underpants and slid the paper figures, cash, and key into the front. Then she put on the cheongsam. The dress was snug, as was intended, even on her emaciated body. It had an upright collar and a high hem with the usual two side slits. On the floor near the bed, she also found black pumps, which were also a shade big.

Vivian walked to the door and slammed her palm on it, shouting for help.

She was surprised when the door opened promptly and Darren Yang appeared. "So you finally woke up. Come on."

Vivian followed him downstairs to the living room. Speedo was pacing quickly around the furniture. A big TV was on, but he ignored it. His spikes had been cleaned of blood. Yang wandered away, apparently considering his duty at the moment fulfilled. Speedo eyed Vivian as he kept on pacing. "What the hell happened to you?"

"Where's Ben?" She looked him over, certain he was still on speed. "And Quinn?"

He ignored her questions. "Talk to me, will you?"

"Maybe I'll tell you what happened if we get better acquainted."

"I guess we will, now that you're Quinn's latest squeeze."

"Like that's going to last very long." She regretted the comment immediately. Most likely, Speedo would pass everything he observed to Quinn. "I guess I didn't mean that like it sounded."

"Sure you did." His tail was swaying faster and knocked over a lamp. "Well, goddammit."

"Where is Quinn? Is Ben with him?"

"Said he was going to his lab and not to disturb him. I'm going out to the garden before I smash all the furniture. Come on."

Vivian followed at a safe distance from the big spikes. She had nothing else to do.

The garden was well lit against the night, with angles to emphasize the variety of colors and to create shadows for an air of mystery. The autumn air was chilly. No one else was present.

"Speak up, will you?" said Speedo. His voice shook, maybe in anger, and his tail swung even faster than before. "I heard Quinn order the Egrets to make sure you can't leave. I'm here by choice. Don't much like seeing somebody imprisoned."

Vivian folded her arms against the cold and wondered if this was a trap, a way for Quinn to test whether she would stay of her own accord. "Come on, where's Ben? Is he a prisoner, too?"

"Just give me a minute. What do you want here? For real? Tell me while Quinn's locked away in his lab."

She hesitated, then decided to take the risk. "I'm nobody's squeeze, you see? I was hoping to get something to sell. Right now, I have to find out how Ben is doing."

"And then?"

"I want to get the hell out of here."

"Something weird happened to you. I was busy at the time, but you looked healthy and well fed when you got here. Now, no way. So what are you? Ace? Joker? What did Quinn do to you? Or is another ace messing with you somehow? What?"

Quinn's voice came from the doorway. "Ah! My little flower, you look so good."

"You want out of here," Speedo said quietly.

"Has anybody seen Ben?" Vivian asked.

"I had Cantonese delivered," said Quinn. "He's chowing down all over again in the kitchen. You hungry already?"

"Yeah, I am."

"I love your look in the cheongsam. Got Ben something to wear, too." Quinn took her hand and walked her into the kitchen. Speedo followed.

Ben looked up from a counter, where he sat on a stool. He was eating with chopsticks out of white containers. He was wearing a gray T-shirt, tan slacks, and sneakers without socks. His eyes followed Vivian, but he said nothing.

Speedo pulled a stool to the middle of the kitchen and sat down with space for his tail. It was swinging back and forth quickly. "Chow down," he said to Vivian.

An Immaculate Egret stood guard near a rear door leading to the outside.

"You are quite fetching," said Quinn. His gaze started at her face and moved down. "Ah, those beautiful legs."

Vivian picked up a pair of chopsticks and looked over the containers that still had food in them. "What happened in the garden? The shooting?"

"I knocked him to the ground," said Speedo. His tail began to swing in sideways figure-8s. "Covered him with my body like a bodyguard should."

Quinn's eyes were shifting quickly as he paced back and forth in a very small space. "The Egrets and Wolves were always a shaky combo. I kept them with me to get drugs out to the street. When a couple of Wolves helped themselves to some 'shrooms a few days ago, I made a deal with the Egrets." His mood seemed to shift and he giggled. "Now those big white birds will make sure the bodies are never found. And the other Wolves won't know what happened. No blowback. We're sitting pretty."

Vivian hoped he was right. She wished she had not been a witness to any of this. "I need to get back home. I'll see you tomorrow so we can talk business."

"Little flower, you are home," said Quinn. "Tell her, Ben."

He spoke around a mouthful of food. "I'm going to work security for Quinn ongoing. There's a guesthouse out back."

"We'll work together," said Speedo. He got off the stool but with Quinn pacing, he had nowhere to go. His tail barely missed the walls and appliances as he stood by the stool.

"And you will live in the main house with me," said Quinn.

Vivian's heart was pounding, but she decided to keep her growing desperation to herself for now. "Of course I will. And thank you for this dress."

"I paid to have some cheongsams brought here. I bought five. The others are in the closet. I will take care of you, little flower. We won't need to talk business."

She forced another smile. "How sweet." She wanted to get Ben alone to talk—a concern she had never faced before. When she tried to catch his eye, he avoided her, so she dropped her efforts for now.

Vivian ate while Speedo talked excitedly about nothing in particular.

Speedo watched her. "Give me another hit," he said to Quinn. "Nobody wants a sleepy bodyguard."

"Ain't that the truth."

"How about a popper, too?" Speedo asked. "And whatever you feel like?"

"What the hell, you're only half human." Quinn reached out and pressed two fingertips to the inside of Speedo's wrist.

Speedo straightened and did an odd little dance on his goat hooves. His tail swung hard, knocking over the stool, smashing into a wall, and then sweeping back to slam into the rear door right after the Egret guard hurried away from it. He shouted about being closed in and wanting air as his tail struck the door repeatedly.

Vivian hoped she understood—and took the risk that Speedo intended what she believed he did. With everyone else watching Speedo, she leaned forward and reached awkwardly up the very short dress to pull out her helicopter of folded paper in case everything went sideways. However, she did not want to leave her body vulnerable here on the floor if she could help it.

Quinn was backing away from Speedo, shouting at him to cool it, and Ben flattened himself against a wall. Yang and two other Egrets came running with their handguns out.

Speedo broke the rear door open to the night air.

Vivian crouched low, waited for his tail to swing away from her, and rushed out the doorway. Speedo yelled louder and whipped the big spikes even wider, crashing against cabinets and drawing more shouts from Quinn and the Egrets.

She stopped to kick out of her shoes and glanced back. Quinn was backing away from Speedo, shouting at him to cool it, and Ben flattened himself on the floor. Yang and two other Egrets came running with their handguns out.

"I'll get her!" Speedo yelled. He gestured for her to keep running.

"Don't shoot her!" Quinn yelled. "Go, Speedo!"

She ran barefoot across the lawn and heard him coming closer. After she had left behind ambient light from the house, he grabbed her and hoisted her over one shoulder. "Where are we going?" Vivian called out.

"Fucked if I know," Speedo said, breathing hard.

Vivian eventually led Speedo to the little apartment Ben had rented. Until today, she and Ben had only needed space for one person. Speedo had found a late commuter train, then a subway, to get close to Chinatown, and then they walked. She had insisted on going home.

"I'm very grateful," Vivian said at the apartment door. She had thanked him repeatedly on the way home. "I know you must be tired but there's no room here. It's not that I'm being rude. There's just the bed and a little space to walk to the kitchen and bathroom."

"You're sure no one but Ben knows this place? And he won't give you away?"

"I don't know anything anymore. I think he'd help keep me safe."

Speedo was still intense, full of energy. "Dammit, I hope so. I'm wide awake. I'll hit the sidewalk, see what I can see, swing by my place. I guess I screwed the pooch on working for Quinn the Eskimo."

"Not if he thinks you're still chasing me."

"Yeah, well. Stay safe."

After Speedo left, Vivian worked the cheongsam off and washed up. She ate some leftover spaghetti, cold, because she was too hungry to wait. Then she stretched out on the bed, expecting to lie awake, given how much she had slept earlier in the evening. She planned to ponder the new life she had without Ben in the long term and figure out another way to make some money in the short term. However, she was exhausted again and slept soundly.

A hard pounding on the door woke her up. The thumping continued, with shouts of "Police!" while she pulled on a T-shirt and a pair of jeans. Still sleepy, she opened the door.

She faced two men in plain clothes, holding their badges up. "Detective Ralph Pleasant, Fifth Precinct," said the older of the two, a middle-aged white man in a rumpled brown suit with a gray necktie. His white dress shirt was stretched out by his paunch. Bags under his eyes made him look tired even at this early hour, and his brown hair was about one-third gray already. "This is my partner."

"Leo Storgman," said the younger man. A joker, he had huge,

curling ram's horns on his head. He was fit, in a dark-blue suit and a stylish blue-and-white tie.

"May we come in?" Pleasant asked, in a tone that said this was barely a question.

"Uh, there's not much room," Vivian said, as a surge of worry brought her more alert.

"We don't mind," Storgman said.

Vivian stepped back so they could enter. Her heart was beating hard as she wondered if the deadly events in Quinn's garden had somehow led them here.

"There's nowhere to sit but the bed," she said.

"We'll stand," said Storgman.

"We're looking for Ben Choy," said Pleasant. "Is he here?"

"No," Vivian said.

Pleasant gave her an expressionless cop stare. "You're what, his girlfriend, significant other, slut of the day?"

"I'm his sister, Vivian."

The two men glanced at each other, apparently surprised. Pleasant brushed past her, looking around.

Vivian decided not to object.

"Ben is alone on the lease," said Storgman. He leaned toward her a little, and his horns seemed even bigger. "Did he sneak you in? That can be grounds for eviction. Where is he?"

"He wasn't here last night." She did not want to add to Ben's troubles, no matter what his lifestyle choices had been.

"And where was he?"

"Sometimes he beds the girl he meets, and stays overnight."

Pleasant returned from a quick look into the kitchen and bathroom. "His file mentions you, but you have no record. We know Ben has criminal associates. Now where do you think he might be?"

"I just don't know."

The detectives turned to each other as though silently considering a question.

Pleasant folded his arms and leaned against the wall. "You want to ask her, what the hell."

Storgman gave her a hard look. "Why did you go to the home of Thomas Quincey, PhD, yesterday?"

Startled, she felt a wave of panic. "I was looking for him. Ben, I mean. They told me he wasn't there."

"We tracked some members of the Immaculate Egrets gang from Chinatown to his home and picked up your arrival, too," said Pleasant. "We couldn't stay long. In fact, we thought you would still be there this morning, and Ben here. So what's your interest in Quincey?"

"I, well . . . I thought Ben might show up if I waited." She waited for them to mention hearing gunfire.

"So you say," said Pleasant. His tone turned hard. "If he's not there, then you won't have any concern with what we're going to ask. Do you know what a confidential informant is?"

"Not really." She was relieved that they did not ask about the gunfire. Apparently they had not hung around long enough.

"We were thinking about offering this to Ben, maybe with a sweetener if he finally gets arrested someday. But you've stayed on the other side of the line. You might want to help because it's the right thing to do."

Storgman spoke gently. "The Shadow Fists are finished with their leaders dead. Quincey is believed to be one of several people aiming to replace them. Street gang warfare is likely. We've recently observed a joker, a faun with a spiked tail, in his company when he leaves home, maybe a new business partner. Did you see him yesterday?"

"I didn't have the run of the place, you see? But what kind of help do you mean? What do you want me to do?"

"We need evidence to prosecute him," said Storgman. "Probable cause for a warrant or exigent circumstances to enter his home in force. Can you tell me if he has illegal substances stored there?"

"Stored there? No, I don't have any idea." That was true, she reflected. She had seen only the garden with the poppies and mushrooms providing raw materials and knew Quinn seemed to have an unending mixture of drugs in his body.

"Are you welcome back there again?" Storgman asked.

"As far as I know."

"Did you hear about something called quiver?" Pleasant demanded.

She phrased her answer carefully. "I think somebody used the term. What is it?"

Storgman answered. "Word on the street says Quincey—known as Quinn the Eskimo—has been making a new hallucinogen. Members of a couple gangs have been seen going to and from his place in recent weeks. We need to verify there's enough quiver on the premises to justify going in. Or a significant amount of any controlled substance. Then we'll arrest him and put him out of business for good."

"I'm supposed to go and find it?" She looked back and forth between them. "Me?"

Storgman nodded, making his big horns rock forward and back. "You'll have a wire and we'll be nearby, listening. Give us the okay, we'll have an entire task force behind us as fast as we can."

"Don't you have undercover people for something like this?"

Pleasant answered. "We've infiltrated a couple of gangs, but no one's gotten close to Quincey."

"If I can do this, would I look good? To the police?"

"Sure," said Storgman. "We'll keep your name confidential for your own safety. But to those of us who know, of course you would."

She hesitated for a moment, steeling herself. "What exactly do I have to do?"

Alone in the apartment again, Vivian felt dazed as she found a small duffel and packed socks and underwear into it. The wire

Pleasant and Storgman had brought her was now wrapped up in underwear in an inside pocket. If she taped it to her sternum as instructed, she was afraid Quinn might find it too soon when he got handsy. She folded several pieces of paper into shapes she could use and put them into the front of her underpants again.

Having her own body was the biggest shock of her life. Instead of mulling over her new life, new surprises kept coming: Quinn's yellow fever, Speedo helping her escape, and now cops convincing her to go back to Quinn.

Vivian was back in the cheongsam and pumps when sharp, loud footsteps coming up the hall got her attention. Worried, she pulled out her paper version of a chain saw on wheels and hoped the visitor was going to another apartment. When knocks were followed by Speedo's voice, she relaxed and opened the door.

"You look good." Speedo was more fidgety than ever and his bloodshot eyes were quick, looking from her to his surroundings and back again. He grabbed the end of his big tail and held it still. "Just want to make sure. Don't mean to be a pest."

"Not at all. Come in." Vivian wondered what to tell him. She owed him big time for helping her escape, but he had been working for Quinn.

"You slept. Now you need food." Speedo was pacing in a very tight space and the spikes kept banging into the wall. "Checked one of my—checked my place. Got a little stash I left there. I need speed. Got to get it pretty damn quick."

"You can go back," said Vivian. "Remind him you were chasing me."

"Thought about it. Yeah, yeah. Maybe. You're okay, good."

"I want to help. I mean, I have to say something and you might get angry."

"Speak up."

"I want to go back."

He stared at her in surprise. "After that long trip home in the middle of the night? What are you thinking?"

Vivian ached to explain, but after a lifetime with Ben in her head, she could almost hear him yelling at her to be careful. "I, uh, didn't like being a prisoner. But I don't have a life right now. No job, no way to pay for this place. Maybe I was too anxious last night."

"The hell you say."

"And Ben's there. If I live there awhile, maybe I can figure out what to do next. I'll tell Quinn I can't live without him."

"Maybe, but I think it's too lame. You got a phone?"

"On the kitchen counter."

When Speedo got Quinn on the line, he held the receiver so Vivian could hear, too.

"Where the hell are you?" Quinn's voice had little energy. He sounded defeated despite his phrasing.

"I caught up to her. She's with me."

"So bring her back."

"She's negotiating. She wants more than clothes, get it? She told me she needs an allowance, a new car, shit like that. And no more locking her in."

"Put her on."

"Quinn? What do you think?" Vivian tried to sound stern.

"You got it! Anything you want! Just come back, okay?"

"I'm on my way."

"I'll bring her back," said Speedo. He hung up. "Yeah, that's the kind of argument he understands. I'll get points this way. And that means the speed I need. Deal?"

Vivian was relieved, even though she knew she was going to enter the lion's den a second time. "Deal."

By late afternoon, Vivian found herself on the front porch of Quinn's house with Speedo.

Darren Yang responded again to the doorbell and frowned slightly when he saw her. "Whatever," he said, and stepped back to let her in. "Quinn's in his lab, big surprise, huh? When he's not in the garden, seems like he's in the lab."

"Where's Ben?"

"In the garden."

She returned to the garden with Speedo and Yang. The Egrets who had tried to keep her inside the house last night were hanging out, eating fresh pizza and guzzling beer. Speedo paced around aimlessly, again with an air of barely contained intensity.

Ben was sitting on the grass alone, also with a slice of pizza. He looked up but revealed no particular response.

Everybody stopped talking when they saw her. Yang moved around her to join the other Egrets.

She felt the need to say something. "Anybody know when Quinn's going to come out of the lab?" It was a lame question.

"No way," said Yang.

"The prodigal daughter has returned," said Speedo. "Dammit, I need speed. Going to go see him." He left the garden.

No one expressed an opinion.

Vivian decided to sit down with Ben but she stopped when the tires of two vehicles squealed to a stop out in front of the estate. Gunfire popped and three of the Egrets fell to the ground.

All the other Egrets dropped to the ground and most pulled out their guns. Ben did likewise.

Vivian also stretched out as more gunfire ripped through the hedge that surrounded the garden and blasted windows out of the house. She understood why Ben was not using his ace. Heavy gunfire would neutralize most of his animals, and she had no idea what shapes he was carrying now.

The Egrets fired back through the hedge, blindly, and Ben joined them.

Vivian pulled up the short dress to get the paper helicopter out of her underpants. She set it on the grass and let her body relax.

Her mind turned the paper into a foot-long helicopter armed with small missiles with a tiny bit of explosive that would go off on contact. She flew up over the hedge, dropped down low, and moved to one side from the gunfire. Two big SUVs, black, had pulled to a stop in the street. The guys shooting into the hedge and the windows in front of the house were Werewolves, judging by the identical Betsy Ross masks they wore. She had designed this helicopter for close spaces and so she did not have any firepower to match their guns. If they left the vehicles, she could try to shoot the missiles into their eyes or at least distract them with shots to some other part of their bodies. She chose to return her mind to her body and let the folded paper drop to the ground.

The two vehicles revved their engines and screeched away.

Vivian remained motionless in the garden while most of the Egrets ran inside the house and out the front door. She saw that Ben was okay, still prone, but three Egrets lay on the lawn with bloody torsos.

Speedo charged back into the garden, followed by Quinn.

"What? What?" Quinn yelled. "What the hell happened?"

"Werewolves," said Darren Yang. "Got to be. They don't know what happened to the homies we killed yesterday, but they must have known this address. I guess they figured out what was wrong somehow."

"I bet it was like a dead man switch," said Ben. "Suppose all of them called separate homies late every night. If nobody calls, they're dead or at least arrested."

"They didn't even try to find out?" Vivian held her dress tight around her legs for modesty as she got to her feet.

The gang members looked at her like she was stupid.

Quinn finally noticed her. He came up to her slowly, with a little grin.

"You came back," Quinn said, and gave her a tight embrace. "Damn. I went to downers last night. Slept late. Time to speed again. But what the hell happened? I treated you right."

"I panicked. Speedo brought me back."

"You're going to stay?"

"I can't live without you," she said, struggling to keep sarcasm out of her tone.

He grinned and put his arm around her shoulders. "You're home again."

"And I got a need for speed," said Speedo. "They often call me Speedo but my real name is Mister Earl."

Quinn pressed his fingers against the inside of Speedo's wrist. "Time to celebrate! My little flower's back."

Several Egrets checked out the three fallen comrades, all of whom were dead.

"Goddamn Wolves," said Yang. "I already got more guys coming. They ought to be here any minute. We got to get these guys to a shed or something until after dark. Damn, I hate this. These are longtime homies. And we got to get word out to everybody else. Got to hit the bastards back hard. And what was that thing in the air?" Yang added.

Vivian busied herself brushing grass from the dress.

"What thing?" Speedo asked.

"I don't know, like a toy airplane or something. I was kinda busy, but I got a glimpse of it." He looked around. "Anybody else? Did they fly it over here?"

A fellow Egret pointed to the air over the hedge. "I thought it went the other way, but I was shooting."

The other Egrets looked at one another but none of them spoke.

"I was occupied, too," said Ben.

"My house!" Quinn screamed. "We got to do something!" Vivian supposed his speed had kicked in fast.

"Plywood," said Speedo. "Call up somebody and get your windows boarded up. Boards and, I don't know, something to fortify this hedge. Call people who know how to keep their damn mouths shut."

"Yeah, yeah. I can do that." Quinn hurried back into the house.

Yang followed him. "I need the phone next."

Vivian decided she should push Quinn regarding the quiver.

Knowing he had crazy drugs in his body was not the assignment. She just had to know if he had manufactured quiver and it was still sitting around. However, with more violence possible, she sought out the nearest bathroom. With the door locked, she saw with disappointment that the sink had a container of liquid soap instead of something she could carve with her fingernails. The shower did not have a bar of soap, either. She worked with toilet paper to create an option more powerful than her helicopter and bigger than her chain saw on wheels, which had also been designed for close quarters. This time she made an earthmover with a raised cab over a tractor engine and long, jointed arms front and back that ended in big claws, the kind for raising old concrete slabs. Then she put a machine gun on the front of the cab, as she considered the drive-by shooting of the Werewolves. Concerned about the flimsiness of the toilet paper, she slipped it into her left sleeve, where she could bring it out more easily. She did not expect to be frisked again, so she moved her chain saw to her sleeve also.

She went in search of Ben while Quinn was occupied. When she found him alone in the kitchen with more delivered Cantonese food, she joined him.

"Crazy, isn't it?" She spoke around a mouthful of food. "All our lives, we wanted this, but it's so different."

"I like it. And we can still help each other with both of us moving in."

Vivian said nothing. She wanted to warn him that she would be the one who brought in the cops if at all possible. However, she was not sure of his loyalties. Certainly warning him straight-out would not be a way to look good to Pleasant and Storgman. "We've had divided loyalties before. I guess it can happen again." That was as far as she could go.

Ben showed no sign he was concerned about what she was saying. "How are you doing with Quinn?"

"If I say I'm going to hate myself, will that do?"

"I still can't get used to seeing you. As yourself, you know. Like you must look at me." He studied her a moment as he ate. "You don't plan to stay long?"

"We're in a stage of life nobody else can imagine. Don't we have to get used to ordinary things, like two of us needing twice the space, twice as much food, clothes for both of us? So twice the money."

"Yeah, we both have to get set up somehow. And there's no telling if the Werewolves might do another drive-by."

"Are you going to help get stuff to protect the house?"

"Hell, no. I'm here to look out for Quinn, like Speedo, and I'll ride with him and the quiver on the way to Chickadee's."

Vivian felt events were likely to speed up. When she had eaten her fill, she hurried up to the bedroom and found her duffel. Listening for footsteps, she turned on the wire from the detectives and opened the braided buttons on her dress to tape it over her sternum. She fastened the dress again and ran a brush through her hair in case anyone asked why she was here.

No one challenged her, however, and she strolled back into the garden.

The sound of vehicles came from the street again, but this time they turned at the long driveway and parked to one side.

Yang and the other Egrets shouted welcomes and went out.

Speedo was alone, pacing around the edges of the garden and talking to himself. Vivian approached him but stayed out of range of his tail. "Are you feeling okay?"

"Got my speed. Got my need." He kept repeating that.

"Do you think we're safe here?" She walked parallel with him. "Just for now, I mean."

"Got my speed. Got my need. Better here than on the streets. Where's there to go? Nowhere to go."

"Why did you help me?" Vivian felt indebted to him and wished he could be somewhere else when she called in the cops.

Speedo spoke fast. "I didn't like seeing you locked up. I'm here for speed, that's all. You wanted to leave, cool. And you decided to come back, that's your beeswax. As long as you're free to come and go, what the hell."

"I guess I sounded crazy, escaping and then changing my mind."

"I'm not always the most rational guy around. So what?"

"Don't you get tired of being here so much? You could, you know, take a walk, do something different."

"Speed's my need."

Yang strode back into the garden from the house, with four guys who had just arrived. They all carried long guns, some more than one. Others had stacks of ammunition boxes. Three wore the distinctive blue jackets with the white Egret emblem on the back. The fourth, a twenty-something of Chinese descent like the others, was in ordinary clothes without a jacket.

"I didn't want to talk out there," said Yang. "But no bullshit this time. They come back here, we got MAC-10s, AR-15s, AKs. And plenty of ammo." He eyed the guy without a gang jacket. "Andy, what are you doing here?"

"I'll do whatever," said Andy. "I've been around for, what, a month or so? I want to get jumped in."

"You said on the phone we need warm bodies," said one of the new guys. "I told him, you want to prove yourself, we're at war with the Werewolves."

"I don't give a shit," said Yang. "Send him out for some beer. No, forget that! Nobody leaves."

"And we got a bunch of guys going to hit some Werewolves hangouts about the time we left to come here."

Vivian went in search of Quinn. She found him in the living room, talking to someone about going to Chickadee's.

When he hung up, he drew her close, but he was still agitated. "Maybe the Egrets were a mistake. The Werewolves followed 'em here. I invent stuff, make it, have a little fun. But I need security, don't I?"

"What's it all about? Do you have anything here they want?"

"Goddamn gang war. They want to be number one with me."

She put one hand against the fabric of her dress over the wire underneath. If she could make the gesture look like old-fashioned modesty, she hoped he would think nothing of it.

Quinn took her arm through his and walked her out to a deck overlooking the rear lawn. "Isn't that pretty?" said Quinn.

A white van backed up a long driveway and stopped near a set of broad French doors in back of the house. Two guys Vivian had not seen got out and opened the rear doors. They entered the house, went to the lab, and walked out with boxes.

"Who are they?" Vivian leaned her shoulder against his, trying to act casual. If she spoke bluntly about the product into her wire, she would give herself away.

"They're from Chickadee's. I used these guys before."

"What is it?" She hoped to sound naïve to draw out Quinn.

He shifted in front of her and kissed her lightly on the lips. "Ha. It's not speed and it's not even rapture. So what does that leave, little flower? You should know." He embraced her and squeezed her against his body. Her arms were pinned by his hug and she felt the wire press against him. "What's that?"

"Nothing." She tried to pull back.

He pressed one hand against the cloth. Then he used both hands to grab the front of the dress and yank, pulling loose many of the braided buttons. Then he reached inside and ripped out the wire.

"Easy," she said quickly. "Let's talk."

Quinn backhanded her face and she stumbled, then fell. "Stupid, ungrateful scum!" He pulled apart the mechanism and dropped the pieces. "You're a cop."

She watched the pieces fall, even more scared now. "No! And I had second thoughts. I haven't reported in."

"Reported to who?"

Before she could answer, he slapped her face. "You broke my heart, slut!" Then he grabbed the fabric hanging loose in the front and lifted her to her feet. He did not look like a guy with much physical strength, but he could be flooding his system with meth or poppers, whatever he wanted, and right now she hardly weighed anything.

Quinn pulled her, bent over, into the garden. As she stumbled forward, she managed to slip the paper figures out of her sleeve. In the garden, she dropped them onto the grass. She moved her mind into the wheeled chain saw.

"Now what?" Speedo said. "I don't get it. You lose interest that fast?"

Quinn dropped her limp body. "Shit, she fainted or something. But she's a rat, a dime-dropper, an informer, a cop, some kinda shit."

Andy shouted, "Go, go, go!" He snatched a MAC-10 from a startled Egret, hit him in the face with the butt, and fired, sweeping across several gang members.

As Vivian drove forward as the chain saw, she realized that Andy was undercover also. The remaining Egrets were the most immediate danger. One was bringing up an AR-15. She drove the chain saw into his leg, bringing him down. He squeezed the trigger, however, and a stray bullet grazed Andy's arm. He fell, clutching the wound.

The Egret screamed, dropping the weapon, and tried to cover spurting arteries with his hands. Quinn stood frozen, shocked. "Get the quiver out of here," Ben called to him.

Another Egret fired an automatic weapon at her chain saw and broke the chain. Vivian returned her mind to her body, then promptly activated the earthmover with claws at the front and back. Vivian hoped the cops would arrive fast after Andy's "go" signal. Now she wanted to make sure the quiver would still be here. She drove to the rear section of the hedge and, using the front claw, broke out to the lawn behind the house.

The guys who had been loading the van had all dropped to the ground. She used the fifty-caliber machine gun to flatten the tires on the van.

When she turned to look behind her, a full-sized grizzly bear was crashing through the opening in the hedge. She knew it was Ben and a wave of fear ran through her as she realized that both their human bodies lay helpless in the garden.

She supposed his plan had been to protect the van, but he was too late for that. If she could hurt him enough for Ben to return to his body, she could go back into the garden herself. Neither of them would harm their real bodies. She fired the machine gun again.

Ben was too agile. He threw himself to one side before she fired and charged her from the side.

When she swung the machine gun as far back as it could go, she realized she had not given it a full 360-degree arc.

Ben grabbed the barrel and yanked hard.

The machine gun did not come loose, but the barrel was slightly bent. When she fired again, the barrel came apart.

Ben had his big front paws under the side of the cab and tried to pull upward. Vivian turned the wheels and accelerated. Ben's grip came loose. She kept turning and grabbed one of his front grizzly legs with the front claw. Though she clamped hard, the claw merely held his leg without damaging it.

She saw him go into a kind of crouch and straighten his rear legs. The front of the earthmover rose up slightly. She swung the arm of the claw back and forth but the cab and cranes made the vehicle top-heavy. As she felt herself falling to one side, she moved her mind back to her body in the garden. Sirens were screaming and coming closer.

She looked up and saw the only three remaining Egrets holding their weapons forward as they looked out the opening in the hedge. Darren Yang was one of them. Then, panicked, they threw themselves to each side.

Speedo was nearby, looking around, trying to assess the situation.

As the grizzly, Ben shoved through the opening in the hedge to the garden. "What the fuck?" Speedo screamed.

Then Vivian, just pushing up to a sitting position, saw that Quinn was on his hands and knees, crawling up to her with his bone needle extended in the fingers of one hand. She had no idea what he wanted to inject, but she knew it would not be good. Scared, she rolled to one side and tried to get her feet under her.

Just as the bone needles were about to reach one of her legs, the grizzly slashed Quinn from behind, ripping open his back. Ben rolled Quinn over and gutted him with his claws.

Yang and the other two Egrets were watching Ben and Speedo, not sure what to do. The cops were breaking into the front door. Others shouted from the driveway as they made a rear approach. One of the Egrets turned to Vivian, raising his firearm. Speedo whipped his tail around, ripping into his belly. The Egret grunted in surprise and fell to the ground, bleeding out.

Yang and the other Egret still on his feet dove out of the way. Vivian remembered she had let the helicopter fall back to the ground just outside the hedge. She moved her mind into it and flew back over the hedge. As Yang and the other Egret raised their firearms toward Speedo, she fired the little missiles into their eyes, where they popped with tiny explosions. Both Egrets dropped their weapons and fell to the ground shrieking, their hands over their eyes.

Seeing that Quinn was dead or at least beyond saving, Speedo seemed to make a new judgment. He charged the grizzly and then turned, whipping his spikes forward. Ben dodged them and faced this new threat.

When Speedo shifted to a position where he was protecting the two motionless bodies, Ben hesitated. They faced off, neither of them making an aggressive move.

Vivian returned to her own body as footsteps thumped up the hall and cops shouted warnings and orders. "Ben!" she screamed as loud as she could. He got the message. The grizzly turned to a small piece of folded paper on the ground. His human body stirred.

Speedo advanced on the blinded Egrets and tore their torsos open. Now that he had killed one Egret, he had to account for all of them.

Cops in helmets and flak jackets ran into the garden with weapons held forward. Pleasant and Storgman came in after them.

"Son of a bitch!" Speedo eyed the little paper figure and then shouted at Ben. "We tangled once before!"

"So you're the Sleeper," said Ben. "Hello, Croyd Crenson."

"You were that Bengal tiger out to get me." Croyd, responding to the cops' approach, dropped to the ground with his hands high.

"I'm Andy Chang, Fifth Precinct, undercover," Andy managed to say to the other cops, through teeth clenched in pain.

Two of the helmeted cops tended to him. Pleasant held his weapon on Croyd and Storgman held Ben at gunpoint.

"You're Ben Choy?" said Storgman. "Don't move."

"Easy!" Vivian called out. She buttoned up the dress where Quinn had yanked it open. "He's the one who killed Quinn."

Storgman told Ben to roll over into a prone position. Once Storgman had cuffed him, he came over to Vivian. "Are you hurt?"

"I'm okay. I want to talk to Ben."

"When your wire stopped transmitting, we didn't realize it immediately. Bad mistake on our part."

"I'm fine. It was only a matter of a minute or two."

"What about this asshole?" Pleasant asked, still holding Speedo at gunpoint. "Who is he? And how do we cuff him without getting in range of his tail?"

Vivian looked at Croyd's face. He was looking back at her with an unreadable expression and she believed he did not want to be identified. "He goes by Speedo. Can I cuff him?"

Croyd gave her a slight nod and the cops came up with several sets of handcuffs. He shifted to help Vivian hook up both his wrists to the last spike on his tail. That satisfied the cops.

The garden was noisy, with crackling and static on radios, orders being shouted, and other chatter among the cops. EMTs came in with stretchers for the dead. Pleasant and Storgman were grilling Croyd.

When Vivian sat down next to Ben, no one noticed. She leaned close and whispered, "I can get you out of this, but you have to promise me something. You're going to leave New York. Period."

"We're New Yorkers, born and bred. I don't have anywhere to go."

"I'm going to apply to the police academy and I can't have you around here, you see? Promise me."

"Look, I can lie low. I know how to stay under the radar."

"Promise me. Right now."

He hesitated. "I'll need some money."

"We can talk about details later. Say it."

He looked into her eyes for a moment. "Okay, Viv, I promise."

He rarely called her Viv. It was a sign of sincerity.

"Take the coin," said Ben. "Our coin. In my pant pocket."

Vivian took it out. "Grandpa gave it to you."

"I'm giving it to you. Keep it in New York."

Vivian closed her hand over it.

"Move apart." Pleasant spoke sternly. "You're not to talk again, understand?"

"Sorry," said Vivian. She stood up and walked over to the detectives. "How long has that Andy guy been undercover? Why did you need me?"

Storgman responded. "He got in with the Immaculate Egrets about a month ago, but he never got close to Quinn before. That's why."

"I get it," Vivian said. "They brought him today because some members got killed."

Pleasant turned to Storgman as he watched Ben. "Bastard never got arrested before but we got him now."

"You don't understand," said Vivian. "He killed Quinn to save me."

"And what were you doing here in the first place?" Pleasant glared at Ben.

"Helping me, you see?" Vivian raised her voice. "Don't arrest him. He doesn't deserve it."

Storgman turned his big ram's horns toward Croyd. "Is that true?"

This time Vivian watched Croyd, much as he had studied her before she avoided identifying Speedo as the Sleeper.

"That's right," said Croyd. "He helped her. Saved her from Quinn."

"I don't know about this," said Pleasant.

"Ben and Speedo saved me." Vivian saw that with Quinn and all the Egrets dead, and Andy wounded in the chaos, only the three of them remained to give statements about much of the violence. "We three wound up dealing with the Egrets."

"We'll sort it all out at the station," said Storgman. "They won't be charged just for being here. We found the quiver in the van. Quinn and the gang members were our targets here."

Vivian was relieved. She was the one the detectives had sent here and she was the one who could vouch for Ben and Croyd. "Detective Storgman," she said. "I'd like to apply to the police academy. This will help, right?"

Storgman lowered his voice. "Your brother might be a problem, but it helps that he's never been arrested. Once I'm satisfied about him, I'll recommend you."

"Thank you." Vivian looked around the garden where so many people had died. She had ridden with Ben during other times of extreme violence but she knew she would never forget this.

Ben caught her eye. Without speaking, they seemed to communicate one more time, as if agreeing they would both be all right.

Swimmer, Flier, Felon, Spy

PART IV

Central Park. Early evening in late spring.

Fine weather. There were, Tesla reflected, good reasons to visit New York City after all.

The park was even more crowded than the weather and time of day would suggest, with people drifting from every direction toward a temporary stage set in the middle of a meadow. Picnicking families, Frisbee throwers, cheerfully barking dogs, and vendors hawking food—all the ephemera of the city's open-air-market atmosphere, competing with the voices being amplified by speakers set up next to the stage.

A woman's voice was saying: "Farewell, thou lob of spirits; I'll be gone."

A Midsummer Night's Dream, Act II, Scene I, Line 16. An unnamed fairy speaks to Puck. The speech was often cut, so this must have been a very traditional performance. Tesla missed attending the theater.

He'd introduced Li Min to several of his favorite plays. The memory of his hand over hers as they sat side by side in the dark in front of a stage nearly made him feel weak. Being in the world made the memories worse. It brought them to him in a way he couldn't suppress as easily as he could at home. Which made him wonder again why he was doing this.

He was grateful for the distraction of a man's voice shouting: "Buy some balloons! *Buy! Some fucking! Balloons!*"

Tesla caught sight of the insistent salesman. He was a slight bald man dressed in clothing that looked like it had been salvaged from a dumpster, clutching an enormous bunch of foil balloons. He was suspended beneath them, his feet dangling perhaps two yards above the ground.

The Quest for the Croyds, Act IV, Scene I, Line 1. The fourth Crenson harangued a crowd of children, tweaked out of his ever-loving mind.

Since taking on this job, Tesla had been surprised when he thought he was being vigilant, he had violated one of his most inviolable rules, he had learned that many of his secrets were hardly secrets at all, and he had been very nearly killed by a tiger.

This, though. This looked like it might be problematic.

A pair of policemen were making their way through the crowd gathering around Crenson. It looked as though they would arrive below him in a couple of moments. It would take Tesla considerably longer, but, sighing, he nonetheless started in that direction.

Someone close to Crenson shouted something unintelligible, and it must have must been directed at the floating man. He released the clutch of balloons, which floated gently up into the darkening sky. Crenson himself hung neutrally in the air for a moment, then began swinging his arms and kicking his legs like a swimmer heading downward, all the while screaming. This screaming was mostly incoherent, but Tesla could make out a few words here and there. "Kill you!" and "Fuck!" and "Get back here!"

This last was no doubt in reaction to the fact that the crowd was withdrawing as Crenson descended, an ever-larger circle moving away from him at a quickening rate.

From the speakers, Shakespeare's words continued, their tone indicating that the players were less acting from conviction than gamely soldiering on. Open-air theater had a history of being performed in some pretty strange circumstances down the centuries, even before the wild card virus.

Another woman's voice broadcast across the meadow, now more difficult to pick out because the entire crowd had become aware something was going on; people were standing and speaking to one another. "Thou speakest aright; I am that merry wanderer of the night." A woman playing Puck. Not so stodgy a performance then.

Tesla pushed his way into the edge of the empty circular space around Crenson just as the police officers reached its center. One of them was shining a flashlight up at him and speaking into the microphone at his shoulder while the other stood with his hands on his hips, clearly befuddled.

Tesla, in his former life as a government employee, had a great deal of experience speaking with law enforcement officials, though admittedly they were more likely to be, say, a vice minister of justice in a Southeast Asian country than an NYPD beat cop working a busy night in Central Park.

The park, Tesla corrected himself.

Despite his long experience, he was hesitant to approach. But the very fact that he stood inside the perimeter of the circle instead of outside it drew the attention of the officer directly below Crenson, who was now flailing about in midair, spitting and grunting. "Hey! You with the horns!" the cop shouted. "You know this guy?"

Decision time. "I do," said Tesla.

"Can you talk him down from there?"

Truth time. "I very much doubt it."

"You don't know how the hell we can get him down from there?"

A deep voice sounded from behind Tesla, and a tall white man brushed his shoulder as he walked toward the police officer. "I can get him down," he said.

Tesla recognized the voice. Even in just catching a glimpse in profile as he walked by, Tesla also recognized the face.

So did the police officer. So did, seemingly, everyone else in the crowd. The man was, at one time, the most famous ace in the world, and still held a creditable claim to the title. He was once regarded as the strongest human who had ever lived, and Tesla would have had to think long and hard to name his rivals for that title as well.

He was despised and adored around the world.

He was Jack Braun. He was Golden Boy.

Tesla fell into step behind Braun, trusting that few eyes would be focused on him.

As they came side by side with the police, Crenson suddenly stopped flailing and turned so he hung head-down, face-to-face with Braun. "Hey!" he shouted. "Hey, everybody, look! It's fucking Tarzan!"

Then he let out a long yodeling yell—a surprisingly accurate rendition of Johnny Weissmuller's famous Tarzan call, not imitating the comparatively anemic bellow that had characterized Braun's efforts when he played the character on television in the early 1960s. Someone in the crowd clapped.

Braun made a swipe at Crenson, but the floating man rose out of his reach with surprising swiftness. "How you been, man? I thought you told me you tried to stay out of the spotlight." Crenson's voice was still shaky, but at least he could be understood.

Braun looked startled. "Do I know you?"

"That Walrus is the only one who ever fucking recognizes me," said Crenson.

Tesla stepped up. "You do know him. That's Croyd Crenson."

"Oh, shit," said one of the police officers. "Call that in."

Braun looked down at Tesla. "Do I know *you*?"

"I haven't had the pleasure, no," said Tesla.

Surprising Tesla and Crenson both, Braun launched himself upward, reached out one hand quick as a cat, and grabbed Crenson by the shoulder. When he dropped lightly to his feet, a howling

Crenson came with him. Braun whipped him around upright and planted the man's feet firmly on the ground, now with a hand on each shoulder.

"People are trying to watch the play," said Braun.

From the crowd, someone called, "Don't worry about it, this is better!"

A pained look flashed on Braun's face. Tesla wondered if he loved theater, too. The man had been an actor, if not a particularly good one, but being an actor didn't necessarily mean one loved the theater.

"Mr. Braun," said Tesla, pitching his voice low. "I would very much appreciate it if you would help me out with a situation involving Croyd Crenson."

Jack Braun looked at Crenson, who was now squirming around in a fruitless attempt to escape. "I'm not helping out enough already?"

"I need to speak to him privately."

"I'd say these two and their friends might object to that," said Braun.

Another voice from the crowd. "Check it out! Here come the horses!"

Tesla looked past the circle of onlookers and saw not just a pair but a whole troop of mounted police officers trotting their direction.

"If you'll humor me for a moment, I'll see what I can do to overcome their objections."

Time to violate another inviolable rule. "Officer, please tell your dispatcher that you have a B618," said Tesla.

The policeman who had been speaking into his radio shook his head in confusion and annoyance. "First, citizens don't tell us what to call in. Second, there's no such thing as a B618."

Braun was watching Tesla with some curiosity. "Go ahead and do it," he said.

The officer considered it a moment, then shrugged. "Dispatch, I've got a B618 here."

A voice squawked back. "Say again? Confirm B618?"

"That's what I said, yeah. B618."

"Stand by."

The two officers looked at each other, then at Tesla. He smiled his closemouthed polite smile. The horses stopped beyond the edge of the crowd, the woman obviously commanding them holding her hand to her ear as if listening to something.

A man's voice, different from that of the dispatcher, came over the radio. "Officer Tripp?"

"Yeah, this is Tripp. Who's this?"

"Officer Tripp, this is Chief of Police Cameron."

"Fuck me," said Tripp, but he had the presence of mind not to hold the TRANSMIT button as he did so.

"Officer Tripp, please describe the men who have apprehended Croyd Crenson."

Confusion warred with worry on the policeman's voice. His partner's hand was on the handle of his baton. "Yes, sir. I have a joker, apparently male, gray-skinned with black horns, no visible hair, wearing a three-piece suit. And I have, um, Golden Boy."

"Good, Tripp, that's good. Now I want you to listen very carefully to me. I want you to thank these citizens for their service and release the suspect into their custody."

"I'm already in their fucking custody," said Crenson.

Officer Tripp ignored this. "Sir? Well, sir, are you sure about that? Do you know this man in the suit?"

"No, Officer Tripp. No, I've never seen him or even heard of him."

"Um, okay."

"And Officer Tripp?"

"Yes, sir?"

"Neither have you."

An amplified voice, not coming from the stage, said, "Disperse. Disperse immediately." The horses began moving in.

Braun took one hand off Crenson's shoulder and used it to grip him firmly by the belt, then turned and looked Tesla directly in the eye. "You want to tell me what this is all about?"

From the stage, Puck closed out Act II, Scene I. "Fear not, my lord! Your servant shall do so."

"Six of him," said Jack Braun.

"One of me," said Croyd. "Those other five assholes are poseurs."

Braun lifted Croyd by the belt and shook him vigorously. "The adults are talking," he said.

"Six is what I was given to believe. This gentleman is the fourth I've met," said Tesla, ignoring Crenson as best he could. This particular iteration was by far the most amped up he'd encountered. Time was indeed growing short.

The three of them were walking west, away from the park, the direction chosen mostly because it was the quickest and most direct away from the crowd still milling around the site of their altercation with the police.

Well, Tesla and Jack Braun were walking. Croyd was floating along in Braun's firm grip, speaking quickly when he spoke, and otherwise sighing loudly.

"Why are you tracking them down, though?" asked Braun. A passing cab blew its horn as Crenson floated slightly out into the street. "Government orders, right? I mean, you're obviously some kind of spook."

"Mr. Braun," said Tesla, "as you'll recall from your own time in government service, I'd hardly be allowed to tell you if I was."

Braun said, "Bullshit. In my time in government service they had film crews following me around and putting up newsreels in every movie house in America."

Which was, of course, true. Tesla slightly reassessed his planned approach with the famous ace. Despite his name—and reputation—this man was not all brawn.

"I'm a free agent," said Tesla. "I was hired to track down the Croyds and bring them all together at one place. Tomorrow night."

"What?" demanded the floating Croyd. "What are you talking about? Who hired you? What place? Why?"

Braun shook Crenson again, then said, "I hope you're getting paid a lot."

Tesla sidestepped a puddle of something that smelled deeply unappetizing. "I assume so. I have associates who take care of that side of things."

"Okay, then, what about our balloon friend's questions? They're legitimate. I know you types sometimes don't know the whos and whys of your jobs, but why are *you* doing it? If you don't even know how much money you're getting paid for what is probably a pretty dangerous job, then you obviously don't need the money. Will you *stop*, already?"

This last was directed at Crenson, who had reached around his back with both hands and was pawing ineffectually at the spot on his belt where Braun had him secured. "You're holding me too tight! I'm gonna hurl!"

A look of disgust passed over Braun, but he did loosen his grip slightly.

Tesla took the opportunity to think about Braun's question. Why *was* he doing it? He still honestly wasn't sure. Perhaps his routines had simply made him bored enough, and the promise of being part of the Sleeper's long history intrigued enough. Perhaps it was something else entirely that he didn't want to admit yet . . .

They had entered a residential area, so the traffic sounds and crowd sounds diminished somewhat, though Manhattan was never quiet. "Where are we going?" asked Braun.

Tesla pointed with his chin. "Someplace private."

"Safe house," said Braun. "Spook."

"I do not maintain any such in the city, alas. But," and here he was interrupting Braun's coming question, "I know for a fact that our friend here does."

Braun swung Crenson around so that he was forced to face the two of them. "How about it?" he asked.

"Safe house? Sure, sure. I know a good one. I need to check it out anyway and see if any of those assholes left any stuff behind."

"Where to, then?" asked Braun.

"You know that newsstand in Jokertown where the guy with the Hawaiian shirts works?"

"You again," said Jube, looking at Tesla. Then he looked at Crenson, narrowed his eyes, and said, "You again." Lastly, he looked at Braun, shook his head, and said, in an altogether different tone, "You again."

Braun sighed. "People are really going to have to get over it at some point. Haven't I paid enough?"

"No," said Jube, shortly.

Most people probably had gotten over it, but Jube, being long-lived, would recall all too well Braun testifying against his fellow wild cards before Congress in the 1950s. The infamous blacklist period.

Jube turned to Tesla. "You've had your joke for the day." Then Crenson. "What can I do for you, Croyd?"

"Jube, Jube, Jube! I need a key!"

The Walrus scratched his head. "Your sleeps are getting shorter, and your personality is getting weird faster. What happened to the key I gave you three days ago?"

"Wasn't me. Look, the blue one. You still got the blue one?"

Jube looked from Tesla to Braun with a what-is-this look on his surprisingly expressive face. But he said, "Yeah, Croyd, sure. I've still got the blue one."

Then he turned and bent over into the interior of the newsstand. There was the rustling of paper, the clinking of bottles, then he turned back, holding a large ring of keys. An octagonal fob on the ring was engraved with the letter C. A dozen keys, all in different shapes and colors, jangled.

Just as his face was surprisingly expressive, Jube's fat fingers were surprisingly deft. He detached a blue key that looked like one for a standard Schlage dead bolt to Tesla, and extended it toward Crenson's outstretched hand. Then he hesitated.

"You with these guys of, uh, your own recognizance, Croyd?"

There followed the longest pause in this particular Crenson's speech Tesla had heard. "They're helping me with a job."

Interesting.

Crenson lurched forward and snatched the key from Jube's hand, almost surprising Braun enough to lose hold of him.

"Okay, okay, okay," said Crenson. "Let's go. Farther uptown but stay east."

Braun shrugged and started walking, pulling the babbling Croyd along behind him. Since this was Jokertown, the pair didn't attract as much attention as one might assume.

Before Tesla turned to follow them, Jube stopped him.

"Got another one for you, if you haven't heard it already," he said.

"I'm listening," said Tesla.

"It's about a know-it-all, a traitor, and a crook."

"I haven't heard it, no."

"No wonder," said Jube. "It's not really funny."

The apartment was a fourth-floor walk-up in a tenement building.

"Looks like this place has seen better days," said Braun as they entered the lobby. Visibility was low, because the only light was what came in with them when they opened the door.

"Do you really think so?" asked Tesla as they began to climb the stairs.

At each landing, they heard different sounds. A low-voiced argument. A slamming door. The skittering of rat feet.

Finally, on the fourth floor, Croyd said, "Look, there's no way to get out of here, no windows, see? Will you let me go already?"

"No," said Braun.

The second-to-last door on the left looked as shabby as the others along the hall except for one thing. Every one of the four locks looked shiny and new.

"You only have one key," said Tesla.

"They're all keyed the same," said Crenson, rapidly inserting, turning, and moving down to the next lock. "Who the hell has time to carry around that many keys?"

"Jube the Walrus," suggested Braun.

"He doesn't carry them around," said Crenson, then, his work with the key done, he pushed the door open. "Ta-da!" he said.

There was absolutely nothing in the room. The bare wooden floors bore scars where furniture had once been pushed back and forth, and the sallow walls bore ghostly outlines of long-gone appliances. An entryway to the right opened into a tiny bathroom with no door.

"This is your safe house?" asked Braun incredulously.

"One of them," said Crenson as Tesla moved to the room's single window. He pushed, hoping to get it up. As he had expected, he could not move it even enough to disturb the dust on the sash. He nodded at Braun.

"Okay," said Braun. "I'm letting you go now, but if you start for the window or the door it won't work out well for you."

"Yeah, yeah, whatever, let's just check to see what we have left here."

Crenson swam through the air to one corner, reached down to put his finger in a knothole with some difficulty, and pulled. He cursed, then looked at Tesla. "You want to give me a hand?"

Tesla pointed at Braun. "He's the strong one."

"It don't need super strength. It just needs normal strength. I'm kind of short on that right now."

Tesla said, "Move back." When Crenson did so, he leaned over and pulled up a portion of the floorboard. He had not known what to expect—cash, perhaps, weapons, drugs. What he found was a bundle of tightly rolled blueprints.

"Now it's time for the big reveal!" said Crenson. "The twenty-thousand-dollar question! Or questions, really; I got two of 'em."

Tesla didn't reach for the blueprints. He did not respond to Crenson.

"Okay, well, you can't stay shut up forever because now's when you tell me this. Who the fuck are you and what the fuck do you want with me?"

Tesla glanced over at Braun, who shrugged. "That's what I want to know, too," Braun said. "Why else do you think I came along on this little adventure?"

Tesla did not hesitate. "My name is Tesla. I am an information broker for a highly specialized clientele who rarely does fieldwork. I am here to convince you to meet me and several others at a time and place I'm sure you don't want Mr. Braun to know."

Croyd had nodded maniacally through this short speech. "A meetup, sure. I can do a meetup no problem, absolutely no problem, Tesla, if that's your real name and I know it's not. Just the matter of the tit for tat, though. The play for pay, or is that the other way around? You know, the quid pro quo."

"I would expect nothing less," said Tesla drily.

"But I don't just need you, I need the big guy here, too."

"It sounds to me like I've found out all I'm going to find out," said Braun. "I've got better things to do than hang around pre-war tenements with spooks and addicts." He started toward the door.

"Wait wait wait!" said Crenson. "Wait—" and here he paused. "What war?"

"What?" asked Braun. "What are you talking about?"

"You said prewar. Wow are there a lot of wars, y'know? I've been in some of them."

"*The* war," said Braun. "*My* war."

"The one where you threw the tank at those guys?"

"That was a different one," said Tesla.

"Shut up," said Crenson and Braun at the same time.

"Just trying to be helpful," said Tesla.

"I'm just fucking with you," said Crenson. "You mean the *big* one! Dubya Dubya *Two*! You keep up with those guys you fought with, right? Veterans all do that."

Braun shook his head. "No, of course not. I don't think any of them are even still alive. The war ended eighty years ago."

"*The* war, you mean," said Crenson. "Like I said, there are a lot of wars, and not all of them are over. And you guys and me, we're about to strike a blow for justice in one that's been going on for fifty years! Which is pretty good, even if it isn't eighty!"

Tesla ran through the list of active conflicts going on anywhere in the world in his head, doing math. "The Kurds, maybe?"

"No!" said Crenson, floating up so suddenly that he struck his head against the water-stained ceiling. "Shit!" He rubbed his head and shimmied back downward. "I mean, the Kurds probably move some product; everybody in that part of the world does. I'm talking about the War on Drugs, partners!"

"Oh," said Braun. "Oh, I am not going to like where this is going. You want us to fight drug dealers?"

Crenson waved his arms and shook his head. "None of that penny-ante bullshit."

"I don't think the Mexican government would agree with you that all drug dealers are penny ante," said Tesla.

"Look, the cartels ain't got shit on the supply we're going to be liberating."

"Liberating?" asked Braun. He sounded genuinely confused.

Tesla wished he was. "You want us to *steal drugs* from drug dealers?" he said.

Crenson giggled. "Even better, even better! Grab that roll, there, the one that's got '1PP' written on it. That one right there!"

Tesla sighed. Clearly, something unpleasant was playing out here. Braun's continued presence complicated things, even if his motivations remained unclear. But he pulled out the roll of blueprints Crenson was wildly gesticulating at.

"Now lay it out, lay it out! Let's take a look at what we're looking at!"

Tesla crouched and spread it open. "Oh," he said. "Of course. 1PP."

One Police Plaza.

"And I again assure you, Mr. Crenson," said Tesla, repeating himself for the third time. "There is not an enormous trove of illegal narcotics locked away in an underground vault beneath the headquarters of the New York City Police Department."

"Biggest motherfucking stash in the world," said Crenson. Sometime in the last half hour, he had begun to sweat profusely.

Braun was leaning against the wall, arms crossed, looking on with what Tesla guessed was amusement. He was smiling at least, even if the smile had a hint of nastiness about it.

"*Think*, Mr. Crenson. Why would they store everything they seized in one place? Why would they keep it at all? There are regularly scheduled burnings in secure locations!"

Tesla wasn't telling everything he knew about how the NYPD disposed of the drugs that came into their possession—their methods were not dissimilar to those of the federal government or of any other large legal authority in the West—but neither was he, strictly speaking, lying. There was no reason to let Croyd Crenson know where the drugs *were* stored, even if they were only stored there temporarily.

Not that that would necessarily be worse than the situation

Tesla found himself in. Because in his deepening delusion, Crenson was absolutely convinced that he was right about his fantasized "stash." And even more alarmingly, he was absolutely convinced he had the perfect scheme to retrieve "as much of it as super buddy there can carry."

Here was the plan, as Crenson had laid it out.

"We go down there, see? We roll up and you use that magic password you used in Central Park, 221B or whatever. They let us in, we make our way down into the sub-basements, brawny rips the doors open, we stuff our bags"—(somewhere, bank bags were to be obtained)—"and out we go!"

And as for the escape plan: "There's always cabs around there!"

Tesla began working on his own plan. He carefully studied the blueprints. He considered what he knew of Jack Braun's powers and what he guessed of the man's motivations and willingness to participate. He listened to Croyd Crenson and watched him closely.

Finally, after Crenson had gone over his scheme once more, spittle spotting the blueprints, Tesla said, "I think we've got it. Let's go."

Braun made a choking noise and raised his eyebrows so high, they nearly made contact with his perfectly coifed hair. Tesla caught his eye and gave him a subtle nod. Braun, in return, gave a none-too-subtle shrug of his shoulders. Crenson noticed nothing of this.

"All right! All right! Let's go! I'm driving!"

"You have a car?" asked Braun.

"How hard can it be to find a car?" asked Crenson.

"I'll call a service," said Tesla.

The concierge at Tesla's hotel arranged for transportation from Crenson's hideaway to police headquarters. The windows of the large sedan were completely black, and when the three of them piled into the back seat, they found that there was an equally impenetrable screen blocking the driver from sight.

The car started moving as soon as Braun closed the door. Tesla had not told the concierge where he wished to go, but he was not surprised that the driver seemed to know their destination. Life in the big city.

Though by this time it was almost midnight, there was plenty of activity around One Police Plaza. The protestors who chanted against police policies around the clock were in their designated area, though at the moment they seemed to be content merely to wave their signs. There were New Yorkers passing by on foot at pace, as was seemingly always the case in this part of the city.

There were police everywhere.

Whereas in Jokertown, no one had paid any particular attention to the three of them—particularly Crenson bobbing along, now tied to Braun's belt as if with the string of a balloon—they were immediately noticed when they exited the car, which sped smoothly away. A number of officers began to converge upon them, but, as luck would have it, Tesla spotted two in particular who suited his purposes excellently.

"Shit," said Crenson. "We forgot the bags."

Officer Tripp and his partner had just exited the main doors of the building. They looked exhausted. Tesla would have assumed they'd just been thoroughly debriefed, but the exact wording of the agreement between the NYPD and the NSA he had abused for his own purposes precluded much in that way. Perhaps they'd simply had their orders to forget everything reinforced.

Well, Tesla was about to undo that reinforcement.

"Officers!" he called. "Would you mind coming over here for a moment?"

The police who had been approaching halted, looking at their comrades with more than a little curiosity. Tripp and his partner, on the other hand, became mildly panicked.

"Officer Tripp, yes? This man"—he pointed at Crenson—"is Croyd Crenson. I believe you'll find that there are a number of outstanding warrants against him, and Mr. Braun and I wish to turn him in to the authorities."

"Hey!" said Croyd. "You're changing the plan!"

Tesla nodded. "I am."

Tripp said, "I just spent six hours being told that I have no idea who you are."

Tesla answered, "*Do* you have any idea who I am?"

Tripp blinked. "Well, no, actually."

"Then know then that Mr. Braun and I are simply concerned citizens, visitors to your fair city, who have decided to do our duty in assisting New York's Finest in their search for a well-known criminal."

"What . . . what about that code and all that?"

Braun said, "I was wondering the same thing, actually." He handed his belt—which looked exceedingly expensive—over to Tripp's partner.

"Ah," said Tesla. "Only one get-out-of-jail-free card in this game's deck, I'm afraid."

"What the fuck are you talking about?" demanded Crenson. "You're fucking everything up!"

"It would seem I am," said Tesla.

"I suppose we're supposed to just take him into custody and let you two go?" asked Tripp.

"Probably for the best," said Tesla.

"Well . . . well, okay," said the officer. Then he signaled his partner and the two of them turned back toward the building, Crenson bobbing along in the breeze behind them.

"221B!" shouted Crenson. "221B!"

"You think he's actually read Sherlock Holmes?" asked Braun.

Tesla said, "I wouldn't put anything past Croyd Crenson."

"Now that you mention it," replied Braun, "neither would I."

Semiotics of the Strong Man

by Walter Jon Williams

March 1999

"EUR looks like it came from outer space
even today," Jack said. "Imagine how it looked in 1944."

"Like Mussolini's wet dream," said Felicia.

"It was pretty badly wrecked in the fighting," Jack said. "Half the buildings weren't finished." He paused, hands in his jacket pockets, and looked around. "They've cleaned it up."

Il Duce had intended EUR as the new modern fascist center of Rome, with massive white buildings standing against the sky like sentries keeping a watchful eye on the people below. Elements of classical architecture—colonnades, obelisks, arches—were mixed with modernist elements such as stark geometries, lack of ornament, and flat roofs. Compared to the rest of Rome, EUR looked like another planet.

EUR had never become the center of Rome, fascist or otherwise, but was now just another industrial suburb with striking architecture.

Its slogan might have been *All Up-to-Date for Nineteen Thirty-Eight*.

Jack and Felicia walked across the Piazza John Kennedy toward the Palazzo dei Congressi, Rome's convention center, a colossal mass set behind a pillared portico, like a brutalist Tara.

"I'd been wounded in the foot," Jack said, "and I was in one of the military hospitals. I had to walk with a cane, but I got a jeep and went with a couple of buddies to see the sights. I remember looking at this half-built thing and wondering what the hell it was supposed to be."

They had actually ended up in the EUR because they'd got lost looking for a whorehouse, but Jack wasn't going to tell Felicia that.

"What was it like back then?"

"Lots of GIs. Lots of half-starved kids, half-starved adults. Refugees come in from towns that had been bombed to death. Rome had been declared an open city, so the damage wasn't as bad as practically everywhere else, but still the German engineers had blown up anything that could be useful to us.

"On the march north I was in Rome only long enough to kiss some girls during the victory parade, but then we came up against the Gothic Line and I got shot in the autumn. When I came back to Rome the weather was miserable and cold, full of rain. Nobody remembers this, but Vesuvius had erupted just before we marched into the city, and I think it affected the weather."

Truth to tell, Jack needn't have gone looking for a brothel that day, because the whole city was a whorehouse by then. Everything and everybody was for sale, and you could get anything you wanted for a price. Silk stockings, wine, grappa, jewelry, paintings, statues, girls, boys, even old ladies if that was your taste. You could dine like a king in a restaurant and then look out the window to watch starving people fighting over cigarette butts in the streets.

He hadn't been in Rome since 1945, and in the fifty-four years since it had become prosperous, with well-tailored men and women strolling around or driving past in shiny new cars. No one starved, not unless they had aspirations to be an actress or a supermodel and starved themselves on purpose.

Even the smells were different. In 1945 the city smelled of garbage, charcoal fires, and cheap perfume. Here in 1999, you could smell coffee, diesel, and money.

And of course tobacco. Everyone still smoked here. Jack lived in California and had forgotten what it was like to live, drink, and dine in a cigarette cloud.

"They feature EUR in a lot of cinema," Felicia said. "Bertolucci's *Conformist*. Antonioni's *L'Eclisse*. Even that vampire flick with Vincent Price, *The Last Man on Earth*."

"I saw that Price picture," Jack said. "It was pretty good."

"A lot of fans of that picture will be here today."

Jack pointed. "Look at that big cupola on top of the Congress hall," he said. "It looks like it was intended as a zeppelin hangar."

"The palazzo is really huge," Felicia said. "But I've been here before, so I can get you where you'll need to go."

Felicia Herman was Jack's minder for the event, an American who worked in Rome with the Instituto Cinema de Genere, which was an organization that studied, preserved, and promoted genre film—what in Jack's Hollywood heyday had been called B-films. Felicia's job was to make sure he arrived at his scheduled events and translate for him when he got there. She was somewhere in her twenties, with auburn hair and dark-rimmed glasses. Felicia had been in Italy long enough to adapt an Italian's minimalist sense of style, and so wore a beige boat-neck linen dress and sandals with comfortably low heels, accessorized with a glossy brown top-grain leather belt and a Prada bag. A few rings but no other jewelry. Everything she wore was tailored and first-class. She might not have a closet bulging with choices, but Jack guessed that what she had was top of the line.

Even in the war, he remembered, the Italians had cared very much how they looked. Threadbare but somehow immaculate.

There had been a reception the previous evening, with officials and movie people, and now Jack was due for a panel discussion. When he'd received the invitation he'd been flattered, and then he realized that he was not to be the subject of any of the programming—it was all about the director Ed Steuben, with whom Jack had made a couple of westerns back in the 1950s. In the past decade or so Steuben had become a cult figure, the subject of serious study by the sorts of people who obsessively analyzed the accidental appearance of boom mikes in dramatic scenes.

"So what's my event going to be like?" Jack said.

"There's no way of knowing," said Felicia. "This field attracts obsessives. It depends on who's asking the questions and what inner itch they're scratching at any given moment."

"I'll try to stay on my toes, then."

Banners advertising the film festival fluttered between the pillars of the Palazzo dei Congressi. Jack and Felicia walked up the stairs and through the immense portico into the entrance hall, which was another striking mixture of epochs and styles, the hall made up of pale rectangles outlined in black, all geometry, but with an enormous colorful mural opposite the entrance featuring stately figures in togas and an enthroned woman—Jack *thought* it was a woman—carrying a scepter.

"Jeez, look at this," Jack said. "You've got to wonder what they were thinking. All this minimalist geometry and then you look at the mural and you think, *These things do not go together.* I don't even know what that mural is supposed to mean." He looked at Felicia. "I know a little bit about architecture, see. And I know it's supposed to make a unified statement. *Do this. Buy this. You're important. You're insignificant.* This says too many things."

Felicia adjusted her glasses as she looked at the mural. "Did you study architecture or something?"

"No. I just built things."

"Like what?"

"Shopping malls. I sank my Hollywood money into shopping malls. And every one of mine says, *Buy this stuff, whatever it is, and you'll be happier.*" He grinned at her. "You can't promise they'll be *happy,* see, because happy people don't want anything, and they won't buy your product. But I definitely promise a rise in the *general level* of happiness."

Felicia looked up at him with an expression that suggested she was reevaluating her idea of who Jack was. "Let me take you to the green room," she said.

She took him into a side corridor, and Jack saw some multilingual signs with arrows intended to direct people into an exhibit hall. "Congress of Wonders?" he asked. "*Wunderkammer?*" He knew some German from his boyhood in North Dakota and he tried to make sense of it. "Wonder Closet?" he guessed. "Is that *us*?"

"No, that's another event. They collect weird shit—they're another set of obsessives, basically."

He peered into the exhibit hall and saw tables and booths filled with a vast array of . . . of *stuff*. Sinister-looking Victorian medical instruments. A bust of Chairman Mao. Giant turtle shells. Old musical instruments. Barrel organs. Things preserved in jars. Costumes and masks from old horror movies. What looked like a mummified monkey stolen from an Egyptian tomb. Vintage jewelry. Mounted skeletons of people and animals. Stuffed birds, stuffed animals, stuffed fish, stuffed crocodiles.

All this visible within maybe fifteen yards, a small percentage of a very large room.

"Did you know Modular Man?" Felicia said.

This seemed a question without a context, but Jack answered anyway. "The android? We never met."

"His head is in there. From when he blew up."

"Wow. Maybe I should, y'know—" He started to go into the room.

"Later," Felicia said. "We don't have time right now."

Felicia got him to the green room on time, and Jack was reintroduced to some elderly people. A writer who'd worked on some of

Steuben's pictures, though not the ones Jack was in. An actress who'd been at Metro at the time, and whom Jack remembered as a vivacious redhead, but who was now a palsied old lady with a cane. The third Mrs. Steuben, who was here because the fourth Mrs. Steuben was dead, along with the first and second. Jack had known them all at one time, but hadn't seen any of them in decades.

The moderator of the panel was an Italian film critic in shades and a striped sailor shirt. Jack had to think this wasn't a good look for him. Apparently Jack was about to be interviewed by the only man in Italy who didn't know how to dress.

Jack was glad he'd worn his Armani.

The critic presented his fellow panelists with his latest book, *Steuben: Man of a Thousand Angles*. It was a thick coffee-table volume, heavily illustrated with photographs and stills from Steuben's films. Jack wondered if any of the pictures were of him.

Felicia handed him a pocket radio with headphones. "I'll be in the translators' booth," she said. "I'll translate the questions and then translate back into Italian when you reply. Keep your headphones on and there shouldn't be a problem."

They were led to the auditorium but couldn't enter right away, because the audience from the previous presentation was leaving. According to a sign, the presentation was titled: *The Eternal Maciste: Toward a Semiotics of the Strong Man*. Jack had no idea what any of that meant.

So many people poured out of the hall that Jack wondered if there would be any audience left. But a respectable number remained, and more entered as the participants waited for the panel to begin.

The hall had walls and ceiling of light wood sculpted into curves, with the spectators' chairs, upholstered in green cloth, arranged into neat rectangles all arrowing toward the stage, like battalions of Mussolini's soldiers advancing on parade. *The Semiotics of the Strong Man*, Jack thought.

The critic opened the session with an introduction in Italian, which made Jack realize he'd forgotten to don his headphones. He put them on, then adjusted the radio set, and finished just in time to respond to the applause of the audience as he was introduced.

The first part of the panel was very formal. The critic would ask a question, and then each panelist would respond in order, beginning with Mrs. Steuben, closest to the moderator, and on to Jack, on the far end. As the title of his book demonstrated, the critic was most interested in the striking camera angles Steuben favored, which he thought were inspired by German expressionism.

The critic seemed to have a problem with the answers he received. Mrs. Steuben described the house she shared with the director and some of its furnishings. The writer worked closely with Steuben on the scripts, but was only rarely on set and had nothing to do with camera setups. The actress said that Steuben's tricks were all to disguise his films' low budget.

"As an actor," Jack said, "I was concerned mainly with hitting my marks and saying my lines. Of course I had to know where the camera was placed, but *why* it was placed there wasn't really anything I thought about."

"I remember," the actress added, "we'd always wonder where the camera was going to be on any given day—I mean, was it going to be in the rafters looking down at us, or looking up through a glass table? We always speculated as we got ready for the day's shoot."

"Not a lot of glass tables in the Old West," Jack said. "But sometimes Steuben would put the camera in a pit, and we'd have to walk over it, or jump a horse over it. I remember once Bill Frawley fell right in and broke the cameraman's arm." He grinned. "There might have been drinking involved."

The audience found that amusing, but the critic did not. Nobody was answering his question about German expressionism.

"Mr. Braun," he said, "a question for you, if I may. There was the famous shot in *Shootout at Sadler's Notch* where the camera was located in a stagecoach while it tumbled off a cliff, with the stunt-men and doubles in the coach being thrown around like crash dummies. I've been unable to discover whether Steuben used more than one camera, or if it took more than one take."

"I'm afraid I wasn't on set that day," Jack said. "I never saw that shot until the picture premiered, and I never asked how it was done. I just thought the stuntmen had really earned their pay."

The critic never managed to get the panel back on its intended track, and the panelists just related stories about Steuben. Jack had very little to say about Steuben, so he told some anecdotes about other directors and said they were about Steuben.

The two pictures he'd made with Steuben were each shot in six weeks on a low budget, mostly at the Corriganville Movie Ranch, and all he remembered was all the hard, grinding work it took to get each picture done on time. He did remember one thing that seemed significant, which was that Steuben never told him how to act, but only what to *do*. He wouldn't say, "In this scene you're overwhelmed with grief after your brother's death"; he'd say, "I want you to walk slowly to this mark and look out the window. Put your arm up on the windowsill at exactly this angle." He hadn't thought about it at the time, because he just did what he was told, but it was clear now that the arm was there to cast a shadow across his face that would make tangible the darkness of his thoughts.

He tried to say this, but he had a feeling he said it badly, because no one seemed to take his point.

The last ten minutes of the discussion was taken up by ques-tions from the audience. Most of them were routine, and weren't really directed at Jack anyway.

Jack was relieved. There were certain questions he dreaded, and they didn't have anything to do with Steuben or his acting career. There had been a time when he was known as the Judas Ace, and he had spent a great deal of mental energy trying to understand how that had come about. He had trusted the people who said they loved him, and who said they had his best interests at heart. But the love was an illusion, and the interest turned out to be self-interest, and Jack had been persuaded to betray the people who actually loved him and wanted the best for him. Hollywood was four-fifths illusion anyway, and Jack had trusted the illusion and not the reality.

But how to say that in a way that people from 1999 would understand? It had been over fifty years ago. Everyone else involved had been dead for a long time.

The dreaded question didn't come up, luckily enough. Instead a man in the front row raised a hand. "Mr. Braun," he said. "You and the other people on this panel have had long lives, but you're different. You still look twenty-five years old. You're still the guy we see in Steuben's old movies."

"I'm a little more handsome now," Jack said, to laughter.

"What I want to ask," the man persisted, "has to do with your relationship with time. You move through time, but you don't change like everyone else. You stay the same person."

The Judas Ace, Jack thought.

"So do you still feel like a young guy who can take on the world?" the man asked. "Do you feel like an anachronism? Are you frozen in time, like the man in those movies? Do you feel old in any way?"

Jack viewed the man with interest. He spoke English, and with a New York accent. He looked at Jack with an earnest expression, as if his question really mattered to him. Like Jack, he seemed to be in his mid-twenties, and was otherwise unremarkable, with dark hair, pale skin, and a pointed face. He wore jeans and a tee marked with the Harvard coat-of-arms. Jack didn't think that meant anything, because Europeans were always wearing tees of universities they never actually attended.

"I think I feel all those things, at different times," Jack said slowly. "We've got this thing called the Information Superhighway now, and whenever people talk about it, I feel like an anachronism. I feel young enough to do whatever I need to do, and I feel old when I try to explain to young people about things I've lived through, like the Great Depression and the New Deal and the Second World War."

His questioner nodded, quite seriously. "And that first Wild Card Day?"

"I lived," Jack said. "So I'm lucky to have memories of it at all."

"Thank you," the man said.

After that there were a few more questions, and then the critic wrapped up the panel by recommending that everyone buy his book.

Jack and the others stood chatting while the audience filed out, and when Jack thought to look for his questioner, the man was gone.

Felicia returned and collected his headset and radio. "That's all till tomorrow," she said. "You've got your *Memories of Steuben* panel, and your *Backstage at MGM* thing, and your signing."

"I think I want to see that Congress of Wonders," Jack said. "Modular Man's head."

"I kind of want to see that myself," said Felicia.

They walked a corridor that reeked of cigarette smoke and went to the exhibit hall. Jack paid their admission with his Amex Black Card.

The exhibits were exotic and strange and had very little in common, except that they all offered things that some subculture was passionate about. One of a set of barrel organs played a tune every ten minutes, operated by a man in an old Prussian uniform complete with spiked helmet. One booth featured a man in a robe and crown who offered to knight people for ten euros. Goths wandered around in mascara and black costume, and a bodybuilder strode down the aisles in sandals and an ancient-looking tunic. "*Quello è Maciste*," someone said.

"So that's a Maciste," Jack said. "Whatever a Maciste is."

"He's like an Italian Hercules," said Felicia. "Dozens of movies about him."

"They any good?"

Felicia considered the question. "I liked *Cabiria*," she said. "That was the first one. Script by d'Annunzio."

"Wasn't d'Annunzio a fascist?"

"More of a precursor. Mussolini stole his whole style from him, straight-arm salutes and all."

Jack found the head of Modular Man in a collection of automata—robots built from the sixteenth century to the twentieth. Some robots blew trumpets, some beat drums, some flapped wings while the clocks in their bellies chimed the hour. They were on exhibit and not for sale, because they were owned by tech zillionaire Lionel Terhune, who was into collecting, not trading.

"I think Modular Man's seen better days," Jack said. The Modular Man head was on a pedestal and covered by a plexiglass cube. The synthetic flesh was scarred and burned on one side of the face, and even the unmarked skin drooped as if it were half melted. Jack looked with interest at the clear plastic dome atop the head, and the little gleaming radar dish inside. Then he looked up to see the pointed-faced man from the panel discussion looking at him from over Modular Man's head.

"I wondered if you'd come to see him," the man said.

"They rebuilt him, right?" Jack said. "He defended the Rox but hasn't been seen since."

"I knew him, a little," the man said. "We kept running into each other. At Aces High I blew him up by mistake, and after he got rebuilt he put me in the hospital."

Jack looked at the stranger carefully. He didn't seem familiar. "Sorry," he said. "I don't understand."

"We had a history, is what I'm saying."

"Okay," Jack said. "Who are you exactly?"

"Name's Croyd. I was there, in New York, on that first Wild Card Day."

Felicia looked at Croyd in thoughtful surprise. "So you're immortal, too?" she asked.

A dubious, pinched look crossed Croyd's face. "It's more complicated than that."

Jack wasn't prepared to believe that Croyd had lived through Wild Card Day without further evidence. He was always meeting people who tried to bullshit him. "Are you an ace, then?" he asked.

The dubious look crossed Croyd's face again. "Much of the time," he said. He made an equivocal gesture with his hand. "See, I *evolve*."

"So what can you do?" Jack asked.

Croyd hesitated a moment, then came to a decision and vanished. Jack and Felicia stared at the space where Croyd had been, and then Croyd reappeared.

Felicia gave a laugh, half shocked, half delighted. "You can turn invisible?" she asked.

"Naw. I can teleport. I teleported just behind you, then jumped back."

"Nice," Jack said. And then he remembered where he heard the name *Croyd* before. "You're Typhoid Croyd!" he said.

Croyd looked pained. "Not anymore," he said. "Like I said, I evolve."

Jack turned to Felicia. "Typhoid Croyd scared the pants off me!" he said. "He was spreading some crazy, mutated strain that could even reinfect someone who had already been altered by the virus." He turned back to Croyd. "I didn't know how contagious you were, so I flew to Australia and found a remote cabin in the Outback and stacked it with canned goods. I didn't want to go through Wild Card Day ever again."

Croyd nodded. "That was probably smart."

"And it was Modular Man who caught you, right? And dropped you in the Jokertown clinic?"

"Yeah." Croyd nodded. "He probably saved my life by doing that, but I didn't see it that way at the time."

"The only thing that scared me worse than you were the jumpers," Jack said. He was still creeped by the thought of his body, with all his powers, being made the plaything of a laughing homicidal teen. "The FBI sent a guy to tip me off, because nobody wanted a jumper to have my power, so I took off to Australia again."

"Another good move."

"Australia's a whole continent, and most of it's empty. You can really get lost there."

Felicia had been watching the two of them, her attention jumping from one to the other like a spectator at a tennis match.

"Wow," she said. "Two legends in the same room."

"Three if you count Modular Man," said Croyd.

"Hey," said Jack. "You want to go get a drink or something?" He turned to Felicia. "Would you like to join us?"

"I would, but I've got an organizational meeting coming up. I can join you after the meeting, though."

"Where's a good place to hang out in the meantime?"

"You could try Palombini on Konrad Adenauer. It's got food, drink, gelato, coffee, and a bar. Leave the building, cross Piazza Kennedy, head straight down the road till you turn right onto Adenauer."

"*Ciao*," Jack said. "See you there."

"I see where you were coming from with that question about time," Jack said. "But what would you say if I asked you the same question?"

"Time moves very fast for me," Croyd said. "I spend most of

my time asleep. When I wake up, it's an all-new world, and an all-new me." He made a fed-up gesture with one hand.

Palombini had turned out to be more of a cafeteria than a restaurant, self-serve except for the bright, spacious bar. Jack ordered a Negroni, and appreciated the large orange slice perched on the edge of his glass—a change from the stingy twist of orange peel served with the American version. He raised his glass and sipped.

"I got a taste for these during the war," he said. "After I realized that the American dollar would buy good liquor instead of that cheap gin they made in Benevento and shipped north by the truckload. The Krauts had shot up most of the wineries on their retreat, so good wine was scarce, but rotgut was everywhere. Grappa I never cared for." He looked down at his drink. "They didn't have big orange slices to spare, either."

Croyd took some pills out of a bottle and swallowed them with his beer. "You know," he said, "when we say 'the war,' we both know which war we mean."

"Yeah," said Jack. His second Negroni was singing in his head, and he decided to set the drink aside for a moment. He'd forgotten how potent the cocktail was.

"We can speak to each other in a lingo that other people won't understand," Croyd said. "Just because of who and when we were."

"Roosevelt box," said Jack.

Croyd grinned. "Chandu the Magician."

"In like Flynn."

"Don Winslow of the Navy."

"Isinglass."

"Allen's Alley."

"Rin Tin Tin."

Croyd guffawed. "That was crazy, when you think about it! A dog as the star of a *radio show!*" He thought for a minute, then added to the list. "Little Orphan Annie decoder rings."

"Melody Ranch."

"'Sighted Sub, Sank Same.'"

"Inner Sanctum."

"LS/MFT."

"'Peace with honor.'"

"Hop Harrigan."

"That was a little after my time," Jack said. "I must have been in the service by the time Hop was flying."

"I never got a chance to serve," Croyd said. He seemed a little melancholy. "I was just a kid on Wild Card Day."

"You would have grown up just in time to get shipped to Korea," Jack said. "Besides, you've seen action."

Croyd sighed. "Yeah. I sure have."

"How many of us are left?" Jack said. "Who were there on that first day?"

"If you're talking New York, thousands," Croyd said. "The whole world, millions."

"How many aces?"

Croyd made an equivocal gesture. "I'm not always an ace, so . . ."

Jack waved a hand. "You're an ace as far as I'm concerned."

"Gee. Thanks." Croyd seemed pleased. "Other than the two of us, the only ace I can think of is the Magpie."

"Oh, yeah." Jack nodded. "I've met her."

"She's kind of a— Oh."

Croyd had noticed Felicia entering the bar. He and Jack, both schooled in the manners of a certain era, rose from their seats. "You guys haven't eaten?" Felicia said.

"Not yet," said Croyd.

"The sandwiches are good."

Jack bought sandwiches and snacks, then ordered another round. Felicia had a single-malt, and Jack decided to shift to wine, and ordered a bottle of Vino Nobile di Montepulciano. Felicia raised her eyebrows. "You going to drink that all by yourself?"

"I hope not," Jack said, and asked the waiter to bring two more wineglasses.

"You should give it a sip at least," he said. "It's DOC-rated, which means it's a traditional vine from a small region, and the wine made with traditional methods."

"You know wine?" Felicia asked.

"I dabble. I own a few wineries." He shrugged. "On a good year, they break even."

"I thought you did shopping malls."

"I branched out."

Felicia picked up the bottle and inspected the label. "You told me your shopping malls say *Buy and you'll be happy*," she said. "What do your wines say?"

"They say, *Let's have a relaxed afternoon in the Eternal City*."

So they did. They sat around the table and told stories. Felicia talked about *Cinema di Assi*, which were Italian action films about wild card heroes. "Pretty bad," she admitted. "They even revived Maciste as a strongman ace, which was maybe the worst idea ever."

Jack told Hollywood stories. His time in Hollywood began when the studio system was at its zenith, and he'd known practically everyone, at least in passing. If he didn't know them well—or at all—he had anecdotes about them, and he had told the anecdotes so many times that they were burnished gold.

"So then Clark Gable turns to William Faulkner and says, 'Oh, do you write for a living?' And Faulkner says, 'Yes. And what do *you* do?'"

"Wait," Felicia said. "You were there with Howard Hawks?"

"Sure. We were duck hunting."

"But this morning you told that story about Ed Steuben."

"Oh. Busted." Jack shook his head. "The truth is I don't have that many stories about Ed. With him it was all business. I was just a prop that he moved around the set to get his effects."

Felicia looked severe. "I hope you can keep your stories straight at your *Memories of Steuben* panel tomorrow."

"If I don't," Jack said, "you can get on my headphones and tell me to find another anecdote."

Croyd opened his pill bottle and took out a couple of tablets, then swallowed them with his Vino Nobile. "I can get confused, too," he said. "I mean, there are so many *me*'s. And then there are all of *youse*. I mean, when I had that talk—I mean, the 'talk'—" Here he used air quotes. "—with Black Shadow, was it the *real* Black Shadow, or was it someone who was *inhabiting* him? I mean, that guy was schizy even before the jumpers showed up."

"Wait," Jack said. "He had multiple personalities?"

"Oh, hell yes. But I don't know whether *he* controlled *them*, or *they* controlled *him*. I mean I can't control who *I* turn into, now can I? But he may have been just a really good Method actor." Croyd gulped the last of his beer, then refilled his wineglass. "He really carried a grudge against the jumpers. I helped him take out several of them. On the one hand, they were just teenage kids, but on the other, well, the most powerful man in the world had to flee to Australia to hide from them."

Felicia gave Jack a questioning look. Jack nodded. *Yes, I ran like a complete coward.*

"Anyway," Croyd said, "if we aren't overrun with jumpers now, it's because Shad did a bunch of them in. Which was strange, because later I ended up trying to make a home on the Rox, which I guess put me in alliance with the jumpers, but—*wait!*" He waved his hands frantically in the air. "I'm getting the sequence confused. Shad and I hunted jumpers *after* the Rox fell, after they'd gone into government service with the Card Sharks. Our little shark hunt was quite the success—"

He gave a nervous laugh, which showed too many teeth. "I'm getting a little unstuck in time here. It's like everything is the past and the present simultaneously. Shad and I made good partners, but I haven't seen him in years. I wonder if he retired, or . . . or if something bad happened to him."

"That reminds me," Jack said, "of the time I met Eddie Ricken-backer. I played him in the movies, and . . ."

"Bentley!" Croyd said. "Have I ever mentioned Bentley? He taught me all about crime, but he was a dog and walked on four legs. Talked good English, though . . ."

Jack sipped his wine while Croyd embarked on rapid-fire remi-niscence. He waited for Croyd to run out of energy, but the words came out like water through a fire hose, and Jack could think of no way to regain control of the conversation. He and Felicia ex-changed sympathetic looks. Finally, when the wine bottle was empty, he rose.

"Croyd, it's been a pleasure," he said, "but I've got to head back to my hotel and make some transatlantic phone calls."

"I've never made a transatlantic call!" Croyd said. "I wonder who I'd call if I did!"

Jack turned to Felicia. "I'm afraid I've gotten a little turned around," he said. "Could you point me in the direction of my hotel?" He turned back to Croyd. "See you tomorrow, yes?"

"Sure!" Croyd gave his nervous laugh again. "I wouldn't miss it!"

Jack paid the bill, and he and Felicia walked out into the blazing sun. He put on his shades. "Talk about multiple personalities," he said. "Remind me never to give liquor to Croyd again."

"I don't think it was the liquor," Felicia said. "I think it was the pills."

"Was it?" Jack shook his head. "That's a shame."

He and Felicia walked to his hotel, and by the time they arrived Jack's forehead was prickled with sweat. He turned to Felicia. "Would you like to come up?" he said. "We can order a bottle or something from room service if you like."

He always asked the young lady to his room, and the results were surprising enough that he'd stopped making bets with him-self about whether she would accept. He was young looking, attractive, well dressed, and rich, which ticked a lot of boxes. On the other hand he was old enough to be Felicia's grandfather, and sometimes he thought that was creepy and sometimes he didn't. He never pressured anyone to do anything. He'd lived a long time; he knew how to wait.

She looked up at him. "Yeah," she said. "Okay."

The rest of the day passed pleasantly, and after nightfall they went to a restaurant in Trastevere that Felicia recommended. After the meal they walked across the bridge and through narrow, winding streets until they emerged into a small piazza, and suddenly there was an enormous portico before them, granite Corinthian columns rearing up behind a baroque fountain complete with obelisk.

"The Pantheon," Felicia said. "It's huge, but you can't get a good view of it because the streets crowd around it. It really deserves to be out in a field somewhere."

"How old is it?"

Felicia considered the question. "Second century?" she guessed.

"Eighteen, nineteen hundred years," Jack said. He laughed. "I wonder if I'll live that long." He took a breath of diesel-scented air. "No reason I shouldn't, I suppose."

Felicia gave him that reappraising look. "That's kind of heavy," she said.

He looked at her. "I don't think I've changed much since the first Wild Card Day. I feel like the same person. I've *learned* a few things—to stay the hell away from politics, and that fame isn't worth a bucket of warm spit, and that I shouldn't ever love anybody—but other than that I'm the same guy."

"That sounds like a different person to me," she said. "A complete reordering of priorities, right?" Her brows came together. "You shouldn't love anybody?"

"They'll die. I won't. That seems unfair, don't you think?"

And besides, Jack thought, they'll take all your money in the divorce, and make you start all over. And how many times could you start over, even in a life that might last centuries?

How many times could he play Tarzan? Three seasons was enough.

Felicia frowned behind her glasses. "That's . . . I dunno," she said. "Aren't you just sort of . . . *grazing*? Sampling things, but without committing to anything?"

"Don't you know my history?" he said. "This way, it's better for all concerned."

Jack was halfway through his *Memories of Steuben* panel, listening on his headphones while Felicia translated the tendentious thesis of an Italian film critic, when Croyd burst through the doors at the top of the hall and charged into the room.

"Jack! Jack! Guys with guns! There's an attack!"

Jack just stared at him for a moment, then pulled off one of his earphones to hear better.

"They're attacking the Congress of Wonders!" Croyd said.

"Uh . . . pardon me?" Jack said into his microphone, then dropped his headset and stood. Croyd was jumping up and down in the aisle, pointing in the direction of the presumed attack. Jack watched the frantic performance and wondered if it, and the supposed attack, had both originated in Croyd's bottle of pills.

Then more people burst through the doors at the top of the hall. There was some screaming and some shouted Italian. If it was a hallucination, then it was a mass hallucination.

Jack hopped off the stage and walked quickly to where Croyd was hopping up and down. Croyd grabbed his arm. "Hurry!" he said. "Lots of guns!"

"Okay," Jack said, and allowed himself to be pulled into the crowd of people fleeing into the auditorium. He took the lead and shouldered his way through the refugees.

"They started by firing a machine gun into the ceiling," Croyd said. "I thought about tackling them myself, but then I realized that I'm not immune to gunfire, and you are." He gave a chattering laugh, and Jack knew he was still cranked.

"How many gunmen are there?" Jack asked.

"Whoops." A backpack had slipped off of Croyd's shoulder and hit the floor. He bent and picked it up. "Of course, I *might* be bulletproof," he said, and gave another nervous laugh. "It's possible! But it's a hard power to test for. I only know that when I stick myself with a needle, it hurts!"

The corridors were nearly empty—everyone who could flee had gone. That made certain choices easier. Jack could jump into the action without having to worry whether bullets bouncing off his golden shield might drop bystanders.

Unless the gunmen had taken hostages. Hostages would complicate matters.

"What are they after?" Jack asked.

"Some of that old-timey jewelry," Croyd said.

"So they're not terrorists, they're thieves?"

"I guess."

"Thieves are easier."

They turned and trotted down the corridor leading to the Congress of Wonders exhibition. Almost immediately three armed men burst from the exhibit hall, each wearing a ski mask. One tripped over the floor sign proclaiming the WUNDERKAMMER! and went sprawling, losing control of a drawstring bag, which slid across the polished floor. One of the others picked up the drawstring bag, and the third turned to Jack and Croyd and brandished a submachine gun.

"*Long live the queen mother of the Albanians!*" he said in accented English, and then fired a stream of bullets into the ceiling above Jack's head.

Jack hunched into his jacket as bits of wood, plaster, and ceiling tile rained down. Croyd jumped behind Jack to use him for a shield.

The fallen thief picked himself up, and the three dashed for a side door and crashed through it. "Did he say *Albanians*?" Croyd said.

"That's what I heard."

Jack went after the thieves in a purposeful trot. The air smelled of burned propellant, and he nearly slid on spent bullet casings. The door the robbers had taken led to a staircase, and Jack could hear them clattering on the stair below. He followed, and when he heard doors boom open, he accelerated.

Hard bright Roman light came through the doors, and Jack saw the thieves descending a ramp toward the street. A red jeeplike vehicle waited by the curb with its doors open, and the three ran toward it. Jack ran as well—not toward the jeep but in the direction it was pointed, where a number of vehicles were parked nose-in to the curb.

Doors slammed, and the jeep-thing revved its engines and lurched into motion. Jack considered his options and chose a blue Alfa Romeo GTV from among the parked cars. He smashed the driver's-side window, reached in, released the parking brake, and then shoved the GTV into the jeep's way.

He thought he'd given the jeep plenty of room to brake, but the driver's reflexes were slow, and with a shriek of tire rubber and an extended cry of metal, the red vehicle T-boned the Alfa and came to an abrupt halt.

Jack was willing to work with that. He walked through a cloud of bitter-tasting tire smoke, stepped to the side of the jeep-thing, got his hands under the frame, and flipped the vehicle onto its side. Window glass crunched, and there was a lot of alarmed Albanian shouting.

The doors on the upper side of the vehicle crashed open. A man came struggling out with a submachine gun held over his head. Jack jumped up, snatched the gun out of the man's hand on the way up, then on the way down knocked the robber on the head with his own gun and dropped him back into the vehicle.

One of the advantages of being very, very strong was that he could jump very, very high. But a disadvantage was that when he hit people, he had to be careful not to smash their heads to pulp. On the whole, he thought he'd judged it rather nicely.

Another head wrapped in a ski mask popped up out of the rear passenger door, and the robber and Jack regarded each other for a long moment. Jack still held the first robber's gun, and by way of warning crushed it between his hands. Fragments clattered onto the pavement.

"Surrender?" Jack offered. The head disappeared into the vehicle. There was about ten seconds of argument between angry male voices, and then Jack heard banging and the sound of broken glass.

It didn't sound as if anyone was surrendering. Jack contemplated the car for a moment, then flipped it onto its roof.

One of the robbers, the driver, had crawled most of the way out of the shattered front window. Another was partway out the rear. A third was still in the car and yelled at the others to hurry up. The fourth, the man Jack had hit, lay inert on the overturned roof and served as an obstacle to the others.

The engine compartment was in the way of Jack's getting at the driver, so he stepped to the rear of the vehicle, picked a robber up with both hands, and tossed him about five yards into the air. At apogee, the robber and his gun achieved separation and the robber tumbled to a hard landing on the pavement. Jack had been careful not to toss him on his head, but he landed on his right hip with a crack of broken bone and gave a yell, then a groan. Jack was already on his way to the next robber.

The two remaining thieves had both gotten out the front window and were running in opposite directions, one west toward Piazza John Kennedy, the other east. It wasn't obvious which of them had the loot. Jack reached into the back of the jeep-thing and wrenched out the spare tire, then threw it toward the man running east. The tire struck the pavement just behind the running man, then bounded up to hit him between the shoulder blades. He landed on his face, and the tire bounced on, heading into traffic.

Jack heard horns and a crash behind him as he turned toward the last robber and began his pursuit. Running was always difficult, because if he used too much power he'd shoot into the air like a rocket, but he managed to control himself and keep reasonably close to the ground. The robber—this was the driver, the one without a ski mask—cast a look over his shoulder, saw Jack about to overtake him, and swung around with his machine pistol brandished in his fists.

"Whoa," Jack said. He slowed and held up his hands. "I don't think that's the smart thing."

The driver glared at him over his mustache. He was half a head taller than Jack, and his bare forearms were covered with tattoos. Rage had turned his neck muscles to steel cables. Jack kept walking toward him. He tried to make himself as big a target as possible, so that if the man fired, none of the bullets would miss and hit some bystander behind him.

"Put the gun down, man," Jack said. Sirens sang in the air. The man backed up as Jack advanced. Jack kept his hands in the air. Jack saw deadly resolution enter the driver's pale-blue eyes.

"Don't," Jack said, just as the man fired. Jack's golden shield flashed with each bullet and illuminated the driver like a strobe. Jack saw the astonished look in the driver's eyes—a look that had grown familiar over the decades—and knew that one of two things would now happen. Either the man would surrender, or he'd fire again.

Albanians, he surmised, weren't very good at surrender.

"*T'qift dreqi nonen!*" the driver shouted, and let fly with another burst.

Jack reached forward, yanked the gun out of the driver's hands, and hit him in the knee with the weapon. The knee bent at an unnatural angle, and the driver went down.

"*Te hangert dreqi,*" the man spat, as Jack crushed his gun into metal scrap.

"Man, that was great!" Croyd said. He had popped into existence at Jack's elbow. "I saw the whole thing!" He cackled. "I appreciate a real professional. You haven't lost a thing over the years!"

"My Armani's shot to hell," Jack said.

Police cars rocketed down the Viale della Letteratura and bumped over the curb to come to a stop. "Hey, Jack," Croyd said. "I'm kinda allergic to cops. I'll see you later, right?"

He vanished, and as police piled out of vehicles and swarmed over the area, Jack kept his hands visible and tried to look harmless. Police came up to him and shouted at him in Italian, and he responded, "Americano, hombre," which was as close as he ever got to a foreign language. They gestured at him to stay where he was.

A few minutes later Felicia appeared on the scene and made some explanations, and the police told Jack they'd speak to him later. Others were trying to talk to the robbers, who glared at them and growled insults. Jack heard references to Mussolini and the queen mother of the Albanians. Felicia listened carefully, then gave Jack a quizzical look.

"They're patriots," she said. "They say they're here to liberate the jewelry of Queen Mother Sadije, which they say was stolen by Mussolini when he took over Albania. They want to return the jewels to Queen Geraldine, who I guess is the current queen mother."

Jack raised his eyebrows. "Well," he said. "That's one I haven't heard before."

One of the police officers had retrieved the bag of loot and emptied it onto the hood of a police car. Gemstones and silver glittered in the sun. Jack and Felicia peered between the police and looked at the jewelry. "That—that doesn't look royal to me," Jack said.

"I'm guessing it's from the 1950s," said Felicia. "I don't think Queen Mother Sadije would have worn a gold brooch in the shape of a poodle. And that plastic thing that looks like three squares of yellow cheese glued together—? No way that's part of anyone's crown jewels."

"Tell them," Jack said.

Felicia offered the officers her opinion, and opened a rapid-fire barrage of Italian as all the police began talking at once.

"Could they have robbed the wrong vendor?" Jack said. "Are the crown jewels still in the building?"

The vendor herself arrived to identify her jewelry, and she assured everyone that they were well-made, expensive vintage items dating from the 1950s, but that so far as she knew none had ever belonged to the Albanian royal family.

One of the palazzo's own security guards came to join the conversation, and that led to another explosion of Italian. Jack heard the words *"Uomo Modulare"* more than once. He turned to Felicia.

"Someone's stolen the android head," she said.

Jack nodded. "Not the Albanian guys, though."

"Someone else. Taken in the confusion, apparently."

"Really." Jack stroked his jaw as he considered this. *Confusion.* For some reason he seemed less confused than anyone here.

"Felicia," he said. "Could you look over my shoulder and see if Croyd is anywhere behind me?"

She was surprised by the request but complied. "Yeah," she said. "Croyd's hanging out between the office buildings across the street."

"In the open, right? Not under an overhang or anything?"

"No. He's just standing there watching us." She tilted her head and looked up at him. "What's this about?"

"I wonder what's in his backpack," Jack said. "He wasn't carrying a backpack yesterday."

Comprehension dawned across Felicia's features. "Wow," she said. "Should I tell the cops?"

"Let me make a move first," Jack said. "Do you have a cigarette?" She shook her head. "Can you borrow one from the cops?"

Felicia managed this without trouble. Jack thanked her. "If you can tell the police what's going on without causing a big scene," he said, "let them know I'm going to try to apprehend a felon. But in the meantime, I'm going to try to give Croyd a surprise."

"Can I help?"

"Not without putting yourself in front of some over-excitable armed police, so no."

Jack turned away and strolled toward the overturned jeep-thing. He examined it, stuck his head through a shattered window, then tore away the hand brake and the steering wheel. Letting them hang from his left hand, he kept his eyes on the ground as he took a few paces in Croyd's direction. He put the cigarette between his lips and then patted his shredded Armani jacket, apparently finding nothing. He continued the mime as he took another few steps, then looked up and let an expression of surprise cross his face as he saw Croyd. He grinned, took the cigarette out of his mouth, and held it up as if it were an exhibit. He walked rapidly toward Croyd and joined him. Office buildings loomed on either side, but these seemed far more conventional than the striking architecture of the older EUR, and Jack concluded they were built postwar. Nevertheless Jack was grateful they blocked the hot sunlight.

"You wouldn't have a light, would you?" Jack asked.

Croyd offered a jittery laugh. "Sorry, no. Never got around to learning how to smoke."

"You know," Jack said, "back in the war, when I'd been out on a dangerous patrol, or on an alert, or after I'd survived a bombardment, I so looked forward to a smoke. I could taste it the whole time."

"You didn't smoke yesterday."

"I wasn't shot at yesterday." Jack gave a laugh. "I know I can't be hurt, but I never got used to someone pointing a gun at me." He flicked the cigarette to the ground. "Oh, well," he said. "Just my luck."

"Yeah. Well. Sorry."

Jack gave Croyd a curious look. "You never mentioned why you came to Rome. I assume it wasn't just to meet me."

Croyd's rasping nervous laugh sounded like a series of ball bearings dropped on a drumhead. "Oh," he said, "this and that. Business. You know."

Flaming anger shot up Jack's spine. Croyd, he realized, thought he was a complete sucker.

He was within arm's reach. "What you got here?" he asked, and reached for the backpack. Croyd vanished just as Jack's fingers closed on the material. He reappeared about fifty feet away, startling some pedestrians, one of whom dropped a shopping bag that broke open on the pavement.

"Jack," Croyd said. "What the *fuck*?"

Jack began to walk rapidly toward Croyd. "What's in the backpack?"

Croyd waved his arms. *"Why do you care?"*

"Care?" Rage turned Jack's hands into fists. "Care about what's in the backpack? Not much. What pisses me off is that you turned me into your patsy."

Croyd gave a chattering laugh. "I was just trying to keep you busy while I did my job, that's all."

"I spent half my *life* being somebody's patsy. Never again. I'm not going to play the sap for you."

Jack shifted the parking-brake lever to his right hand, judged his distance, and threw it as hard as he could. Croyd vanished before the missile reached him, and there was the sound of breaking glass from the street beyond.

Though the lever had been hurled in fury, Jack hadn't expected it to land. The attack was a test, and Jack was happy with the results.

Jack guessed that Croyd's talent was a short-range teleport. If Croyd could jump longer ranges he'd be gone by now. And he also figured that Croyd had to spot his landing before he jumped, and

he'd been looking at Jack, so he knew Croyd had reappeared behind him. Without hesitation he turned and launched himself at
Croyd, who was only twenty feet away. Croyd's eyes grew wide,
then his glance darted over Jack's shoulder and vanished again.

Jack was happy to do this all day. He spun around again and
headed for where Croyd had reappeared, maybe fifty feet away.

He called down the lane between the buildings. "Who are you
working for?"

Croyd waved his hands. "Falls under the category 'eccentric
millionaire.'" As Jack came forward Croyd backed up at a kind of
trot.

"If he's got money, why didn't he just buy the head?"

"Lionel Terhune won't sell!" Croyd said. "Terhune's in the ac-
quisition stage of being a billionaire, he's not interested in relin-
quishing his possessions right now. He's gonna build a museum
or some shit."

Jack scooped up a city trash can with his right hand—it had a
gold badge with the image of a she-wolf and the letters SPQR—and
he hurled it overarm for Croyd's head. Garbage trailed behind it
like a comet's tail. Croyd saw it coming, glanced over his shoulder,
and popped across the street into a long, narrow green space that
served as a lane divider on the Viale della Civiltà Romana. Jack
heard screams and the sound of brakes as the trash can smashed
its way across the road, but he paid no attention and kept his focus
on Croyd.

Anger simmered in Jack's blood. He crossed the road into the
green strip with its small trees and its bushes trimmed into button
shapes. "Your guy knows Albanian monarchist terrorists," he
called.

"The Albanians were supposed to do the entire heist. Then the
boss heard you were going to be here and thought he needed more
firepower, and I, ah, became available right then." Croyd cackled.
"It all came together, man!"

Keeping an eye on Jack, Croyd was backing across the eastbound lane of the Viale della Civiltà Romana. Behind him was a long office building, brown and beige instead of the blinding white seen elsewhere in the EUR. The building had a garden reaching out to the sidewalk, protected by a metal fence with steel pickets, and when Jack crossed the road he reached for the pickets and tore a pair free. He put one in his left hand to join the jeep-thing's steering wheel, and hefted the other in his right like a spear. He could see Croyd's head swiveling to spot his next jump.

"Let's see what else we can bring together," Jack said, and threw the picket. Croyd vanished, but Jack had seen him spot his landing, on the roof of the long brown building, and he whipped the second steel picket backhand to where he guessed Croyd would appear. The picket made sawing noises as it spun through the air, and Jack saw Croyd's silhouette on the roof standing just above where the picket struck the parapet. There was a deep resounding crash and the parapet disintegrated into flying fragments mixed with shards of steel. The silhouette flopped out of sight.

"*Oww! Jesus Christ!*"

Jack gave a triumphant laugh. *Make me a patsy, will you?* He bounded over the steel fence and jumped as high up the building as he could, which turned out to be three stories. He clamped his fists on a window frame, then pulled himself up the fourth story, smashing window glass and hoisting himself upward.

People inside the building stared at him. Many of them seemed to be wearing naval uniforms, and he wondered if he was climbing the exterior of the Naval Ministry or something.

He heard sirens approaching. Apparently Felicia had alerted the police to what was happening—or maybe the bystanders had.

When Jack gained the roof he saw Croyd limping away. *Lovely,* Jack thought. In his sights.

"What are you trying to do, man?" Croyd complained. "Kill me?"

"You could always surrender," Jack offered.

"Can't do that. Too many people want me."

"Then drop the backpack."

Croyd had come to the far parapet of the roof, and Jack could see he was scanning for a landing again. Jack threw the steering wheel backhand, like a Frisbee, and it hit Croyd in the back. Jack heard a crunch, which was possibly the Modular Man head breaking, and Croyd yelled "*Oww!*" again and pitched forward off the roof.

"Nuts," Jack muttered. He hadn't exactly intended to throw Croyd four stories to the ground; he'd just hoped to lay him out on the roof. He ran to the parapet and looked down.

No Croyd. Apparently he'd made a jump to safety from midair.

He made a diligent search for Croyd in the urban landscape below but failed to find him. People in naval uniforms had come dashing out of the building, and a few carried firearms. Police cars whirled along the streets. Jack sighed. It was time to face the music.

He raised his arms, jumped the four stories, and landed in a burst of golden light that dazzled his onlookers. Keeping his hands visible, he approached the navy men, who shouted at him in Italian.

"Americano, hombre," he said. "*Comprende* Croyd?"

It was a long afternoon. Felicia turned up to translate; otherwise he might have spent the night in jail. Turns out that he had vandalized the headquarters of the Italian Coast Guard. The auto wheel that he'd thrown at one of the Albanians had bounded into traffic and caused a car to sideswipe a bus. The hand-brake lever had smashed someone's rear window.

Nobody complained about the trash cans. Apparently Romans were used to having their trash containers disappear.

The owner of the Alfa Romeo GTV turned up screaming. "Why my car? Why mine?" he bellowed. "Why not destroy the Fiat Panda? It was sitting right there! No one would have missed it!"

"Somebody who owns a car as beat up as that Fiat," Jack said, "might not be able to afford to replace it. But anyone who can pay for a GTV can afford good insurance."

This upset the GTV's owner even more, but Jack's reasoning

seemed to earn a degree of affection from the police, who'd prob-ably had more than their share of grief from citizens who could afford GTVs. One cop offered him a cigarette, and he took it.

It was the first cigarette he'd had since he played Tarzan, when he was urged to quit as an example for the kiddies.

It was early evening before the police let Jack go, and then he had to deal with a mob of reporters who wanted his story. Fortu-nately he'd learned a few things about public relations in the last few decades.

"My memories of Rome and its people from 1944 are very strong," he said, "and I came here to renew my acquaintance of your beautiful city and meet some old friends, but then the con-vention center was attacked. I became mixed up in the action, and I chased down the perpetrators, and all but one are now in cus-tody. The police can tell you the rest. I'm going to bed."

He barged a way through the reporters, Felicia following in his wake, then found a cab that took them away.

Jack stayed in his hotel room only long enough to shower and change out of his ruined clothes, after which he and Felicia en-joyed a late supper at a restaurant in Pietralata, with a view of barges and pleasure craft going up and down the long curve of the river. The scent of tobacco warred with the aroma of rich sauces. Prosciutti hung from the ceiling and swayed gently in the night breezes, and when Jack ordered a martini, he found a piece of Parma ham perched on the edge of the glass. After a couple of drinks, a selection of cured meats, and some buffalo mozzarella, Jack began to feel the day's hard edge begin to dissolve.

"I suppose the Amex Black Card will have to put things to rights," Jack said. "I'll repair all the damage, except for what hap-pened to the Alfa. That jerk's on his own."

Felicia gazed at him from behind her glasses. "Is today typical for you? Does this sort of thing happen all the time?"

"This is what happens when I stop *grazing*," he said. "A whole lot of breakage." He shook his head. "I'm relieved that no one but the robbers got hurt. I'm glad *you* didn't get hurt."

She sipped her Kir Royale. "You took care of them so quickly. I ran out of the palazzo and everything was already over."

"I wanted to knock them out before they started shooting." He regarded her. "What shall we do after supper?"

She smiled. "Graze?" she said.

He raised his martini. "Here's to grazing." He drained the glass and signaled for another. "I've got to take the edge off," he said. "Croyd got me so angry."

"I got that impression. I don't blame you, though." She waved a hand. "He hung out with us just to make it easier to steal."

Jack sighed and looked down at his plate. *Isinglass,* he thought. *LS/MFT. In like Flynn.* He should have gotten out his decoder ring to find out what was going on.

"Hell," he said, "I thought I'd made a friend."

Swimmer, Flier, Felon, Spy

Tesla's resources, as vast as they were, were not infinite. Sometimes he needed information to which he did not have immediate access. Usually, as now, this was when he *intuited* something. Intuition did not make Tesla comfortable.

But as he had met the various Croyds and the people whose lives had intersected with his—theirs?—down the decades, something had started nagging at him. Something about the plan to reunite them—in more senses of the word than one—that suggested he was overlooking something very important.

During the year or so he had spent intensively studying psychology, Tesla had read a great deal about multiple personality disorder, and the delicate and sometimes dangerous process of treating it. Now he found himself involved with such a situation, lacking expertise and—more disconcertingly—lacking *information*.

In his various incarnations, Croyd Crenson had, at certain times, possessed the potential to harm himself and others. This wasn't new information. Many aces and jokers had tremendous powers that might threaten entire cities. New York itself had been under such threat many times before.

But now something altogether new had happened. This angry and unhappy man had fractured, and the angry and unhappy men that resulted might together do something that so far Crenson had never done. He might take the lives of thousands of people, should the process of reintegrating these disparate personalities go badly.

And Tesla knew nothing about how the wild card virus interacted with multiple personalities.

The people who treated the maladies of wild cards—both mental and physical—were notoriously closemouthed about their methods and the data they collected. Medical case files on individual wild card patients were kept even more confidential than those of nats, protected by not just HIPAA but also loyalty and, frequently, camaraderie.

If there was anyplace he might find information to help him understand and prepare for what he hoped was the imminent meeting of the Croyds, it would be in the records of the Jokertown clinic, which had stood for over half a century as a street clinic, an emergency ward, a cutting-edge research hospital, and a psychiatric facility. It was one of the few places Tesla had never had success in data mining.

He thought carefully about who might be able to tell him something—anything—about jokers or aces with psyches or even bodies that were at one and at war. He knew of one. He just had to find her. And her location, he was confident, would be available to anyone who had a legitimate reason to search the files of the Jokertown clinic.

Tesla picked up the phone in his hotel room.

"Yes, sir?"

"I need to be an epidemiologist specializing in community psychological effects of the wild card virus with a long-scheduled appointment to examine the records of the clinic in Jokertown."

"Yes, sir."

What followed was a simple act of espionage. What resulted was a name—the name of a woman who was perhaps unique in all the world in knowing what it was to be more than one ace at a time, though now she was a lonely nat, living quietly on her own. Her name was Patty.

Party Like It's 1999

by Stephen Leigh

December 31, 1999

Oddity glanced into the "spare bedroom" of Oddity's lair, set in the labyrinthian tunnels under the Bowery. During Prohibition, the tunnels had been used to run liquor to various illegal speakeasies. The speakeasies were long gone, abandoned or repurposed, but the tunnels remained underneath the streets, if you knew where to look for the hidden entrances.

Wrapped in a cocoon of blankets against the cold, Croyd was there now on New Year's Eve, asleep and oblivious to the fact that, above them, most of New York prepared to welcome the turn of the century. He'd been there for three months now; Father Squid had asked them to take in Croyd as his church was still under construction after the fire. Patty shook her head and shut the door behind her.

The lair was cold in winter—too much space for them to heat it all evenly—though for a New Year's Eve, the weather was fairly temperate: clear, with a high that day of forty-three, though the temperature was dropping slowly, now down into the upper thirties. Patty was still wearing Oddity's oversized, hooded cloak, masking their piebald and ever-shifting body where muscles and tendons and bones migrated randomly, the pain of their movement something that Dominant always had to endure, making Oddity whimper, groan, or shout without warning.

It would be Patty's turn to be Passive next in the rotation. *Tomorrow,* she thought privately. *What better way to start the new century?*

Patty sighed again as she entered their lair's main room. The warmth there was a small relief, but not enough that she shed the cloak. She caught of glimpse of Oddity's face in the glass of a framed picture as she entered. Oddity's reflection in the glass was a horror-show rendition of a human face: over-large, twisted and distorted, with portions of all three of their features and pigmentations—Patty's pale British Isles coloration against John's more Mediterranean cast, and traces of Evan's dark skin (because he was Passive at the moment and largely submerged into Oddity) here and there. One eye was Patty's, the other John's, and the lower lip definitely Evan's, though their features continued shifting restlessly, disturbingly, and agonizingly.

She sat on the couch. Today's edition of the *Jokertown Cry* was there on the coffee table in front of her, a banner headline just below the fold blaring:

MILLENNIUM BUG TO CRASH SYSTEMS?

And underneath, in smaller letters: **Have the fixes worked? We'll know at midnight.**

Patty picked up the remote alongside the newspaper and turned on the television; *ABC 2000 Today* with Peter Jennings appeared, Times Square and its new ball of Waterford Crystal in the windows behind him. Jennings was speaking to Lisa Stark regarding airline traffic as midnight arrived in Cairo; Lisa told him that everything around the world was running smoothly with no indications of any Y2K issue rearing its head. Patty closed

Oddity's eyes and tried to rest as well as they could as the commentary droned on.

She must have succeeded, since she was woken by the TV inexplicably going silent and alarms shrilling throughout the lair. Oddity's eyes opened to darkness. "What the hell . . ." Patty said aloud.

[Check the electric panel in the kitchen,] she heard John say from Sub-Dominant. [Something's tripped the circuit breakers.]

Oddity pushed off the couch, feeling their way out of the main room and down the hall toward the kitchen. As they approached the kitchen, they heard a crackling like wet wood in a fireplace. A flickering of blue light accompanied the noise. They smelled acrid smoke; something electrical was on fire in there. "Shit," Patty/Oddity said, afraid that something was massively wrong, though she had a strong suspicion she knew the source of the mayhem: a trail of Croyd's blankets carpeted the hallway, leading from the back room where he'd been sleeping.

The kitchen's fire extinguisher was on the far wall; she wondered whether they were going to be able to easily reach it. Oddity peered into the fitful gloom of the kitchen. They saw movement near the fuse box; in the next flare of sparks, Oddity saw Croyd clearly—but not the Croyd who'd come to them three months ago as what looked like someone who'd been dipped in glue, then had rolled in prickly pine needles. This new version of Croyd was topped with a small, hypermobile head that appeared to be able to turn nearly 180 degrees in either direction, attached to a spindly humanoid body with thin arms and legs but massive thighs, like those of a human-sized grasshopper—a grasshopper that looked as if it'd been built of steel. His head and naked body gleamed, as if Croyd had been plated with polished stainless silverware. If he had genitalia, they weren't currently visible. His eyes were large and black, like a shark's.

Croyd's arms were inside the fuse box, his hands tearing at the guts behind the panel without any apparent fear of the electricity it held. The main electrical line had been pulled out and disconnected; Croyd fed the sparking, frayed ends of the cable into his mouth as electric flares and sparks fell in a bright rain, dancing across the tiled floor. Croyd sucked in fountaining sparks like a parched man drinking from a spewing garden hose.

[That's it! We never let Croyd back here again!] John shouted in their head.

"Croyd!" Patty called out and the creature's head rotated impossibly, staring at Oddity with those bulbous eyes speckled with emerald against midnight black. Hair-fine spines lifted on his head, twitching and sparking. "Croyd, what are you doing?"

Then Croyd crouched on his massive legs—Patty was certain it *was* Croyd, one of the blankets from his bed was still snagged around an ankle—and bounded away at jaw-dropping speed, leaving the blanket behind and eluding Oddity's grasp as they tried to grab or at least block Croyd to keep him in the kitchen. Claw-tipped feet like those of a large dog slid and clattered on the tiles as Croyd half ran, half leapt into the hall. Oddity pursued, following the sound of items crashing and breaking. "Croyd, dammit! Stop this!"

Croyd was in their main room, racing around at terrifying speed and knocking over everything in his path. Whenever Croyd's legs, hands, or body touched metal, sparks showered from the point of contact, guttering to the floor. The TV had fallen from its stand to the carpet, the shattered screen littering the rug with glass shards; the fencing mask that Patty had placed atop the TV rolled into a corner with what looked like streaks of smoke on the steel mesh. Small fires were alight around the room. "Croyd! Please stop this!"

Croyd gave no answer. Probably, Patty realized, he *could* give no answer, given his current form. After all, she wouldn't expect a creature who drank electricity to be able to speak English. Croyd tore across the room one more time, rebounding off the walls, and headed for Oddity in the doorway. Oddity braced for the impact, arms out, but at the last moment Croyd bounded onto the recliner in front of the toppled TV and jumped. Oddity/Patty made a belated adjustment, but Croyd was faster. He catapulted over Oddity's head and past them, the claws on his feet (and on his hands as well, she noticed) scraping against the tiles. As Oddity turned, they heard a metallic crash, accompanied by a wild showering of sparks as Croyd slammed hard into the steel front door of the lair. Dead bolts slammed back into their mechanisms as circuits shorted; the door swung open and Croyd was out and through into the dark tunnels beyond.

"Croyd!" Patty/Oddity shouted again, starting to pursue him when she heard John's voice in their head.

[Fuck him, Patty. You need to take care of the fires here first.]

[John . . .] Patty began, but he didn't allow her protest to continue.

[Look, you're tired and hurting. I'll take care of things. Let me take over Oddity.]

[No,] Patty told him, knowing John would just let Croyd go if he was Dominant, not caring what that might mean for anyone else. But John was right: They needed to at least put out the fires first. [I'm fine. You stay in Sub-Dom for now. On open ground, Croyd's moving too fast for us to catch him, anyway.]

[We need to take care of our own problems before you worry about goddamn Croyd,] John told her.

And, from Evan, [. . . stop it both of you no more arguing or I'll take Dom myself . . .]

Patty/Oddity gave a sigh that was nearly a groan.

[The virus gave us what we thought we wanted,] she told him, told John. [We're about to start a new century that way.]

[Yeah,] John answered, his voice flat and burdened with self-loathing sarcasm. [Happy fucking New Year to us. Welcome to the goddamn twenty-first century. Whoopee. Pour us some champagne, Patty, why don't you?]

Asshole, she thought, though she said nothing that either of the other two could hear. [. . . we can never be alone and never without the agony never never never . . .] Evan whispered from deep down in Passive.

Patty had no answer to that. Oddity hurried back into the lair, going into the kitchen and snatching up the fire extinguisher. They pulled out the locking pin for the trigger, tossed it aside, and began to spray the fires with the foam.

It was a good hour later before Oddity extinguished the fires that Croyd had accidentally caused, made sure all the ashes were cold, and left the lair. The lair was still a sodden, soot-laden mess. Patty had allowed Evan—who had experience with electrical work—to take over control of Oddity long enough to reconnect the main electrical line to the fuse box and reset everything and restore power to the lair. With Evan back in Passive to rest again, they'd turned on the battery-powered police radio that Harvey Kant in Fort Freak had given them, listening to the police calls as they worked.

There were reports of power outages nearby in Jokertown: blocks going dark as power relay stations around Jokertown failed. A few news stations were speculating that these incidents might be symptomatic of the millennium bug that various pundits had been discussing for the last year—the possibility that the switch from 1999 to 2000 would result in cascading breakdowns of computer-controlled systems like the power grid. The Fort Freak police station itself was currently under generator power only, undoubtedly causing chaos in patrolling Jokertown on this night of all nights.

[We can't ever bring Croyd here again, Patty,] John complained from Sub-Dominant. [It was obviously a mistake this time. Evan should never had told Father Squid we'd do it.]

[. . . sorry I'm sorry I didn't expect it would be a problem . . .]

[Croyd's usually at his best when he first wakes up,] Patty reminded them. [It's usually later in his cycle that he gets belligerent and dangerous, when he's fighting sleep and taking drugs. This isn't his usual pattern. Not at all.]

[But we all know Croyd can be dangerous. You can't argue about that, Patty.]

Down in Passive, Evan stirred, wisps of his thoughts rising like fog in their fused consciousness. [. . . at least Croyd has a new shot at life every time he sleeps not like us we're trapped here in this horror of a body with no way out no way out ever . . .]

That was a sentiment that Patty had also heard John voice occasionally. It troubled her, though she understood the attitude. Intimately. Oddity's ever-shifting body caused immense pain to the person who was Dominant within Oddity and controlling the body. The Sub-Dominant personality was somewhat sheltered from the pain; very little of Oddity's torture came to the person who was Passive—which was why the three of them rotated, so that none of them were Dominant for too long.

The three of them were locked forever in a torture room too small for them, in which their body parts were constantly and painfully shifting and merging.

It wasn't a situation conducive to fostering affection. They had loved one another deeply and sincerely once, but that love was tattered and worn after decades inside Oddity.

Patty wasn't sure that what any of them felt now was "love" for the others. She missed that, often.

Jokertown (given that crowds of jokers were decidedly not welcome in downtown NYC) had put together its own "Millennial" festivities for the turn of the century—though Evan always mentioned that, for some, the twenty-first century didn't actually begin until *next* year, with 2001. The Jokertown festivities were taking place in Sara D. Roosevelt Park, with the centerpiece being Jokertown's own "ball drop"—though their "ball" was actually a sculpture created by Evan over the last several months whenever he was in control of Oddity: a two-story-tall steel-and-copper image of a fanciful Ouroboros. The ancient symbol of a dragon eating its own tail signified infinity and the cycle of birth and death. The passage from 1999 to 2000 would be signified at the moment the dragon's mouth closed on its own tail and touched off a large fireworks display.

Oddity re-locked the door of the lair, moving through the maze of tunnels until they reached the hidden stairs on Pell Street near Bowery. Oddity walked down Pell to Bowery before turning left and heading uptown toward Roosevelt Park. The streets were crowded with joker revelers with a smattering of nats mixed in, though it was difficult to tell one from the other since the majority of revelers were masked. It had been four or five decades since mask-wearing in Jokertown had been the fashion, but masks had become fashionable once again as the world approached the turn of the century.

Many of the revelers were openly drinking with several of them already intoxicated, talking too loudly and wandering all over the sidewalks or out into the streets. There, traffic was hopelessly snarled due to many of the traffic lights being out. Nat or joker, though, most were careful to stay well away from Oddity in their cloak and fencing mask, allowing Oddity to move in their own clear space. If someone did happen to jostle them, they quickly apologized and moved on.

More than once in the long walk, Patty was tempted to take John's offer to take control of Oddity, as tendons, muscles, and bone migrated inside them. Oddity moaned, whimpered, and wailed as their body shifted and stabbed at them from the inside. People stared as they passed, with whispered comments.

[You don't have to be a goddamn martyr, Patty. Let me have Oddity. Evan's been down in Passive for a few days now. Go on. Trade places with him.]

[No. We need to find Croyd.] *Because you'd just leave him out there and who knows what would happen then.* She didn't say the words. Couldn't say them, knowing it would just start another internal shouting match.

Three blocks on, Oddity reached the corner of Hester and Bowery, where Jube's newsstand sat. The lights were out there: All the buildings around them were dark, the streetlamps were stubbornly dark, and the traffic lights weren't working. None of the cars packing Bowery and Hester were going anywhere soon, though that didn't stop the drivers from punctuating the night with the blaring of angry horns.

Jube had placed a battery-powered lantern on the shelf of his newsstand, casting a warm yellow light over the piles of newspapers and magazines and revealing his walrus-like body behind the counter, attired as always with his porkpie hat and garish Hawaiian shirt. They'd known Jube since May 1974. That was when the three of them had been infected with the wild card virus while sleeping together, to wake the next morning as Oddity. Over the decades, as the people they knew and Jokertown itself aged and altered, vanished or died, Jube never seemed to change at all. His breath smelled eternally of buttered popcorn.

"Happy New Year," Jube called out loudly to Oddity as they approached, his deep voice competing admirably with the car horns. "At least, let's hope so, if they ever get the electricity fixed. Patty?" he ventured. "You in charge of Oddity tonight?"

"For the time being," she answered. "Good guess, by the way."

Jube nodded. "Hey, you know what I just learned?" He grinned at them and Patty sighed.

"No, Jube," she said resignedly. Knowing Jube, she also knew he wanted the standard setup line. "What did you just learn?"

"Did you know that boomerangs are Australia's biggest export—people are just throwing them away."

Patty managed a groan at that, helped by ribs clashing under the cloak, but Jube was still grinning.

"And you know what else?" he said. "Boomerangs are also Australia's biggest import. When you throw them away, they just come back. Get it?"

This time, the groan was louder. "Keep trying, Jube. One day you'll find your comic timing."

Jube chuckled, and the odor of popcorn and butter wafted through the mesh of the fencing mask. "Need a copy of the latest *Cry*?" he asked. "It'll give you the schedule of events for tonight. There's some new music group calling themselves the Jokertown Boys playing soon—gotta say I hate that name, though at least the musicians actually *are* jokers. I'm told they're just kids barely out of high school, since Jokertown can't afford an actual name act—but word is that they're decent enough."

"Don't need a schedule right now, thanks." Oddity glanced up Bowery and to the right where it appeared that Roosevelt Park at least still had power, the streetlamps revealing packed crowds moving slowly north toward the booths, the main performance stage, and the looming curves of Evan's sculpture of Ouroboros visible over the top of tree branches, the snake's red eyes glowing. "I understand power's gone out in several places."

"That's what I hear from the radio." Jube pointed to an ancient transistor radio on a rear shelf. "Officer Long and his new partner—a nice young woman by the name of Yakami Smythe—stopped by maybe fifteen minutes ago on their way to patrol the park and said the same. The first blackout I heard about was down by Bowery and Division; then over around Elizabeth Street and Fort Freak. The last ones have been up this way—we lost power maybe five minutes ago, which is why all those idiots are honking their horns. Maybe that thing people were worried about is actually happening and none of the computer systems will be working after midnight, eh? Making the 'year' field two digits rather than four was a lousy choice from the start." Jube leaned over toward Oddity, his voice lowering slightly. "I'm also hearing reports of people being injured by some strange fast-moving, metallic joker in conjunction with these outages." Jube stroked a tusk as he glanced at Oddity. "That might be something you could handle."

[Croyd,] John declared firmly from Sub-Dominant. [The son of a bitch.] Patty had no doubt John was right. Given what they'd seen in the lair's kitchen, the outages were likely caused by Croyd feeding on electric power supplies. She was thankful that the fencing mask meant Jube couldn't see any expressions in Oddity's ever-shifting face, not that they'd have been easy to read in any case.

"I'll keep an eye out for that joker," Patty said. "Don't want anyone getting hurt, especially tonight."

"Ah," Jube commented, still stroking a tusk thoughtfully. "That's good. You take care of lots of things around here that the authorities don't or won't." Jube shrugged. "We need you in Jokertown. We're grateful you're here."

Inside, John snorted disdain. [Like we have any choice. It's that, taking the Black Trump virus, or suicide.]

Shut up, John . . . Again, Patty didn't say the words. The Black Trump virus, otherwise known as Xenovirus *Takis-B*, had been created as a potential cure for the wild card virus, though its success rate was low: just below 25 percent, and it was actually more likely to outright kill the patient than cure them. All three of them were well aware of that. "Thanks," Patty answered. "A Happy New Year to you, Jube."

"Yeah. We have a whole new century to explore starting later tonight."

[Not until next year,] John interjected sourly. [Evan's lectured us about that a few thousand times.]

[Just shut the fuck up, John. No need to be more of a pain in the ass than you are already,] Patty said, then to Jube through Oddity: "Hope it'll be a great one for all of us."

Oddity left Jube's stand and continued striding up Bowery. Half a block on, most of the streetlamps were alight. They could see the glare of stage lighting near the main stage at the north end of the soccer field, still a few blocks away. The PA system there was blaring Prince's 1982 hit song "1999." The streets flanking the park, Chrystie and Forsyth, had been blocked off to vehicular traffic, causing further traffic jams in the surrounding area. Oddity walked up Bowery toward the Dime Museum along with the growing crowd of pedestrians.

Their internal conversation was louder than the noise and clamor surrounding them.

[This is totally useless, Patty,] John insisted. [Frankly, I don't give a fuck where Croyd's gone or if he cuts the power for the whole damn city and electrocutes himself in the process. We're not his goddamn babysitters. Like the song says, the party's over.]

[What happened to you, John?] Patty answered wearily. [You used to care about other people, and especially those who are jokers. Where have your empathy and your compassion gone?]

[Burned away by almost thirty years in this body. Where's *their* compassion for *us,* eh? When do *we* get a break? Tell me that. The cops hate us. They call us a "vigilante" and worse. They arrest us whenever they get half a reason and sometimes when they don't even have that. Then we gotta call Pretorius to get us out again.]

[Are the cops entirely wrong?] Patty retorted.

[What do you mean? I know who you mean and that's an old, hoary argument.]

Patty/Oddity sighed audibly. From Passive, Evan's voice rose before Patty could answer. [. . . we've argued this a million times already let it go it's all ancient history and no one cares no one cares at all . . .]

[*Enough!*] Patty shouted to both of them. [I'm sorry I brought it up. I just . . .] She stopped herself there. [We made it our job to protect the jokers, so let's do that. If we can find poor Croyd, at least something good might come of tonight. That's all I care about.]

They continued walking, Patty ignoring John's continuing angry objections. *I love John, but I really don't like him when he's this way. But there's no way for me to leave the room or shut out his voice. Or for him or Evan to do the same when I'm bothering them.* She worried what that might mean, if not now, in a year or five or more. *How long before we all go mad inside Oddity and whoever's Dominant takes the Black Trump virus or resorts to pills or a gun?*

Patty forced the thought away.

Ahead, they could see the Dime Museum, adorned with banners painted in bright primary colors and illuminated by flood lamps; Patty nodded and quickened their pace. The lights meant Croyd had not visited this block yet, which meant that maybe they could find him nearby. Charles Dutton, the skull-faced and skeletal proprietor of the museum, was standing out front as one of his employees—his neck and torso unusually large and a mouth funneled like a cheerleader's cone—was calling out in booming, carnie-barker voice to the increasingly thick crowds moving toward Roosevelt Park.

"Come in, one and all; admission's a mere two dollars and fifty cents. You still have time before midnight to see everything. Come in, come in! View the wonders of Jokertown spread out before you in fantastic, realistic dioramas. See Earth battling the terrifying Swarm. Marvel at four authentic shells from the famous Turtle. Gasp at Jetboy dangling above the city as he attempts to stop the criminal mastermind Dr. Tod from releasing the wild card virus over New York . . ."

Dutton nudged the barker with a bony elbow and pointed to Oddity as his gaze rested on them, standing a head above most of the others on the street in their fencing mask and black cloak. The barker joker responded, "And here's an extra treat: Oddity, whose talented hands have sculpted many of the wax figures you'll find inside. Come in, come in!"

As the barker continued his pitch, Dutton waved in those wanting to enter. "Evan?" Dutton asked in a voice that was more a rasp as Oddity approached.

"Patty. Sorry, Charles. Evan's resting in Passive, but he says to tell you he'll stop by as soon as he's Dominant again. He has some new ideas for the Church of Jesus Christ, Joker, fire diorama."

"Excellent," Dutton replied. "Tell Evan I'll look forward to that."

The barker continued to exhort those passing by, most of whom were staring at Oddity as if they were a walking exhibit.

"Can we ask a favor, Charles? Do you mind if we go through the museum's back halls and out the rear entrance to avoid the crowds? We're going to the park. Oh, and have your staff prepared for the electricity to go out. Maybe soon."

Dutton's yellowed, stiff skin folded above the sockets of his eyes. "Oh?"

"It's Croyd, but let's just keep that between us," Patty told him. Against the din of the barker, she quickly told him of Croyd waking, his new appearance, and his apparent appetite for electric power. "If you see him, don't even bother to try to stop him; he's awfully damn fast in this incarnation, dangerous if he touches metal, and I'm not certain he can hear or understand anyone talking to him. He's been hitting the power substations and he's heading this way."

Dutton nodded. "I'll have someone on my staff make sure our generator's ready, in case. I hope you find him."

"So do I," Patty said, "before he ends up hurting himself or others."

Sara D. Roosevelt Park was a roiling, restless sea of movement and noise. The rear staff door of the Dime Museum let them out on an alley that, in turn, fed onto closed-off Chrystie Street at Lion's Gate Field. Chrystie was packed solid with pedestrians; there were booths set up on the field displaying everything from artwork to masks to food and drinks. Oddity moved into the crowd; the crowd made way for them, eyes regarding Oddity from behind their masks, either with sympathy (from the jokers—often obvious by their bodies) or with wariness (from the nats).

At least half of the jokers in the park wore no masks at all. After all, here in Jokertown it was also fashionable to flaunt your difference from the normal people unaffected by the wild card virus. There were trash barrels and signs set up around the park: JOKERS! UNMASK AT MIDNIGHT! the signs proclaimed. THROW YOUR MASKS AWAY IN THE NEW CENTURY! SHOW YOUR FACE IN THE 21ST CENTURY!

[Yeah. Like we're going to do that. No one wants to look at our ugly, eternally shifting face. Hell, I can't stand looking at us myself,] John commented.

[. . . not our fault our faces were fine Patty's was so beautiful I still remember it and how we'd be together the three of us . . .]

[Enough!] Patty told them. [Let's worry about Croyd and what he might do.]

[I still say fuck Croyd and let's go home,] John responded. Patty decided to ignore that; John went silent.

Oddity was three long blocks from the main stage on Four Aces Field between Rivington and Stanton, with Evan's sculpture yet another block north at the end of the park near East Houston. Nearby street musicians were competing, and losing, with the great echoing roar from the massive PA system set up for the Jokertown Boys on the main stage. Oddity continued north on Chrystie, figuring that Croyd might be attracted by the glare of lights at the main stage as well as the overwhelming decibels.

"Oddity?" The call was accompanied by a faint salty scent.

The query came from a booth along Chrystie, with a banner stating CHURCH REBUILDING AND MAINTENANCE FUND: OLPM duct-taped above it—*OLPM:* Our Lady of Perpetual Misery, also known as the Church of Jesus Christ, Joker. Father Squid slid out from behind the booth. Oddity moaned as Patty brought their body to a halt. "Father," Patty said. "How's the collection going?"

The tentacles that made up the priest's nose wriggled like Medusa's hair as he shrugged. His hands spread wide, revealing webbing between the fingers and palms studded with small round suckers. "Rather slower than I'd like, I'm sorry to say. But I wanted to thank you for the very generous contribution you made to our fund. That has helped enormously."

Father Squid held out his hand. Patty took the priest's hand, pressing the flesh carefully. Softly. "It was our pleasure for all you've done for Jokertown and those like us."

[Bullshit!] John growled. [You're just trying to assuage guilt with money, Patty. And how did we get that money? It's not like anyone pays us a salary. No, we just take it from the criminal element here in Jokertown. Steal it from those who stole from others. We've hurt lots of people over the decades, deliberately or accidentally, but hell, we've done good, too. Saved joker lives even if we had to resort to violence at times. That's what we had to do, and as far as I'm concerned we fucking don't have any reason to apologize. Remember that.]

Patty didn't answer John. She released Father Squid's hand. "We'll add more to the fund when we get a chance," she told him. Under the tentacles, Father Squid smiled and the scent of a salt sea grew stronger.

"Bless you," he said. "All three of you." He glanced over toward the church's booth. "And I'd better get back . . ."

He stopped as a pop in the air intruded and a figure appeared alongside the priest: Quasiman, or at least most of him; his left arm was missing. As Oddity looked at Quasi, his right forearm also vanished.

A few heartbeats later, both returned, and Quasi clutched at the priest's cassock with his right hand, pulling at him. The hunchback with the deformed and twisted limbs was also the handyman at Father Squid's church, and the priest's sometimes protector as well. It was Quasi who had pulled the priest from the arsonist's fire that had destroyed the original church. "Father," Quasi said, his voice slow but clear and insistent, "we need to go. Now."

"Why? What's wrong?" the priest asked. "Is something going to happen?"

"We have to go," Quasi repeated.

"Why?" Father Squid asked again. "I'm talking to Oddity. What's so urgent?"

Quasiman's tight grip on the sleeve of Father Squid's cassock released as his entire right arm vanished as if taken by a cosmic eraser. "Darkness," Quasiman said slowly. "Panic. People running. Sparks and fire."

[Darkness? Is Quasi talking about Croyd taking out the electric?] Patty wondered.

[That's my bet,] John answered. [The lights going out in the park could easily cause panic. Look what it's done to street traffic around Jokertown.]

[. . . Quasi is a precog he can glimpse the future we know Croyd was heading this way . . .] Evan agreed.

Father Squid was staring at his rumpled sleeve. "Father," Patty told him. "Maybe you should listen to Quasi. We can talk some other time."

Father Squid looked at Oddity quizzically, then shrugged, glancing around the park as if searching for what had triggered Quasiman's sudden fear. "All right, Quasi. Let me get the donation box and we'll head back to the rectory. Oddity, thank you all again. Happy New Year to you."

Patty watched them go. A roar of applause and approval came from the area of the main stage. Oddity heard the sound of a pop band and saccharine vocal harmonies—the Jokertown Boys, Patty presumed—over the PA system. They turned that way and began walking, more quickly now.

The noise level and the press of people increased as Oddity approached the main stage. The Jokertown Boys consisted of five members, all young males, one on guitar, another on drums, another on keyboards, and the remaining two holding mics and singing. They were all harmonizing as Oddity approached the stage.

The audience slowly parted in front of Oddity like the Red Sea before Moses; the stage crew in front of the bandstand watched them warily as Oddity stood in their own clear space to the left of the stage.

Lu Long, an Asian officer from Fort Freak—a massive torso and clawed hands; a head like that of a Chinese dragon; dragging a thick prehensile tail—was watching them as well from where he was standing at the other side of the stage. There was another uniformed officer with him—Yakami Smythe, the new partner that Jube had mentioned, Patty presumed. Patty wondered if Officer Smythe wasn't a nat. She had no visible joker qualities, nor any noticeable ace abilities. She was entirely normal: a woman perhaps in her mid-twenties, short black hair pulled back tightly under her uniform cap, dark eyes with epicanthal folds, and a hint of Japanese skin coloration—given the name, Patty figured her father was heavily English and her mother Japanese. Patty also had to wonder if someone at Fort Freak had paired them together thinking (wrongly) that there was no difference between someone Chinese and someone Japanese.

Officer Long was also known as Puff, though Patty knew the man hated that nickname. His saliva was flammable, and Long had the capability of igniting it when he spat. Oddity also knew it was a joker-ish ability: Puff could summon up no more spit than any normal human, which meant he could emit a flaming goober and little more. He also wasn't as strong as his chest made him look, though his tail could be dangerous.

Long's gaze as he glanced at Oddity was decidedly unfriendly. He nudged Officer Smythe and tilted his head in Oddity's direction as she glanced at him. He said something close to her ear, and her gaze fixed on them with decided interest.

The Jokertown Boys' song ended in a cluster of high, close harmonies and crashing cymbals; the crowd responded with a roar of applause. One of the members—with a patch over one eye and two horns protruding through dark hair, wearing a sequined tux and gloves—stepped forward to the front of the stage. A raven was perched on his shoulder as a spotlight swiveled to pin him in its glare. He was greeted by shrieks of "Roger! Oh, Roger!" from the teenage girls nearest the stage.

"Thank you all so much," Roger called back to the audience. "We have lots more to come. Right now, though, let me introduce the members of the group. That's Jim, also known as Gimcrack, on keyboards; Alec 'Alicorn' shredding on guitars; Dirk, whom we call Atlas for obvious reasons, on drums. And, of course, Paul, aka Pretty Paulie, on main vocals." Roger paused between each name for applause and more shrieking from the mostly female fans. "I'm Roger Ravenstone, and this is my trusted assistant Lenore," he said, gesturing to the raven. "Lenore, do you have something to give our fans?"

Lenore gave a hoarse caw, then spread large black wings and took flight outward, the spotlight following its path. With each beat of the raven wings, a rain of glitter fell over the audience as if shed by the raven. It circled above the audience (adorning Oddity's cloak in the process) then returned to Roger's shoulder, where it shook itself, spreading more glitter over Roger's tux.

"We have a special guest for you right now: our own good friend and 'stage mom,' Cameo. She's going to take you to a place where there isn't any trouble . . ."

A woman emerged from the curtains stage left, spit-curls of golden hair frothing under a top hat, a choker around her neck with a cameo at the center. She was dressed in a 1940s-style evening gown with low-heeled shoes covered with bright-red sequins on her feet. She lifted a microphone to her lips, and it was unmistakably Judy Garland's voice that emerged from the speakers. "It's not a place you can get to by a boat or a train," she intoned as the band started to softly play behind her. "It's far, far away. Behind the moon, beyond the rain." Then, singing: "Somewhere over the rainbow / Way up high . . ."

That was as far as Cameo and the Jokertown Boys got. The main stage and the entire park to the south suddenly went dark as—near Lion's Gate Field—a storm of sparks and crackling sounds exploded across the field like fireworks on the ground. Screams and shouts of alarm from those in the park shattered the sudden night gloom. Patty could hear wails of pain and terror erupt from those nearest the explosions as people trampled one another in an effort to get away from the commotion.

[Croyd's here!] John shouted. The stage crew leapt onto the stage as the Jokertown Boys and Cameo gaped wordlessly at the sputtering bright display before them. Roger Ravenstone was shouting uselessly into a dead microphone and waving his hands while Lenore cawed and careened overhead; other members of the Jokertown Boys flailed at instruments that were no longer working. Even through the chaos, Oddity could hear Atlas's drums, sounding thin and pale now in comparison with their previous thundering. Some of the fans nearest the stage tried to climb onto it only to be pushed back by the crew and roadies as the musicians were hustled away toward the rear. More of the crowd ran past on either side, bumping helplessly into Oddity as they fled.

Roosevelt Park was wrapped in night except where Evan's huge sculpture of Ouroboros loomed high overhead in the north, still framed in colored spotlights, its open mouth gleaming a fiery red as it came ever nearer to eating its own tail and setting off the display of fireworks that would mark the arrival of the New Year. The spotlights there cast multicolored curves of strong shadows back toward them. Patty/Oddity surged that way, pushing aside those who were in their way as gently as possible. [The glow will draw Croyd. We gotta deal with him, Patty, before more people get hurt—and not worry much about whether Croyd is hurt in the process. Now. If you won't do it, I will. Just let me take Oddity.]

[. . . we installed an electrical panel there Patty at the apex of the sculpture we had the electricians tap into one of the main outside lines that's where he'll go . . .]

Patty felt John's presence pulling at her, attempting to drag her down from Dominant. Already exhausted and hurting from being Dominant in Oddity's body, she struggled to remain in control but found herself falling away into Sub-Dominant as John took over control of Oddity.

"Get out of the way!" Oddity roared suddenly, their arms flailing wide, any gentleness gone. Even Patty, no longer Dominant, could feel them striking those pressed around them. "Move, dammit! Let me through!"

Oddity saw Puff and Smythe heading to intercept them. The dragon's massive prehensile tail lashed over the ground in front of Oddity, blocking their path. Smythe just stood there alongside Puff, staring at Oddity. Half a dozen jokers were sprawled on the ground around Oddity, getting up slowly. "You're not going anywhere, Oddity," Long said. "In fact, you're under arrest for assault."

"Fuck that, Puff," John replied. "You have bigger problems. Those reports of an odd-looking joker around these power outages? They're true." John pointed Oddity's left arm at Evan's huge sculpture. "And that's where he's going to show up next, because there's still power there. You want to actually do some fucking good for a change? Then get more cops up here to keep everyone far away from the Ouroboros sculpture."

"Yeah? Well, we don't take orders from no vigilante asshole," Long retorted with a snarl. He spat, and John watched the flaming ball of saliva land near his feet. Long's tail lashed again; John reached down, grabbed the scaled length, and pulled hard. Officer Long went down hard, cursing as Oddity started to move past him, still shouting at the crowd.

But Oddity had only taken a few strides when they heard a woman's voice shout "*Kaba!*" behind them. With the word, as if it were an incantation, their way was blocked by a wall growth of thick cattails springing up as tall as Oddity from the ground in front of them and curving around to either side. Oddity looked behind: Yakami Smythe was smiling gently at Oddity as Puff tried to rise ponderously from the ground.

"I can make the wall as thick as I want and surround you entirely," Smythe commented. "I know you're very strong, but I can keep adding new cattails and brush until you're exhausted."

"Maybe," John answered, "or maybe you're just talking shit. I don't know. But while you're ignoring the real problem, just like Officer Puff there, other people are going to get hurt or worse. It's your choice, Officer. We're going there." Oddity pointed to Evan's sculpture. "You can follow us and arrest us there if nothing happens. But something *will* happen. We guarantee that."

Smythe glanced at Puff, who growled something unintelligible accompanied by a stream of gray smoke from his snouted face. She turned back to Oddity, and the encircling cattails withered and died in an instant. "All right," she said. "Go on. I'll help Officer Long get back on his feet and we'll follow you."

Ahead of Oddity, the nearly completed circle of the massive snake rose three stories into the night, scales of engraved stainless steel welded to a flat black body studded with glittering LEDs, the colors shifting and changing with the computer program Evan had created. The eyes of Ouroboros were a sinister, unrelenting red, like staring into the heart of a volcano. At the top of the circle nearest the tail, LEDs counted down the hours, minutes, and seconds until the calendar would flip from 1999 to 2000. As Oddity looked up, the numerals shifted to 00 02 59. Steam vented from the mouth of Ouroboros; the gears inside moving another click closer to completing the circle and setting off the fireworks.

A crowd had gathered around the sculpture, though they were warily regarding Oddity's lumbering approach more than the representation of Ouroboros. Oddity waved cloaked arms—the left one mostly John; the right mostly Patty—at them, both forearms that protruded from the cloak patchworked with Evan's darker flesh. "You're all in danger here!" Oddity shouted at them. "Leave! Leave now before you're injured! Go!"

John pushed Oddity to move faster, which sent pain racing through the body as muscles and bone shifted in response. Oddity howled, roaring in mingled pain, fury, and frustration as they came closer. The crowd broke, scattering as they fled to either side of the park or north onto East Houston. Oddity chased the stragglers, herding them away from the sculpture, which was still illuminated by colored spotlights.

Behind him, Officer Puff was shouting. "Oddity, you bastard. I'll throw so many charges at you that Pretorius won't ever get you out . . ."

John glanced back over Oddity's cloaked shoulder to see an enraged Puff lumbering toward Ouroboros spewing globules of flaming spit that fell like sad, failed meteors to the ground and expired. Officer Smythe trailed behind him.

Behind the duo, there was a movement in the darkness: moving faster than seemed reasonable, Croyd's flexible head atop a too-slim and too-metallic body. "Puff! Smythe! Behind you!" John shouted, pointing. "Watch out!"

Smythe turned too late at Oddity's warning; Croyd was already skittering past her before she could react, but Puff lashed out with his tail at the last moment. The heavy tail struck Croyd and sent him spinning away into the metal fencing around Evan's sculpture.

A furious explosion of sparks and flames erupted, sending the last few onlookers fleeing in panic. Croyd shook himself, then climbed the fencing effortlessly, long fingers laced in the chain links, followed by a glittering, hissing waterfall of half-molten metal. When he reached the top rail, Croyd hesitated momentarily and leapt, further and higher than John thought possible, landing at the base of Ouroboros. Croyd paused there; John could see him staring up at the snake rising far above, the mantis-like head craning and turning.

"Fuck!" they heard Puff mutter as he and Officer Smythe came up behind them. "That little bastard's fast and athletic as hell."

"He is that," John agreed. "I'm also not sure it's safe to touch him, given all the electrical energy he's absorbed and what happens when he touches metal. As for handcuffing him, well . . ." John stopped, leaving that to cops' imaginations. Smythe grunted, and Puff expectorated flaming spit.

"You know that joker?" Puff asked. Inside, John heard Patty: [John! There's no reason to tell him it's Croyd.]

"No clue," John answered. "It's not like we know every person living around here. What about the two of you?"

Smythe shrugged; Puff shook his dragon head. "All I know is that there were reports of someone of his appearance near the outages, and we were to apprehend him if we saw him."

"Then be our guest, Officers," John said, waving a hand toward Croyd. "Don't let us stop you from making the collar."

Puff just stared at Croyd, but Smythe laughed—she had a nice laugh, John thought. It reminded him of Patty's in happier days. Through the mesh of the fencing mask, John saw Croyd crouch on top of the fence. He seemed to be sniffing the air, like a dog on the scent of something, and the mantis head swiveled eerily, the body remaining still. Then, before either Puff or Oddity could react, Croyd leapt over them to the base of the sculpture, tearing off sheets of metal as if they were no more than cardboard, tossing them to fall like meteors with glowing molten tails, clanging harshly on the blacktop. John saw Croyd crawl inside, every touch causing more sparks to spray. John caught glimpses as Croyd started climbing up the steep incline toward the head. [Evan? What's in there?]

The reply was faint. [. . . gears and supports mostly but the electrics and computer controls are up near the top that's where he's going there's live high voltage there and the fireworks are set close to it also I don't know what will happen when he gets there . . .]

They could hear Croyd's quick ascent inside Ouroboros, clawed feet clattering on the steel and igniting more quick fires inside that were visible in the gaps in the scales and supports. John put Oddity's head into the narrow hole Croyd had gone through and peered up. The darkness was interrupted by meteor showers wherever Croyd touched steel. [John!] Patty called out. [Please don't go in after him. It's too dangerous.]

[It's also too small for us,] John agreed. With the exception of the sputtering illumination Croyd was causing and the faint glow from the rear of the LEDs, it was too dark and confined inside the sculpture to maneuver. Evan might have some idea of how the supports were set and how to climb up without good lighting, assuming they could even fit inside the interior, but confronting Croyd in an enclosed metallic space seemed a horrible tactic. John pulled his head back out and looked at the two police officers, shaking his head. "I think the best we can do is wait and watch," he told them. "And it'd probably be better if we did our watching from a little more dis—"

That was as far as John got. There was a deafening roar as flame and blinding electric fury exploded from the mouth of Ouroboros as the fireworks went off all at once inside the sculpture. The ring of Ouroboros shuddered and shook, metal groaning and shuddering as shattered pieces of the sculpture rained down around them. The body of the snake sagged as if it were made of heated wax. John saw a large chunk of the dragon's scales falling from high up on the sculpture's framework, with Officer Smythe directly underneath and oblivious to the danger. Oddity surged toward her: As Smythe suddenly noticed the plummeting steel and raised her hands above her head in futile protection, Oddity roared and pushed her out of the way. The steel hit the ground a scant handbreath between then, burying itself deep in the blacktop. Smythe stared wide-eyed at Oddity over the fragment between them.

Oddity heard Puff cry out as Ouroboros's tail collapsed directly in front of the cop. John pushed at the steel framework as it fell, causing the arc of the snake's tail to narrowly miss crushing Puff underneath its weight, though it brushed the Fort Freak cop hard enough to send him sprawling and unconscious, with some of the framework draping itself over Puff's legs.

Hissing, colorful explosions hurtled out from the wreckage in every direction: up into the air or smashing into the ground or fuming at head level. Their blinding, loud explosions echoed from the buildings around them. The grass and the wooden benches around Oddity were smoldering.

There were no lights on anywhere nearby.

Then the fireworks stopped. The world around Oddity went eerily still and dark, though John, through the afterimages in Oddity's eyes, could still see the glare of Manhattan. The bright spheres of distant firework displays appeared above the skyscrapers to the southwest: over Liberty Island, John assumed. Other displays could be glimpsed between the buildings around the park.

Smythe was still looking at Oddity, breathing hard. "Happy fucking New Year," he called out to her. Smythe shook herself, then rushed to where Puff was sprawled on the ground.

The head of Ouroboros was staring at Oddity with its shattered, broken body stretched up behind, the fires reflecting golden on its scales and the mouth stained and streaked black with soot. Inside the head, Oddity could see a naked, all-too-human Croyd, curled up in a fetal position.

[He's not dead, is he?] John heard Patty ask.

John sidled closer. He touched Croyd's head with a tentative forefinger, snatching his hand away quickly as soon as they touched him. When no sparks followed, when John felt no new pain, he reached out again, this time pressing fingertips (Patty's, he noted) to the side of Croyd's neck. He could feel a strong pulse throbbing in the carotid. [Not dead. Either unconscious or asleep again.]

[And Puff?]

Smythe had crouched down in front of her partner. "How's Puff?" John asked.

"He's breathing," she answered, "but he's not conscious. I've put in a call for a bus. Hopefully they can get through all the traffic. Can you help me get the wreckage off him?"

"I can do that. Stand back for a moment."

Oddity walked over to where Long was sprawled. They reached down, lifted the snake's tail, and tossed it away from Puff. The metal structure sounded like a dozen car crashes as it hit the blacktop. They crouched down next to him. "His breathing's strong," John told her as Smythe knelt down next to them. "Some nice cuts and bruises, and he'll probably have a hell of a headache when he wakes up."

They all heard the sound of approaching sirens.

[Let's get Croyd and take him back to the lair,] Patty suggested. [The cops will take care of Puff.]

[They'd take care of Croyd, too,] John answered. [He doesn't have to be our problem, Patty. He's *not* our problem.]

[. . . no that's not right Fort Freak doesn't like Croyd any more than they like us they're scared of Croyd and what he might do Patty's right we should take him with us two against one John . . .]

John sighed. "I gotta go," he told Officer Smythe. Rising, he went to the mouth of Ouroboros. Grasping the jaws, groaning with the effort and pain, he bent the steel jaws far enough to reach in and drag out Croyd.

"Who is that?" Smythe asked.

"Croyd," John answered. He slung Croyd's sleeping body over one massive shoulder, then began walking south into the darkness of the park. Behind them, he heard Smythe's voice.

"Thank you," she said. "You very likely saved my life and Puff's. I won't forget that, and I'll make certain Puff doesn't, either." She paused. "Is it like this a lot around here? I think I may want to reconsider my choice of career."

"That might be wise," John told her without looking back. "I wish we had that choice."

January 24, 2000

It had been a long day working on the wax figurine of the Harlem Hammer for a new display in Dutton's museum. Evan, as always when working for Dutton, was in Dominant, with Patty in Sub and John in Passive. The day had been chilly, the temperature steadily below thirty degrees Fahrenheit all day; at 9:30 P.M., it was still the same. Oddity's breath hung before him in a white cloud, and much of the fencing mask was rimed with their frosty exhalations.

Oddity unlocked and opened the heavy steel doors of the lair—still scorched with soot on the plates where Croyd had run into it on New Year's Eve. Evan kept the cloak wrapped around him, given the chill in their underground rooms, but he put the fencing mask in the kitchen sink so the frost could drip off.

[We should check on Croyd,] Patty suggested. [We've been gone for most of the day.]

[He's probably still sleeping,] Evan said. [After what happened New Year's Eve, I suspect he'll sleep a long while yet.]

Patty said nothing more and John was silent as well, but Evan moved deeper into the lair toward the room where they'd put Croyd after the New Year's misadventures. He opened the door; the bed on which Croyd had been sleeping when they'd left that morning was empty and the blankets were neatly folded on the mattress. There was a folded note on the blanket. Oddity picked it up and read the short message written there.

Thanks. I'll always remember what you did. I owe you for the food; I'll pay you back.

Evan moved through all the rooms in the lair, puzzled. Croyd didn't have a key for the lair. Evan knew the front door had been locked when they'd returned to the lair. He checked the two "back doors" into their warren of tunnels—both of them were still locked and barred, and the only keys for those locks were the ones that Oddity carried under his cloak. In the kitchen, it looked like Croyd had eaten nearly everything in the fridge and pantry. Other than that, nothing was missing, and nothing had been disturbed.

It was as if Croyd had never been there. [How the heck did he get out?]

[No idea,] Patty answered. [And we have no idea what Croyd woke up as this time.]

Croyd was gone. Somehow.

[I'll check the security camera,] Evan said. Oddity went into the computer room where the orange gumdrop of the iMac G3 they'd bought in '98 sat on the desk. A VHS videocassette recorder was humming on a shelf behind the iMac; on the TV monitor next to the iMac, they could see the front door of the lair from outside. Evan stabbed at the STOP button, then rewound the tape, fast-forwarding after they saw themselves leaving the lair. [Wait!] Patty said a few minutes later. [Back up a bit.]

Evan rewound until they saw movement on the monitor, then started playing the tape once more at normal speed. [There . . . That's gotta be Croyd.]

"Oh, my God," Evan said aloud. "That's impossible." Evan rewound again before playing the tape back in slow motion. On the monitor, they watched as first a hand, followed by an arm, passed through the steel plates of the door. A body followed, seemingly as insubstantial as a ghost and naked. Once on the other side of the door, Croyd—in appearance, now just a normal human being, albeit one who could walk through solid doors—looked directly into the camera. He waved at them, smiled, and blew them a kiss.

[Well, that explains everything,] Evan said. [That's a handy little trick the wild card's given him, and a nice new body to go with it. I wish we had such luck.] Jealousy, resentment, and irritation all mingled in Evan's comment. As he spoke, Oddity moaned helplessly as organs and bones shifted deep inside their mingled body, waves of agony that made Evan hunch over and cradle Oddity's body with their arms. Evan/Oddity cried out, allowing Patty to move from Sub to Dominant, moving Evan down to Passive as

John rose to Sub-Dom. The pain momentarily receded from Oddity's body with the change, becoming bearable again; then, as always, it returned, relentless. Patty fisted Oddity's hands and gritted their teeth against the torment.

On the monitor, Croyd moved out of the camera's line of sight and was gone.

[. . . not right not fair at all Croyd can always escape what he is eventually but we can't escape can't do that not ever not ever this body is a prison and we have a fucking life sentence . . .] Evan ranted from Passive.

[We hear you,] Patty responded. [We understand. But what choice do we have?]

[There *is* a possible way out that doesn't necessarily involve all of us dying,] John answered. [We could try the Black Trump virus.]

[. . . are you kidding that only has a twenty-nine percent cure rate it would just kill us all . . .]

[I'm only pointing out our options,] John responded.

[I don't want to do that or to commit suicide,] Patty answered. [What I want both of you to know that is that, like all of us, I sometimes hate being what we are. I wish we could escape the eternal torture. But that doesn't mean I hate either of *you*. Yes, sometimes I'm angry and resentful of what happened to us, but I still love you, John, and you, Evan, no matter what. I've been thinking about that a lot since New Year's Eve. Whatever happens for us going forward, I can't hate or blame either of you.]

Patty ejected the videocassette and put a new one in. She hit RECORD.

[It's a new year and a new century,] Patty continued. [If Oddity's a life sentence, at least none of us is alone in this prison cell. We still have one another.]

[I still love you, too, Patty, and Evan also, but it's not the same as it was,] John answered. [It never will be.]

Patty went to the bookcase and pulled out a photo album. She laid it on the desk, opening the cover and paging through it, knowing that Evan and John would also see what she saw: snapshots from the late 1960s and early '70s, photos of the three of them before that morning in May 1974 when it was Oddity who woke in the bed the three of them shared.

Patty, John, and Evan: They called themselves a throuple. They were complete and content that way. In the photos, they were almost universally smiling, arms around one another. Happy. Looking forward to every day, to continuing to share what they had with one another.

[It may never be that way again for us,] Patty said. [But I remember. It's what keeps us alive. We *all* should remember. We *have* to. It's the only way to hang on. I'd like to see some more of this new century. I hope both of you do, too.]

[. . . still have each other yes I remember I do even if I don't always show it . . .]

There was nothing but silence from John. Patty called out into that void.

[We did good on New Year's Eve, John. We saved at least one life and probably more: Croyd, Puff, Smythe, and likely several others in the park. Think of all those people around Evan's sculpture that John scared away—how many of them might have been injured or worse? And we've seen how incredible Evan's work at Dutton's has been. Heck, we've heard locals call us the Protector of Jokertown. But . . .]

Patty paused, and Oddity took in a long, shuddering breath before she continued. [I remember that night when the wild card changed us. I remember that I was dreaming about us, about how much I loved being with the two of you in the same bed. We all know that, at least sometimes, the wild card seems to take personalities into account when it changes those who have been infected. I have to wonder if maybe *I* wasn't the cause of us being the way we are, that maybe I was the only one who was actually infected and the virus felt my dreams when it activated and snared the two of you, when otherwise both of you might have woken up the next morning as you were.]

[You don't know that, Patty. You *can't* know that.] John finally spoke.

[. . . Patty none of this was your fault you can't think that it's nobody's fault not yours or John's or mine it just the damn virus . . .]

[I hear you,] Patty told them. [But however we came to be this way, if it's my fault or John's or Evan's or just some cruel accident of fate, I still want to be here with both you. No matter how much our existence hurts. There's still good we can do. There's still reasons for us to be here.]

[You're sure of that, Patty?]

[I am.] She tapped one of Oddity's fingers on the photo album. [Remember this. Remember us. Hold on to that.]

[I'll try,] John responded. [I just can't promise how long that will be.]

[. . . I remember I do it's been twenty-five years so far what's five years or ten or more? . . .]

Oddity closed the photo album and returned it to its place on the shelf, feeling tendons snarling and complaining in their right calf as they did so. [None of us can promise how long we have,] Patty said. [This body can't last forever; I think we all understand that. All we can do is the best we can with what it gives us. Are we together on that?]

[We're *always* together. We don't have a choice.]

Patty managed to push aside Oddity's pain enough to laugh wryly at that.

The rare amusement sounded loudly in Oddity's head.

Swimmer, Flier, Felon, Spy

PART VI

Tesla was brushing his teeth when he heard the discreet knock at his hotel room door indicating he would find his breakfast tray in the hallway. He finished his task and washed his hands. The hotel robe he was wearing fit perfectly and was quite comfortable.

A cart was parked in the hallway set with a covered plate, a pot of coffee, and a bottle of chilled orange juice. Instead of the folded newspaper he had expected, there was a brightly colored pamphlet. Tesla took the lot into his room and set it on the desk.

Upon removing the silver cloche, he found a steaming goat cheese omelet sprinkled with freshly cut chives and a slice of sourdough toast. His favorite breakfast.

He poured cups of coffee and juice, then picked up the pamphlet. At the top, it read "Aluth Avurudda Street Festival! April fourteenth!" April 14 was today's date.

Aluth Avurudda. That did not immediately bring anything to mind, but instead of opening his storehouse of memories, Tesla simply unfolded the pamphlet. Aluth Avurudda was better known outside of Sri Lanka as Sinhalese New Year, and the advertisement promised music, food, and games of all types in the Tompkinsville neighborhood.

Tompkinsville was on Staten Island, Tesla recalled.

Turning the pamphlet over, he found a note appended with a round, elegantly curved paper clip. The note was written in sepia ink, the handwriting of someone who took great care with their penmanship, even to judge by just the two characters written on the heavy cream paper: "#5."

On the one hand, Tesla was growing more and more annoyed that so many people in the city seemed to know not just how he conducted his business but what his particular business, just now, *was*. On the other, he could not fault the hotel's service in saving him the trouble of tracking down the fifth Croyd Crenson.

He picked up the phone. A woman's voice answered, "Transportation to Staten Island, sir?"

"Something subtle, please," said Tesla.

"Of course, sir."

"Did you know," Tesla said, feeling unaccountably chatty, "I've never been to Staten Island."

"I'll make a note of it, sir."

The submarine sank back below the waters of the Hudson River under Tesla's watchful gaze. He had known that the number of submersible vehicles plying the waters around Manhattan and its environs was far greater than what most New Yorkers suspected, but he had been surprised by how luxuriously appointed the submersible the concierge had arranged had been.

Tesla was learning all sorts of things about moving about the city.

He turned and walked along the riverfront, following crowd sounds and music. He could smell spices on the air, but he was confident that it was not that iteration of Croyd Crenson he would be meeting soon.

Hundreds of people were gathered along several blocks of a cordoned-off street. At a quick glance, the number of jokers was about what one would expect in any such gathering in New York. Aces, of course, were not so obvious, and the information he had been given had not included any identifying details. Croyd Crenson could be almost anyone in sight.

Then he saw a sign with a broadly drawn picture of a joker with eight arms all pointing in the same direction. Above the joker was the legend CROYD'S CARICATURES! CREATIVE! COMICAL! CHEAP!

The ability to draw eight caricatures at once. Well, it was only slightly odder than emitting the aromas of various spices.

Following the crowd around a corner, Tesla saw a packed stall between one selling delicious-smelling tomato pies and another offering colorful scarves. The stall was large enough so that better than half a dozen patrons were sitting in chairs surrounding the eight-armed artist of the poster, who was slowly rotating on a stool within a smaller circle of easels.

Croyd Crenson, for surely this was him, worked at a manic pace. This Crenson was less of a talker than the others, only occasionally grunting out short sentences. "Chin up" and "Look at me" and "Your ears are enormous, I can use that."

He was using the typical tools of a seaside caricature artist: colored markers and cheap poster-sized sheets of paper. At least, that was how he was working on seven of the easels. The eighth was something else altogether, a portrait in oils of a joker woman whose skin was covered with fine red hair, evincing a rare eye for color and light and a rarer talent for the subtle geometries used by the finest portraitists.

Tesla took his place at the end of the line, which was moving quickly to match Crenson's speed. Like a skilled hostess on a busy night at a crowded restaurant, Crenson knew how to keep customers moving in and out.

There was a jar stuffed with $20 bills—a mix of the old Jacksons and the new Tubmans—set on a small table by the entryway to the stall. Tesla paid the price of admission and took a seat. Crenson rotated on his stool, head whipping from patron to patron as his arms flew. He paused for the barest fraction on seeing Tesla. "You sure you want a caricature?" he asked. "You kind of *are* a caricature."

Tesla raised an eyebrow.

"Yeah, yeah," said Crenson. "Takes one to know one." He sketched the outline of one of Tesla's horns then turned his head away, though he kept drawing, as he was drawing on all seven of the easels simultaneously.

None of the other sitters paid any particular attention to the exchange. Most were looking down at their cellphones except when Crenson told them to look up. "For God's sake, look at me!"

Tesla said, "The portrait there is quite an accomplishment. Did the subject sit for it?"

"Commission piece," said Crenson, which was not exactly an answer.

"So it's not for sale?"

Crenson looked at him sharply. In this guise, his features were even, his eyes bright and his skin smooth, his hair a thick tangle of blond. Except for the eight arms radiating out from his torso, he would have been accounted a handsome man.

"I'd be open to a bidding war," he said.

"The person who took out the commission would no doubt be disappointed to hear that," said Tesla.

"I've disappointed her before," said Crenson.

"It interests me to learn that you do commission work of that quality," said Tesla. "I have a group portrait I'd very much like you to undertake."

"You decided that just now sitting here?" said Crenson, suspiciously.

All the while, he kept turning, drawing with seven of his eight hands, muttering to the sitters, once making change when someone came in who wished to pay with a $100 bill, this last causing

Crenson some agitation. "Who the fuck comes to a street fair expecting to change hundreds?"

"I'm taking the opportunity I see before me," said Tesla, answering Crenson's question the next time the artist came around to him. "You're obviously quite gifted, and I believe you would have a special interest in the subjects."

Again, Crenson reacted with suspicion. "What's the catch?"

"Nothing in particular. Nothing a man of your obvious talents can't handle."

"I'm expensive," said Crenson.

"You're drawing caricatures for twenty dollars each," countered Tesla.

"I fucking hate mysteries."

"But you like money. Money you can use to buy, say, better art supplies. Or anything else you might need."

"You know how much a tube of high-quality cadmium blue costs?" asked Crenson.

"I do not," said Tesla.

"Me either, I just got into this business. You might say I recently discovered my own talent."

"And I have just discovered it as well. If you will deign to consider my offer, I've thought of something you might think of as that catch."

"Go ahead," said Crenson.

"You have to meet me and the subjects at a certain time, at a certain place. You have to come alone. And bring whatever supplies you might need."

"You've got my attention."

"I can offer you ten thousand dollars cash upon completion of the painting."

"I was thinking five, so you've hired yourself an artist."

"I'm pleased to hear it," said Tesla.

"Name the time and place."

"If you'll give me your card, I'll write the directions on the back."

"My card," said Crenson, snorting a laugh. He ripped a corner off one of the poster sheets he was drawing on.

"Hey!" said the man whose caricature was taking shape on the page.

"Shut up," said Crenson, handing the torn slip of paper to Tesla.

Tesla pulled a pencil from inside his jacket, sharpened it with his nails, and wrote down the pertinent information. Then he rose from his stool.

"I'm not finished with your drawing," said Crenson.

Tesla looked at the easel for the first time. It showed a face with what were recognizably his features, if more than a little exaggerated. There was a smile on the illustrated face that resembled Tesla's own in no way whatsoever. A tiny body was below the head, riding a bicycle, the fast turn of the pedals indicated by a puff of cloud blowing beside the rear wheel.

"I quite like it as it is," he told Crenson. The eight-armed man grunted, deftly tore the sheet free with one hand, and rolled it into a cylinder.

"Cardboard tubes are another twenty," said Crenson.

"I'll just take it as is."

"Right, well, I'll see you when I see you," said Crenson, and waved in the next person in line.

"Tonight," Tesla said.

"Tonight?" Crenson sounded both annoyed and delighted. "You better have my money."

Now just one more left to find. Tesla decided to try one of the tomato pies at the next stall, then visit his employer, who might have a lead for him. He needed to be informed of the current status of the search and the meeting spot anyway. But food was both pleasure and necessity.

The pie was exquisite, the tomatoes, tamarind, and curry blend delicious. Then, dabbing his lips with a napkin, caricature tucked under one arm, he wandered the fair and thought about his quarry. One more Crenson to find. One more to somehow convince to come together with all the others to an end that Tesla was only beginning to envision.

He caught sight of a laughing joker woman examining the wares of a jeweler. She had fine red hair over her whole body and a prehensile tail. It was the woman from Crenson's portrait.

She turned to hold a bauble up to the sun to admire in the light, and Tesla caught sight of a lanyard hanging around her neck. From it depended a visitor's credential for the United Nations. Tesla had once worn such a lanyard himself, though his had not identified him as a visiting dignitary from Sri Lanka.

There was no record of Croyd Crenson ever having visited the United Nations. If he *had* been there, and it would not have surprised Tesla to learn that he had, it almost certainly had been under clandestine circumstances.

What was certain, though, just from public records, not even the private secure ones Tesla had access to, was that Crenson had traveled the world. He remembered what the other Crenson had said about having been in the wars. Then he remembered what he said about having disappointed whatever "her" had commissioned the portrait of this woman.

Croyd Crenson. A striking joker woman. Wars. Sri Lanka.

There was a story there.

The Bloody Eagle

by Mary Anne Mohanraj

Sri Lanka, 2003

She found him in the jungle, sleeping.

Nikisha's first impulse was to run—her second, to kill him. He
was no one she recognized, and in their territory, where no stranger
should dare to come. He had to be an enemy, and her duty to the
movement was clear.

But the man looked so helpless, fast asleep and naked as a baby,
curled into a tight ball, snoring a little. A slight hiss of air, mingling
with the sounds of the jungle at night, the incessant chittering of
monkeys, the whirring thrum of the tree frogs. And if her sister
Udhya had been there, Nikisha would have had to admit that the
fact that he looked like a film star might have factored in—nut-
brown skin, a sleek fall of black hair, and finely drawn features.

Udhya wasn't there, of course. And the truth was, Nikisha had
never actually killed a man. Not on purpose, anyway.

She pulled the kaetta out of its sheath to have it ready. Nikisha
didn't need the knife, of course, wouldn't even try to use it. But in
the last bloody year, she'd found that there were plenty of men
willing to press themselves on a young woman, alone, without

protectors. Having a large kaetta at the ready served to save her from needing to prove to them that they couldn't touch her. It was for their own safety, really, though they'd never admit it.

She settled down on her haunches, watching. He couldn't sleep for that long, and when he woke, she had questions.

When she'd finally become a big girl at fifteen, Amma insisted on holding a party, no matter how much Nikisha protested that in the year 2000, such a thing was hopelessly outdated, not to mention humiliating. Amma called their cook, Soma, to the dining room, and rattled off a long list of instructions: celebratory dishes to make, auspicious elements for the occasion. "I want Marina's biryani, you understand? Yours is not so good; everyone knows hers is the best. And there has to be plenty of cutlets—we don't want anyone to think they need to be careful with their portions . . ."

Nikisha held her tongue while Soma was in the room, but as soon as she went back to the kitchen, the words burst out: "Amma, you're basically announcing to the world that I'm menstruating . . ."

"Chee! Don't talk like that!"

"Oh, my God!" Nikisha threw up her hands in frustration. "You won't even talk about it, so why would you want to throw a party for it? It doesn't make any sense."

Udhya nodded silent agreement, knowing that she'd be having the same argument with Amma in not too long—they were only nine months apart, as close as sisters could be in that, as in most things.

"Aiyo! You don't understand what you're saying. You should be happy about this. I was thrilled when I attained age. My parents threw me the biggest party the village had seen, almost as fancy as a wedding. If anything, you should be mad at your father; he's the one refusing to let me do this properly."

Appa winked at Nikisha from across the dining table, and then retreated behind his newspaper again, saying only from its shelter, "Money is tight these days, you know, kunju. The economy is bad; patients don't have as much money as they did, so we have to extend credit. And we need to save for the girls' schooling . . ."

"Credit, credit. You're a soft touch, Manesh. As for schooling! Tcha!" Amma had a master's degree in accounting herself, did all the billing for the medical practice, so it wasn't as if she was against school. But she hadn't actually ever applied for a job or worked outside the home, not since marrying the local doctor. "Schooling is all well and good, but getting Nikisha properly married is the priority. Do you want her to grow wild? You indulged the girls too much; it's your fault they're so spoiled."

"Yes, yes, kunju," Appa said soothingly from behind his paper. "But I only have two darling daughters, no? Whom else should I indulge?"

Nikisha smothered a grin; it wouldn't help her case. She'd probably lost anyway—when Amma made up her mind, she was the famed unstoppable force. Everybody else had better just bow their heads and try to make the best of it. Maybe she could at least get Soma to make her some cashew milk toffee for the party; it was her favorite sweet, and Amma usually said she ate too much of it, and it would make her fat. Maybe if she got really fat, Amma would realize no man would want to marry her, and they could cancel this party?

Fat chance.

The weeks passed, and party preparations continued like clockwork, every obstacle smashed by the force of Amma's will. Finally the day arrived, and Nikisha was trussed up like a prize pig, in a choli blouse too tight, pushing her small breasts up to best display. "Chee! You have no bottom to speak of," Amma said with disappointment. "There's just no way to get the proper shape to the sari."

"It's all right, it's all right," her sister Saila said, as she jammed more and more gold bangles up Nikisha's arms. "She's such a pretty girl, no one will notice. She has your eyes, you know—the eyes that captured a doctor! Our little Niki will do just fine!"

Amma shook her head in reluctant agreement. She gave Nikisha one last tug on her sari, spun her around, took a long look. "Good. You look beautiful." Nikisha couldn't help feeling a little proud at her mother's approval, even if she still simmered with resentment, too. And then suddenly, Amma's eyes were filling with tears. "Ah, how did the years go so quickly? My baby is going to run off and leave me now."

"Amma . . ." Nikisha said, awkwardly, not sure what to say to that. Her mother was never sentimental like this.

Saila laughed, breaking the tension, "Don't be ridiculous. You go, Niki—enjoy your party. I'll take care of your foolish mother."

Nikisha fled the room gratefully, bangles jingling, leaving behind the sound of Saila's gentle scolding.

She survived the party, too, somehow, the leers and snarky comments of the uncles, the discomfort of the teenage boys dragged to it. Nikisha was careful to steer clear of the kitchen, where Amma and her sisters had soon fallen deep into very serious weighings of the merits of this boy or that. Which one had a family history of drunkenness? Which one had passed his exams with flying colors? Which one already had an uncle in America, who'd promised to get him a programming job at IBM?

Mostly, she tried to keep her sari from falling off—the embroidery made it itchy, so she kept tugging at it, and that loosened the folds, and even though Amma had stuck a huge safety pin through the big folds, there was only so much a safety pin could do. Eventually, Nikisha retreated to the bedroom she shared with Udhya, closing the door. Maybe no one would notice she'd gone?

It wasn't long before her sister slipped in. "Hey—are you managing all right? I brought you a plate."

A plate piled high with cashew milk toffee. Nikisha reached out for it eagerly. "How'd you manage to sneak this past Amma?"

"She was distracted by scandal! You know the Ponnadurais' daughter, the one who got married last year?"

"Rani, right?" Nikisha liked to eat her candy slow, let it crumble and melt on her tongue. If she had to, she could make a single piece last half an hour. With this much milk toffee, she could stay in here happily for the rest of the party.

"Right." Udhya reached out and grabbed a piece herself, popped it in her mouth. Two bites, and gone. "Turns out her husband is gay—he's been in a relationship for years, on the sly, and just got married to keep the family happy. When she told him she was pregnant, he broke down and admitted everything."

"God, what a nightmare for her." Nikisha wondered if she should reach out, text Rani—but she barely knew the girl. How awful.

"The whole family's humiliated—that's why they're not here, not wanting to show their faces. Rani's moved back home with her parents, and I guess she'll raise the baby there. No one wants to dissolve the marriage with a baby coming, but it's just a mess all around." Udhya brightened. "Hey, maybe we can use this as an example?"

Nikisha raised a skeptical eyebrow. "Don't rush us into marriage, because he might be secretly gay?"

"Hey, every little bit of ammunition helps."

Nikisha shook her head. "I think, *But Amma, I'm too young; I have to concentrate on my studies,* is still the best approach."

"Maybe for you!" Udhya flopped back on her bed, heedless of her carefully pinned half sari. "No one will believe that I'm taking my studies seriously enough to matter. I'll be lucky if I pass my O-levels. When you're a rich doctor, with a beautiful house of your own, you'll let me come live with you, right?"

"Always," Nikisha said, smiling. Udhya was often ridiculous, but she also made everyone laugh. No one could keep a frown on their face when she was around.

— — —

She was all alone now, though. Oh, the movement had control of a few small houses in the village nearby, and if she wanted, she could walk there in twenty minutes. Somebody would likely still be up, planning at the big table, arguing over endless cups of milk tea and cold vadai.

They'd been so united when she first joined, a glorious unified brigade. But as the months passed and they made little headway, the cracks became more evident—Tamil squabbling with Sinhalese, Muslim with Hindu, the Vietnamese refugees alternately courted and abused . . . it was a mess. Better to be out in the forest alone, patrolling, even if normally there was nothing to patrol for.

The hours of the night passed quietly. Nikisha had settled in cross-legged, leaning against a tree trunk, watching the handsome man. It was strange—he slept deeply, but his body wasn't still—it shivered and shook. Leaf-filtered moonlight wasn't the best for seeing by; at one point, though, she could have sworn that she saw fine red hair springing out all over his arms, legs, even his face. She almost crept forward then, to touch the hair, and make sure it was real, but before she could make up her mind to that, it had disappeared again, as if absorbed. Nikisha shivered, gripped by memory.

After the party, Amma had made it clear that removing body hair was no longer optional. "Chee chee! Such a hairy girl. No man will marry you if you look like a jungle ape." From puberty on, Nikisha was obliged to shave the hair on her legs and arms. She'd tried creams and epilators, threaders and waxes.

The salons were expensive and a little embarrassing, so mostly they managed at home. She and Udhya took it in turns to do each other's backs, and debated whether they could safely skip the light dusting on their stomachs. Better take it off, too, just to be safe. What if Amma makes you wear a choli for Meenakshi's wedding?

It was tedious, but so were many other aspects of being a girl.

Best to just put your head down and get through it as best you can, looking forward to life's rewards.

Those rewards could be sweet—by the time she was seventeen, Nikisha had met a boy. They hadn't gone further than discreetly holding hands during secret evening walks on the beach, but even that was thrilling—the warmth of Nikhil's fingers pressing against hers sent chills down her spine. How strange, that electric transmission.

Udhya was particularly delighted by it all—"Nikisha and Nikhil—it's perfect! Your wedding invitations will be so beautiful." She doodled an elaborate "N&N" on her schoolwork, surrounding it in curlicues and twining flowers.

"Oh, shut up," Nikisha said, pretending to be angry. She snatched the page up and shredded it—what if Amma saw? Secretly, though, she couldn't help fantasizing. Nikhil wanted to be a doctor, too—they could open a practice together, maybe move to the States. She'd bring Udhya with them, of course, and Amma and Appa, too, if they wanted to come? Something to dream on.

But all dreams eventually ended. For Nikisha, it started with the smallest thing—Udhya complaining that she didn't feel well. Such a common occurrence that she barely noticed it—Udhya frequently had a mysteriously upset stomach, or a terrible migraine, or it was her time of the month and the cramping was paining her so much—generally whenever there was a test scheduled at school.

That day, Amma was having none of it, and chivvied them both out the door. They kicked up the dust as they walked down to the Holy Family convent school, but Udhya's feet dragged more than usual. The neighborhood was starting to be lit up with Christmas decorations, lights strung around shop windows, little fake evergreens covered in red balls, plopped into planters.

It all looked bright and festive, but Udhya was clearly taking no joy in it. "I'm really not feeling so good."

Nikisha frowned. Her sister's face looked clammy, despite the relative coolness of the December day. "When we get to the school, go straight to the nurse's office. I'll tell your teacher. Lying down for a little while should help."

Udhya nodded, looking miserable, and when they got to school, followed her orders. She generally did; it was part of why they got along so well. Nikisha was bossy, and Udhya didn't mind being bossed.

By the time they got to the school, Nikisha wasn't feeling so good, either—she gave the message to Udhya's teacher, Sister Mary, and then headed to her own classroom, but she only made it through a few classes before she was forced to go to the nurse's office herself. It felt like her heart was pounding; she could almost hear the blood rushing through her arteries and veins.

The nurse frowned over her glasses: "I've sent Udhya home already—your mother says your father is coming home to take a look at her. You'd better go, too. If you girls have something contagious, I don't want it spreading around the school."

It was only a few blocks' walk, but Nikisha was dizzy, staggering by the time she got back to the house. Soma was out in the front garden, talking to the driver, but one look at Nikisha and she hurried over, exclaiming. "Niki—come, come. Let's get you inside. Raj, get the door!"

He opened the door to a scene so horrific, Nikisha couldn't make sense of it at first. Soma screamed, and the sound echoed through the halls. Amma was on her knees, her hands pressed to . . . something. Some twisted thing, in schoolgirl uniform, but with arms and legs gone dry and desiccated, withered away . . . and the face!

A skull looked back at Nikisha, a skull with gray-brown skin barely pulled across the bones, and it couldn't possibly be anyone she had ever known, anyone she had loved. There was no world in which that was possible, and her legs crumpled underneath her then, and Amma was lunging forward, over the thing in the white uniform, pulling her from Soma's arms, holding her close.

Nikisha was falling down a long, dark tunnel, but Amma was

there. Everything would be all right. Amma was a force of nature—nothing could stand in her way. Amma would keep them safe.

The man's shivers had grown more pronounced. He twisted and arched, moaning, and that was almost enough to send Nikisha away, back to the others. She had no obligation to this man. But she remembered; her whole body remembered, what it was to suddenly shift and morph, to become something other, something horrific. This must be the wild card, and this poor man would wake to learn he'd lost his beautiful form forever. What strange shape would emerge, if he survived this?

Nikisha kept vigil. There was nothing else she could do for him.

She woke, eventually, to nightmare. Appa was sitting by her bed when she woke, murmuring prayers. His stethoscope hung uselessly around his neck, and his dark hair was streaked with gray that Nikisha didn't remember from before. There was no wink or smile from him when she opened her eyes, not even a sigh of relief. Just grief, weighing his shoulders down. When Appa took her hand, he squeezed it a little too hard.

"We thought we'd lost you, mahal. You bled—you bled from everywhere, even the pores of your skin. I don't know how you could survive losing so much blood; I was sure you were lost to us, too."

"I'm here, Appa," Nikisha managed to say, through a mouth dry as dust.

He called out for Soma then. "Bring us some milk tea. Nikisha's awake."

Udhya was gone, which was incomprehensible.

Nikisha was still here, which should be cause of celebration. She'd survived the virus that killed 90 percent of those it touched. But her body had changed. Now her skin was entirely covered with a fine reddish fur, like that of a monkey. Even her face. She'd lost a few inches of height, but gained a tail—strong and prehensile, as it turned out. Soma brought in a cup of milk tea and instinctively Nikisha reached for it with her tail—she would have grabbed it, too, if Soma hadn't shrieked and dropped the cup to shatter on the floor. Appa bit his lip, then sent Soma to get more tea, and a broom and dustpan.

Amma wouldn't look at her. For days, while Nikisha regained her strength, while she curled under the covers and sobbed for Udhya, for Nikhil who would not want her now, for everything she'd lost, only Appa and Soma came into her room. She left the room only to stumble down the hall to the toilet, then back to bed again. Five days, before Amma finally appeared in her doorway. Her hair was pulled up tight in a bun, face drawn and haggard, and she held a razor in her upraised hand, like an exhausted avenging angel.

"We will fix this," she said.

Nikisha didn't object at first, grateful to have Amma there finally, even if she were colder than she had ever been before. Amma would fix whatever of this could be fixed; Nikisha had faith in that. Soma came, bearing white towels to spread over the bed, and a bowl of warm water, and shaving cream. Nikisha bent her head to let Amma shave the back of her neck, her back and shoulders, the parts of her arms that she couldn't reach, that Udhya had always done for her. She bent her head and tried to cry without motion, without sound, not to disturb Amma at her work. Fine red hair fell like rain, until the towels were blanketed in a sea of red.

Nikisha did her belly, then her own legs, as she always had, and her feet, which proved more difficult, curving around the bones. Her toes had grown longer; she thought perhaps she could use them more effectively now, if she ever got out of this bed, if she were allowed to leave this house. She was feeling better now, stronger. She was a little curious even, to learn what this new body could do.

They left her breasts and pelvis and buttocks alone—that would all be covered by clothing, thankfully. Which also meant they could avoid the question of the tail. For now.

It was hard not to flinch away, when it was time to shave her neck and face. Amma grabbed her chin and held it in a grip of iron. Nikisha closed her eyes and set herself to endure, while the blade whispered along her forehead, her cheekbones—it nicked her once, and she couldn't help a slight jerk away with the pain. Amma's fingers dug in harder then.

"You're not actually bleeding. Hold still."

Her left cheek stung so, it was hard to believe, but Amma didn't lie. You always knew where you stood with her. Nikisha endured the blade along her cheek, her neck, finally her chin. "We'll have to use depilating cream on the ears," Amma said fiercely. "Every day. We will do this *every day*. Soma will help you after today."

"Yes, Amma," Nikisha said meekly. Maybe it would be all right. Amma knew best.

The man's face was changing now. The sun was rising, making it easier to see, and Nikisha watched the transformation, fascinated. First the color drained away, until he was white as a Norwegian. How could a little color make a man look so different? Then it flushed back again, but instead of a uniform brown, now his skin became a patchwork of whites and creams and tans and browns, speckled and . . . feathered? Yes, feathers were sprouting, erupting, all over his skin. His coloring became more defined: reddish feathers at the top, gray-black feathers on his face, and his torso was now white with black spots. Reddish-white legs still seemed mostly human, aside from the feathers, and the feet as well.

Nikisha's eyes had avoided his private parts, as much as they could, and now they were modestly shielded by feathers, so it was unclear whether he still had the equipment of a man. Nikisha hoped so, for his sake—men set such store by it, she couldn't imagine how he would react otherwise.

Back to the face, which was growing longer, more pointed, his nose turning black and hardening into a what was clearly a bird's beak. The hair at the top of his head had morphed into feathers as well, red and black, rising into a dramatic crest, and Nikisha suddenly realized what he reminded her of—a changeable hawk-eagle, one of the island's native birds. She didn't know why they were called changeable, she should ask Udhya if she knew—oh.

Sometimes, still, she forgot, and then knowledge punched her in the gut, just like that, and she was doubled over, fighting not to wail aloud her grief.

He was awake. The sun was up, his eyes had opened, and bright-yellow eyes had locked on hers. A hand reached up, touched his face, the beak, and rage filled those yellow eyes. Nikisha's hand slipped to the kaetta's hilt again, and she raised it, just enough to make sure he could see it.

He coughed, then propped himself up a little on one elbow, tilted toward her. His chest was broader now, strongly muscled. "I don't want to hurt you." His voice was high, fluting, like a bird's, and she could tell it startled him, though he went on without pausing. He was handling it all much smoother than she would have expected. "My name is Croyd. Croyd Crenson."

Not a Sri Lankan name, of any sort. Yet he had looked like one of them—how strange.

"Can you tell me what day it is, please? What the date is, I mean?"

"It's December third."

"Three weeks," he said, groaning a little. "I've been asleep three weeks. I'm lucky nothing in this jungle tried to eat me." He was pushing himself up now, staggering to his feet. Unsteady, perhaps because of the weight at his back, pulling him off balance. "And no wonder I'm starving. Please, can you help me find some food, and some clothes? I'm at your mercy."

Those were wings attached to his spine, folded now but unmistakable. They were huge—when he extended them, they'd likely be three times as wide as his current height. He was going to be quite the marvel in the camp. And maybe—maybe they could use him. Nikisha would have brought him food and clothes regardless, for pity's sake, but if he were just a man, she'd have had to sneak them out. Those wings—they changed everything.

Amma dumped a stack of cardigans on Udhya's empty bed— "Lucky it's winter," she muttered. No teenager Nikisha knew wore cardigans; those were the kind of clothes old women wore with their saris because they were always cold. Amma had Nikisha tie her tail down, wrapped around her waist; with that, a long cardigan seemed enough to disguise the tail. It wasn't easy to tie down—sometimes the tail seemed to have a mind of its own, responding to her mood with motion. But if you applied enough pressure, you could get anything to hold still.

Nikisha winced as Amma tugged the rope tighter around her waist. "We could just tell people I got fat over Christmas. You're always saying I'm going to get fat." Pushing back against her mother, but in a halfhearted way, out of habit more than anything else; Amma didn't bother responding. Nikisha had very little appetite these days, and had been losing weight precipitously. Her waist was quite slender now, which made it even easier to hide the tail.

Shaving and depilating her entire body took long enough that Nikisha had to get up an hour earlier every day. The fine red hair grew back very quickly; by dinnertime, she had a stubbly shadow all over her skin. No going out for dinner with friends. She didn't really have friends anymore anyway. She'd been so close with Udhya, they've never really needed anyone else, and her casual friends didn't know what to say to the girl who'd lost her sister so tragically. A heart attack, at such a young age!

Amma wouldn't let them tell anyone the truth, of course. If people knew that Nikisha's family carried the wild card in their genes, that either Amma or Daddy or both of them were carriers, then no one would let their son marry her. That was a fact that Nikisha couldn't even try to argue with. She'd thought about telling Nikhil the truth—but she thought he might suspect something, because he'd started avoiding her after Udhya died. Maybe people didn't believe the heart attack story; rumors were probably flying around the school.

Nikisha didn't know—she kept her head down, did her work, tried to pretend everything was normal. It was hard, though, with Amma walking like a ghost through the house. Sometimes Nikisha would wake to find Amma standing by the bed, just staring at her in the middle of the night. Sometime Amma would mutter curses on the disease, as if she were still in the village, like her grandmother, rather than a modern woman of the capital. Demon, yaksani, why won't you leave my daughter alone? Return the child to me! Aiyo! Sometimes Nikisha tried to talk to her, to calm her down, but that rarely worked. Usually, she just buried her head more deeply under the covers and pretended to be asleep until Amma wandered off again.

December became January. Christmas lights came down, and tensions rose in the capital. It seemed like more and more cases of the wild card were emerging, a flood of cases, and no one was quite sure why. Sri Lanka hadn't been hit hard by the virus up until now, but something seemed to have changed. Newspaper and TV pundits linked it to the thousands of Vietnamese refugees that an earlier liberal government had welcomed in—the wild card wasn't contagious, but who knew who might have been sleeping around, introducing more disease into the Sri Lankan gene pool? Accusations flew, marriages broke up, and by February, the conservative government had started implementing stricter measures.

Nikisha overhead Soma talking to her father: "Aiyo! Did you hear? They're requiring jokers be registered now, saying they're going to make them live in separate areas. What will that mean for Niki?"

"Don't worry, don't worry, Soma. No one will know about our Nikisha. Just focus on doing a nice job with that chicken curry, eh? I'm still hoping I can find a treatment for her, something that will reverse the effects . . ."

Her father was spending all his spare hours with his books, but Nikisha thought that was a fool's errand—so many scientists and giant research companies had tried to cure this disease, how likely was a single internal medicine doctor on a tiny island to make any headway? Maybe it gave him some comfort, though—he'd kiss her cheek after dinner, not seeming to mind the stubble, and head to his study to bury himself in his books. Nikisha wouldn't take away anything that gave him comfort, even if it was only false hope.

Then the news came down, a clear order from the government. "Jokers are not allowed to marry or have children without government permission." It was also clear that permission was unlikely to be granted. That was what broke Amma in the end.

That night, Nikisha woke to Amma standing over her bed once again, but this time, she carried a massive knife in her hand, the kaetta that Soma used to chop coconuts in half.

"Amma?" Nikisha asked, still bleary from sleep.

"Shhh . . . shh . . . It's for your own good, mahal. Just hold still, this won't take long. Amma promises, it won't hurt."

"What won't hurt, Amma?" Nikisha was wide awake now, had dragged herself upright in the bed, her spine pressed back against the headboard.

"The tail, the tail—it's the demon taking over." Her mother's voice was soft and soothing, as if she were talking of everyday things. "Everyone will know soon, summer is coming, we can't hide it for much longer. And the hair, it just keeps growing and growing." Now her voice rose a little, its pitch going sharper, fiercer. "The demon killed Udhya, and it's killing Nikisha, little

Niki, my firstborn, my precious daughter. We have to cut the demon out! I'll be quick, I promise, you won't feel a thing, and then Appa will come and sew you up, and nobody will ever know we had a demon in this house—"

Amma lunged at her then, grabbing Nikisha's right shoulder with her left hand, in that same iron grip she'd always had. The one she used when she had to hold a wailing child still for a vaccination, or remove a splinter with a sharp sterilized pin. And Nikisha was smaller now, after her card had turned, not nearly strong enough to stop Amma.

"Amma, no!" Nikisha shouted, was screaming now, surely Appa and Soma would hear, would come running.

But Amma was so fast! Amma yanked, flipping Nikisha over in the bed, so that her tail sprang free of the covers, flailing in the air. The kaetta was already slicing down, swinging! It was only in the last seconds that Nikisha's tail whipped around Amma's wrist, stopping the swing inches away from its target. "No!" Nikisha screamed. And then Amma was screaming, too, dropping the knife, falling to the floor.

Appa rushed in, with Soma close behind, and Nikisha pulled herself upright in the bed. Why was Amma—oh, God. Blood everywhere. Blood pouring out of Amma's eyes, her ears, her nose and mouth, make it stop, make it stop, please!

And it stopped. As soon as Nikisha shaped the thought in her mind, the blood stopped gushing out. Appa had Amma's wrist in his fingers, heedless of the blood, and when he looked up, Nikisha felt as if her heart would stop—but he nodded. It was all right. Amma was alive. Unconscious, though. Soma was silent, her eyes wide with horror.

Appa looked at Nikisha, at the fallen kaetta on the floor, at the tail still whipping wildly behind her, as if all of her grief and turmoil were manifest there. "Kunju, rasathi"—his voice broke. Rasathi, his little princess. He hadn't called her that in years, not since she was a little girl. "I—I packed a backpack for you, with clothes and money, and a letter for introduction, just in case. It's in my closet. You'd better go."

"Appa?"

He glanced back at Soma and then turned to Nikisha again. His meaning was clear—this secret was going to be too big to keep. His eyes looked a thousand years old, full of knowledge no human father should carry. "Now, rasathi. Hurry."

That was the moment her childhood ended.

The letter had led her here, to this guerrilla group deep in the jungle. They'd enlisted her in the cause—why not? Nobody else would help her. Months had passed, and now here they were, December again, with Christmas just around the corner.

After explaining the situation and getting permission from the unit leader, she'd brought out a sarong to Croyd—she didn't see how he could wear a shirt with those giant wings.

"Do you need help tying it?"

"No." And indeed, he seemed quite deft. "I've spent time in this part of the world before. There was a woman once—never mind. It was a long time ago." He looked sad, and Nikisha felt an unexpected pang of pity. She was lonely, but he seemed far lonelier, somehow. The loneliness pulsed off him, in waves.

"Well, come eat. You'll feel better."

"Will anyone mind—?" he trailed off, gesturing at his feathered form.

"We're all jokers here," Nikisha said, her tail whipping out. She'd learned how to adapt her clothes for the tail, with a lot of help from the local tailors, and had better control of it now, too. These days, it mostly stayed neatly coiled around her waist—visible but unobtrusive. Sometimes people didn't notice it for quite a while, and clearly Croyd hadn't either, because he blinked surprise at the sight. He seemed reassured, though.

"Is it far?" he asked.

"No—maybe fifteen minutes' walk. Although maybe you could fly there faster." If she had wings, she would want to try them out!

He shook his head. "That's all right. I've flown before. I'll walk with you this time."

Flown before. Nikisha frowned—she'd thought that Croyd was like all the rest of them, dealing with the disease newly emerged. But maybe he was something different? Her stomach rumbled then, breaking her train of thought. Eat now, think later.

She hadn't known a man could eat so much. Even though dawn had broken not long before, the cooks had already started on preparing breakfast—there were hundreds of people in their unit, so they needed to start early. Nikisha liked a simple breakfast: fresh fruit and a little bread. She served those to Croyd, then added to his plate stringhoppers and sothi, pol sambol and fish curry. He demolished all of that, which the head cook seemed to take as a challenge.

Now the cooks were making egg hoppers, a rare treat, and a chicken curry that had been simmering for lunch was added to the table. Croyd ate at least three more meals' worth of food—Nikisha had no idea where he put it all—while Charu, the head cook, watched with satisfaction. The eyes in the back of Charu's head meant that he could keep an eye on the diners while he mixed up another batch of hopper batter . . . there were sometimes advantages to being a joker chef.

When Croyd was finally done, Nikisha asked, "So, we have a proposition for you. If you're willing to talk to the leaders . . . ?"

Croyd said, "Of course. I owe you all—for watching over me while I slept, and for feeding me now. If I can help you, I will."

Nikisha quirked an eyebrow and said, "Better wait to promise anything until you hear what they want."

Croyd nodded. "Fair enough."

It had been just past midnight when Nikisha left her parents' house; her father saw her into the car and gave the driver instructions. They drove up from Colombo, up into the hill country, past Kurunegala, all the way to Dambulla and beyond. She tried to doze, but despite exhaustion her mind kept throwing up images of horror, jerking her from sleep.

Dawn was just breaking when the driver dropped her at the small village referenced in her father's letter. The rock fortress of Sigirya rose not far away, looming over the landscape; Nikisha wondered what the story of that doomed king might signify for herself and her journey.

The unit leader—they called him J.R.—read her father's letter by the light of a flickering bulb, his brow furrowed. When he finished, he looked her over, seeming unimpressed. "You're welcome, of course. We don't turn any jokers away. And your father's been helping raise funds for us. We appreciate his dedication to the cause. It's always good having doctors in support. But from what he said, it seems like you don't have any particular talents that would be useful to us."

Nikisha almost didn't say anything, didn't do anything. Was it a talent, what she'd done to Amma? Part of her wanted to forget it had happened, lock it away in her mind forever. But her pride had flared, to be dismissed this way. Just another man, seeing a young woman, a girl, thinking her a nuisance. He thought her worthless, and if Udhya had been here, he'd have thought the same of her. Before she could think twice about it, Nikisha stepped forward, leaned across the table, and grabbed his wrist. "Bleed," she said, in a quiet voice, and blood started to gush from his nose.

She hadn't really expected it to work. Her mother's voice echoed, a cold whisper, demon. Nikisha let go, shocked, and the blood slowed and stopped. J.R.'s eyes had widened; he grabbed a shirt hanging off the back of his chair and used it to mop up the blood on his face, the spatters on the table, on her father's letter.

"Well. Maybe we have something to talk about after all. What else can you do?"

She shrugged. She didn't really know.

He nodded. "We'll find out. You could be useful to the cause." He stepped to the open door, called over a girl, and told her to help Nikisha get settled in. "We'll start exploring the scope of your talents tomorrow. Get some sleep."

They were clearly still very new, this organization. Most of their unit was still set up in the jungle. The girls had their own area, with a single large shelter hastily thrown up, and reed mats on the dirt floor for sleeping. When one of them had to use the pit toilet, another woman went along to stand guard, protecting their modesty. Nikisha had never used a pit toilet in her life, certainly never had someone else possibly watching her use one, but after the events of the last week, it was one small humiliation in a sea of horrors, not even worth worrying about.

Under J.R.'s direction, she explored the scope of her powers, testing them on hapless volunteers. If she was touching someone, she could make them bleed. From a distance, she could heat their blood, make them feverish and ill. Maybe heating wasn't exactly what was going on—the others called her Yaksani, disease demon. They meant it as a compliment, and saw her as a great weapon for the cause. Nikisha wondered what her doctor father would think of his daughter's new skills.

Nikisha settled in, training in hand-to-hand combat, use of weapons. Could she actually take a life? In self-defense, probably, but could she do so on command? She wasn't sure, but it didn't hurt anything to learn how to defend herself.

She soon discovered that attempts at preserving the girls' modesty was mostly a sham. The joker girls all seemed to be wild junglee girls; they acted as if it didn't matter what they did, or with whom. Since now none of them would be allowed to legally marry, maybe they had the right of it. One or the other of them was always sneaking off (and sometimes, two of them together); the other girls seemed to think it was all a big joke.

For months, Nikisha mostly kept to herself, but eventually

found a young man as well; slender as a sambur deer, with a deer's skittish ways and two small pronged horns spiraling out from his forehead. Rajiv was immensely gentle. When he touched her breasts under cover of darkness, by the light of the rising moon, Nikisha could almost forget . . . everything. Most of the time, she'd rather not think at all.

There were other movement groups scattered around the island, but theirs was one of the largest, and comprising mostly young people, the student wing. The leaders called them the Young Demons; they'd taken the pejoratives hurled at them and made them a badge of honor, a rallying cry. But Nikisha couldn't hear the phrase without hearing her mother's whispered words, sending a cold shiver running down her back.

As they cleared their plates and rinsed their hands clean in the back of the kitchen, Croyd offered, "I'd heard that a resistance group was forming; that's why I came to Sri Lanka. I'd been traveling through Southeast Asia, visiting relatives of a woman I once knew; from the news reports, it sounded like things were getting pretty bad here. In my last form, I could pass for a nat and a native of this country, but my hearing was greatly enhanced—I thought I might be useful in gathering information. But then I just ran out of time; I fell asleep before I could do any good."

"That probably would have been helpful," Nikisha admitted. "We're not great at gathering information. This isn't a subtle group."

She started leading him toward J.R.'s house. The unit members had all moved into the village over the last year, but most of them were in shared quarters—only J.R. had a house to himself. It was fair, since he had the responsibility for leading this unit. Most of the time, other people were in there anyway, huddled around the dining table, plotting. She added, "We can't just keep going as we have been—an attack on a military warehouse here, disturbing a supply train there." She frowned—sometimes it felt like they were children, playing at revolution. "Everything we do is too small. Even though some of us can do quite a lot of damage, it's just not on the scale of a government military. They shrug us off, as if we were ants, and every successful attack leads to stronger crackdowns."

"I heard that jokers here lost the right to vote last month," Croyd said soberly. "Shocking. Surely that won't last, though."

Nikisha shrugged. "I'm not a strategist or a politician. The others, they argue about it. But it's clear that we can't go on as we have been."

Were they on the right track? Sometimes, when she heard J.R. or one of the other leaders talk, she was caught up in their stirring rhetoric. All of Sri Lanka's people coming together to protect the jokers among them. Tamil, Sinhalese, Middle Eastern Muslims, Malays, Burghers, ethnic Chinese, Vietnamese, and more—they would form a true Unity Party, wrest the government away from those who preached hatred of the Other, the ones who'd risen to power on a sea of populist rhetoric.

Other times, though, especially in the first months after she'd joined the camp, she worried that their tactics made her no better than the enemy. If she used her powers to hurt, to kill—was that righteous? Or just expedient?

When Rajiv was killed in a set of reprisal attacks, her resolve had hardened. The government butchers gutted him, as if he'd been a deer in truth, an animal, and left him dismembered in pieces by the side of the road for the rebels to find. They'd even laid him out on a pile of banana leaves, as if he were being served for a holiday feast.

Nikisha couldn't claim to have been in love with Rajiv, or even to have known him that well. But everyone in the camp was appalled by the callous horror of the soldiers' actions. And Rajiv had held her together for a little while, when she was falling apart. That was worth something. Now his gentleness was gone forever.

She'd gone to J.R. after his death, and asked to be shifted to more active duty. She was willing to use her powers to kill, if need be. J.R. took her at her word. The first time he'd sent her out with a team to take down a military target, she hadn't hesitated before setting the soldiers' blood boiling. Nikisha had never been sent close enough to actually lay hands on anyone, so she wasn't sure if she'd been responsible for any deaths. If she had, her Appa would be shocked; he wouldn't recognize his daughter. But in the weeks after Rajiv's slaughter, she hadn't been able to make herself care.

Nikisha explained to Croyd, "We're planning a big coordinated attack now." She paused, then added, "I'd better let the leaders fill you in on the specific details, but I'll warn you—I'm not sure they'll let you leave once you know the plan." Was this a betrayal of the cause? She didn't think so. "They're not going to hurt you, or force you to help; we're sworn to behave better than they do. We don't hurt anyone who doesn't deserve it. But if you won't help us, you may be detained here until it's all over."

Croyd stopped still in the street. "That might not be an option for me. How long will that be?"

The big attack would take place on Christmas Eve, when everyone had their guard down for the holiday. "Three weeks."

He frowned, then said, "Three weeks should be doable, especially if your people can get some medication for me. Nothing too exotic—I just need amphetamines."

"That shouldn't be a problem." J.R. had connections everywhere, it seemed, and maybe her father would help. They wrote to each other every month now, though she told him nothing about the blood on her hands.

His letters to Nikisha were a lifeline to her old life, though even there, nothing was the same. He wrote Amma had been doing worse, had stopped eating for a while. He'd hired a new woman, a nurse, to live in the house with them, to make sure she didn't wander off when Appa was gone. Soma had fled long before, declaring herself terrified that Nikisha might come back and murder

304 Mary Anne Mohanraj

them all in their sleep. No one cooked in that house anymore—all their meals were made in local restaurants and delivered by tiffin carriers on bicycles. If she were to go home again, Nikisha wasn't sure she'd recognize the place.

Croyd nodded. "All right, then." He grinned suddenly and said in an oddly robotic monotone, "Take me to your leader." Then, in his normal voice, he added, "I always wanted to say that."

The attack would be four-pronged. The biggest element was the one they'd be assigned to, the attack on a large cantonment, a massive military installation. Several units were coming together from all over the island, the Young Demons, eight hundred of them, divided into groups of roughly twenty-five each.

Other groups would simultaneously enact other attacks. One group would abduct the prime minister. Another would rescue one of the leaders from jail. The last would attempt to capture the city of Colombo, attacking police stations, gaining arms and ammunition from each. They'd take the prison, the radio and TV stations, and several residences of government officials. With the government and media under their control, the military decimated, they could do some real damage, and hopefully, win serious concessions. All they wanted was to be full citizens again, with the same rights and privileges as everyone else. That didn't seem too much to ask.

J.R. turned to Croyd after the recap. "Understand?"

"Yes, that all seems clear enough."

J.R. nodded toward a quiet dark-skinned man who sat cross-legged on the veranda just outside, placidly weaving together a palm leaf basket. "Sanjeevan has told me you're an honest man who wants to help—he has a talent for telling such things now."

Croyd nodded. "I do want to help, but I'm not sure how this body will be of any use to you. I can hardly gather intelligence in this form." A shiver passed across his shoulders, and then he shook it away, stilling his body. "Where do you see me in this?"

J.R. said soberly, "We don't have enough fliers. They have helicopters. We need some way to knock those out of the sky."

Croyd frowned. "Even assuming I can fly well enough to be of use during a long battle, which isn't at all clear to me yet, I don't know that I'll be much good against a helicopter—especially if it's carrying men with rifles."

"That's where our Yaksani comes in," J.R. said, gesturing to Nikisha. "Get her close enough, and she can boil the pilots' blood in their cockpits, maybe even before they get off the ground. You might be able to take out much of the air force in one fell swoop."

"Might," Croyd said, raising a feathered eyebrow.

J.R. shrugged. "No plan survives contact with the enemy. We think it has a good chance of working."

"Can I think about it?" Croyd asked.

J.R. hesitated, then said, "Of course. Maybe we could send you two out on a few scouting missions in the meantime? That'd be helpful, too."

Croyd nodded. "That should be possible. Now let me tell you what I'm going to need in return . . ."

After the meeting with J.R. ended, Nikisha led Croyd out, over to the men's barracks. As they walked, Croyd kept touching his beak. It would be funny, if he didn't look so distressed every time he did it.

Nikisha asked, "Is it so awful?" Her tail whipped around in the air behind her, responding to her mild irritation.

Croyd frowned. "I'm sorry. I know you're all jokers here." He gestured out, to the whole camp. "But I never really get a chance to get used to it. I only become a joker once in a while. Mostly when I wake up, I look . . . well, I can pass."

"That must be nice," Nikisha said, in as neutral a tone as she could manage.

He shrugged. "Sort of. Then I'm trying to stay awake as long as I can, and the uppers can really mess with my brain. That's not really a great option, either."

She quirked a smile. "Well, this time you get both, so that's something. If you decide to help us, that is."

Croyd laughed. "You have a pretty grim way of looking at the world."

Nikisha shrugged. "That way, you're never disappointed."

They went to Sigiriya to practice, sneaking past the security guards with the help of some of the others. There were cameras to avoid, but only at the base—once they'd started climbing, it was just a matter of being careful with footing in the dark. It took close to an hour to make it to the top, and when they finally got there, Nikisha couldn't resist climbing up onto the king's stone, standing high over the landscape. How proud King Kasyapa must have been, looking out over the island he'd come to rule. How terrified, too, knowing he'd stolen it from the rightful heir, who would soon return to topple him from his high perch.

"Are you ready to fly?" Croyd asked.

Nikisha nodded. She stepped forward, reached up to put arms around his neck, then jumped up a little, wrapping her legs and tail around him as well. His torso was notably broader than hers; she nestled against his chest. It was easy to cling there, as if her new body were designed to climb trees, or climb people. Croyd wrapped powerful arms around her, securing her even more tightly, and then, without a word of warning, he was running forward, throwing himself off the edge of the high stone tor, wings snapping open.

They fell for a gut-churning moment, and Nikisha had to fight the instinct to boil the blood of the one who'd done this to her. But then Croyd's new wings caught the air, and he was flapping firm, powerful strokes, taking them up instead of down. They circled Sigiriya in a widening gyre, gaining height with each turn of the spiral, until they were so high, Nikisha imagined she could see Kandy in the distance . . .

They coasted then, catching long downdrafts and updrafts, playing in the breeze. At one point, Croyd mischievously sent them tumbling, and Nikisha dug her fingernails into the back of his neck in response. He laughed, and then she was laughing, too, despite death and loss and all the sorrow of the past few years. In the sky, none of that mattered.

She could feel when he started to tire, and she whispered, "Down there," pointing to a clearing by a lake. One of the old reservoirs built by ancient kings, but no buildings nearby—just the jungle, waiting silently for them. They coasted down, down, finally coming to a stop on the shore, scaring away some geese that honked irritation as they went. Croyd staggered a little as they landed, and Nikisha leapt off, landing on her own two feet. Feeling oddly bereft without the warmth of his body against hers, the twinned beating of their hearts.

"Are you all right?" she asked. "You must be tired."

Croyd shook his head. "I've only been awake for two days—I'm not tired at all. Just needed a moment to adjust to using my legs again." He folded his wings smoothly at his back.

"Well, that's good—we weren't very practical with that experiment. It'll be a long walk to get back to base." She frowned. "Unless you can take off from the ground?"

Croyd said, "Maybe? It'd be hard, carrying you, too—you pull my weight further forward than my body wants. We might just crash if we tried."

Nikisha stepped forward, catching that same mischievous spirit that had led him into barrel rolls in the sky. She smiled slowly and put a hand on his chest. Ah, there—there was his beating heart, blood pulsing through its four chambers. She could feel it rushing, and gave it just the smallest push with her power. Let his blood run hot for her. "Are you saying I'm fat?"

"Yes, exactly," Croyd said, eyes bright with laughter. He couldn't kiss her, not with that beak, but he reached out and pulled her to him, his head coming down so his beak rested on her bare back. He traced a pattern there, delicately, and Nikisha shivered in response. Cold in the night air, heat in her blood, her bones. She wanted to be hotter still. Nikisha pulled him down then, to the sandy shore, and for a little while, they both gave up on thinking.

They carried out a few actual missions in the next weeks, small scouting trips. Nikisha practiced using her powers from the air, trusting Croyd to keep her airborne and safe. She could feel the people below her, in the dark, little pinpricks of moving blood and heat. They hit a military convoy, trucks winding along a high, hilly road, and when she boiled the blood of the lead driver, he lost control of his truck, sending it tumbling, falling down the side of the hill. The others stopped, climbing out of their vehicles in some hapless effort to help the man. Nikisha and Croyd didn't wait to see the result—they'd fulfilled their task, another test run, and swooped away in glorious triumph.

By the second week, word was starting to get around. The soldiers murmured in their barracks about Yaksani, the disease demon, who attacked them from the air.

J.R. said, "We're going to have to be careful—it's a good thing Christmas is soon. If we use you too much, they'll start hunting you. Maybe we should just wait at this point—assuming Croyd has decided to help us?"

Croyd popped another pill in his mouth, grinning widely. "You keep these coming, and I'm your man. Anything for you and sweet Yaksani."

J.R. nodded approval—by this point, everyone knew that Nikisha and Croyd were together, and no one seemed to care. So different from how she'd grown up, when Amma was forever warning her and Udhya of the price that would be exacted, should they cross the line. Maybe being a joker meant that you lived by a different set of rules. Maybe having your sister die in a breath, having your mother try to hack off your tail, having her life in your hands and her blood pooling around you—maybe all of that meant that worrying about how people might talk about your sex life just wasn't relevant anymore.

It was, after all, a great sex life. With every day that passed, Croyd seemed to grow a little wilder, more manic, and Nikisha found herself pulled along by his excitement. For so long, she'd been sunk in a dark hole, but he pulled her up—literally, flying her up into the sky. Croyd had mastered the art of taking off from the ground, even with Nikisha clinging to him, and once they'd gone high enough, he could use the downdrafts and updrafts to rest his wings, giving full attention to what his hands and hips could do in the air. A lot, as it turned out.

Risky behavior on several fronts—mostly Nikisha remembered protection, but sometimes they got a little carried away. And more immediately, when Croyd was truly distracted, they might slip out of an updraft and start tumbling to the ground. Once, Croyd's urgently flapping wings pulled them up from collision mere seconds before they would have hit—but that didn't lead to any more caution on either of their parts. He slipped her one of his pills instead, and soon, she was flying, too, even when they were on the ground. Everything else in the world just dropped away, and they were two bodies intertwined, moving to the beat of their blood. It was all going so, so well.

And then disaster struck.

December 21. The camp was in a furor with the news that one of the district leaders had acted early, launching an attack against the Peradeniya police station. Three constables were killed, but the real problem was that jokers had attacked in force, in full daylight, and the populace had witnessed the attack. The people were demanding action, the government was mobilizing frantically.

J.R. paced behind his table, ranting to a small group of key personnel, a group that included Nikisha and Croyd. "These fools! Now they've declared curfew and it's going to be ten times harder to move into position. All the police stations will be warned, so who knows if we'll be able to get arms and ammunition from them? The entire fourth prong is in danger of failing."

His second was a young woman whose skin and eyes had gone entirely black when her card turned, and who preferred to be known only by her joker name of Karuppu, blackness. She had further news for them all. "The army is mobilizing. They've called up reserve units and are reinforcing their weaker stations— stations we had targeted previously. We have to rethink the entire attack plan, and then we have to make sure that we communicate it to everyone. Everyone who wasn't captured already—and who knows what they'll give up under pressure." She finished grimly, "Pray to whatever gods you believe in that there isn't a leak, because then we'd be truly done for."

J.R. added, "It's all over the TV and radio now, the newspapers are printing bloody reports as we speak. We'll lose the initiative, and worse, the sympathy of the people. We have to move up our plans, act while they're still sorting themselves out."

"How soon?" Croyd asked. He wasn't looking so good these days—his leg jittered a little, almost all the time, and he blinked frequently, as if trying to clear his eyesight. Nikisha thought that maybe, for his sake, it would be better if the attack came sooner.

"Tonight," Karuppu said. "We'll take the day to plan and spread the word, and then as soon as darkness falls, we move."

— — —

The first attack went like clockwork, just as they'd planned. They'd been partnered with a mobile strike force of twenty-five of the Young Demons, a group of students so excited to work with them that they'd taken an emblem for themselves, the bloody eagle, symbolized by a feather dripping blood, painted onto arms, clothes, even faces. Nikisha and Croyd stooped in first, from the air, and Nikisha sent out her power in a sickening wave, as strongly as she could. The soldiers in the barracks cried out, groaned, fell from their bunks to the floor, and the Young Demons rushed in, taking their weapons, tying them up.

No unnecessary loss of life, that was the plan. As J.R. said, it would only harden resistance against them, make their job more difficult in the long run. But before they could glory in their victory, Karuppu was there, running in to shout in Nikisha's face— "Go, go! The third force needs backup; they're breaking."

So she and Croyd were up in the air again, with a leap and a mighty beating of his wings, and she was almost laughing, giddy with the triumph, plus the pills she'd taken before this final battle. Wasn't it all wonderful! And then, moments later, stooping down again, a little northeast, to where the third force were embattled. That was when everything started falling apart.

Half the force or more was on the ground. Nikisha couldn't simply send her power out—it would be indiscriminate, as likely to hit one of their own as an enemy. They hadn't thought this through. She'd have to lay hands on them, but that was all right. She'd been training in hand-to-hand combat for a year now, had a gun strapped to her thigh, she could handle herself.

As soon as they touched down, she slipped from Croyd's grasp and was running, dodging, weaving her way through her fallen comrades, reaching out to grab an enemy soldier's arm, and there! There it was, contact, and then he was bleeding, falling to the ground, and she couldn't, wouldn't pause to stop the bleeding. She was on to the next one—bleed!—and then another.

She was a whirling, spinning top, a disease demon born of legend. Her head felt so light, her bones, Nikisha almost felt as if she could fly. She wasn't Nikisha anymore—she was Yaksani, and they would see her power, they would fear her. For Rajiv, for Udhya, for herself and her comrades and all the pain that they'd endured, for Amma and Appa and everyone who had been hurt by the Takisian disease, she would punish those who, instead of reaching out to help, had made it worse with their selfishness and greed and fear and hatred.

And they had noticed now, they were calling out her name—Yaksani, *Yaksani*! Calling out her name as they ran away and oh, how funny, that they were frightened of a little girl like her. It made her want to laugh, it made her tail curl itself in a tight corkscrew of delight. She stopped still in the middle of the courtyard, and that was almost the end of her. Because she might be a disease demon reborn, but she wasn't invulnerable—she wore no armor, just a tunic and pants, nothing that would stop a bullet.

Not everyone was running away—one man had dropped to one knee, raised his rifle, and taken aim, and that would have been the end of Nikisha if Croyd hadn't been watching, hadn't intervened, falling down from the sky to sweep one giant wing into the man, knocking him aside. The gun had no chance to go off. Croyd grinned at her, in the dim lighting of the courtyard, and Nikisha grinned back, bloodlust thrumming through her. She felt invulnerable, with her changeable man, her changeable hawk-eagle by her side.

And then the other soldier, the one they hadn't seen, took his shot, and Croyd crumpled to the ground.

"*No!*"

Nikisha didn't remember rushing over to his side, didn't remember putting her hands on the gaping wound. In his belly—that was bad, she knew that much. Gut wounds were bad. If they perforated the bowel, he was likely dead. But if not—she pressed down on the wound, applying pressure. Nikisha was suddenly thinking sharply, more clearly than she had in weeks, since she started taking Croyd's pills. More clearly than she had since her card had turned, her sister had died, since that morning when everything had changed.

What had she been doing? She had killed people tonight, and probably before tonight, and none of it had seemed real, none of it was something she had chosen. She just went along, because it was easier, and now Croyd was bleeding out in front of her—oh.

Blood. She hadn't caused this wound, but if she had power over blood, just maybe . . .

Oh, please. And she was praying now, praying the way she had when she was a child, the way her father had when he sat by her bedside. Hail Mary, full of grace, the Lord is with you. Give us this day—No, that wasn't right, but it didn't matter, the words weren't important. Maybe no one was listening, but what mattered was her intention—that's what the priest had always said. And right now, Nikisha intended to heal.

The blood stopped. Her hands were still red, covered in Croyd's blood, but it had stopped pulsing out, as if her two small hands were a sufficient barrier. But she couldn't count on that forever. She dared to take away one hand, to rip at her clothes until she'd pulled a strip of fabric free. Nikisha bound it around the man, lifting him up, tucking it beneath the point on his spine where the wings attached, then back around again, tight as she could make it. There. That might be enough to hold.

Karuppu grabbed her arm, dragged her to her feet. "Come on!" Nikisha would have protested, but two of the cadre were already at Croyd's side, lifting him up, carrying him out. She put her head down and ran.

It wasn't just a defeat—it was a rout. Communications had fallen apart, so two-thirds simply didn't attack when night fell.

Between that and the increased government preparation, the Young Demons had no chance.

They counted themselves lucky that most were able to flee. Some disappeared completely, crossing the ocean to India, seeking refuge among those teeming masses, leaving friends and family behind.

The government forces continued to search for the leaders, offering rewards for information to the general populace, but jokers had their powers to help them evade capture. It evened the playing field, just enough. Eventually, hopefully, the government would grow tired of hunting for them.

As for Nikisha, she crouched in the Dambulla safe house, watching over Croyd. He slept, snoring a little. Whatever it was she'd done to his blood had triggered the end of his cycle; he'd fallen into deep sleep, not waking even when the surgeons stitched up his wound. The bullet had gone through and through, missing anything major, which was the main reason he'd survived. But Nikisha had helped.

She watched over his sleep, in thanks for what he'd done for her. She'd saved his life, but first, he'd saved hers. She was curious to see what new form he'd take in his next transformation; after just a few days, the feathers had started dropping from his wings. Nikisha collected them in an old rice bag, though she didn't know why. Maybe she'd use them to decorate a mask to hang on her wall, the kind the woodcarvers made to ward off demons. Demons like Yaksani. The thought made Nikisha want to laugh, but she stifled the urge; it wouldn't go over well right now.

Around her, arguments swirled, as those who'd survived dissected everything that had gone so terribly wrong.

"We'll regroup," Karuppu said vigorously. She was leader of the Young Demons now, with J.R. captured, imprisoned. "Regroup, rebuild, and when they're not expecting us, we'll strike again. If it hadn't been for that early attack . . ."

Nikisha tuned her out, hugging her knees to her chest, rocking back and forth gently by the side of Croyd's sleeping form. She wanted the pills; she was shaky with desire for them. But she wasn't going to go through Croyd's clothes looking for them, or ask Karuppu to help her get some more. Whatever this group of jokers decided to do, Nikisha wanted to be free of them. She was done with revolution. This was never what she'd wanted for her life.

Of course, now would be a bad time to try to leave, but once things had calmed down a little . . .

When the final transformation came, three days later, it was swift. The last feathers fell in a cascade, surrounding Croyd's torso on the reed mat. He'd grown tall and thin, his skin shifting to a light tan, with a hint of olive underneath. Hair sprouted on his head, dark and thickly curled. His beak disappeared, and in its place grew a rather handsome nose—in fact, overall, Croyd Crenson had become a good-looking man, the sort you might see in a Bollywood film.

Nikisha found him much less attractive this way. This wasn't the joker who had helped her fly so high.

She'd brought a mirror for him, and when he opened his eyes finally—dark pools an ordinary girl might drown in—Nikisha handed it to him silently. He'd want to know. Croyd gazed at the face in the mirror for a little while, looking pleased, then put the glass down beside him, propping himself up on one elbow, in a gesture that was uncannily reminiscent of his previous waking.

"It's good to see you again," Croyd said, smiling with a peaceful calm Nikisha hadn't seen in weeks. He glanced around the small, dark bedroom, lit only by a burning mosquito coil and the light of the cold December moon. Karuppu argued with the others in the next room, her voice sharp and angry. She was always arguing. "I take it we didn't win?"

"Pretty much the opposite," Nikisha said wearily. "It's going to take months before they're ready to try again." She hesitated, then added, "Resources are stretched thin; they might not be able to get you your pills anytime soon."

"Ah," Croyd said. He pushed up into a cross-legged sitting position, facing her, a lost look in his eyes. "I don't really get to plan on timelines that take months. Not anymore." Croyd frowned. "I'm probably not going to stick around here." He hesitated, then added, "Unless there's some other reason for me to stay?" Croyd reached out a hand to her; it would be cruel not to take it. Nikisha curled her fingers around his; she felt the pulse beating there, the warmth of the blood coursing beneath the skin. Her heart beat a little faster in response.

Nikisha wavered—they had had something. Maybe they could leave the Young Demons, make something new? She'd been dreaming of going back home, seeing if she could do anything for her mother. Nikisha could finish her exams—or maybe that would be too difficult, and she'd have to try to study abroad.

Either way, she could write about what had happened here, try to publicize what the government was doing to jokers, shame them on the world stage. That was how Gandhi had won independence for India, after all—so much of his strategy had to do with public shaming. Maybe she could do something with that, too. And Croyd could come with her—the way he looked now, certainly, no one in her father's household would object, and with the help of some drugs from the clinic, they'd have a few weeks to make plans . . .

Croyd's hand disappeared.

It didn't really—Nikisha could still feel the weight of it, the warmth. If she wanted to, she knew that she could still make his blood race. But his hand had camouflaged itself against her hand, the reed mat, the pile of feathers. Effectively invisible.

"Well," Croyd said softly. "That's new." His hand faded back into view—he made it disappear again, then come back, and he was laughing now, inviting her to share in the pleasure of it. Life with Croyd could be an adventure—Nikisha could see that. Always changing, always something new around the corner.

She just couldn't. The deaths, the killing, even saving Croyd's life—it was all too much, a dark wave that threatened to drag her out to sea. Nikisha was tired. Aching for Udhya and Rajiv, heart-sore with the deaths she'd caused. She wasn't a little girl anymore, but still, she wanted to go home and confess to her father. Could he still love her, even with so much blood on her hands?

"I'm sorry," Nikisha said softly. She let her hand slip out of his, and for a moment, Croyd looked stricken. It must be a lonely life he led, constantly changing. But she couldn't go with him just to ease his loneliness—that wasn't enough for Nikisha, and in the end, it wouldn't be enough for him, either.

Croyd shrugged, smiling faintly, as if he'd gotten used to letting people go. "Maybe someday we'll meet again, out in the world?"

"Maybe," Nikisha said. It seemed unlikely, but she wouldn't deny a drowning man a spar of hope. Her time of the month had come while Croyd lay sleeping, and the truth was, Nikisha had welcomed the blood that told her she needn't maintain ties with the man. Croyd had invited her onto a seductive, exhilarating path, and for a time, she'd followed willingly. But the excitement came at too high a cost; enough was enough.

Nikisha could heal now, like her father. She had so much to learn. She'd go to him, ask him to teach her. There were too many broken people in the world, and they were all in need of healing.

Yaksani would have to go to sleep. It was time for Nikisha to go home.

Swimmer, Flier, Felon, Spy

PART VII

Just as Tesla had told the aquatic Croyd Crenson who sought him out, finding him would be no trouble at all. He simply visited Jokertown, for what he hoped was the final time on this trip. He needed to see his . . . acquaintance? He didn't know what to call Jube the Walrus, but they were certainly becoming familiar with each other.

And since Jube kept the ring of keys to Croyd Crenson's safe houses, *they* were clearly far more than acquaintances. It seemed likely that Jube would know precisely where the man who stood on water was staying in the Bronx.

The only wrinkle would be getting the information from him. He'd proved somewhat prickly at his and Storgman's previous visit to the newsstand.

"Back again so soon?" Jube asked by way of greeting, his blue-black skin almost glimmering in the sun. "What do you have there?"

Tesla realized he was still carrying the caricature of himself. He was unaccountably shy about revealing it.

"Come on, you're here for something from me, so let me see it."

What could it hurt? Tesla unrolled the caricature and held it up for Jube's inspection. To his surprise, Jube cackled in delight.

"You found the eight-armed Croyd, I see," he said. "What'd you do with the crook?"

"He's in a holding cell."

"I bet he doesn't like that." But Jube nodded. "Smart, though. But then, that's your defining characteristic, being smart. Which is why Crenson's drawing is so delightful. I can't imagine you on a bike. It would be like me riding one." He gestured at his large humanoid walrus body, unsuited for the frame of a bicycle in every way.

Tesla couldn't suppress a sniff of amusement.

"So, I suppose you're looking for another one," Jube said. "I have to tell you, I'm protective of the Sleeper. I've known him for a long, long time. But I'm beginning to think you feel the same. Protective. Not many people understand him."

"I am beginning to, in theory, at least." Tesla thought of the plans forming in his mind. "I'm surprised to say you might be right about the protectiveness. I need to get them all together, not just because I was hired to do so."

It was more explanation than he'd ever given anyone for what and why and how he did a job. Tesla was changing—being changed by this hunt, understanding himself better, too—and he wasn't sure he liked it.

"The one in the Bronx is who came to me initially," Tesla added. "You have his address?"

Jube stroked his chin with his large fingers. "I'll give it to you for the picture."

"Of me?"

"That's the one."

"Fine, but for that, I'd also like to know where the final Croyd Crenson is. I need to find him today."

Jube shook his head almost sadly. "He's been moving around so much, he's a real force of nature. I've heard about it, but he hasn't been to see me. I can't help you there. But I do have the address you need."

Tesla wasn't in the habit of compromising. But he rolled up the picture and passed it over.

"This is going in my private collection," Jube said proudly. He reached into a pocket and produced a piece of paper, which he handed to Tesla. It had an address in the Bronx written in pencil, a fine pencil. "Figured you'd be back," Jube said. "Good luck today. Now, you ready for your joke?"

Tesla braced.

Tesla found the building in the Bronx with little trouble. Jube not being aware of the last Croyd Crenson's whereabouts worried him, but he had much of the day left to deal with that problem. Perhaps this visit would provide a lead.

He knocked on the door and a voice he recognized as his employer called, "Come on in, the water's fine."

Tesla resisted the urge to roll his eyes and did as told. The scene inside the small apartment was . . . unexpected. In contrast with the worn, nearly empty safe house of the floating Crenson, it was comfortably appointed with bookshelves and furniture. Not that Crenson was using them. There were splashes of water on the wooden floor.

"In here," came another shout.

Tesla went up a short hallway and stopped at an open door. It was to a bathroom, based on the checkered tile visible.

"Like I said, in here," Crenson said. "Don't be shy. I'm clothed."

Tesla stepped into the bathroom. Where he found Crenson currently standing on top of the water filling a large claw-footed tub. His pupils were the size of dinner plates as he bobbed up and down slightly on the water.

"Good thing you finally showed up. I've been getting sleepy.

You don't have any speed, do you? I'm almost out. There's coffee in the kitchen, though."

His speech was far more rapid than at their first meeting.

"I came to give you a time and place. You need only stay awake until midnight."

"Good good, I can do that. You found everyone?"

"I have one more left." Tesla rattled through the men he'd found. "I don't suppose you have any idea where the elusive final Crenson might be."

"That asshole blew me all the way out to the Hudson, so no, I didn't keep tabs on him." Crenson looked nervous, bobbing in the water, which Tesla realized also had bubbles in it. Croyd Crenson was standing on a bubble bath, and he hadn't even blinked at the oddity of it. "You sure you got this? You can bring him tonight?"

Tesla decided to ask about this Crenson's intentions. "One of the others thinks you intend violence," he said. "Do you?"

"Not unless they hit first. Besides, you said you'd figure out what I'm after. You're really sure you don't have any speed?"

"I'll see you this evening. You remember that place? Where it all began?"

"I remember it better than anyplace on earth," Crenson said, sounding almost sad. "I'll be there."

Tesla sat in his hotel room later that afternoon, thinking about failure.

He had one Crenson left to find and zero leads. He'd returned here hoping that perhaps some helpful soul would have another pointer for him like that morning's. No such help arrived.

He considered lifting the telephone and asking for the day's newspapers.

He considered going for a walk, but it had begun to storm outside.

He considered what he'd lost. It was becoming clearer to him, without him necessarily wanting it to, that part of the reason he'd left his hidden home in the first place had to do with Li Min. Being in the world made him want to be in the world with her.

All those years ago, he'd come home after learning from his contacts that she was a spy to find her already gone. She'd left her things behind. It took him three years to realize she wouldn't return and to put them into storage.

He was only now realizing she would never show up on his doorstep, no matter the breadcrumbs he trailed, no matter how long he stayed there. Thinking about Croyd Crenson—about these multiple Croyd Crensons—had allowed him to do something he had never tried before. He put himself in her shoes, as best he could.

He did not know if her love for him had been real or not. He knew that his for her had been and still was. He could imagine that she would assume he would feel betrayed (he had, but). That he would hide in ego and that his commitment to his country would outweigh his commitment to her (it didn't). Maybe she even believed he would turn her in (he wouldn't).

It was entirely possible she believed he hated her for her deception. Many men would. He'd never gotten the chance to tell her that he could never do so.

Now, using his powers of deduction and some luck, he'd located four Croyd Crensons and had them set for the meeting tonight with the fifth.

But this was worth nothing unless he found the last, most elusive Crenson. The search for the sixth was proving much more onerous than the rest. Tesla did not know whether that meant the missing Crenson was even more paranoid than the others, if he was simply keeping a low profile, or if indeed he had holed up somewhere and gone to sleep. He hoped the last wasn't the case, or his entire job would be that worst of all things. A failure.

There was no extra time to be had. The Crensons would grow

increasingly unstable, and if any one of them slept, who knew what the result would be? No, it had to be tonight.

Thus far, he had depended on logic, on research, on his own wits, on luck. But now logic had failed him. His research had turned up nothing. Luck seemed to have abandoned him altogether. Tesla elected not to think about his wits.

And, of course, it was now storming so heavily he'd not be able to traipse around the city hoping for a lead. The morning skies had been fair and clear. The floor-to-ceiling windows of his room showed a dark sky and sheets of rain. Hail crashed against the windows.

In the distance, then, there came the unmistakable shattering of glass. His own windows remained intact.

The phone rang.

Tesla answered. "Yes?"

"Sir, you have a visitor. He insists on coming up to your room. We are having difficulties keeping him in the lobby."

Fascinating. Not a little troubling, given the specialties of this particular hotel. Tesla started charging up his horns. "Send him on up," he said.

"Sir, there's been some rather extensive property damage."

"I'll take care of it."

"The manager wishes to speak to you once you've finished your meeting, sir."

It could be assumed that any hotel, even one so specialized as this one, would have a manager. But Tesla had never encountered him or her or them. "I look forward to that conversation," he said.

"Doubtful. We're sending the gentleman up, sir."

The phone went silent. Outside, the wind subsided and the sky began to lighten.

Tesla suspected that the failure he had contemplated and feared might have been preferable to whatever was about to happen. He recalled, in that moment, Jube's mention of his being a real force of nature. Of the aquatic Croyd saying that he had a power strong enough to blow him out into the river.

Tesla had allowed himself to become distracted by the only thing capable of doing so. Thoughts of Li Min. He did his best to push them aside for now. He continued charging up.

A few moments later, he heard footsteps in the hall. He positioned himself so that he was not in front of the door.

His intuition proved correct when the entire door, hinges, and frame exploded inward, across the room, and out through the long windows. The loud shattering of glass was accompanied by an uptick in the wind. This time, however, the wind was blowing *inside* the room.

Tesla put his back to the wall next to the bed. He balled his fists so tightly that his fingernails drew blood from his palms. He was prepared to fight for his life. He was not prepared to die. He had a little to live for, yet. He had hopes.

A slight, dark-eyed man with a sallow complexion rounded the corner. He was wearing nothing but a pair of jeans, not even shoes. He was soaking wet.

He caught sight of Tesla and white sparks flew from his eyes.

"Who the fuck are you and why the fuck are you trying to track me down?" asked the man, and here, Tesla did not doubt, was the sixth and final Croyd Crenson. And with the possible exception of the mining Croyd he'd met deep beneath New York's streets, the most dangerous.

Or at least the most powerful. And danger and power needn't necessarily go hand in hand. Perhaps there was a way through this encounter that wouldn't lead to any more violence than that which had already occurred.

"My name is Tesla. I am a contractor. I was hired by another of the men you woke up with several weeks back to find you and convince you to meet with him tonight. I've been seeking to locate not merely you, but all of you."

A puzzled expression crossed Crenson's face. "All of who? Wait . . . wait, I'm remembering now. My mind gets messed up sometimes. Who were those other guys?"

Humid air poured in from outside of the windows Crenson had destroyed. Sirens sounded in the distance, but when were there not sirens sounding in the distance in this city? Even if they were headed here, they would not make it in time and would not know how to effectively intervene. So how could Tesla respond that wouldn't lead to a sudden flight and fall to the street below?

He decided on the truth. "Those other guys were you."

Another flash of sparks from Crenson's eyes, then, "That's right. That's right. And this other one wants to kill me! Isn't that right?"

There was a noticeable drop in temperature and the wind picked up, if more gently this time.

"No. No, that's not quite right," said Tesla, though of course he still didn't know if he believed the aquatic Crenson's motivations were pure. He had suspicions. Miner Crenson certainly had said he meant to end them. He answered with caution. "I think some of you want different things."

"Then what is this meeting about?"

"I believe he's worried. The one of you who hired me."

"About what?"

"About . . . diminishment. I am worried about the same."

"What the hell is that supposed to mean?"

Tesla rubbed his temples with his fingertips. He was still holding the electrical charge at the ready. "You were infected with the virus on the very first day, isn't that right?"

Crenson looked confused. "Yeah, sure. Jetboy. The blimps."

"And since that time, in the past three-quarters of a century, your life has been a constant cycle of sleeping and waking, always with some new expression of the wild card."

"Plenty of people know that."

Tesla went on. "But in all that time, in all those iterations, has this ever happened to you? Have you ever woken . . . split?"

Crenson slowly shook his head. "I don't think so. I would remember that, wouldn't I?" And for the first time in Tesla's meetings with the various Croyds, the man sounded sad.

"I'm sure you would," said Tesla. "It must have been startling. To say the least."

"I hated them. I just woke up and hated them. I thought there was going to be a fight, and there was a little bit of a scuffle. But we mostly just busted out of there running in different directions. Mostly running. I might have . . . Uh, yeah, I accidentally blew the swimming guy into the Hudson. But he seemed to move better then anyway."

"Why do you think you hated them?"

"*They hated me!*" It was a shout.

"So you all hate one another?"

"They're stealing my life!"

And there, perhaps, it was.

"That's what diminishment means, Mr. Crenson."

"That doesn't explain shit."

"I have come to believe that each of the Sleepers who woke several weeks ago shares just one part of the essential core of Croyd Crenson. You are, none of you, complete."

"Mystic mumbo jumbo," said Crenson.

"If there's one thing we've learned in the past seventy-five years, Mr. Crenson, isn't it that there is far more to the world than we ever suspected?"

Crenson shrugged. "Some people suspected it."

Which was a remarkably astute observation, but exploring it would serve only as a distraction. Tesla felt like he was firmly on the track of something. He kept moving toward it. A renewed sense of purpose. A grasp on the situation that had eluded him.

The picture began to take shape.

"You don't believe in the soul?" Tesla asked.

"Sure I do. I knew a woman once who could suck your soul right out. Leave you comatose."

"Then consider the possibility that your soul has been split. Split into six equal parts that are now faltering on their own."

"Bullshit. I'm not *faltering*. You should see what the lobby of this hotel looks like."

"I believe that a close examination of the structural damage you've caused is in my near future, yes." Tesla made sure he was pressed tightly to the wall. "But that doesn't mean you aren't faltering."

More white sparks from his eyes. "What do you mean?"

Tesla hazarded the question. "What makes you, you?"

Crenson's eyes rolled, which was better than the alternative. "What the fuck, you some kind of philosopher now?"

Tesla extended one hand. "Think about the question; you must have, over all these years. When you wake in a different body—and in this case in six different bodies—what makes you Croyd Crenson?"

"What makes you a pain in the ass?" he grumbled. "Who knows? If I knew that, I'd be charging money to tell people the answer. I'm me."

"And that, Mr. Crenson, is why I'm here and what I want to ensure. I want to make sure you are still you the next time you sleep and wake. Do you believe me?"

There was a long pause. Then, "Sure, horns, I guess I do, though I don't have a fucking clue why. What do you want from me?"

"I want you to meet the others at midnight."

"We'll kill each other."

"Some may try."

Wind blew through the hotel room. Crenson tilted his head. "What the hell? Sounds like a party."

Nearly all was in place. It was a delicate structure of a plan, depending on Croyd's memories and not a little to do with the Sleeper's feelings about, of all things, the New York City public school system. That was where it had all begun, in an institution that still told tales of Crenson.

The Boy Who Would Be Croyd

by Max Gladstone

October 2019

His name really was Clay.

I want to make that clear. Kids can be cruel, even at Xavier Desmond High, and sometimes teachers who don't understand that call the kids the names they call one another, because they want to seem in-the-know or even, yikes, cool, and end up giving a child's passing cruelty a sort of official stamp. That's how a puffy kid gets called Muffin all through senior year, even by his English teacher. You try to watch for things like that, but even the best teacher only knows so much about what's in their students' heads. You might think you understand, because you used to be that age and you think things don't change so fast that you don't know what's up, but they do change, and you don't know.

My point is, that was his actual, honest name: Clay Calvados.

But he did look a bit like clay, in the potter's studio, on the wheel: gray and unfinished, droopy. A little wet, a little soft. Large eyes. He looked like if he touched things with his bare skin he'd leave prints. He wore thin gloves everywhere, even to shake hands, and long sleeves and jeans even in summer, and big sneakers with the laces undone. Billowy clothes, hand-me-downs or Goodwill finds meant to last. You couldn't see the shape of him under all that.

It was even the name on his birth certificate. Most kids at Xavier Desmond turned their wild card early—or it turned them—so they ended up with card names young. My card didn't turn until after high school, and it left me looking normal so long as I'm paying attention enough to pass, so that's another thing about their lives that I don't understand. Imagine coming back from freshman summer with skin made of rock, or praying mantis arms. So they take joker and ace names early—joker names for the most part, since there are more jokers obviously. Or they give one another joker and ace names, but you have to be careful with those, since card names are often a skip and a jump away from teasing. When my card turned, it left me stretchy and bendy, like rubber. That's how Robin Ruttiger became the Amazing Rubberband! But the kid with the big sideburns who can set his hair on fire, in, you know, a superpowered way, not an unhealthy-relationship-with-lighter-fluid way, if everyone calls him Burnside, is that a joke or not? And is it his joke?

Clay just had the odd luck of that name on his birth certificate, and of looking shaped to fit.

He was a nice kid, by all accounts. As a guidance counselor you learn fast that most kids, like most people, are more confused and scared than particularly good or evil. They're muddling through and trying to figure themselves out. Even the ones with super-powers.

Not that a confused and scared teenager with superpowers doesn't pose a particular set of challenges.

But Clay was not, to be honest, on my radar. He'd never come to my office hours asking for help with a class, or how he could become an engineer or a chef. In a perfect world every kid would meet a guidance counselor once or twice a week, even the ones who just sort of coast along with B averages and muddle through lunch period and JV basketball. They all deserve care. But in a perfect world, I'd meal prep on the weekend so I wouldn't come home too late and too tired to cook and end up grazing dinner from yesterday's leftover pork fried rice. Lots of things would be different, in a perfect world.

But we live in this one. Clay knew me by sight, and I knew him. And he and I might have gone all his four years at XD without having more than a casual lunch-line conversation and the standard senior-year college-and-test-prep talk, if not for Elgar Zadornov, if not for IHeartTonya, if not for David Constantinopolis, and definitely if not for Croyd Crenson.

Or if Mrs. LaJolla had not asked me, of all people, to fill in when she had to attend her third granddaughter's wedding. To teach . . . geometry.

It will be easy, she said. Geometry is just a matter of thinking consistent thoughts about space, she said. Anyone who can't do that, can't do anything else, either, she said.

I suggested, in the careful way people suggest things to Mrs. LaJolla, that a district-supplied sub might be a better fit.

"Nonsense." (Mrs. LaJolla reads a lot of British novels and talks like them sometimes.) "Each and every time the district sends a sub, a week later I receive a panicked letter about how Lisa Patil has porcupine quills, or how Burnside incinerated the sub's jacket. No stamina. No grit. We used to have subs with integrity in this city, subs who got their teeth caved in and smiled about it."

I wasn't sure, I allowed, still carefully, that masochistic tendencies were a good indicator of substitute-teacher quality, and offered to show any prospective substitute around Xavier Desmond, introduce them to the kids, ease any prospective panic, et cetera.

"You're a better fit, Ruttiger. You *understand* these kids."

Most objections encounter Mrs. LaJolla like a civilization encounters an out-of-context problem. That is, it's generally a pretty final sort of thing.

So two weeks later, on a fine autumn afternoon, I was teaching geometry.

I'd never taught geometry before, so I was not sure what a successful geometry class was supposed to look like. Maybe it was a good sign that, ten minutes into the lecture, half of them were staring into space and the other half talking among themselves. But I didn't think so.

Mrs. LaJolla had left me notes, which I tried to follow. But while geometry might be a matter of thinking consistent thoughts about space so far as Mrs. LaJolla is concerned, there's a little more to it than that from my perspective. For example, you're supposed to know what SAS congruence is, and things like that. Then, ten minutes into the lecture, Lisa Patil asked, pointing to a diagram I'd copied to the board from Mrs. LaJolla's handwritten notes: "But Mr. Ruttiger, how do you know *those* angles are congruent?"

It was a good question. Mrs. LaJolla's notes were not enlightening. Mrs. LaJolla could have answered Lisa's question offhand, but she wasn't here and I was. So Lisa and I tried to figure it out, while the rest of the class stared out the window. Pretty soon we ran into a dead end, only for Burnside to raise his head and say, "That's dumb, it's obvious, can we move on?"

So Lisa and Burnside got into a fight about angle congruence, which the other kids did seem to find more interesting than my lecture. A few students in the back offered suggestions, meant more to egg one side or the other on than to contribute. There was a personal subtext to the whole thing: The teacher's lounge gossip ran that Burnside and Lisa Patil had been dating earlier in the semester, or seeing each other, or perhaps publicly denying that they had ever seen each other. Reports varied. But however personal their motives may have been, the substance of the argument was all geometry, and everyone was involved, and that was more than I could say for my lecture.

Everyone was involved, that is, except for Clay.

He had come to class slumped over, red-eyed and hollow-faced and looking as if he hadn't slept for a week. When I called roll he stared at me as if I'd grown a second head and was turning purple. But he said, *here,* and I gave him space. That seemed like the kindest thing I could do. When a kid's that sleepy, you can't lecture them awake. The only way to help would be to go back in time, and not even aces can do *that.*

Clay tried to stay awake. He had a liter bottle of one of those awful neon JOKERFÜL energy drinks, and finished half of it in the first five minutes of class. He had a paper clip in one gloved hand and dug it into the skin of his wrist, between the cuff of his shirt and the hem of his glove, to stay awake. The paper clip came away slightly damp. He shook his leg. But it didn't work. Five minutes after attendance he started nodding and bobbing asleep. Each time he'd sit up straight, eyes wide, dig the paper clip into his wrist, and try, for the minute or so he could manage, to look as if my cover version of Mrs. LaJolla's geometry lecture was the latest Zorro movie trailer.

Maybe if I'd paid more attention I could have cut the whole mess short—but to make different choices I would have had to know things I didn't know until later, which brings us back to the time-travel problem.

I don't know exactly when Clay fell asleep, but he was out by the time Lisa and Burnside were standing on their desks, shouting about the opposite angle theorem. Lisa's spines were all up and sharp, Burnside's hair was browning the ceiling tiles, and I had stretched myself up to stand between them, doing my best to moderate, if not the conversation, then at least the way their powers were channeling their enthusiasm. I didn't want to have to explain to Mrs. LaJolla why her classroom had burned down. Or the school.

Then Lisa made a particularly good point, more about Burnside's romantic graces or lack of same than his geometry expertise.

Burnside flared, briefly. He got it under control, but the gathered students staggered back, running into desks as they did. One of those desks was Clay's. Clay himself had slumped back in his chair, mouth open, asleep, but his JOKERFÜL was still on the desktop.

Clay was out. Stone-cold-snoring out. But he wasn't out enough to sleep through the shouts, the screams, the destruction of his desk, and the ice-cold soda in his lap.

His eyes snapped open. He jerked awake with a shout.

And he was different.

Clay had a round, unfinished face. That is, he used to have. Now he had cheekbones. Maybe he always had them, but something about the way he held his face suddenly made me notice them. His eyes were sharp—bright, fixed, calculating. There's a line from, I think it's Sabatini: "He was born with a gift of laughter and a sense that the world was mad." Not words that had ever come to my mind when I saw Clay before. They came to my mind in that moment.

When I said "he jerked awake with a shout" just now, really I meant, with a curse. It had been loud enough to cut through the noise of the argument, and now the whole geometry class was staring at him. And so was I.

His gaze darted around the room, alert but without panic. A guy I used to know back in Ohio, who was in the marines, used to talk about *situational awareness*—another phrase I had never before associated with Clay. He still had that smile, like someone had just told him a cruel joke. Finally he focused on me. "Who are you working for? Zadornov? The Greek?"

"The Greek?"

His brow furrowed. "What's today?"

"Tuesday." I wasn't sure what was going on, but working with so many kids who've turned their cards, you get a sense when caution is required. You never know when someone's going to flip, lose control, or manifest in a way they haven't before. It's not like we get owners' manuals to these bodies when the card turns. I edged toward him. Carefully. "Clay, are you all right?"

"The date," he said, forcefully. He patted his pockets—found a pen and a set of house keys. The joke, his mouth said, was crueler than he'd expected, but still funny. He looked around him, saw Stephanie Choi's phone abandoned on her desk, snatched it, powered it on, and checked the date. Stephanie squawked—he didn't flinch, just tossed the phone back onto her desk. "Good. There's still time." And he backed slowly toward the door. "I'll be going now. As you were." With a nod to me, to Burnside and Lisa on their desks, and to the class.

"Clay." I was close to him now—just out of arm's reach for a normal person. My arms have more reach to them than most, but even people who should know that don't know it deep down enough for the body language to translate.

But Clay didn't seem to know me at all. He looked different. More different. His skin drier, his jaw sharpened. His nose had an aquiline bend I'd never noticed before. "You don't look right. Maybe you should go to the nurse?"

"Thanks but no thanks," he said. "I have a bad history with doctors. A lot of needles under the bridge. I don't want to interrupt your little . . . whatever you have here. I'll just leave you to it." He tipped a hat he wasn't wearing—and ran.

I'm not proud of what I did next. A proper teacher, I'm sure, would have any number of ways to handle a student running out the back door without losing control of the portion of the class who had *not* just tried to take an unexcused absence at a dead sprint. Call security. Call the principal's office. Intercom the front desk.

But before I was a guidance counselor—no matter how briefly, no matter how I try to forget—I was . . . Well, I don't like to use the word to talk about people who aren't firefighters or trauma nurses or something, because really the long-johns-and-logos business isn't the same kind of thing at all, but I'd been a hero. At least that's what they said on television.

When you're a hero and someone runs, you chase.

Clay barreled ahead of me. I'd seen him on the basketball court once, and I do mean just once, the time the JV team suffered three rolled ankles against PS 116 and Coach Ickles had to put *someone* in. He wasn't a kid who set foot-speed records. I'm not in training anymore, but I should have caught him easily.

I didn't.

He rocketed down the empty hall, knocking over trash cans in his wake. I stretched my legs up high to step over them. "Clay, stop! Whatever's wrong, we can talk it over."

"Let it go, Stretch. I have places to be." He cornered hard down a side hall. My legs were too long to turn easily at speed. I tripped over my own shins, which is easier to do than you might think when you've stretched your shins four feet long each. As I fell, I shot out my hands and grabbed two nearby door handles. I let the force of my fall stretch my arms even further—aimed . . . and *snap!* Shot down the hall, and landed in front of Clay.

I stretched my body wide to make a wall. "Clay. Look, I'm not a geometry fan, either, but let's take a deep breath, go back to the class, and—"

He ran into me. Just got his shoulder low like he was ready to charge the Giants' defensive line, and . . . *bam*.

But really it was more of a *whump* with a bit of *sproing*. When I make myself big and stretched out, it doesn't do me any favors density-wise. It's impressive and intimidating if you don't know what you're seeing, but I'm really just 168 pounds of guidance counselor, even if I am spread out to the thickness and elasticity of a trampoline.

So I folded up like a blanket, limbs and torso in a confused heap on the ground, all over Clay. I was scrambling to get off him—blocking the hallway with my body was an old strategy from the *American Hero* days, the idea being that if the other guy was so dumb as to dive into me, I could wrestle them into submission, drawing myself rubber-tight around them. But of course Clay was a student, so really what I wanted was get off of him as quickly as possible.

He didn't know that. Perhaps he thought my panicked scrambling was me trying to choke him out. He certainly reacted that way. But he didn't move as if being covered in living rubber was the weirdest thing that had happened to him this year, or even this week. As I tried to wriggle away, he found my arm, did something my old wrestling coach would have thought was extremely clever with it, and dug his fingers into a spot near my neck. I went limp. Muscles I didn't know I had stopped working, and I was a puddle on the floor. It was like jiujitsu, only jiujitsu doesn't work on me. Or, I didn't think it did.

Clay was standing over me. In that moment he looked almost normal. I mean, almost like he usually did. Damp and unformed, big-eyed and kind of scared. He looked down at his hands, as if he wasn't sure what he had done.

The numbness was wearing off. I could feel my limbs again—my body remembered the general shape of human anatomy enough to speak. "Clay."

A moment of confusion: a boy who'd fallen, staring up. Then his eyes were sharp again, and his jaw, and his mouth had that here-we-go-again smile. "Sorry, Stretch. You've got the wrong guy. The name's Croyd."

Then he was gone.

By the time I sorted out which parts of me used to be legs and which arms, Clay had pulled the fire alarm and escaped in the confusion. I hoped I could find him in the crowd outside while the fire department cleared the classroom building, but it was a crisp day in early autumn, and kids are kids, and Jokertown kids even more so. They scattered through Roosevelt Park while teachers fought for order. I couldn't see a thing.

I got up into the trees, displacing a battle between some miniature Picts and a gang of tattooed sentient squirrels, and scanned the park for any sign of Clay. I didn't expect much. I was pretty sure that he had already left the neighborhood.

I couldn't stop thinking. It's a problem I have sometimes. I was thinking about Clay, who was a nice quiet kid, and I was thinking about how big New York could be even if you'd grown up here, which I hadn't. I was thinking about how he'd changed. And I was thinking about what Beatrice LaJolla would do to me for losing one of her geometry students. I had a sense it might be viscerally anatomical.

That's when I saw my landlord.

She was perched in the tree next to mine, drinking a large diet soda. Wearing dark glasses and a trilby lined with aluminum foil. Her overstuffed messenger bag rested on the branches beside her.

"Howdy, Rubberband." She toasted me with the soda.

Jan Chang is . . . Look, there are a hundred thousand ways I could finish that sentence without exaggerating, but you wouldn't believe most of them. You know that internet art project they used to have, Humans of New York? She's the greatest-hits version. She wears dark glasses because of her electric blue eyes, and I'm not using *electric* figuratively. The tinfoil hat was entirely in character, though she's not usually that literal, for practical purposes. She doesn't usually put off that much voltage, but when she gets excited little Tesla coil arcs jump between her hat brim and the tips of her ears. "Sparkplug," I said. That's Jan's card name. She uses it about as often as I use mine. "I thought diet soda was a conspiracy?"

"Counterprogramming," she said. "It does mess up your glycemic index, and contributes to a whole rash of cancers and dementias, but that part's been emphasized in public health communication because Hollow Earth psychoactives don't want you to know that it *also* interferes with their dream access rays." She took a big sip, grimaced. "The things I do for the cause."

"Did you know it's illegal to climb trees in New York?"

"The mycophroageal spores that reptoids use to influence mass gatherings are heavier than air." She pointed down at the kids. "See?"

"It's a fire drill."

She shrugged, potato-potahto. "What's your excuse? You look like a puddle."

"I was." I explained, dejectedly, about Clay Calvados, the chase, and the escape. By the time I was done, the building had been cleared and students were milling back inside.

"Croyd," Jan repeated. She had finished her soda and swung herself down to the ground.

"I must have misheard him."

"As in, Crenson."

"It's a common name."

"It's not. Did you just teach a *geometry* class to *the Sleeper*?"

"No. I don't know. He's one of Mrs. LaJolla's students. And I've lost him." The sun, for all its crisp autumn radiance, might have been a million light-years away. I felt cold. "We're going to have to call the police."

"To look for Croyd Crenson."

"To look for Clay. He's not the Sleeper. He has family. He has friends—I think. One or two." I didn't know who they were. I rubbed my arms and tried to think happy non-cop thoughts. Puppies. Nice, clean, uncomplicated forms, on good paper, and a new pen. "The first call will go to Fort Freak, but if he's on the run, he won't stay in Jokertown. And with nat cops involved . . ." I didn't want to finish that sentence. Jan didn't need me to. "I lost a kid."

"He ran out on you."

"He's out there all alone."

"He's the Sleeper. If half the stories I've heard about that guy are true, I don't think there's anything we can do for him that he can't do for himself."

"He's not, though." I remembered that look in his eyes, the moment's indecision before he said his name. He didn't know what he was doing. Whatever he was, he was scared. "I don't know what's going on. But I have to help."

Clay's family lived in a fourth-floor walk-up in what newspapers call a bad part of town. What they meant by that, of course, is that it's a part of town that's not made to make nats or out-of-towners feel comfortable—it's just fine if you're a joker, so long as you don't act like an idiot. Of course, cheap rents have driven more nats to Jokertown in the last ten years or so—which puts more pressure on the locals, elevates tensions and everyone's blood pressure.

I'd been as jumpy as any nat when I moved to Jokertown, but by now I knew this area pretty well. I'd first come here when Jan and I were trying to save Zargoza's Bakery a few years back, and some of my students lived around here, so people recognized me.

As we approached the crumbling brownstone, an old slug-man basking on the front steps and smoking a cigarillo tipped his hat to us. Jan tipped her hat back, smiled with a little spark in it, and we climbed the old but well-swept stairs to 4B.

It sounded like there was a minor Disney war on in 4B—shrieks, running feet, bouncing springs, and a woman's strained voice: *Don't touch the remote* and *Julian, apologize* and Spanish that was too fast for me to catch. No doorbell. I tried to knock. It didn't seem to register. Jan rolled her eyes and knocked loud enough to be heard two floors down.

From inside: *Coming!* The war subsided into muffled protests and giggles. After some manipulation of a dead bolt, the door opened on two chains.

The woman behind the door was maybe twenty, with big hair in curls and rich dark lipstick and a round face tight with worry. "Excuse me. Do I know you?"

"Ms. Calvados?" I said. "My name is Robin Ruttiger. I'm from the school."

But before I could finish the sentence there were four arms around Jan and me, and she was crying.

"I'm sorry," she said, after the tears had dried. "I'm Carlotta Calvados, Clay's sister. Mami's at work." Carlotta had a supernatural ability to dry her eyes without smudging her makeup. "It's just that you're always hoping it just works out, you know? Mami and Steve and Clay had a big fight yesterday. Clay went out, didn't come home. He does that sometimes. I wish he wouldn't, I tell him not to, but he says he just needs to be someone else. He goes to a friend's house, or he walks all night, you know, and I worry. I called the school this morning and they said he was there so I thought it was okay. But then they called me, and now . . ." She closed her eyes and took a deep breath some yogis I know would envy. "So he's in trouble?"

Jan and I were sitting inside the crowded Calvados family living room on a sofa whose springs had given up the battle long ago. The sounds of the city blew in the open window: distant traffic, sidewalk radios. Two of the younger kids arguing about the political contours of various factions of Lego ninjas while a third stood on her head. They should have been in school, I thought, but it didn't seem like a good idea to mention.

I've been in a lot of rooms like this since I started working in Jokertown. Big plants in big pots, stacks of magazines, cut flowers springing from the necks of old wine bottles. Nothing thrown away. In some parts of Manhattan this wallpaper print would have been extremely hip. It had gotten that way by starting in the 1970s and lasting until it came back around again on the guitar.

"So your brother," Jan said, "isn't the Sleeper."

"What? I mean, excuse me?"

"Croyd Crenson. The Sleeper. Isn't . . . your brother?"

"He wishes."

"Was that what the fight was about? Clay wishing he was the Sleeper?" Jan's question, not mine. I didn't know Clay well, but I was starting to get an image in my head—from the Legos, from the wallpaper, from the chorus of the family, and from the image of him walking alone, late at night. Not an image of him, exactly. A collage with a Clay-shaped cutout at the center. What I'd seen back in Mrs. LaJolla's classroom was not a psychotic break. Psychotic breaks don't magically teach a fifteen-year-old jiujitsu.

"When we were kids, he used to play Sleeper. I'd be the Turtle. If we ran into trouble, he could just fall down, get 'knocked out,' and jump back up with powers that could save us. I thought it was kind of silly, right, like the point of the game is you figure out how to use the powers you have, but he always wanted to be different."

"So the fight was about that?"

"It was about IHT."

"Something-hormone therapy?"

"A band. Or a singer? IHeartTonya. A Korean supergroup idol thing, but Russian? They're in town for a show at the Garden, and Clay had a line on tickets for forty bucks that go for like four hundred. He usually works that night but he'd get someone to cover his shift, you know. But Steve went off about responsibility and how he saw Nirvana for twenty bucks back in the '90s like that was relevant, and Mami and I tried to calm them both down but it got hot and Clay stormed out."

"And you don't know where he might go."

A shake of the head. Tears brimmed her eyes again.

"It's okay, Carlotta," Jan said. "We'll find him." And while Carlotta's face was buried in her tissue, Jan gave me a big nod and pointed with her head toward the back of the apartment.

"Carlotta, would you mind if I looked through Clay's things?"

Clay had the back corner of his bedroom, a twin bed across from his brothers' bunk beds. I had to pick my way through Legos to get there. A curtain hung on the wall near his bed. You take your privacy where you can, in a situation like that. Under the curtain, he'd hung a bulletin board covered with pushpin photos of IHeartTonya: willowy and pale, vivid dark hair, cheekbone architecture, a costume aesthetic like Gothic cathedrals made out of taffeta, perfect skin, claw-length nails. All of that I expected, but her expression took me by surprise: wide-eyed, sky-gazing hope. I didn't think anyone had looked like that since the '90s. And certainly not in Russia.

There were printouts, too. Clunky formatting, links in weird places, a website not built to render in pen and ink. IHeartTonya Manhattan debut, get All the Details Here. Tickets on sale for Thursday. Renting out the top two floors of the Mandarin Oriental for her entourage. VIP reception Tuesday before the big show. Want to share the music in my heart with all my fans.

The quotes made her sound very real and very fake. People who are good at that business can be both at once. I'd had a taste of it when I was on *American Hero*, and in my own personal fifteen minutes afterward, before Terrell and I broke up. You believe the things you say, you are the person you make yourself out to be. If you're lucky, you never have to find out whether you're lying.

I imagined Clay drawing the curtain back when there was no one else around, and watching her, and wondering.

His pillow rang.

I lifted it by the corner. A white rounded rectangle glowed through the striped cotton pillowcase. The ring was a snatch of song, a few bars looped like a dance track in the kind of club where I didn't spend much time anymore. I couldn't make out the words, which sounded Slavic. I thought of IHeartTonya. I fished it out— a cheap Android handset, a call from UNDISCLOSED NUMBER. I turned to bring it back to the living room, but Carlotta was already in the doorway, her hands outstretched, her eyes wide and tearful. She must not have known it was here. I gave her the phone.

"Clay? Clay honey, you have to come home, we're so worried, Clay, Mami's worried, Steve's worried, where are you?" Her voice shook. Someone spoke on the other end of the line.

Carlotta looked confused, hurt. She took the Android from her ear, handed it back. "It's for you."

I took it. Thumbed the speaker and held a finger to my lips, looking at Carlotta, at Jan. I wanted them to hear. I wanted whoever this was to think we were alone.

"Stretch."

The same voice from the hall. The same edge. I've run across a lot of kids who've been hurt, who've had to carry more than anyone should, without being able to trust anyone else to help them. Bring that forward a while. Bring that forward sixty or seventy years. "Clay."

"That's not my name."

"Then where did you get this number?"

Nothing on the other end of the line. You used to be able to hear the copper, like a distant ocean. Now you get digital silence.

"You're not Croyd Crenson."

"Then who is?" My turn for silence. "I get it. You have a job. So do I. But you're cramping my style. This isn't your scene. You'll just get civilians into it."

"I'm trying to help you."

"Then stay back. Let me do what I do. Or, if you have to do whatever it is you think you're doing, do it better."

"Clay. Croyd. We can help you."

"I wouldn't mind help. But there are the civilians to think of. You and your pals can't even cover your own tracks."

I felt cold. Gooseflesh hits me harder than it hits most people. You can follow the ripples. "What do you mean?" But I was moving already toward the window in the living room, facing the road.

Jokertown does have a case of the gentrification, but black Lexus SUVs still aren't common, and this one hadn't been there when we came in. Through the tinted windows, I caught the flare of a lighter.

I don't need to breathe anymore, not the way normal people do, with lungs filling and emptying. Oxygen just filters through my skin. I still do breathe, though, most of the time, because once you get in the habit it's hard to stop. But once in a while you get that old limbic fear-trigger, and your breath stops, some evolutionary memory reminding you that the predators can hear.

I opened the window. I don't know why. Maybe I meant to do something stupid. Maybe Clay, or Croyd, calling me a civilian stung some pride I didn't realize I still had. I didn't have a plan.

But the Lexus was watching. Its lights flashed, its engine roared, and it was gone.

"How do we know," Jan asked, later, in her murder room, "that he's *not* the Sleeper?"

When I say "murder room," that might be giving you the wrong idea. Jan is not a murderer—unless I'm due for a chilling and brutal revelation at some point, I guess, in which case this will just be ironic foreshadowing. Jan thinks violence, while sometimes unavoidable, almost always plays into the hands of sinister forces from the counter-Earth. She is conscientious, and kind to animals, except when ordering pizza. But there is a room in the basement of the decaying building she inherited from her dad that she does not show to the dates she brings home, because even Jan recognizes that it's more than a little suggestive of homicide.

Mostly it's the bulletin boards. She must have a pallet box of them somewhere because a new one shows up every few weeks, to be placed on an easel or nailed to any blank span of wall or ceiling that remains, or, in a pinch, on top of other bulletin boards.

From the bulletin boards, by a galaxy of pushpins, hangs her scrapbook. Grainy pictures, tabloid article outtakes, graffiti snapshots, annotations in bold red marker, whole encyclopedia entries, five books, a hubcap, what I really hope isn't an original Picasso sketch—she's pinned them all and webbed them with yarn as if they might fly away.

I don't think it's all conspiracies. She has her whole family up on one of those boards. I think this is what she needs to do, to let her mind work.

She'd found a fresh board for what she insisted on calling "this case." So far it held the snapshot from Clay's school file, a picture of his family, the Lexus, IHeartTonya, and, under one industrial-grade pin, a stack of photos and artist's renderings an inch thick, labeled, in Post-it: "The Sleeper."

"We know Clay's not the Sleeper," I said, "because he's Clay. I've seen him in school every day for two years. You just met his big sister. We went to their apartment. We saw his bed."

"Those could be paid actors."

"You're suggesting the Sleeper's been a student at Xavier Desmond for two years, without nodding off once. How many amphetamines would that take?"

Jan narrowed her eyes as if she really was considering the problem. I've never met anyone as smart as Jan, but her brain is like a rocket. Whether it takes you to Mars or vaporizes a city depends on where it's pointing.

"I saw him wake up. As Croyd. I'm pretty sure that's against Sleeper rules."

"Maybe he was faking it. Maybe he found some way to take a break as the kid."

"A break?"

"Maybe he wanted not to be the Sleeper for a while."

"Carlotta was not an actor. That Lexus was real. There's a kid in trouble, Jan."

"I know." She took off her glasses and pinched her nose. Her eyes were blueshot. "But have you seen the Sleeper in the last two years?"

"Jan. When's the last time you slept?"

"It just so happens," said Fred Minz, from the couch, "that I have seen him."

I didn't mention Fred earlier because, until he spoke, I had forgotten he was there. He distended the pale-green upholstery of Jan's murder room sofa, a taut man-globe in a cavernous Giants jersey, eating homemade beer-battered onion rings.

With some people, you can forget that they're in a room because they have no presence, no personal gravity. They slip through the cracks in your attention like change between sofa cushions. Fred Minz can disappear, too, but for the opposite reason. His personal gravity is so strong not even light can escape. I don't mean that he's arrogant or self-absorbed. What he is, most of the time, is satisfied—with his onion rings, with his inevitable progress through the world, with each of the successive get-rich-quick schemes he propagates through Jokertown. He doesn't need you to notice him. When his card turned, Fred was already an adult—grown, traveled, and mixed up with shady characters. That might explain it. Then again, Jan turned as an adult, too.

Fred's ace is that he turns into the animals he eats. It's not that he *can* turn into them, it's that he *does*, unless he tries really hard not to. Fred, being Fred, once told me that staying human feels like holding in a fart. He doesn't eat much meat these days, except on special occasions, and he was a three-steaks-fried-in-butter kind of guy before. He used to be a chef, but it's hard to be a chef if you can't taste what you're cooking, and he never could keep himself from snacking. Most guys would take that hard. Fred's response to enforced veganism and losing his career had been to shrug, heat up two deep fryers, and start looking for vegetables to coat in beer batter. He had been Jan's tenant when I met them both, though he had the same kind of notional relationship to rent that I did. Jan sometimes joked that he went with the building.

So when Fred said, "I have seen him," it felt kind of like an alien murder robot had de-cloaked in the middle of a UN meeting—just to offer a bit of color commentary.

"You've seen my student? Clay?"

He shook his head: one movement left, one right. "Nah. The Sleeper. Gets around. I saw him at Ape and Louie's, maybe a year

back. He was red all over like a newspaper. We shot what is collo-
quially referred to as the shit. Nice guy." *Crunch.* Another onion
ring bites the dust.

"You know the Sleeper?"

One more head shake, one more onion ring. "He's not a guy that
a guy knows, if you know what I am saying. But you can recognize
a guy so as to have a conversation with said guy without the pair of
you being on what I would term know-a-guy basis." He wiped his
hands on a paper towel and leaned even farther back in the couch.
He laced his fingers behind his head. The sleeve tattoo on his big
right arm peeked out from under the jersey cuff. He'd had that one
done in Brooklyn to cover up some other work he'd had done in
Kuala Lumpur, "back in what is commonly identified as the day."
The sleeve consisted of three ample women, naked, intertwined,
lashed by waves. Fred called them his sy-reen-ees. "But this guy
was definitely the Sleeper, and he was definitely not a high school
kid as of one year previous. And even if I had not the pleasure, I
would say that I think you are going about this in the wrong way."

Jan crossed her arms. "I'm listening."

"You want to work through this like it was a multiple choice.
Crossing out such options as are impossible and on like that. But
with the Sleeper, there is no impossible. He has been young and he
has been old. He has had every kind of face, and he has had no
face at all. He told me he was a cockroach once, like your guy
Gregor Samsa." *Crunch.* "As far as we know, he ain't never been a
lady, but maybe he just has not happened to be one yet, or maybe
he was and never told nobody. He could have turned something
psychic, or he could have swapped bodies with your kid while his
own is still in bed somewhere, or it could be a shapeshifting sort of
situation, or maybe he's spreading a virus again, only the virus is
him, and all of us is gonna be Croyd Crenson by this time next
week. Maybe he's the moon. You can't figure out someone like
that. He can't even out-figure himself. You just got to start with the
things about him you know won't change."

"But everything about him does."

It's hard to tell when Fred is thinking, as opposed to when he's dozed off. His jaw slacked open. I thought he might be about to snore. Then, with an oracular breath: "We ain't all ourselves," he said. "We got to find someone who knows him. So we got to see the theater dame."

Ape and Louie's was, Fred reminded us with a critical once-over of our outfits before our journey uptown, a "swank joint." He himself had changed into a fresh jersey. I don't really have an up-scale mode these days—it's a matter of attitude as much as of actual clothes; I could be head-to-toe Alexander McQueen and still look like a teacher after hours—but Jan had put on a tuxedo-print T-shirt, which had to count for something.

I spent the subway ride staring out at flashes of construction light in the dark, and thinking about Clay walking alone at night, without anywhere to go. I don't know if everyone has times like that when they're in high school and I guess probably not, but every one of us who has builds a wall around that experience in their own way, to stop it from leaking into the present. Sometimes those walls leak. I remembered how it felt: not knowing who you are, not knowing what you are, except that somehow, no matter how many people surround you, you're alone.

Ape and Louie's on 40th and Seventh was founded in the 1960s by Louie Ueda and Joe Donnelly, based on a steak joint where they'd both worked in Boston. Louie was the chef and a nat, and Donnelly was the house manager, and bartender, and a chimpanzee. Sometimes the card turns that way. Donnelly chose the name because he thought it was funny.

I'd been there a few times back when I was younger. The place hadn't changed, and I loved that. This city wiggles under you—sometimes it feels like all it is, is change—but if you're careful you can find places that feel time the way a big old tree feels the breeze.

The more slippery the world seems, the more important it is to remember that there are things deeper than time.

As I stepped into Ape and Louie's, with the dark wood paneling and the white tablecloths and Zeke the Squid tickling the piano keys with his tentacles in the corner, with photos on the wall of Sinatra and Sondheim and Patti LuPone and Mandy Patinkin and Jerome Robbins, I thought about the Sleeper. About how Ape and Louie's never changed, and how Croyd Crenson woke up every day a different person, a stranger to himself, with the whole world in front of him. He didn't age—though how could you tell?—but he was never the same.

Then again, he could wake up dead any day.

What did that mean for Clay?

I tried not to think about that part.

When Ape and Louie founded the joint they'd wanted to make a classy, sophisticated kind of place where Broadway stars could hang out, which put them in a dilemma, because even in the '60s it was hard to swing classy and sophisticated on a Broadway paycheck. So they made a deal—if you were in a show, you could eat at a discount. Actors came for the food and drink, and tourists came to see the actors. There were few of either at two thirty on a Tuesday afternoon, though, so it was easy to pick out Fred's "theater dame," seated at the bar, ignoring something cold and clear in a martini glass while she read a paperback romance.

I recognized the cover typeface. Mrs. LaJolla read the same series—billionaire aces and innocent well-meaning young women who'd been in the wrong place at the wrong time, or the right one at the wrong the other, or vice versa. The woman looked elegant and alone, looked it so well that she might have been playing it onstage. Her jeans were modern but the heels could have fit anywhere in the last sixty years. She looked like an actress at the top of her game. She looked like she lived in a different world from the rest of us.

Then she knocked her martini glass onto her jeans.

"Shit!"

And I realized, as she mopped at her jeans with a linen napkin, that I knew her. So did Fred, apparently. "Abigail! Long time no see!"

Though perhaps not well, to judge from the way she jumped up and back, one hand raised to ward him off, and a fork in the other. "Oh, no, Fred Minz, don't you come one bloody step closer. Back. Again." He complied without lowering his arms—he'd been about to go in for a hug—or the voltage of his smile. "I have had more than enough of a day to add to my own trouble by transforming into a heifer or a chicken or a-a zebra!" She pronounced it so it rhymed with Deborah. Still British. Abigail Baker had lived in New York for years, but she'd never lost her accent. She had picked up a few Americanisms, new vowel sounds and turns of phrase, without meaning to. She picked up a lot of things without meaning to. That's her ace: Other people's cards tend to stick to her fingers.

Now Fred looked concerned. "Abigail, has someone fed you a zebra?"

She blushed. "Not—not to my knowledge, but then nobody—ow!" A bright-blue spark jumped from the bar's footrail to her shin, and she jumped, tipping over a chair at a nearby empty table. "Nobody," she finished, righting the chair with an actress's composure, "has fed me electric eel either, recently, and yet here we are." She gestured expansively; a spark jumped from a beer tap to the fork I don't think she realized she was still holding.

"That," Jan said, "would be my fault. Sorry." She raised one gloved hand and waved with her fingers. "Hi. I'm Jan."

Jan's disarming smile might be her real ace, and the electricity and the shock-glow eyes a distraction. The smile doesn't work on everyone, but I've seen it hit women I could have sworn were straight as Nebraska roads. If, on the great theater lights board of Abigail Baker's heart, the two sliders marked "flustered" and "furious" were riding at maximum, some invisible tech seemed to have swept "furious" down to about a three, made sneaky adjustments to a number of other sliders and dials, and perhaps hit a switch. Abigail adjusted her hair again. Differently. She set down the fork. "Hello. I mean, hi, anyway. I'm terribly—it's just that, well, your friend here, and I, to put it mildly, let's say our aces do *not* mix, it happens to be something of an oil-and-fire situation, and I have been particularly clear about my desire for him to notify me before he decides to just, you see, it's all something of an— Oh, no. Am I growing horns again?"

"I sent you a text," Fred said. "But you did not text back."

"I am in *Chicago* tonight and I would rather Roxie Hart not appear with a tail, thank you very much."

"I'm sorry about Fred," Jan said with the ease of someone who's had a lot of practice with those words. "He's going to wait at the other end of the bar. But we were hoping . . ." She trailed off and turned to me.

I don't think Abigail had noticed me, really, before that moment. We'd only met a couple of times, and I wouldn't expect her to remember the random guidance counselor she'd happened to meet while helping out the Xavier Desmond drama club. But then, half of her business is people, and the other half is memory. "Assassins. At the high school. The girl with the fake mustache. Not you yourself obviously—Rubberband, right?"

"Ruttiger," I said, "Robin. Yes. I'm sorry to barge in on you like this, Miss Baker."

"Please, I must have said Abigail, or anything really, so long as it's not Abby, always makes me think of a convent. Anyway—are you . . . with . . . ?"

"He's my . . ." What was the right word? "Friend."

"My condolences."

"Hey!"

"Abigail." Teaching and acting have a lot in common. There's the audience, of course, but there's also the voice. You have to know how to speak—to students as a group, to a particular kid who's come to you with a particular problem, to a curriculum committee asking why you do this or don't do that. One voice I have down pat is the tone you use with another adult—a parent, say—when a kid needs help. Just like with acting, it helps if you believe. "One of my students is in trouble. I *think* it has something to do with . . ." I couldn't finish the sentence. How would I feel if someone came to me asking for help with something Terrell-related?

But she saved me. "Croyd." A flick of a sad smile. "You needn't look so stunned, Robin, it's not as if it's the Sunday crossword. I mean, my life's quite exciting on its own, but Roxie Hart is not likely to put a student at sufficient risk to bring you down here in the middle of what I rather do think is a workday. Croyd always did live more of a profound-risk-to-life-and-limb sort of existence, one jump ahead of the head man and all that." I don't know if you've seen her videos or interviews, but she has this bubbling-fountain energy, like she's not quite finished, either with what she's saying in the moment, or with herself in general. It's what made the Roxie casting work, though the critics called it "against type" when it was announced. So it was a surprise to see her look, not tired, not old, not the ways those words are used against women, but . . . grown-up. "What did he do this time?"

"I need to find him," I said. "I think one of my students is in danger."

She considered, with a long, harrowed expression, then drained the dregs of her martini. "Well. Let's go. We can talk on the way."

We took the subway to the Upper West Side. Fred, by Abigail's request, stayed at the other end of the car. He spent the ride chatting with a subway break-dancer between shifts.

Croyd had bolt-holes all over the city, Abigail said—but this was where he'd been living when they last met: an old doorman building, which we entered through the basement maintenance entrance, using a key she was surprised to find still worked. "Croyd's a money-comes-money-goes sort of person, understandably given his general habits, and somewhere between our first encounter and our last, it seems to have come. He told me he wanted a way in that he could use even if he came back looking different from when he left." She refused to let Fred share the elevator with us to the top floor, and Jan stayed with him, taking the opportunity to examine the basement for concealed Hollow Earth access points while Abigail and I rattled up.

I'd told her the story on the subway, and as we waited for the others in the marble hall in front of the thick oak door, she repeated it back to me, double-checking its particulars. "That all does sound rather like Croyd," she said, "but, if you'll forgive me, only rather? You're sure you have his words right, his tone of voice and all that? I don't mean to doubt, you know, but I was watching a documentary, and it turns out eyewitness accounts aren't altogether reliable at all, our brains invent things, and then miss other things, and there was this remarkable bit with either a gorilla or someone in a gorilla suit. That is. I don't of course mean to say I doubt you, you understand. But did it happen, just like that?"

I believed so. I've never claimed to have a perfect memory. But then, I've noticed that books where people claim to have perfect memories are generally also the kind of books where at the end you learn the narrator's been dead the whole time, or something goofy like that. I'm not smart enough to pull any of those tricks, so don't worry.

"It's not unlike Croyd, I suppose. Croyd at times, I mean. He changes. That is, I guess, the only truly stable thing about him. Some days Croyd is a master criminal, and some days he's failing to run a pirate DVD business. And there are days when he's both, when the cunning plan turns out to have been a disaster all along, or the other way around. So in a way this all sounds just like him."

"And in another way . . ."

"Well. Exactly. It does not sound like him, quite, does it? The way you have him talking, Stretch and so on, it's all a bit actor-y, like someone who saw too many Bogart movies. And that voice, the mid-Atlantic accent, that's a posh American boarding school accent, and Croyd is not posh. He has this way of speaking that is so matter-of-fact, even when he's speaking about, or to, the most wonderful things, people. It draws you in. You find yourself matching its cadence, its rhythm, and when you do, you find that it doesn't lower the wonderful and horrible things he's seen to your level. It raises you to theirs." She came back from wherever memory had taken her. "So, what would the detective shows call it, the *modus operandi* is right, but the, would it be, *modus vivendi*, the mode of living, is just wrong."

"He sounds like a great guy. Croyd, I mean."

She looked at her shoes, then at the door, then back at me. "He's the spirit of the midcentury. He's the last man in New York who smokes in bed. He's all stories. And what people miss when they look at him is, it's all real. That's his life. It scares him and he loves it and he's always changing, and he'll never change. And . . . You're wondering what happened."

I wasn't. Or I was trying not to. But I didn't interrupt her, either.

"We tried, is what happened. Twice, I suppose, though the second time barely counts. We were hardly together. He did bring me here, he gave me keys . . . I think, perhaps, he was worried. Not for me, at all. But I got the sense he was, all of a sudden, aware he was alone. You might think, ah, she wanted to chain him down, isn't that always the line, here comes dear Yoko the specter of death. But the truth is, when we were first together I was young and in New York and I barely knew who I was, what I wanted. He was clearer. But he was wrong, and I think . . . I think he understood that in the end. And as for me, well—haven't they been down there entirely too long?"

I was just having visions of black Lexuses when the elevator began to rattle up from the basement. Fred emerged, and Jan, apologetically. "I was certain I'd found an entrance," Jan said.

"And?"

She shook her head. "Just another vending machine."

"Well," Abigail replied with a smile, "hopefully this will clear matters up."

She crossed her fingers, then tapped a key code into the console beside the door. It flashed green. It's odd watching an actress when she's not onstage, because her real emotions are subtler than the ones she means to project. Croyd hadn't changed the code since they were last together: that brought relief, and pain, and a little shock to be feeling either.

She selected a complex, antique-looking key from her key ring and inserted it into the lock. "Home sweet home."

But before she could turn the key, the door drifted open on its own.

"That's funny, isn't it? I mean," she said, "the keypad was in fact engaged."

I slipped inside.

The place was empty. Of people, I mean. (Abigail, it turns out, isn't the only one who tends to pick up other people's habits.)

I guess I expected a cave of wonders, the accumulated trophies of, what, more than eighty years, Ali Baba's cave and Sherlock Holmes's study all in one. But if this apartment had been bought to serve as a sort of shadow gallery, the owner never managed to get it there. Half the front hall had been finished with velvety green art deco wallpaper; the other was bare to the plaster. One wall of one bedroom was all books; not bookcases, just books, piled on their sides from floor to ceiling. Another wall was boxes, taped shut. The bed was a mattress on the floor. The formal dining room was empty except for a table made of plywood across pillars of bare cinder block. The desktop was scattered with papers: blueprints of something that looked like a hotel, business cards, a notepad. A rotary phone. A tallboy of neon-colored JOKERFÜL, dew collecting on the side.

"We must have just missed him."

Abigail frowned. "Croyd would never drink this stuff. Corn syrup and taurine and who-knows-what-else. Amphetamines, certainly. But not this."

Jan had donned latex gloves, and was sifting through the papers. "Blueprints of the Mandarin Oriental. Notes, in code. I might be able to break it, given time." A notepad and pencil rested next to the rotary phone. She used the pencil to side-shade the notepad, which was an old-fashioned trick, but then, Croyd Crenson seemed to be an old-fashioned sort of person. A message emerged: "DAVE," and an address, also on the Upper West Side, not far away. "Weird. The handwriting's not the same as on these other notes."

A first name and address did not seem like much to me, but Abigail's face darkened. "What were those names your student mentioned, Robin? Before he ran."

"Zadornov. Sadornoff? Something like that."

"No, the other one."

"He didn't mention a name. He just said something about 'the Greek.'"

"I should have thought even Croyd at his most desperate would not stoop to working with *him*."

"Who?"

She pronounced, with a scorn usually reserved for bedbugs and certain politicians: "Dave the Greek."

"Oh!" Fred chipped in from down the bar, where he was drinking a Pabst and listening to everything we said. "I follow him on Snapfeed!"

This news did not seem to brighten Abigail's day. "David Constantinopolis is a species of detestable, opportunistic, and vulturous—though I think that's rather an insult to the vulture community—a giggling scavenger-breathed species, at any rate, of paparazzo photographer that I used to think blissfully foreign to the States."

"He is fukkin' hilarious." Fred had pulled out his phone. "He

got this shot one time where I guess Salma Hayek tripped or something and her bazongas just went—ow!" Jan had applied the heel
of her boot to the top of Fred's foot. "I mean, he's great. Just look
at this guy."

"When I met the man," Abigail continued, as if Fred had not
spoken, "I assumed he would infest your entire country like a sort
of semi-human kudzu, but so far the infection has been blissfully
contained to Manhattan." She took a centering breath. "He is, at
any rate, a photographer. Only a bit in reverse. He takes photographs. Then you pay him money not to publish them. At which
point, if you have not paid him enough, or if he thinks it's funny,
he proceeds to publish them anyway."

"Robin." It was Jan this time. She tapped me on the shoulder.
She was holding, like you'd hold a dead rat, Fred's phone.
Alfred E. Neuman's three-eyed visage leered from the case. What,
me worry?

The phone was open to Snapfeed. A lizard-faced personage
with multicolored hair, who I assumed was @dave-the-greek, had
posted a selfie one minute and twenty-seven seconds ago: leaning
out an open window, his hair blowing in the crisp fall breeze off
the river, a big sly self-satisfied grin, a peace sign I was pretty sure
was meant as ironically as the hashtag captions. Hashtag blessed
hashtag fall, hashtag sweater weather, hashtag basic, and I didn't
read the rest of the paragraph. Because my eyes jumped back to
the street behind and below him, which was weirdly in focus, the
way the backgrounds in cellphone pictures are.

Giant Lexuses are not quite so rare in the Upper West Side as
they are in Jokertown, but this one looked familiar. And the five
men getting out of it—two in black suits and overcoats, and three
in tracksuits, all some serious military brand of buff—looked like
goons from a Tarantino movie. The lead suit had a big black beard
and was smoking a stubby cigar. I remembered the cigarette lighter
flare behind the tinted windshield of the Lexus outside the Calvados residence in Jokertown.

And—as if that wasn't enough—there in the upper-left corner of the frame, that could be the back of Clay's army surplus jacket, walking away.

"Thank you," I told Abigail. "Thank you so much. But . . ."

"I understand." She smiled sadly. "Go. I'll lock up here."

We reached Dave the Greek's apartment not quite too late.

The Lexus was still there, parked on a street that led down to Riverside Park. The window out of which Dave the Greek had taken his selfie appeared to have been broken—there was glass on the sidewalk, weird for that part of town. Four goons—the two wearing what I could now see was Armani, and two in tracksuits—were dragging an extremely limp man in a loud toucan-print shirt toward the waiting Lexus. I couldn't tell for sure it was Dave the Greek, because of the bag over his head.

We drew back around the corner before the goons noticed us. But I needn't have worried. They were, suddenly, distracted.

The final tracksuit lurched into view, dragging a much-less-limp figure in an army surplus jacket. Clay.

Or, possibly, Croyd.

Clay tried to dart away, but there was a scuffle. Tracksuit had a bundle under one arm, so he was somewhat encumbered, but he was still at a distinct advantage, because Clay's hands appeared to be zip-tied behind his back.

Croyd, or else Clay, didn't seem bothered by the bruise around his eye; he didn't seem scared at all.

The Armani with the cigar snapped something impolite to the tracksuit. Tracksuit barked back something I didn't understand, either, but seemed to amount to: You try dragging this kid along and see how you like it.

"What are they speaking?"

Jan volunteered: "Counter-Earth dialect?"

Fred: "Russian."

"Same difference."

"We've got to *do* something," I said.

What, though? They were halfway down the block, and probably armed. These guys didn't seem the type to settle for nonviolent intervention and mediation.

While I was still thinking, Clay, or perhaps Croyd, took the situation into his own hands.

It happened like this: Cigar marched over to Tracksuit and drew something from his long black cashmere coat that looked a bit like electric hair clippers. And when he was near enough—well, back on *American Hero,* one of the events involved breaking out of restraints, mostly so the producers could get a few gratuitous shots of all of us tied up and wriggling for the late-night crowd. It wasn't a problem for me, because of my card, but we all got trained. You can break out of zip ties even with nat wrists, so long as the zip ties aren't specially designed, and you don't mind a bit of pain.

Well, these ties weren't special, and Croyd, or else Clay, didn't mind.

He moved fast. His arms were free. He grabbed the hair clippers from Armani and shoved them into Tracksuit, who dropped, shuddering. Then he grabbed the bundle under Tracksuit's arm and ran. Armani chased him. I think that, too, was part of the plan. The other goons, if armed, wouldn't want to miss him and hit Armani. Bad for job security. But Clay's legs were shorter than Armani's, and while Clay's body might be twenty or more years younger, he wasn't exactly an athlete. Even with a head start, Armani would catch him before the corner. I didn't think that had been part of the plan.

"Fred, I need a boost."

With a jump off Fred's shoulders, I could—just—reach the top of a nearby lamppost. Falling stretched my arms out, and the elastic snap-back threw me into the air, high enough to reach the next lamppost, and so on. It's awful on the joints, but hey, I don't really have those anyway, and it beats walking.

Besides, people don't expect it. Not a bad choice with guns involved. I am pretty bullet-resistant, but bullet-*resistant* isn't the same as bullet*proof* and you never want to test something like that.

Armani did catch Clay, but not until the corner. They were fighting, and it wasn't going well for Armani, for all his size and general military-thug-ness. Terrell once told me, you can train all you like, but the only way to learn how to fight is by fighting. And Croyd Crenson had been in a lot of fights.

Still, Clay had taken a big fist to the gut and might have been in trouble if I hadn't crashed into Armani from behind. (There was a commotion behind me—Jan and Fred, maybe, occupying the others.) Armani and I were a tangle of limbs, and he was a dirty fighter—but his skull bounced off the pavement and no matter how badass you are, brains don't like bouncing off things.

He went limp. I unwound myself.

Clay—or Croyd—stood there, with a look on his face like he was waking from a dream.

"Mr. R?"

"Clay." I felt sure, then. "You can trust me. I don't know what's going on, but we can figure it all out together. Your sister's worried about you."

His eyes were wide, clear, and brown. Then a door behind them closed, and he looked old and young at once, and tired. Very tired. "Sorry, Stretch. I have a job to do."

There was a spark between us.

I had forgotten the Taser.

I came to in the back of a taxicab, and then again, later, on Jan's murder couch. Tasers hit me harder than most people. Something about the hydrostatic micromuscular whatever that jiggers my morphic whatnot.

There had been cops, whom Jan and Fred dodged. The Russians seemed to have concentrated their efforts on escaping the cops,

too, with Tracksuit and Armani—to the extent, even, of abandon-
ing their target.

Both times, when I drifted back to consciousness, I'd heard a
low groaning sound, and assumed it was me. It wasn't until I re-
constituted my torso and sat up in Jan's basement that I saw Dave
the Greek, tied to a chair. He looked much the same as in his photos, minus a couple of egregious youthifying filters. In person he
looked more like a trim uppers-and-cardio forty-something—
apart, of course, from the shifting tie-dye vortex of his skin. His
complexion reminded me of a screen saver, if you remember those.

"We were not certain what we should do with him," Fred said.
"So we thought we would ask you."

I didn't know how they managed to get a rubbery puddle of
Tasered me and a stoned iguana man across town, even in a New
York taxi, so I asked.

"Fred told the cabbie," Jan said, "that it was a 'sex thing.' " She
made the air quotes with her fingers.

"And I waggled my eyebrows. It always seems to make a difference. Everybody respects a waggle of the eyebrows." Fred had significant eyebrows, even if you ignored the piercing.

And here I'd been proud of myself for noticing that the bundle
Clay/Croyd had stolen from the tracksuit was a hotel staff uniform with a Mandarin Oriental name tag.

"Fascinating." Jan pinched Dave's cheek, slapped it, and the
colors gyrated. She knelt, checked his leg below the trouser cuff.
His skin there had the same melted-Life-Savers effect. "Microsuc-
tion arrays on his fingertips, too. A sort of chameleon morph. Core
infiltration strategy."

"Not wearing a shirt like that." It looked even louder in
person—a houndstooth pattern composed of interlocking neon
toucans.

"He must gain access to a secure area using disguise, then strip
and rely on chromatophores to conceal him. Hard to hide a camera
that way. But these days cameras can be very small."

Next to her, Fred was doing his own thing. A thin trail of normal-looking drool leaked out the corner of Dave the Greek's mouth. Fred swiped his fingers through the drool, sniffed it, then shrugged and stuck his finger in Dave's ear. Dave didn't twitch. He moaned, but he was doing that anyway.

"Fred!"

"I am observing vital signs. Your boy here has got himself down in a k-hole. Probably something the Russkies did to him, so as they could get him away without a fuss. He will be feeling no pain, and nothing else neither, for a while."

"How long?"

"That does depend on the dose. Those guys do not look to me like the type to worry over milliliters. He will be fine. Eventually and probably. Hey, buddy!" Another moan. "Not talking for a while, though. It is a shame."

"Would speed help?" Jan asked. "I don't have any, but I know a guy who knows a guy. Except that he's a girl, and the other one's a ghost."

"Not if you want him to answer questions in an accurate and non-hallucinatory fashion."

"So we're back where we were before. The Russians are a Rosicrucian front, and there's a generation-old Rosicrucian-anthroposophist feud, which would explain the pop music link, given Swedish dominance in international pop lyrics composition. But the sphere-conjunction is still months away, which means it's early for dramatic intervention—"

I'd stopped listening when she mentioned pop music. You may have put the puzzle pieces together already, but you have to understand, I'm telling this story so it makes sense and you have most of the relevant information. I, meanwhile, in the last twenty-four hours, had been Tased, judoed, and subjected to a high-velocity encounter with an Armani-wearing goon, all of which was somewhat discombobulating.

But the pieces did assemble. I felt cold. I had been worried about finding Clay before he ran afoul of cops who weren't as understanding as the Fort Freak crew. Armed goons were a whole different threat level. But then—I thought of Clay wandering the city alone. He'd been in deep for a while. Maybe this was only finding his depth. Still, someone had to go in after him.

And it all came back to the music.

"IHeartTonya's at the Mandarin Oriental." Fred and Jan turned to me, curious, which I guess was understandable. I'm not usually the parlor scene guy. "Clay had an IHeartTonya poster on his wall, was fighting with his stepdad about wanting to see the show. He got a Mandarin Oriental uniform from Dave the Greek. What if he tried to sneak in to see her?" I remember those architectural cheekbones, the wink of an ice-blue eye. "Maybe he did, and he ran into Croyd Crenson. And then . . . something went wrong."

"Something?" Jan sounded more skeptical than I thought was reasonable for someone who'd just been talking about Rosicrucians and sphere-conjunctions.

"I don't know. Crenson is too much of an X-factor to say more. But I think Clay is trying to finish Crenson's mission."

"What mission?" Fred, this time.

"I don't know. Look, we have a Russian pop star my student loves. We have an infamous blackmail photographer kidnapped by Russian goons. And then we have Croyd Crenson, thief for hire, trying to visit the same photographer, about some Russian guy. Zadornov. They all go together somehow. I'm sure of it."

Jan poked Dave the Greek in the temple. The pressure wave rippled across his scales. "This guy's good at getting pictures. Why would he need Crenson?"

"Maybe he had the pictures, but lost them. Maybe he hired Crenson to get them back."

"He didn't have backups?"

"Maybe not? My point is, Clay has a Mandarin Oriental uniform. If I'm right, he'll be looking for a way to break in to IHeart-Tonya's suite, and do . . . whatever Crenson was hired to do. And we have to help him."

"I thought," Jan said, "that you were for sure going to say *stop him*."

"We know, more or less, where he's going. If we could just figure out when—"

"Or we could, you know, just let the kid who may or may not be the Sleeper be the one to break into the mobbed-up Russian pop singer's hotel suite? Because he has the skills for the job, and we do not have said skills?" Fred raised his hands to ward off Jan's I-don't-believe-you look. "I am simply suggesting a suggestion."

"We don't know how Clay ended up like this," I said. "Maybe whatever's turned him into the Sleeper stops in the middle of his run. When he's surrounded by tracksuits. What then?"

"Huh."

"He's just a kid, Fred."

Fred is a big guy. His exhalations carry a lot of weight. "Okay. I will see what I can do."

In a sensible universe, Fred's phone call to an old buddy who manages in-house catering at the Mandarin Oriental would have revealed that IHeartTonya's gala reception for New York's elite music scene would be held the next night, or the night after that. This universe, though, hasn't been sensible since the first Wild Card Day, and if you've read history, you know that it wasn't all that sensible before then, either.

The gala reception was that evening. There were event planners, there was a guest list, there would be ice sculptures and passed hors d'oeuvres and a Sommeli-Aire, which Fred told me was kind of like a bartender but for breathing.

But it was all happening this evening, and any time spent complaining would be better spent in preparation. IHeartTonya's first show stateside was almost sold out, and the rest of the tour was selling. The new album had, apparently, buzz. More people absolutely *had* to be there, to see the princess in person. So we were in luck. An expanded guest list meant an expanded catering roster, and Fred and his two buddies would be welcome. "Donnie owes me big time," he said when he hung up the phone, by way of explanation. "I sewed him up after the Peruvians caught him in Cambodia, when the only way he looked like he was getting out of there was in a large number of dime bags. He is good people."

So there we were. Jan, Fred, and I, in white shirts and black slacks, with little name badges on our chests, in the palatial penthouse ballroom of the Mandarin Oriental, with New York at our feet, and tuna crudo on the trays we carried. Dave the Greek we left recovering in Jube the Walrus's living room. Jan and Jube had been next-door neighbors since forever and when she explained the situation—Russians, ketamine, et cetera—Jube had smiled a big husky smile. Ah, so you want me to *tripmaster*! This I have not done since *1978*! He'd been halfway through setting up his stereo system and blacklight array when we left. Dave the Greek seemed to be in good hands. Or, flippers.

I probably should go all gossip column on you, describing the party, who was there, who wasn't, what they were wearing, what they weren't. The fact is, I didn't much care. For one thing, I had a job to do. For another—look, I used to be just a little bit famous. It's like any other drug, I guess. When you dose for the first time, you learn if you really need it, if it's your scene. Me, it fit like someone else's skin. With gravel sewn inside.

I mean, sure, on a per-item basis the tray of seared tuna and wasabi foam and dots of caviar that I was carrying cost more than I'd spent on lunch in the last year, and I missed *that*. But as the room filled, I saw again and again that look, that calculating edge on the faces of the guests, the work required to be the people they were in public. Some people enjoy that sort of thing, the way some people enjoy lifting heavy weights or getting tied up in special clothing. But it wasn't my scene.

Fortunately I didn't have to *be* here, not as me. I was scenery, a fixture. Unwatched, I could circle the floor and keep tabs on the entrances and exits. So far I had not seen Clay. Two of the big guys in black suits near the door looked familiar, though that could just be the breadth across the shoulders marking them as goon-type Pokémon. I hadn't gotten a good look at the tracksuits, though. Those could be the guys. I hadn't seen Armani Cigar yet. He didn't seem the type you'd trust at public parties. Too much of a risk he'd put out his cigar in the eye of another guest.

So I circled the floor, passing out tuna and caviar, and with every minute I felt more like we had made a horrible mistake. We didn't know for sure Clay was here, that he would be coming at all. What if he waited to break into the hotel after hours? But security after the party would be back to its routine. Things, and people, are most vulnerable when they change. This was the best chance for Clay, or for Croyd. The ballroom adjoined the presidential suite, and the two floors underneath all seemed to have been rented out by the IHeartTonya tour. They'd brought a town's worth of entourage, and probably booked a bunch of empty rooms to cushion them from other guests. Or to show off.

The ballroom's kitchen staging area was a hive of worker bees in Mandarin Oriental uniforms—Clay would sneak in through there, then out through the connecting doors to the suite. Fred was watching the staging area, since not even the Peruvians could move Donnie to give Fred a front-of-house position. Jan was on the ballroom floor, being chatted up by a pair of agreeable twins, but she was near the door to the suite at least. That left me, circling, circling, watching, watching, for that mop of brown hair, for the damp gray unfinished skin.

As I looked for Clay, I paid less attention than I should have to my path through the ballroom. I let the current carry me, out and back, out and back, smiling vacantly at the guests who emptied my serving platter.

Which was why I didn't notice the crowd thicken around me until it was too late. Human currents drew me down past the point of neutral buoyancy, where it became easier to get further into the crowd than to get out. I tried to work free, but my efforts only drew me toward the unseen center—until, at last, I found myself blinking and breathless, my tray of tuna miraculously unspilled, before a pair of architectural cheekbones.

Tatiana Valskaya. IHeartTonya herself, in the flesh, and in some kind of royal-purple outer-space princess dress.

It's common to claim, when you meet a superstar in person, that they're larger or smaller than you imagined. The truth is stranger than that. You know exactly how these people look. You've seen their faces on billboards, on movie screens, on tabloid pages. *They* look exactly right, and so do their costars and handlers and the members of their family. It's *you* that isn't right. You are the one who's larger, or smaller, than you thought.

"Tuna crudo?"

I wasn't expecting her to look my way—I didn't look at the guy with the passed hors d'oeuvres back when I was her age and an idiot, and anyway she was talking to someone famous, one of the endless strong-jawed Chrisses they find to star in those EC Comics horror-movie serials. But she turned away from him, made eye contact, beamed.

"How wonderful!" Her speaking voice was rich and light at once, aerial. Most pop performers don't take that kind of care of their instruments. I liked her for that, and for the other things. "These are delicious. Keep them coming. Come back with them." She took three, and passed one to her Chris, who looked confused. "Have you tried them?"

I had. "I love the wasabi."

"And the lemon! Such careful balance. Please, come back with more. Though I know you have so many to feed."

"Well," I said, risking the joke, "it is your party. I'll manage."

And she laughed at that, as if it really was funny, and not just the best I could come up with at the time. I wanted to stay. It was foolish, but for the first time in years I missed being a person who belonged in this room, on the other side of the serving tray.

But that wasn't why I was here. Even as the pang hit me, I saw movement in the corner of the room I'd been trying to watch without obviously watching. The door that led back to the penthouse suite was open. I saw a dark-haired and gray-skinned kid in a Mandarin Oriental uniform dart through.

I stammered an excuse, turned away from those cheekbones, and made for the door. The crowd was dense, but I couldn't lose Clay now. I let myself go wiggly to get through, and trailed a stir, a number of turned heads. Attracting the wrong sort of attention, but I could worry about that later.

I ditched my serving platter on the bar; the door to the suite was swinging shut. I slung my hand out—fast, far—and caught it. I was through.

The suite and ballroom were connected by a service hallway, and at the far end of the hall another door was closing. I ran and caught that one, too.

Beyond the door lay the penthouse, and beyond the penthouse walls, the jewel forest of the city.

The penthouse was, you know, what those things always are. Bland and elegant, a sort of lush sandblasted aesthetic. The decor doesn't usually feature a fistfight near the door to the second bedroom. That would add too much distinctive character. But Clay and two tracksuits were doing their best to remedy this lack of interior decorating panache.

Clay/Croyd could fight, sure. But whatever you've learned from movies, it's hard, in real life, to win a fight against someone much bigger than you, and it's almost impossible to win a fight against *three* someones-much-bigger. Clay had taken one guy out already, even so. I recognized the moaning form as one of the men involved in the Dave the Greek kidnapping—but another had caught him from behind and the third was using Clay's stomach like a heavy bag. Or trying. Even in Jokertown, heavy bags don't squirm and kick back. Often.

I tackled the guy from behind. We went down in a heap. He had some kind of big-time grappler training. You can tell from how a guy falls, from the shapes his limbs seek out by reflex. Most of that stuff is not designed to work on people who only have joints and bones by force of habit. Croyd knew how to make his jiujitsu or whatever work on me, but this guy hadn't put in the hours. I got an arm snaked around his throat and squeezed, carefully. Normal human brains have a real thing about blood flow. They get grumpy when it stops.

I unwound myself from his unconscious body in case Clay—or Croyd—needed help. My worry was misplaced. At Xavier Desmond it feels like we're always telling our kids to seize the day. Some of that must have sunk in. Clay had seized a nearby lamp and applied it, forcefully, to his attacker's head. Then followed up with a boot to the groin.

We looked at each other over the bodies.

He was breathing heavy, his hair a tangle. He looked alive. I tried to find in his face that self-consciousness I'd seen on the street corner, the kid I recognized. But I'd never seen him in his element before. I didn't know what his element *was.*

"Thanks, Stretch."

"We have to get out of here."

"I have a job to do first." A pause, and there, I was sure I saw it: the twitch of uncertainty. "But I could use some help."

"It's not worth it, Clay."

"You don't get it, Stretch. There are lives at stake."

Knockouts don't last long in real life. Tracksuit and his friends were already twitching awake. I'd always been bad at this sort of thing on *American Hero*. I heard the snare drum, the overdone voiceover: *Okay, Ruttiger. Time for a snap decision.* So I said: "Let's do it."

You know those people who stress in the lead-up to a decision, but once it's made they never doubt, they just roll on like a boulder going downhill? Yeah, I always envy those people.

Clay / Croyd reached for the handle of the closed bedroom door. I stretched out my hand and got there first. "I'm bulletproof. Mostly."

He backed off: *Be my guest.*

I opened the door.

Have I mentioned how much I hate Tasers?

After a bright-blue shock it's hard even to keep my eyes on the same side of my body, let alone pointing in the same direction. Whatever I've got instead of a visual cortex struggled to assemble the sense data into a picture, an image of the world. But I saw, swimming over me, an Armani suit, a big black beard, an unlit cigar clenched between flat teeth. A rush, then a scuffle, a young voice cursing with the fluency and inventiveness of a very old man.

Armani lit his cigar. He had been waiting, I guess. Hadn't wanted to warn anyone he was there. When he inhaled he got that itch-scratched expression people have when they've been counting the minutes to light up. He breathed out a smoke ring.

They'll lose the nonsmoking deposit, I thought.

"Put them," he said, "with the other one."

There's always a moment, as I wake up in a new hotel room, during which I have no idea where I am. Memory rifles through a deck of half-remembered half places. Is this your card?

I hadn't been Tased on the floor of too many luxury hotels, though, so this time around it was a pretty fast sorting job.

Fine motor control—the sort that lets me have a head—was still too much to ask of my taxed pseudo-nervous system, but I gathered my eyes into more or less the right position and extended a lumpen pseudopod to look around.

"Hey, Stretch. You've looked better."

"Same to you."

Clay was zip-tied to a chair. At least it was a high-end, four-star-hotel chair. Whoever had done the tying must have remembered that Clay had a way with zip ties, because they'd added duct tape. Big bruises flowered around Clay's eye, and he needed to ice his jaw, but he didn't look too bad, all things considered.

"You should feel it from the inside." But: "They seemed in a hurry. Zadornov mentioned 'accomplices.' Your friends? I came here alone."

"That's Zadornov? With the cigar?"

"Elgar Zadornov. Tonya's head of security."

"Elgar?"

"His parents were music lovers."

That only raised further questions, but those questions could wait. "Where are we?"

"A room near the penthouse. Locked in. They either hacked the hotel systems or got special access. Zadornov was being cagey when he explained it to the muscle."

"You can speak Russian?"

"A little. But he was speaking English. A lot of the muscle are local boys bused in from Brighton Beach. Zadornov knows better than to trust their grasp of the mother tongue in the field."

"This is the field, now?"

"For him. Intelligence background. FSB. Old habits die hard."

I craned my pseudo-neck up higher. This room was furnished in the same sandblasted elegance as the penthouse suite, just less of it.

And there was a body in the bed.

No. Not a body. He was breathing. Just, slowly. His eyes were closed. He was wearing a housekeeping uniform—not all that different from Clay's. And he was tied up. But his skin seemed to be made of ribbons, or ropes, all coiled together.

"Who's our friend?"

Clay acted like he hadn't heard my question. He was wriggling against the tape, without success. "Any chance you could grow an arm there, help me out?"

"I have a few questions first."

"Come on, Stretch. They'll be back soon." I kept watching him. He exhaled. "What do you know already?"

"Dave the Greek took pictures of Tatiana Valskaya that Zadornov doesn't want people to see. Dave's used to evading civilian security, but not guys like Zadornov. They found him, somehow, and stole the photos back. Maybe they stole his computer."

"Negatives," Clay said. "Can't hack analog. Most of Dave's targets are American celebs. They don't go in for wetwork like the Russians do."

"And Zadornov didn't destroy the negatives for . . . some reason."

"Blackmail."

"Of Valskaya?"

"Of whoever else was on the film." Clay shrugged, which is hard to do when you're tied up like that. "Pop's a competitive business. Waste not."

"And how did you come into this?"

"I—I was hired." He returned his attention to the tape, without success. "To steal the negatives back."

"I don't mean Croyd. I mean you, Clay."

"I keep trying to tell you, Stretch—"

"You called me Mr. R, back at Dave's. And I've never met Croyd Crenson. He doesn't know my name."

"I must have heard it as I escaped the school."

"From whom? And how did Croyd Crenson know Clay Calvados's phone number?"

"I don't know who that is."

"You called me on his cell, to warn me off your tail. Because you wanted to protect your family. There is a cave in your mind and you don't want to look inside, but it's still there." He twitched, straining against his bonds—wanting to turn away from me. "You have Croyd's memories. His skills. But you don't talk like him, not really. You talk like you think he would."

"You're wasting time, Stretch. We have to get out of here." He was sweating. The firm set of his features, the sharp line of his jaw and the aquiline nose, softened, then jumped back into focus, like televisions used to when you didn't have the rabbit ears quite right.

And I saw it then. I don't know why I hadn't seen it before—except that seeing properly takes distance, and time, and a will to not-know. Or maybe I was just slow. I had, after all, been Tased twice in the last twelve hours.

"Clay," I said. "Look in the mirror."

There was one, full-length, on the wall. He looked into it. Into a face that was young and old at once.

"Now look at the man on the bed."

Once you got past the fact that his body seemed to be made of ropes, he looked a bit like Sherlock Holmes in old movies, tall and thin, with a high forehead, a sharp jaw, an aquiline nose. But sleeping, there was a kindness to him, a sense of laughter I never associated with Holmes.

Clay glanced at him, then away, as if the sight burned.

"You don't touch people, Clay. You wear gloves and you don't take them off to shake hands. Your sister knows you disappear sometimes; she thinks it's just you blowing off steam. But there's more to it than that, isn't there? You have an ace in the hole. Something you hide, because it scares you."

"You don't know what you're talking about."

"Clay. You haven't done anything wrong." Well, if you didn't count breaking and entering, pulling the school fire alarm, multiple counts of assault . . . but all that could wait until we weren't being held prisoner by mafia goons. "I'm not here for Croyd Crenson. I'm here for you."

He looked scared. Wary. Young. I wonder if he'd ever heard that in his life before. It's easy for a kid to slip through the cracks. To think he doesn't matter, even to himself. If that was your life—fear of who you were, of what you could do—and you had the option to be anyone else in the universe, wouldn't you take it?

And what if you woke up with the chance to be Croyd Crenson? Not the real man, not Abigail Baker's ex, not the kid who'd changed forever one afternoon in 1946 and never had an easy night's sleep again, but the hero? The one you'd always chosen when you played aces with your sister in Roosevelt Park, because if you were in trouble, you could wake up and be anyone else?

Kids have big feelings.

"When you touch people, you . . . learn from them. You absorb their memories. Is that it?"

He nodded, once.

"But what happened two nights ago was different. You fought with your stepdad about the IHeartTonya show. You stormed out, and maybe you thought you could just go by the hotel. See if you could sneak in. You tried, and you met someone else with the same idea. The Sleeper."

He turned, tenderly, back to the man on the bed. Toward the face of which his was a reflection.

"I didn't mean it." That was Clay's real voice, not the Cary Grant echo. "He helped me. Let me tag along. He was—he seemed to know everything. And he was funny. He'd make a joke and I'd get it five minutes later, but not so I felt dumb or anything but so I felt smart for figuring it out at all. And then . . ." He shuddered. "There were men with guns. The guy with the cigar—I've never been that scared, Mr. R. Croyd laughed about it all, but the guns were real. And when he pushed me down, to get me into cover . . ."

"You touched his skin," I said. "And you . . . became him."

"He collapsed. It never happened like that before."

"Fear does that," I said. "Adrenaline. In unusual circumstances people can do things they never thought they could. It's the same with our powers."

"Usually I just—when I touch someone, by mistake, they get a sort of headache, and I hear what they're thinking. That's okay at first. But when I go to sleep—I wake up and I can hear them in my head, all day. Like, they think they're me, or I'm them. I talk like them, I . . ." He shuddered. "I just shout them down. I try. But this time, when he went limp, I heard his voice right away. *Run!* In my head. I ran so fast. I was good at it, too, like he was telling me what to do, how to move, where to go. Bullets whizzed past overhead. They couldn't touch me. But I—I left him." He sounded ragged. Terrified, of himself. Poor kid.

"You were scared," I said. "He'd led you into trouble. He wanted you to be safe."

"He got me out." Clay licked his lips. "But then I thought . . . if he was so strong in my head at first, what would happen when I went to sleep? And I felt so guilty. Could I save him? Was he even still . . ." He couldn't finish that sentence. "I stayed awake all night. I didn't know where else to go, so I went to school. I was so tired."

"It's all right," I said. "It's all right. We'll be okay." I wasn't sure how.

"Mr. R," he said, "I don't know what to do."

"Can you get over to the bed? A touch started this. Maybe a touch can reverse it."

He tried to scoot. The carpet was too deep for the chair to shift without toppling.

"Hold still," I said. "Let me try."

A normal human body was still beyond me, but I'd managed my eyestalk pseudopod just fine. I pushed in Clay's direction, and a rubbery tendril stretched out toward him. Closer. Closer. It felt like straining to reach something with my tongue, if my tongue were seven feet long, but at least I had a grip.

I pulled. Clay scooted. The chair moved one foot, two feet. The tendril felt like it would tear free of my body at any moment. Three feet. Almost.

The chair caught on the rug, and tipped forward. With all his strength and his limited leverage, Clay lunged.

The chair twisted under him. His head struck the duvet—and as the weight of the chair carried him over, he craned his neck, to brush with his cheek the limp hand of the man on the bed.

The chair hit the ground hard, and so did Clay. From the door, I heard a question in Russian. After a moment's silence, it was repeated.

I don't, as I think I've said, have to breathe the way most people do. I held my breath anyway.

It happened faster than I expected, his waking up. But I guess he's had more practice than most. Physically, he didn't change at all. The sand of a beach at low tide is still there even after the ocean rolls back in. He wasn't, in his face. And then he was.

He blinked. The ropes of his arms and hands shifted, split, wriggled, and his bonds fell to the bed. He sat up, and raised a hand to his face, as if surprised to find it was still there. "That," he said, "is new." He grabbed the back of Clay's chair, and righted him—taking care, I noticed, not to touch his skin. "You still with us, Clay?"

"I'm sorry," the boy said. "I'm so sorry."

His smile was sad. "You came back. Not many would." He pulled a small sharp object out of a concealed compartment in his belt buckle and sawed through the tape and zip ties.

"I didn't think—"

"You're here." I could see what Abigail meant about the way he spoke. Like sinking pillars through sand to reach bedrock. Then he turned those eyes to the puddle that was me. "I don't think we've been introduced."

I raised another tongue-like pseudopod and waved. "Robin

Ruttiger. I'm Clay's guidance counselor. I usually have—more of a body."

"I've been there," he said. "Guidance counselor?"

Outside, more Russian. Harsher. Clay stood, rubbing his wrists where the zip ties had cut in. "From high school. He came looking for me."

The man's eyes were old and young at once. The effect was sort of the inside-out version of the way Clay looked when he was being Croyd. That was a boy who remembered being old; this was an old man who remembered being young. He had been in school on Wild Card Day. I wondered if anyone came looking for him. "I remember," he said, with some surprise. "Or did I dream I was a butterfly?"

I didn't know how to answer that. "We have to get out of here."

He considered the ceramic lamp on the bedside table—an intricate twist of porcelain. "Once we finish the job."

"That plan hasn't worked out well for you so far," I pointed out.

"Third time's the charm," he said, and pushed the lamp off the table.

Let's make a long story short. The lamp shattered. The Russians came in to investigate. They weren't ready for three people, or for two people and one awkwardly mobile puddle. We left them in a heap in the bathroom, sans knives and guns and phones, tied up with lamp cords and telephone wire.

The plan was for Croyd to lift the negatives while we kept Zadornov and his goons occupied, if necessary. The how of the theft concerned me, but not Croyd. "Let me worry about that," he said when we reached the door of the penthouse suite, and with a wink, he unraveled. The thin cords that made up his body slipped and slithered under the door, dragging his uniform along for the ride. He opened the door from the inside, with a grin.

He led us down the hall, past the closets, to the main room—but stopped short at the sound of an argument.

"Our friend," Fred said, "went in here, and he has not come out."

"Your caterer's delinquency is not my responsibility." Zadornov. I peered around the corner. He was looming over Fred, a lit cigar clenched between his lips. More goons watched, with an air of threat that Fred did not seem to register. Jan was there, too—she'd taken a step back, positioning herself between Fred and the goons, but she wasn't crackling with electricity, at least not yet. She'd left her twins behind for my sake. I felt touched.

"I am not," Fred blustered, "any kind of delinquent, friend, and you had better understand at this moment that if you have messed with our boy, the union will hear about it." He sounded like he was enjoying himself. "And if you think you can high-roll your way out of this, mister, you do not understand the fundamental truths of New York City, which are as follows—"

Zadornov moved. His Taser crackled into Fred's midsection, and Fred slumped forward, twitching. Jan cried out and lunged for him. One of the goons grabbed her. There was another blue spark, and *he* fell back, twitching. They don't call her Sparkplug for nothing.

She just had time to look smug before another goon tackled her from behind.

I lost all sense of proportion, of mission, of subtlety, and rushed into the room, wrapping myself around the guy who had tackled Jan. Fortunately, when she shocked *him,* she didn't get me at the same time. In one corner of the room I was vaguely aware of Clay engaged in heroic fisticuffs—good for him!—and of Croyd, slipping into the bedroom. The distraction plan seemed to be working out, which was a pleasant surprise.

Of course, I was all tangled up in goon, and now Zadornov was approaching me with his Taser in one hand and a gun in another.

I could hear the *American Hero* soundtrack now: the snare drum, the announcer. *How's Rubberband going to get himself out of this one?*

Then, on the ground behind Zadornov, Fred began to change.

Fred left food service, I remembered, because he couldn't help snacking, which was a problem, considering his ace. He could hold in the change, of course, as long as he was focused. But we'd been working this passed-hors-d'oeuvres reception, and the tuna crudo *was* delicious.

Have you ever seen an Atlantic bluefin tuna? I hadn't. I always figured that fish were pretty small, on average, except for sharks, and the really weird ones in the aquarium. Tuna always looks small on the sushi belt. But it turns out that bluefin can grow twelve feet long and weigh as much as a small car.

Zadornov might be a professional, a skilled operator, experienced and trained. But I guess that even in Russia they don't train people on what to do when they're taken out at the knees by a one-ton fish in the middle of a hotel suite.

Welcome to America, I guess.

Things got wacky after that. Wackier, I mean. Zadornov went down, lost the gun, cracked his head on a table. Croyd emerged from the bedroom, presumably with the film—I was too busy with my goon to check—and, seeing the chaos, grinned and launched himself into it, his body split into whiplike strands, wrapping around goons' necks and slamming them into one another. I saw him and Clay fighting back to back. Then I had to get busy with my side of the room.

Jan helped me up; a goon tried to jump her from behind and I rubberbanded him in the throat. Together, we made our way past overturned furniture to Zadornov, who was still trying, to his credit, to do something about the giant tuna. Whatever he was trying, it didn't seem to work.

I held him, and Jan zapped him. I try not to indulge in schadenfreude, but I will admit, it was nice to see him drop.

And then it was over. The goons were down. Zadornov out. Croyd had the film. Fred had managed, with some difficulty, to reassert the existence of his own legs and head. He still had fins and scales, but at least he could breathe. Clay was grinning. I don't think I'd ever seen him smile before. Not as himself, I mean.

"Friends," Croyd said, with a courteous air. "May I suggest a retreat?"

"Lead the way."

And he did.

I thought that would be the end of it. I wanted it to be the end. We escaped into the night, before security or the goons or the cops, who also must have been called, could catch us. My last glimpse of Croyd that evening was of a ropy hand raised in salute—and then we were alone.

I didn't like the thought of what Dave the Greek would do with those photos, of what might happen to Tatiana Valskaya afterward. Clay was safe. He was himself. I saw him back to his sister. I saw them hug, and cry. That was enough for me.

I tried to tell myself that when the celeb gossip sites went wild two days later. "IHeartTonya, Secret Joker!" Under some specific wavelength of light, which seemed to have been used in her lighting setup even though it was specifically forbidden in her rider, Tatiana's skin turned iridescent, transparent, her organs visible, her muscles shimmering crystal. I tried not to look. I felt sick to my stomach. To see someone's personal life just—out there like that, without her consent. To have played a part in it all.

So when I got a text from a mysterious number—a selfie of Croyd Crenson, eyes bloodshot, holding up a handwritten sign asking me to meet him at Madison Square Garden at four o'clock before Tatiana's show—I almost didn't answer. Almost.

He was there, twitchy from coffee and NoDoz and exhaustion, with an amphetamine edge to his smile. He offered me no expectations, but he did offer a lanyard, which I draped over my head. VIP. Backstage pass.

We drifted through security, through a warren of tunnels,

through the cavernous theater. He flashed his badge whenever we were challenged, and when we reached Tatiana Valskaya's dressing room, I felt resigned to the inevitable.

"Let's get this over with," I said.

"You figured it out?" Croyd sounded a little disappointed. He was still a kid, in some ways. So much more than that. But still, also, a kid.

"Not until I got your text."

"We thought you should know."

"So should Clay."

"He does." And Croyd opened the door.

A diva, in the hours before she steps onstage, seems to be standing a little too close to the lens. She's gathered the presence to awe twenty thousand people across a stadium, and now it's all directed at you. Plus, stage makeup overwhelms up close. Tatiana Valskaya did not look like a woman whose dark secret had just been blasted all over the internet. She looked happy. "I was worried," she said, "when you didn't come back. At the party, I mean."

"Where," I asked, "is Uncle Elgar?"

"On a flight home to Moscow. Having failed so utterly to protect my honor." She had perfectly formed teeth, and knew just how much she showed them when she curved her lips.

"He's old-fashioned," I guessed.

"The whole family is," she corrected. "But in Russia these days, one must be a realist. Elgar is . . . a true believer. But sometimes a true believer is bad for business, as you see."

"Russia's not a good place for jokers these days. From what I hear."

"Which the international community ignores so long as it is convenient for them to do so, and tuts about when they must, while nothing changes. Perhaps this will change things. Or start."

"I heard that ticket sales are through the roof for the rest of your tour." I didn't know how far to go. "It's a funny coincidence, isn't it? That even with the rider, and all the trouble your family went through to hide the fact you aren't a nat, someone just happened to set up the wrong stage light for your dress rehearsal. When Dave the Greek was there, ready, with a camera."

Actors, on-screen, have a way of making their smiles go hollow when some lie of theirs has been revealed, some twist uncovered. That's a trick of communication. It's harder to see in real people. I couldn't find it in Tatiana Valskaya at all. "In Russia, these days, one must be a realist."

"And outside of Russia."

"Russia, Mr. Ruttiger, is a state of mind."

"I know how that is," I said. "I'm from Jokertown." After a moment of silence, of her looking at me and me looking back: "What about Clay?"

"An accident. I spoke with him earlier. Gave him a backstage pass. I wanted to ask you—I would like to help with his education, in some discreet manner?"

"We'll figure something out," I said. "What about the rest of the people on Dave the Greek's film? The ones who didn't plan to have their secrets exposed?"

"Oh," Croyd said, "they'll be fine. Turns out Uncle Elgar accidentally wiped the negatives."

"They were analog."

"Funny how that happens."

"What do you get out of this?" I asked him.

"A bit of Russia, and a bit of Jokertown."

"You were paid."

He nodded. "And I had a chance to help someone be themselves. Two someones, counting Clay. He's a good kid. I wish . . ." He looked away. "Help him out, okay?"

I remembered Abigail Baker, back at Ape and Louie's. He never knew how long he'd be asleep, or what he'd be when he woke up. But he couldn't stay out in the cold forever. "I will. You can help."

"I'd like that."

It wasn't a yes. But it was more than I expected. More than he did, too, to judge from his reaction.

"And that leaves you," Tatiana said. "Mr. Ruttiger. What do you want?"

I thought about Russia. And I thought about Jokertown.

"I wanted to help Clay. I've done that. Now . . . Now I'd like to rest. It's been a long week."

"Stay," she said, with that million-candlepower smile. "See the show."

I did stay. And at the climax of the opening number, when the lights flared and she hit the high note and became a crystal statue onstage—even knowing what was about to happen, and what she'd done to get there, I cried in my seat.

I worked with Clay every week for the next two years. That part's less dramatic, there are fewer Russians, but it's true. Tatiana Valskaya came through to pay for his college. Clay came back to XD after his first semester at Swarthmore to introduce me to his boyfriend. And I gather that he and Croyd Crenson did stay in touch.

I never saw Croyd again. Not that I'm aware. But you never know. Maybe Zadornov, or one of his local boys, tracked Croyd down and took some back-alley revenge. Maybe he and Abigail worked something out in the end. I hope that's what happened.

But he could be anyone, anywhere. That insect reading a newspaper on the seat next to you on the subway. The old gray-scaled man up front at a protest. The boy with a spray paint can and a wild grin. We're all changing all the time, forever. That's the one thing you can count on—that when you lie down, you get up changed.

Even death is just another sleep.

Swimmer, Flier, Felon, Spy

PART VIII

"I meant to ask earlier," said Tesla, looking up at the sign deep below the city. "Why geometry?"

"I hate geometry," said Knees.

"When did you ever have to do any geometry?" asked Nose. "Anyway, it's just because that abandon-all-hope thing has been done to death."

Fair point.

"Still, a fairly obscure choice," said Tesla.

"Picked it up when I was doing classics at NYU," said Nose.

"Here we go," said Knees.

Nose had baited the hook, and Tesla did the man the favor of biting. "You studied at NYU?"

"For a little while," said Nose. "Had to drop out. Too smelly."

"You live in a sewer," said Knees.

"Smells better than the Classics Department," said Nose.

Tesla smiled. It was genuine, even though he also knew it was what was expected of him.

"Anyway, here you are again, and this time you found your way down without any weirdo help," said Nose.

"Found his way *out* last time without any weirdo help, too," chimed in Knees.

Tesla and Nose both looked approximately where the boy's invisible face must be.

"What? I'm not a weirdo. You two are weirdos. Electric horns and being able to tell when the last time somebody had garlic bread was by sniffing them."

"Garlic bread's pretty easy," said Nose. "You could do that. Well, maybe. Do you even have a nose?"

"We've been on this guard post for three years and you're just now thinking to ask me that?"

How old *was* Knees? But that was not the question at hand.

"I was wondering if you two might do me a favor," asked Tesla.

"Oh!" said Knees, his tone brightening. "That's an easy one!"

"No," said Nose. "No, we won't."

As expected.

"Anticipating that that might be your answer," said Tesla, "I wonder if instead I might hire you to do a job for me."

"Man," said Nose. "There are a lot of factors to take into consideration with a question like that."

"We'll do it for a lot of money," said Knees.

Tesla asked, "To be paid into the anarchist collective's general fund?"

"Nah," said Nose. "We operate on a favor-based economy down here."

"You just told me you wouldn't do me a favor," said Tesla.

"I look at you," said Nose, "I don't see 'anarchist.'"

"I consider myself apolitical. Isn't that close enough?"

"Nope," said Knees. "Anyway, you were talking about giving us a lot of money."

"Very well," said Tesla. "I need you to break a man out of prison

who will no doubt fight you kicking and screaming the entire time
and bring him to a meet point at midnight tonight. Make sure to
take something to keep him tied up."

"Really," said Nose. "That's a big ask."

"It is," said Knees. "So, seriously. A *lot* of money."

There were as many methods for preparing a clandestine meeting in the shadowy world Tesla inhabited as there were shadowy
denizens. One factor was time. How long in advance should an
operative arrive at the meet point?

Tesla knew of one CIA operative, a joker with the head of a
crow, who was said to have lain motionless on a cliff top in a con-
tested part of the Levant for six days spying on a terrorist camp he
was scheduled to visit, learning its rhythms and methods. Tesla
didn't have that kind of time.

So instead of six days, he took six hours.

The prewar building that housed the school on 93rd Street had
been refurbished in the 1970s—Tesla did not bother calling up the
exact year—which had done nothing to improve the uninspired
lines of its architecture. The important thing about the building
now was that it would be empty.

Well, that was one important thing. The other, much more cru-
cial fact was that it was the birthplace, in 1946, of the Sleeper.

Not of Croyd Crenson, of course. Crenson was fourteen years
old in the autumn of 1946, just beginning ninth grade, when the
future fell out of the sky in the form of alien microbes. Unlike so
many, the boy had not died. Unlike so many others from his era,
and nearly unbelievably considering the events of his life, the man
he became had not died, either.

Not yet.

The alarm systems used by the New York City public school
system were woefully out of date and trivially easy to overcome.

Tesla ran a current through his fingernails and disabled them as soon as he entered the building. He was encouraged by the fact that they had been active. That meant there were no custodians or overworked teachers or harried administrators in the building later than usual.

Tesla didn't hold out much hope for the building's survival.

The gymnasium doubled as the lunchroom, so Tesla was able to find it by following the smells of institutional cooking and puberty. It was barely large enough to house a regulation basketball court. The backboards were cranked up high against the ceiling, parallel to the floor. Those would be good spots. Not enough. Not nearly enough, but they would do for a start.

He made a circuit of the darkened, cavernous room. He had chosen rubber-soled shoes, but even so, soft echoes of his footsteps bounced off the walls. One wall featured windows placed high up. He walked to the center of the room, where a circle was painted on the floor for basketball tip-offs. He carefully sat the rucksack he had carried on the long walk from the hotel precisely in the center of the circle.

It was now close to seven o'clock in the evening. There would be, with little doubt, enough time to make his preparations. Unless one of the Croyds decided to show up early as well, upsetting Tesla's primary plans.

The smell of smoke came to Tesla then, and he sensed heat coming from the floor at one end of the court. Flames leapt up in a jagged oval, and Tesla was glad that the systems he had deactivated included the fire alarms.

The floor fell away, or was burned away—or perhaps, given the oven-like heat that now filled the room, it had even *melted* away. Rising up from the floor on a pillar of stones and bricks and other glowing-hot detritus, the Croyd of the jeweled eyes roared, "Where are they?"

Tesla performed the mental operations required to set aside his primary plans and enact one set of secondary plans, these based on the fact that this particular Crenson had shown up at this particular time.

He had taken dozens of variables into account. Which Croyd arrived first and which last. What would their demeanor be? Would they come seeking violence—as this Croyd certainly was—or seeking some other sort of resolution? Would they come alone or with allies? Would they come at all?

The situation was far too fluid for Tesla's liking. But it was the situation he faced.

He walked over to one wall, where injection-molded plastic chairs were stacked atop rolling racks. He lifted one, set it down on the floor, then put his foot against its seat. He kicked, and the chair slid across the polished concrete surface to come to a stop just short of Miner Croyd.

"You're quite early," he told Crenson. "If you'd like to take a seat, I'll be with you as soon as I can."

The onyx-skinned man held out one hand, and it glowed briefly. The chair—plastic seat, metal legs, and all—liquefied into a steaming puddle.

"Or," said Tesla, "you may stand if you prefer."

"I will be listening," said Crenson. "I will feel the fall of their footsteps." And with that, he sank back into the floor. The glowing rubble coalesced, but the heat coming from it did not subside.

Potentially problematic.

But there was little to be done except complete his preparations as he had planned. He went to find the cranks that operated the basketball backboards.

At eleven forty-four, eleven minutes ahead of schedule, the sound of an elevator bell rang from the wall next to the kitchen. A vertical line of light seven feet in height appeared, then a set of familiar doors opened, revealing the crowded interior of the elevator.

There was the hunched operator, who looked even more annoyed than the first time Tesla encountered her. There was Nose, also looking annoyed. If Knees was annoyed, well, there was no way to tell from a grubby pair of feet. Floating at the top of the elevator, secured to Nose's wrist by a chain and a pair of handcuffs, was the floating Crenson.

"You owe us another four thousand dollars," said Knees as Nose began the difficult process of maneuvering Crenson out into the gymnasium.

"I already paid you."

"Yeah, well, once we got this guy, we decided to pay the expedited rate."

"And return," said the operator.

"Hey! Hey! It's my old partner!" said the floating Crenson. "Thanks for springing me! But that wasn't part of the plan! Was it? Did you get the goods?"

Tesla reached into his pocket and pulled out a clear orange bottle labeled with the logo of a pharmacy chain that had branches on what seemed like every other corner in the city. "No," he said, "but I brought you these." He tossed the bottle in an arc. Even though his hands were still cuffed and he was only halfway out of the elevator, Crenson caught it deftly.

He could not, however, manage to open the bottle while shackled.

"Let him go," said Tesla.

"Gladly," said Nose. "This guy hasn't shut up since the doors opened in his cell."

Nose pulled Crenson down, produced a key, and unlocked the handcuffs. Crenson floated up a few feet, ignoring everyone and even falling silent as he read the label of the pill bottle, grinned, twisted off the cap, and took a dangerously large handful of pills.

"Thank you," Tesla said to the Troglodytes. "Sincerely."

"Sure," said Knees. The pair of them had retreated to the elevator. "We'll put the four grand on your tab. Come see us next time you're in town, you can pay us off then." The door started to close. "Good luck with whatever it is you're doing, Sparks."

Just as the elevator shut, Nose said, "Let's call him Ozone."

The floating Crenson began to sing. "I'm gonna be hiiiiiigh, as a kite!"

Not if Tesla had anything to say about it.

And so they came, one by one. The aquatic Crenson who had hired Tesla, walking with some difficulty on dry land. The artist with eight arms. Preceded by the smell of cardamom, the Crenson whom Tesla had encountered in the restaurant.

A few minutes after midnight and they were all there except for the Crenson with the weather powers. Neither had the Miner risen up again from the floor.

Except for the floating Croyd, the Crensons kept their distance from one another, arrayed around the gym floor.

"God, I hated dodgeball," said the eight-armed Croyd.

"But you'd be so good at it now!" said floating Croyd. "You'd catch the ball every time!"

"And you would be an easy out," said the aquatic Croyd. Then he turned to Tesla. "Two short."

"Not to worry," said Tesla, electing not to fret about what the subterranean Croyd was up to just yet. "I'm confident we'll have a full house. Now, though, it's time for you to reveal the purpose of this gathering to me and these . . . gentlemen."

The aquatic Croyd looked around the gym. Tesla had not bothered to turn on the overheads, so the only light was the ambience from the windows high above.

"He doesn't know," said a voice from the doorway that led to the interior of the school. "None of us know shit. Because we're fucking 'diminished.'" The Croyd who could control the weather was standing there, this time fully dressed and dry.

The first Croyd whom Tesla had met slowly nodded. "That's

right. That's right, I don't know. But it seemed like the right thing to do, somehow. It seemed like maybe if I didn't do that this time I . . . we . . . might not wake up again."

"No worries!" shouted floating Croyd. "I've got the goods!" He pulled the pill bottle from his pocket and shook it. There was no sound. "Oh shit," he said. "I guess I took them all."

A miniature volcano erupted at mid-court. The subterranean Crenson burst up from the floor, landing a few feet clear on one knee, a fist against the concrete. He looked up and his eyes burned. "Time for all you imposters to die," he said.

This was, of course, a delicate moment. Tesla reached into his pocket and pressed a button on a key fob.

"What's that smell?" asked the cook.

He should have expected that.

The fiery Croyd extended one arm and a blazing bolt of light flashed toward the floating Croyd, who showed a surprising amount of dexterity in avoiding it. A jagged hole showed where the light had struck the wall.

"What the fuck, man?" shouted floating Croyd. "I just offered you pep pills for free!"

He was slurring his speech. This was overdue. If anything, thought Tesla, the man should be asleep by now. The pills were devastatingly potent.

"None of that!" shouted weather Croyd, and raised both hands. A gale-force wind arose, blowing the onyx-skinned Croyd across the court to crash into the wall where the elevator had been.

"Seriously," said the cook. "What is that smell?"

The men fell silent and still.

"I don't smell anything," said the eight-armed Croyd after a brief moment.

"It's coming from up there," said the cook, pointing at one of the basketball hoops. "And from the other one, too!"

Floating Croyd was close to one basket. He swam through the air until he could tangle his fingers in the net. "There's some kind of spray can or something up here," he said. "Can speed come in spray cans? I've never heard of that."

"It's gas!" said weather Croyd. "*He's* trying to kill us!"

"No!" shouted Tesla, but the man whipped one arm around in a semicircle. The windows shattered and a gale-force wind blew. Tesla was sure that the sleeping gas had been dispersed.

Along with his plan.

The plan had not been devised using any of Tesla's usual methods. Instead he had depended on something he usually barely acknowledged he possessed. Intuition.

This was of a piece with the unusual nature of the job he had undertaken, with the uncharacteristic, even impractical methodologies he had adopted over the past few days, and with the memories that kept blooming up at unexpected moments. Tesla decided, as the six Croyd Crensons turned their attention to him, that he would undergo an intense bout of self-analysis when this was all over.

Should he survive.

Surprisingly, the first attack came from the cook, who simply took a handgun from his pocket and fired it at Tesla. The shot went wide. So wide, in fact, that it winged the eight-armed Croyd, who cried out in pain and slapped several hands to one of his shoulders.

So much for putting them all to sleep at the same time and place and waiting to see what happened.

The two real threats in the room, the Croyds of lava and wind, stalked toward Tesla. But when the subterranean Croyd released another magmic bolt, it was aimed not at Tesla, but at his opposite number. The weather-controlling Croyd raised his arms and a rushing stream of water met the bolt, an explosion of steam occurring where the two met.

The gym descended into a tumultuous melee, every man present seemingly bent on killing someone, anyone—even if it meant, in a quite literal sense, killing himself. Every man except for the aquatic Croyd, who shambled around the perimeter, shouting into the chaotic fights erupting. "Stop it! Stop it! We don't have to die!"

"And I wasn't trying to kill any of you!" Tesla shouted in response. "I'm trying to—" What? What was he trying to do?

"I'm trying to save you."

And myself.

None of them paid him any mind except for the cook, who took his time in aiming more carefully. He was still no great shot, but Tesla felt the bullet pass through his jacket and graze his ribs. He bit back a scream and threw himself flat on his back, hopefully gaining a measure of protection while still being able to see what was going on around him.

So as Croyd Crenson, in aggregate, tried to kill himself, only Tesla saw a figure in black ghost into the gymnasium through the broken windows. It appeared to be a man in some sort of tactical body armor, and he was very agile. He swung from rafter to rafter until he was directly above Tesla, then dropped to the floor with a rope extending upward, a controlled fall.

The cook took another shot, this one at the newcomer. It hit the man dead center in the chest. The stranger grunted and took a step back, but otherwise seemed unaffected. Instead of paying any attention to who had just shot him, he took a strange-looking gun from a holster at his waist and looked down at Tesla. He was wearing a gas mask and goggles.

He shot Tesla with what looked and sounded like a lightning bolt, directly in the face.

Tesla did not die.

Instead, he felt a huge surge of energy, heard an enormous roaring inside his skull, experienced something between agony and ecstasy. He started to scramble to his feet, but the man who had shot him put one foot on his chest and pushed him back down.

"Wait for your moment," he said, projecting to be heard over the explosions, gunshots, screams, and crashes coming from every direction.

"What was that?" demanded Tesla.

"That," said the man, removing his mask and goggles. "Was not General Tso's chicken and steamed dumplings." The man was Tesla's delivery driver from Virginia. "That was a gift from an old friend. An apology."

Li Min, Tesla thought, and a wave of emotion stronger than any lightning bolt passed through him. *Li Min has been keeping tabs on me. All these years.*

The man pressed a button on his belt and was drawn swiftly into the rafters. Smoke obscured the ceiling. Tesla did not see him make his way out of the gym. Tesla did not see the man ever again.

As he stared up, the floating Croyd swam into the air just above him. "Motherfuckers are *shooting* at each other!" he shouted.

The sensations Tesla had been experiencing resolved into a headache and a revelation. He stood.

"Stop this!" he shouted. "Stop this now!"

Astonishingly, all the Croyds turned to look at him.

"Or what?" asked all six of them simultaneously.

"Or this," said Tesla.

He spread his arms wide and turned in a slow circle. The overcharge the delivery driver's weapon had birthed in his head manifested in a surge of electricity that reached out in every direction, striking each Croyd and holding them still, but also, to Tesla's horror, striking the walls, the ceiling, the floor. Debris began falling from above. The concrete buckled where the subterranean Croyd had manifested.

Bolts danced and crashed. The sound was terrifying. All of the Croyds, not just the erstwhile balloon salesman, hung suspended in the air. All but the subterranean Croyd were immobile, and that one's efforts to raise his hands were futile.

Tesla tried to stop. He had never felt such power, though it was of a kind with what he had possessed for years. Of a kind, but nowhere near of a scale.

Looking down, he saw that he was suspended in the air himself, arcs of electricity lancing from his feet, which were now unshod. His clothes were tearing away. He spun.

And then, as suddenly as it had started, the lightning stopped.

The collapse of the gymnasium did not.

Tesla's fingers were hard enough to dig through the rubble without splintering. He wore only the ragged remains of his trousers. He worked frantically. The authorities would surely arrive shortly, and Tesla had to know if he had just murdered six men. Or one man.

He heard a murmur beneath a stack of lunchroom chairs and scrabbled in that direction. Before he could throw the first one away, something caught his eye in the debris.

It was a fortune cookie.

He could not resist. He swiftly picked up the cellophane-wrapped confection and tore it cleanly apart. The paper inside was folded, larger than a standard fortune. Nor was it printed in watery red or green.

Instead, there were three lines of Hanzi characters rendered in the blackest ink, the hand flowing and delicate and as recognizable to Tesla as his own memories. The hand of a woman, the hand of a scholar, the hand, no doubt, of a high-level operative of the Guoanbu, the Ministry of State Security of the People's Republic of China.

It was, on the face of it, simply an address in Macao, one of the PRC's special administrative districts. Tesla read more than that, though. He read an invitation. He read a plan.

He read a promise for the future.

He made a careful note of the address in the files he kept in his mind.

Again, a shuffling from below the chairs.

Tesla took a box of matches from his pocket and prepared to set the message—the fortune—alight. Then he threw the matches away and put the slip of paper in the right pocket of his ragged trousers.

Only then did he heave the pile of chairs to one side to see which of the Croyds had survived.

He saw no onyx-skinned man consumed with rage. He saw no man capable of swimming from New York to Washington, consumed with doubt. No comparatively innocent artist, no homicidal cook, no hopeless addict. He did not see a man capable of raising the wind.

He saw, curled naked in the rubble, a boy, perhaps fourteen. He was of average build, freckly-faced, with straight brown hair. His eyes were closed, but Tesla knew they were blue.

Not half a dozen tormented men, then, just one boy, sleeping.

He looked like he needed it.

© MINESH BACRANIA

GEORGE R. R. MARTIN is the #1 *New York Times* bestselling
author of many novels, including those of the acclaimed se-
ries A Song of Ice and Fire—*A Game of Thrones, A Clash of
Kings, A Storm of Swords, A Feast for Crows,* and *A Dance with
Dragons*—as well as related works such as *Fire & Blood, A
Knight of the Seven Kingdoms, The World of Ice & Fire,* and *The
Rise of the Dragon* (the last two with Elio M. García, Jr., and
Linda Antonsson). Other novels and collections include *Tuf
Voyaging, Fevre Dream, The Armageddon Rag, Dying of the Light,
Windhaven* (with Lisa Tuttle), and *Dreamsongs Volumes I and II.*
As a writer-producer, he has worked on *The Twilight Zone,
Beauty and the Beast,* and various feature films and pilots that
were never made. He lives with his lovely wife, Parris, in
Santa Fe, New Mexico.

georgerrmartin.com
Facebook.com/GeorgeRRMartinofficial
X: @GRRMspeaking

About the Type

This book was set in Palatino, a typeface designed by the German typographer Hermann Zapf (b. 1918). It was named after the Renaissance calligrapher Giovanbattista Palatino. Zapf designed it between 1948 and 1952, and it was his first typeface to be introduced in America. It is a face of unusual elegance.